Further Titles by Christopher Nicole from Severn House

Black Majesty Series

Book One: Black Majesty
Book Two: Wild Harvest

The Dawson Family Saga

Book One: Days of Wine and Roses?
Book Two: The Titans
Book Three: Resumption
Book Four: The Last Battle

The McGann Family Saga

Book One: Old Glory
Book Two: The Sea and the Sand
Book Three: Iron Ships, Iron Men
Book Four: Wind of Destiny
Book Five: Raging Sun, Searing Sky
Book Six: The Passion and the Glory

Bloody Sunrise
Caribee
The Friday Spy
Heroes
Queen of Paris
Ship With No Name
The Sun and the Dragon
The Sun on Fire

The Russian Quartet

Book One: The Seeds of Power
Book Two: The Masters
Book Three: The Red Tide
Book Four: The Red Gods

THE SCARLET GENERATION

THE SCARLET GENERATION

Christopher Nicole

SEVERN HOUSE

This first world edition published in Great Britain 1996 by
SEVERN HOUSE PUBLISHERS LTD of
9–15 High Street, Sutton, Surrey SM1 1DF.
First published in the USA 1997 by
SEVERN HOUSE PUBLISHERS INC., of
595 Madison Avenue, New York, NY 10022.

British Library Cataloguing in Publication Data
Nicole, Christopher, 1930–
The Scarlet generation. – (Russian saga ; 5)
1.English fiction – 20th century
I. Title
823.9′14 [F]

ISBN 0-7278-4968-9

Typeset by Hewer Text Composition Services, Edinburgh.
Printed and bound in Great Britain by
Hartnolls Ltd, Bodmin, Cornwall.

Amid the groves, under the shadowy hills,
The generations are prepared; the pangs,
The internal pangs, are ready; the dread strife
Of poor humanity's afflicted will
Struggling in vain with ruthless destiny.

William Wordsworth, *The Excursion*

THE BOLUGAYEVSKI FAMILY

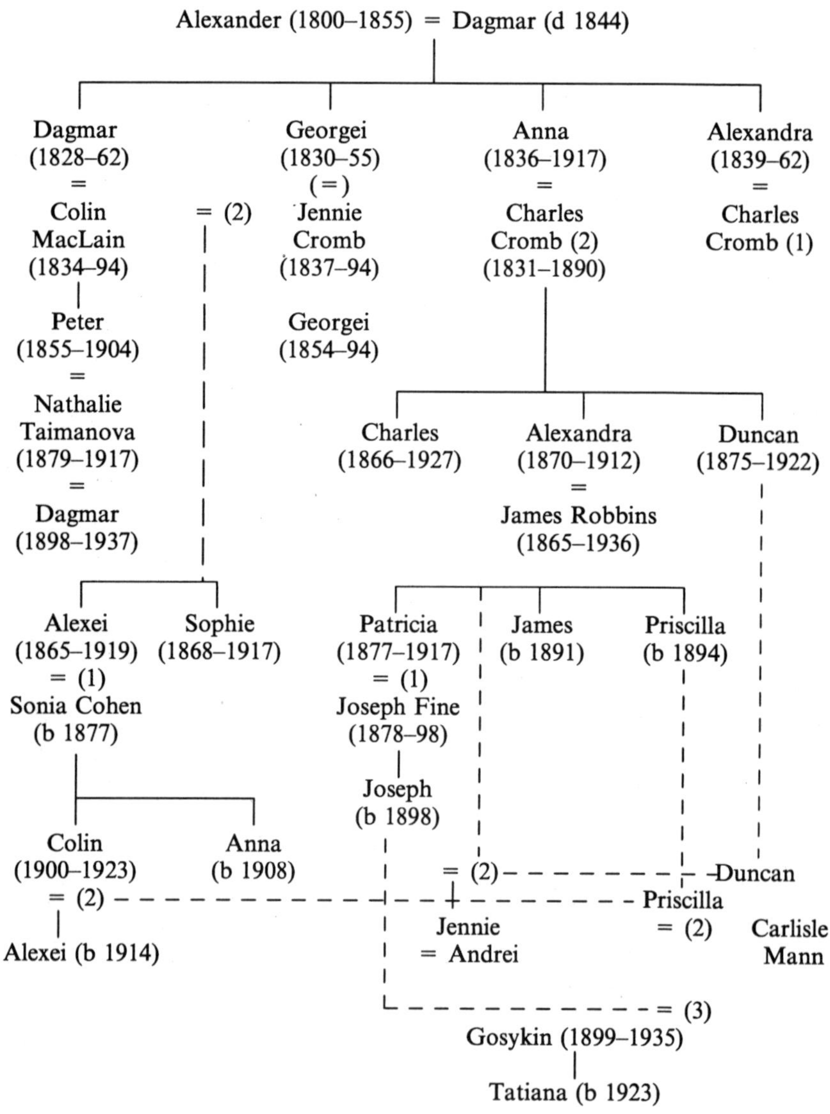

CONTENTS

Part One

Those Who Would Die

Better one suffer, than a nation grieve.
John Dryden, *Absalom and Achitophel*

Chapter 1

The Calm

"Ra, ra, ra!" the crowd shouted. "Ra, ra, ra! FDR for ever! Ra, ra, ra!"

Alex Bolugayevski and his friends looked down at the people from the windows of the Boston General hospital. "It's not really legal, of course," said Oliver Wenck. "Three terms! It's not constitutional."

"It makes them happy," Alex suggested. Although the young men were all in their middle or late twenties, all wore the white coats of housemen, and were all friends, having been through medical school together, Alex Bolugayevski stood out, not only because he was the tallest at some inches over 6 ft, and the biggest, or because he had bold, handsome features and crisp yellow hair, but because he was tangibly different from his fellows. Several of them had ancestors from Eastern Europe, some even from Russia. But none of them had as a mother a princess of the old Tsarist regime, or a stepfather who had spent several years in a Stalinist prison. Or was entitled to call himself prince, if he chose. Nor did any of them have the prospect of inheriting a sizeable chunk of the Cromb Shipping Line Inc. Some of them often wondered why Alex chose to spend his time following the backbreaking routine of an internee at Boston General instead of sitting behind a large walnut desk, telephone in each hand.

"But you didn't vote for him," commented Elaine

Mitchell, tapping the button pinned to his coat. Elaine was the only woman in the group. Herself tall and willowy, attractive rather than pretty, with curling, dark hair, she aspired to be a surgeon, providing she didn't give up medicine to marry Alex Bolugayevski, which she fully intended to do if he would ever get around to asking her.

"My family are Republicans," Alex pointed out.

"And you always vote the family way," Elaine suggested.

"Of course! Don't you?"

"Never!" She found the idea of so tightly knit a family fascinating, but also terrifying; her own was so relaxed. Her sister lived in California, and they only met a couple of times a year, but when they did, conversation, relationship, continued as if they shared a room. The concept of still living at home after the age of 21 amazed her. It gave her goose pimples to think that she might one day belong to a family with such a background, and who seemed to find it necessary to be within touching distance of each other on a year-round basis – and which was ruled by a princess! She had only seen the Dowager Princess Priscilla from a distance or in photographs in the glossies, as Alex had not yet got around even to taking her home, but he had promised to do so after the election – to celebrate Wendell Wilkie's victory. Now she wasn't sure he would still wish to do that.

What did one say to a princess? She had heard that the Princess Bolugayevska, as she had been in her heyday, had been considered one of the most beautiful women in the world. Well, obviously that had to have been some time in the past – the Princess was well into her forties now. But she was still a princess.

"Is that by inclination, or habit?" Alex asked, as he fetched their coats.

"It's an American custom," she explained. Well, he ought to know that, having lived here for 15 years. He did not even have a trace of a Russian accent. But Elaine knew all about how he and his mother and his now dead half-sister had escaped from Russia during the great Civil War. Even if Alex could remember very little about that, it was still an incredibly romantic background from the point of view of a young woman who had been born, brought up, and educated in Concord and Boston.

But he *was* taking her home, she realised, as having said goodnight to Staff – they would be back on duty at dawn the next morning – and to the other internees, he escorted her out into the chill and boisterous November air. People surrounded them, shouting the praises of Franklin Roosevelt, jumping up and down, setting off firecrackers, laughing and shouting, utterly friendly because Alex had wisely removed his Wilkie button and Elaine still wore her Roosevelt. "Do *you* think it's unconstitutional?" she shouted, as they fought their way through the throng. "A third term, I mean."

"It's democracy," he assured her.

Elaine clung to his arm as they climbed the hill swaying against each other. "I'm scared stiff," she confessed.

"They're human."

"Well . . . there are humans and humans, aren't there. Do they know about me?"

"No."

"Shit!" she muttered. But she had created this scenario. She had pushed as hard as she dared, short of actually inviting this gorgeous hunk to bed, and well brought-up young ladies did not do that sort of thing, even when they have shared the intimacies of examining male and female reproductive organs together – their subjects had either been very dead or very sick, which is not conducive to romance. Now was the moment of fruition.

She was out of breath when he pushed through the gate. The house was big, four-storeyed and square, and glowed with light. There were two expensive cars parked in the drive to the right. Even in the November darkness it was easy to see that in the spring the garden would be a blaze of designed colour. She was in the domain of a Russian princess!

The door was actually opened by a butler. Elaine wasn't sure whether or not she should curtsey. "Rollo, this is Dr Mitchell."

"It is a pleasure, Dr Mitchell." Rollo revealed no surprise at the unusual title, in a woman. "May I take your coat?"

Elaine allowed herself to be divested of her tweed herring-bone. "He's English," she whispered to Alex.

"All butlers are English," he told her.

Rollo was walking in front of them to open double doors. "Mr Alexei and Dr Mitchell," he announced, rather, Elaine thought, as if they were at a grand ball. She had never heard Alex called Alexei before.

Alex had taken her arm again, much to her relief, and urged her into the brightly lit room. It was large, and there was a roaring fire in the hearth at the far end. There were only three people present, but one of them was a surprise, it appeared, even to Alex. "Alexei, darling!" Priscilla Cromb came forward. "Isn't the result disappointing!"

"Absolutely! Mother, I'd like you to meet Dr Elaine Mitchell."

Again Elaine was not sure whether she should curtsey. It was early evening, and perhaps the Princess dressed for dinner every evening. The dark-green taffeta gown with the plunging décolletage, in which a gold chain with a sapphire pendant nestled with devastating effect, was sufficiently breathtaking, but even that magnificence was meaningless when she got her eyes up to the Princess's face. The contours were basically soft, flawlessly carved into the most superb beauty, but rendered even the more compelling by the traces of hardness at the edges of her lips, the cool ice-blue of her eyes. Elaine could not discern any lines other than a few crows' feet at the corners of the eyes, while the décolletage indicated that even at 46 the Princess Dowager still possessed the sort of figure any woman half her age might dream of. "Dr Mitchell?" Her voice was soft, but her eyes flickered towards her son.

"We work at the hospital together," Alex explained.

"How nice," Priscilla said. Elaine realised that she had not actually been welcomed.

"But I must warn you, Mom," Alex went on, "that she voted for Roosevelt." Elaine cast him a hasty glance, both to ascertain that he was joking and in amazement that anyone would dare address this supreme creation as "Mom"! But he was smiling.

And now Priscilla Bolugayevska-Cromb was smiling as well, and doubling her beauty. "We accept all sorts, Dr Mitchell."

"Elaine, please, Your . . ." she bit her lip.

"Call me Priscilla." Priscilla took her hand and led her into the room.

"My husband, Joseph."

Joseph Cromb was also dressed for dinner, in a dinner-jacket. Elaine began to feel like a tramp. He was a tall, somewhat thin man. His face was handsome, the aquiline features revealing his Jewish ancestry. It was a strong face, more obviously so than that of his wife, although both indicated powerful personalities. Elaine knew that this man had been imprisoned by the Russian Communists for several years. She had no real idea what that meant, but it sounded pretty grim. Yet there was no obvious sign of ill-treatment, in his face, at least. "My pleasure, Dr Mitchell," he said and, to her utter consternation, kissed her hand. No one had ever done that to her before.

"And now I would like you to meet Sonia Bolugayevska," Priscilla said.

She was really addressing her son, who had been staring at the other woman in the room. Well, Elaine thought, she was certainly worth staring at. Sonia Bolugayevska was well past 60 but there remained traces of her once great beauty in the firm lines of her chiselled features, in her carriage – she was a tall woman and must once have had an eye-catching figure – and even in the traces of glowing black in her curling gray hair. "Aunt Sonia?" Alex stepped forward, and she embraced him.

"Sonia and I shared the same husband, once," Priscilla told Elaine, and smiled as the young woman was obviously out of her depth. "Not at the same time, of course. But we were both Princesses of Bolugayen." Living history, Elaine thought.

"Dr Mitchell!" Again Elaine felt like curtseying.

"But, Aunt Sonia, to see you here . . ." Alex was clearly overwhelmed.

"I invited Sonia to visit us for a while," Priscilla said. "I didn't tell you, just in case she decided not to come."

"Oh, how I wanted to come!" Sonia said.

Priscilla rang a silver bell and Rollo appeared instantly, carrying a tray of glasses of champagne. Priscilla raised hers. "So, I drink to old times."

"Old times!" the others said.

How I hope they are going to talk of them, Elaine thought.

"Time was when we smashed our glasses after each drink," Alex whispered. Elaine goggled at him. Rollo topped them up.

"Now let us all sit down," Priscilla said.

"I was most terribly sorry to hear about Mr Trotsky, Aunt Sonia," Alex said.

"Thank you."

"Trotsky?" Elaine asked. "Oh, I'm sorry. I didn't mean to interrupt. But wasn't he the Communist leader who was assassinated a couple of months ago?"

"Yes," Sonia said.

"Did you know him?"

"I was standing beside him when he was killed," Sonia said.

Elaine opened her mouth and then closed it again. Being a doctor meant that one had to be acquainted with death, but always at second hand, as it were. "Gosh!" she said. "But weren't you in danger?"

"I don't think so," Sonia said. "There were a lot of people around. The assassin was on a suicide mission. Well, he didn't die. Not then. But he was arrested immediately."

"Gosh," Elaine said again. "But . . . why? I never did understand that. Who would want Trotsky dead?"

"A man called Josef Stalin. Have you heard of him?"

"Oh, yes. He's the President of Russia, isn't he?"

"No. He is the Chairman of the Communist Party in Russia, and thus Prime Minister. He tells the President what to do."

"But why should Mr Stalin wish Mr Trotsky dead? I thought he was a friend of Stalin?"

"He was Stalin's bitterest enemy," Sonia said.

Priscilla decided this conversation had gone on long enough. "Will you stay to dinner, Elaine?" she asked.

"Oh, well, I'd love to . . . but I'm not dressed."

Priscilla looked her up and down. "We shall be informal, tonight," she decided. "But I am sure you would like to freshen up."

Rollo was waiting to close the doors behind Elaine and leave the family in privacy. "She seems a very nice girl," Priscilla remarked. "Is she a very special friend?"

"She could be," Alex said.

Priscilla looked at Joseph. Over their very long association, which had begun a good many years before they had been able to marry, Alex had insensibly come to regard Joseph almost as a true father; he could not remember his real father, the previous Prince Alexei Bolugayevski, who had died fighting against the Communists in 1919, and although he had respected his first stepfather, the American financier Carlisle Mann, he had always felt that was a temporary arrangement, because his mother's true lover had gone missing and was presumed dead. But since Joseph's return from prison in Russia he had entirely accepted him as head of the family. All of which Joseph knew very well. Just as he was aware that this was a crisis long in the making, in that this was the first young woman Alex had ever brought home. Now he smiled, easily, seeking to defuse the tension. "So tell us, Alex," he said, "are your intentions honourable, or strictly sexual?"

"Honourable, I would hope. If she'll have me. I haven't asked her yet."

"Well, I think you need to get to know her a little better before you do ask her," Priscilla said. "All of us need to do that."

Alex knew what his mother meant, even if he did not agree with her. However well she appeared to have re-adjusted herself to being a Boston matron, he knew that in her heart and mind she remained the Princess Dowager of Bolugayen, and would always remain so. Equally, as Princess Dowager of Bolugayen, she was certain that however complete seemed the domination of Stalin and the Communist Party over Soviet Russia, so historically unacceptable a situation must one day come to an end; she believed it would be sooner rather than later. And however impossible it might for anyone else to envisage such a collapse of the Communist regime being followed by a reversion to the society of Tsarist Russia that she had known and loved so briefly, just before the start of the Great War, that was what she intended to aim at. It followed, therefore, that in her agenda the woman her son married would one day herself be Princess of Bolugayen. This was not a business to be undertaken lightly. As for whether Elaine might consider such an agenda as totally unacceptable, Alex knew that would never cross his mother's mind. "I do intend to get to know her better," he promised, without specifying what he had in mind. "Now, let's talk about you, Aunt Sonia." He sat beside her. "What are your plans?"

Sonia looked at Priscilla. In the strangest manner, the two women were the oldest of friends. Alex's father, as Prince of Bolugayen, had divorced Sonia Cohen, ostensibly because he suspected her of adultery, which had never been proved, but really because, as Alex knew, it had been pointed out to him that the high command he sought in the Tsarist Army could not be obtained while he remained in the social wilderness through his marriage to a Jewess. The parting had naturally been bitter, and the bitterness had been increased when Alexei had promptly married a 17-year-old girl who not only happened to be roughly a third of his own age but was also his niece. If ever two women had cause to dislike and distrust the other it had to have been Sonia Cohen and Priscilla Cromb. But the exigencies of war had thrown them together.

When Bolugayen had been overrun and destroyed by the marauding Reds they had been taken prisoner together, suffered rape and mistreatment together, and however much their paths had diverged since – Sonia seeking her future in the maelstrom that had been Russia in 1919, and appearing to emerge triumphant, and Priscilla being forced to flee and become a political refugee – they had remained friends.

Now, while Priscilla had at last found stability and happiness with the man she had always loved, Sonia's world had come crashing down with the murder of the man she had never loved but had faithfully served for 20 years. Yet when she looked at the man who was, in effect, her stepson, there was no defeat in her eyes, only anger. "My plans," she said, "are to seek vengeance for Leon's death."

The dinner conversation was, predictably, about events in Europe. Elaine had not been following very closely what was happening in Europe, although she was of course aware that a war was raging over there, even if raging seemed hardly the right word. Nazi Germany appeared to have overrun the entire Continent with the greatest ease, except the Iberian Peninsula, and of course Soviet Russia, with which they had an alliance. They had attempted to bomb Great Britain into surrender, but had failed to do so, and now the conflict seemed to have sunk into a kind of stalemate although there was apparently some fighting going on in North Africa, between the British and Germany's allies, the Italians. Elaine had voted for Roosevelt not only because he had done so much to bring the country out of the dark years of the Depression, but because part of his platform was a commitment to keep the United States out of the War.

Now she was surprised to learn that although the Crombs were second generation Americans, and, she had supposed, third generation Russians, they were actually British by descent, and revered their ancestors, especially the man they regarded as the founder of their branch of the house, the Scot Colin MacLain, who had been wounded and taken prisoner during the Charge of the Light Brigade, not a hundred years ago, and whose marriage while in captivity to the Russian Countess Dagmar Bolugayevska, had created this branch of the family. They were thus wholeheartedly in support of Britain against the Nazis, and equally condemnatory of the Soviets for agreeing virtually to give Hitler a free hand.

"What do you think is going to happen?" she ventured.

Joseph sighed. "Sadly, it is difficult to see what can happen for the better, as long as this country remains isolationist. The British certainly can't lick Hitler all on their own, any more than I believe he can beat them, at least by invasion. But if he were really to get his U-boats to work he can slowly strangle Britain, and if it went on long enough they'd simply have to make peace on his terms."

"You're talking about a war of several years," Alex said.

"Oh, at the very least. It's a pretty gloomy prospect."

"And you think if we went in, we could win?" Elaine asked.

"Absolutely."

"But so many people would be killed . . ."

"So many people are being killed, Dr Mitchell," Sonia

Bolugayevska said. "If not in battle, by execution. It is an unthinkable scenario."

She was seated on the Princess's left, and Priscilla squeezed her hand. "But at least you are safe, here, Sonia, for just as long as you wish to stay. You simply must put thoughts of vengeance out of your mind."

"Never!" Sonia said.

Alex borrowed his mother's car to drive Elaine home. She wasn't at all sure whether she hadn't dreamed the evening; certainly she have never drunk so much champagne and wine at one time – the car seemed to be floating high above the street. Alex appeared to be absolutely sober; she supposed he was used to it.

The car braked to a stop beside the kerb. There was still a great deal of celebratory noise in the city, especially down by the water, but this street was empty. "I'm sure I didn't thank your folks enough," Elaine said. "It was a simply marvellous evening."

"They enjoyed entertaining you. I enjoyed entertaining you."

They gazed at each other, each just visible in the gloom. "I'd ask you up," Elaine said. "But . . ."

"Tell me this but."

"Well, in the first place, my apartment isn't very elegant. In the second, it's pretty crowded; there are two other girls up there."

"Ah!" he said. "Can't you send them out?"

"At this hour? You must be kidding!"

"Well, in that case . . . goodnight."

Elaine waited for the kiss, and duly received it, but it was chaste and formal. Shit, she thought. I've blown it!

The Reichschancellory in Berlin glowed with light, hummed with music, exuded excitement. Inside was crowded with bare shoulders and heaving breasts, glittering jewels and medals, elegant uniforms, mainly dark blues and blacks, while the walls glowed with the red, black and white of the huge swastika flags draped there.

"A most impressive display of Teutonic splendour, wouldn't you say, Countess?"

Anna von Holzbach turned sharply. The man was speaking German, but with a foreign accent, and his tunic was dark green, with red collar and cuffs and shoulder straps. "How do you know I am a countess?" she demanded.

"I know a great deal about you, Your Excellency." This time he spoke Russian. "About the entire Bolugayevski family."

Anna inhaled, slowly, while she surveyed him; she could not remember ever seeing him before. But he was Russian, and therefore to be hated. For all her name and background, Anna Bolugayevska von Holzbach was not really Russian at all. Her father, the last true Prince of Bolugayen, Alexei Bolugayevski, son of Colin MacLain Bolugayevski, had actually been Scottish, and her mother had been the Jewess Sonia Cohen. Fortunately, for her present circumstances, she entirely took after her father and was tall and strongly built; now that she was in her mid-30s she could almost be described as matronly, although she had never been a mother. Her features, too, were pure Bolugayevska, bold and strong and handsome, as her curling yellow hair was also a trademark of her family. Thus, as she had long been separated from her mother – who she knew thought her to be dead – and as no one in Germany had thought to look beyond the utter Aryanism of her appearance, she remained welcome in the very inner circles of the Nazi Party.

But she would not remain so if this lout were to spread her background about. She was not afraid, physically. Although the Jews had been turned into second-class citizens by the regime, forced to emigrate or remain to be locked up in special camps, as she was married to one of Hitler's favourite young men, and a man who was one of Germany's new heroes for his exploits in the campaign which had driven France out of the War and Great Britain out of Europe, and as she was herself one of Hitler's pleasures – he delighted in entertaining her to tea, which always left her breathless with anticipation and frustrated with his total apparent lack of sexual interest in her – she could not imagine that were it suddenly discovered she had a Jewish mother would involve her in any personal danger. But the social consequences would be unthinkable. She looked the Russian officer up and down. "We do not seem to have been introduced."

He clicked his heels and bent over her white-gloved hand. "Feodor Ligachev, Your Excellency."

"And you are . . ." she studied his insignia. "A captain?" Her tone was contemptuous.

"I am an assistant military attaché at the Embassy."

"Ah. And you claim to know all about me. Tell me what you know about me?"

"I know that you are the daughter of the late Alexei Bolugayevski, one time Prince of Bolugayen."

Anna waited, almost holding her breath, but he didn't immediately continue, so she remarked, "That was a long time ago, Captain, and I long ago turned my back on my family. I am Frau von Holzbach, now."

"That is good to know," Ligachev said. "As we are now by way of being related."

Anna raised her eyebrows. "I do not think that can be possible."

"My father, Ivan Ivanovich Ligachev, is your cousin Jennie's second husband." Anna was speechless. "Is that not a happy turn of events?" Feodor Ligachev asked. "As your father was our enemy, while Colonel von Holzbach and his people are our friends."

"That must be very nice for you," Anna said, and sighed with relief as she saw her husband coming to her rescue.

"What did that fellow want?" Alexander von Holzbach asked, as he swept his wife into a Strauss waltz. Alexander von Holzbach was a handsome man, tall and well built, his somewhat bland features given strength and purpose by the dark blue tunic with its high collar, and the various insignia pinned there, not to mention the Iron Cross, First Class, which hung from his throat. Like all German officers following their great victories in Poland and the West, he was a romantic figure. But Anna would have found him so in any event. With her father, and her brother, he had fought for the White armies seeking to overthrow the Bolsheviks following the end of the Great War. Following their defeat in the Great Civil War, Alexander had accompanied Prince Colin, as he had become on the death of his father, to France, to eke out a meagre living driving taxis while they had dreamed of regaining supremacy in Russia. And when Colin had been murdered by the Red assassin Andrei Gosykin, shot down in cold blood while she had lain in bed only a heartbeat away, it had been Alexander who had swept her up and fled with her to safety in Germany, to become a Nazi hero.

Anna had not known what to make of Alexander then. For one thing, they had only met the very afternoon Colin had been shot. And she had been so wrapped up in her brother, who had returned to her life after she had already supposed him dead, that the fact of his real death obscured every other consideration, and certainly every other man. But Alexander had promised revenge, and through his relationship with the rising Nazi Party in Germany, such revenge had seemed possible.

It had been a long time coming. Gosykin himself had fallen a victim to the great purges instigated by Stalin, but his wife and daughter still remained as objects of hatred to be brought down. That Jennie Gosykinya was Anna's own first cousin only made her the more hateful. But her hatred extended to all Russia and all Russians, beginning with Stalin himself.

Hitler had promised they would be wiped off the face of the earth. He had not been thinking so much of revenge – no Russian had ever harmed him, personally – but in getting rid of what were to him hordes of sub-human Slavs to create living-space, *lebensraum*, for the German masses. But then he had signed a mutual aid pact with Stalin. Anna had hardly been able to believe it. Alexander had explained it, of course; it was necessary to be friends with Russia while Germany dealt with the West. But that had been accomplished, more than six months ago, and still Germany and Russia seemed the best of friends – which was why such a lout as this Ligachev was at a Chancellory ball. "He claimed to know my background," she said. "Would you believe it, his father is now married to Jennie Gosykinya!"

Alexander frowned. He cared nothing for the antics of Jennie Gosykinya, a woman of whom he had only ever heard, not met, but he knew his wife's background better than anyone else. "He knows about your mother?"

"I don't think so. He didn't mention her."

"Bastard!" Alexander said into her hair as he hugged her close. Although they had been intimates for nearly 17 years, from the moment he had found her kneeling naked beside her dead brother's body, he still adored her. Anna, now 33, was a most beautiful woman who had perhaps just about reached an apogee – with her height and strong build she was liable to become overweight as she grew older. But it was more than her physical attraction. She was a countess, the descendant of princes. That gave her an aura. And he was afraid of her; she possessed a quality of intensity he entirely lacked. "But he will soon be history," he whispered.

Anna pulled her head back. "Tell me."

"Not here. Would you like to go home, early?"

"Tell me," she said, as soon as they had entered the door of their apartment.

"Keller told me tonight," Alexander said. "My orders will arrive tomorrow. The Balkans."

"The Balkans?" Anna was astonished. "Whatever for?"

"Well, the Italians have got themselves into their usual mess while trying to occupy Greece. Now it seems that the British are sending men into Greece to help. So, ostensibly, we are sending forces down there to assist the Italians."

Anna went into the bedroom. "There will be little glory in that." She stood before her full-length mirror while she reached behind herself to unbutton her gown. "Do not the British always run away?"

He joined her, and took over the unbuttoning himself. "I said 'ostensibly'. As for the British, the sooner they run away the better." She turned, in his arms, as the gown slipped away from her breasts and gathered round her thighs. "Keller told me, in the strictest confidence, my pet, that the Fuehrer has made up his mind to move against Russia."

"There! All set?" Jennie Ligachevna smiled at her daughter.

They made a splendid pair. Jennie Ligachevna was the daughter of Patricia Bolugayevska-Cromb, the wayward countess who had sided with the Russian Communists and been exiled to Siberia before managing to escape and flee to the sanctuary of England and the arms of her cousin Duncan Cromb. She had carried with her her infant son, Joseph, born to another exile, the Jew Joseph Fine, in the wilds of Siberia. Jennie revered the memory of the mother; she could no longer revere the memory of the half-brother she had once adored. He had turned against Soviet Russia and indeed, herself. She did not know the truth of the articles he had written about his experiences in the gulag, the Soviet prison in which he had been confined for several years. She did not wish to believe any of it.

Jennie Ligachevna had known very little of what to believe over the past few years. When she had eloped from England with the handsome, dashing Soviet agent Andrei Gosykin, defying her family but not her background – her mother Patricia would have done the same thing, she was certain – the world had seemed at her feet. Welcomed in the Kremlin by Lenin himself, as the first true Russian aristocrat ever voluntarily to return to the Soviet state, she had been the happiest woman in Europe, she had had no doubt at all. Lenin had shared exile in Siberia with Patricia Bolugayevska, and a lasting friendship had grown up between them. Even Lenin's death so soon after her arrival had not in any way interfered with the even tenor of her new life. She had been made almost a member of the family of Lenin's successor, Josef Stalin, for whom Gosykin had then worked.

There had been a difficult time: her brother Joseph's so strange visit to Russia in search of her which had apparently resulted in his being sent to prison for several years – if that were true – and the tragedy of her Aunt Sonia and her lover Trotsky, disgraced and then banished. She had been horrified at the news of Trotsky's murder, last autumn, by an unknown assassin – even Uncle Joe, as she referred to Stalin, had claimed not to know who had been behind it – and only relieved that Sonia had managed to survive.

Her real personal crisis had occurred several years ago, when her husband had been arrested for treason, tried, condemned and shot. His execution had been one of the first resulting from the murder of Uncle Joe's close friend Sergei Kirov. Jennie had been utterly shocked. Andrei had denied having anything to do with that murder, but it had been carried out by an associate of his, a man named Leonid Nikolaiev, and when the facts had been put to her by the Party investigators, that the man she had loved, the father of her daughter, should have turned out to be a traitor to the Party, a professional murderer, who had (as it had been proved), only married her on orders from Lenin, she had been left prostrate with grief and humiliation.

Jennie did not know how she would have survived without the aid and encouragement of Uncle Joe. He had even offered to let her go back to the West, if she wished. But how could she do that? The West was the enemy of the Party. And of everyone in the West, her own brother Joe and his wife Priscilla were the most implacable of those enemies. She had nothing left in the West. Uncle Joe had understood, and had himself bestowed upon her a second husband, one of his very best friends.

In a perfect world Jennie would never have chosen such a man as Ivan Ligachev as her husband. She would, indeed, have preferred his son. But she was no longer in her first youth – she was 35 – and although she retained much of the beauty she had inherited from her mother, the glowing auburn hair, the boldly handsome features, the tall strong body, she no longer possessed the spirit. Ivan Ivanovich, stolidly unimaginative, earthily passionate, provided the security not only of a man about the house but of a prominent Party member. Being married to Ivan guaranteed her future.

More important, it had guaranteed the future of Tatiana. Jennie's only worry was Tatiana. For Tatiana, the events of the past few years had been even more traumatic than for herself. The father she had been brought up to love and admire had suddenly been accused of a host of crimes and shot. Tatiana even took after Gosykin, in many ways. Her height came from both of them – she was 5 ft 10 inches tall. Her body also perhaps came from both of them, with the thrusting breasts and strong thighs of her mother, the suppleness of her father. And if her face was pure Bolugayevska, her curling black hair was pure Gosykin. But where was her mind?

Jennie knew that her daughter was an enthusiastic member of the Comsomol, the Party youth organisation. Descended as she was, at least on her mother's side, from a long line of soldiers, she delighted in the martial displays, the drills, the gymnastics, which were so important a part of the picture Uncle Josef was intent upon presenting to the world of Communist youth. With her figure, the sight of 18-year-old Tattie leading a parade wearing only vest and shorts could bring all of Red Square to its feet. But she had never brought any of her fellows home.

Partly, Jennie knew, this was because of Ivan. Ivan was what would be known in England as a groper, and one of the women he most liked to grope was his own stepdaughter. It was embarrassing, and Jennie knew it also embarrassed young Feodor, but in a male-dominated society such as Russia there was nothing anyone could do about it; the one time she had tried to remonstrate with him he had slapped her. She had promptly slapped him back and he had never tried that again, but she did not consider the situation was worth a fist-fight.

Soon enough Tatiana would find a man of her own. Jennie even had some hopes that it might be Feodor himself. But Feodor was away in Germany as an attaché. So now she smiled brightly as Tatiana hefted her backpack. If there was one thing the girl definitely looked forward to it was summer camp outside Brest-Litovsk. And this year there was the prospect of a friendship. Her friend Galina Shermetska's daughter Sophie was going to camp for the first time. Galina lived in the apartment above, but hitherto Sophie and Tatiana had not been at all close. Well, Sophie was only 15, three years the younger, and with her spectacles and nervous demeanour she was as much unlike Tatiana as it was possible to imagine. But they were going to camp together. "You will look after Sophie," she said.

"Mother, I will do what I can," Tatiana said. "But this year I am camp captain. I have to look after all of the girls. Not just one."

"I know you will do your best, darling," Jennie said, as she kissed her goodbye.

Summers in Russia were more important than anywhere else, Tatiana Gosykinya thought. Perhaps even more so than in Scandinavia, or the Arctic, because of the immensity of Russia. And especially Belorussia. Other countries were divided by seas and mountains; Belorussia had only rivers, and of course the great swamp, known as the Pripet Marshes. In the winter, it was an unending, flat, sea of snow and ice, broken only by huge forests. In the summer it was equally unending, but now it was a mass of waving cornstalks.

Over the past year it was also exciting because of its proximity to what had once been Poland. Poland had been partitioned between Germany and Russia following the brief war of 1939, as it had been, between Russia, Germany and the Austro-Hungarian Empire, without a war at all, at the end of the Eighteenth Century. It was possible for a Russian to wonder if Poland had ever actually been meant to exist. But its non-existence had brought the borders of Soviet Russia adjacent to the borders of Nazi Germany. This was not a cause for alarm, as they were constantly told, not only by the Party faithful but by Premier Stalin himself, and Tatiana totally accepted whatever her Uncle Joe told her to believe. Thus she assumed that the Nazi-Soviet Pact, so strange, and indeed, so unnatural for either side, had been a necessary step in preserving the strength and safety of the Russian State. Besides, the facts were obvious enough: Germany was engaged in a life and death struggle with the British Empire, and was thus fully preoccupied.

Nonetheless, where two such mighty forces actually touched each other, it was necessary to be armed, and there was a vast Soviet Army, or Front, as the Russians called it, encamped in and around Brest-Litovsk. This was always fun. Tatiana loved soldiers, or at least, watching them performing their marches and manoeuvres. In the course of time she fully intended to be a soldier herself. But until that moment arrived, she wasn't sure she actually wanted to get too close to one; she wasn't sure she actually wanted to get too close to anyone. Of course, these summers required a total intimacy. She had not liked the thought of that the first time she had been required to attend one, two years before. And it had been every bit as bad as she had feared. Everything had depended upon the desires, and the strength of character, of the tent captain. In her first year, Tatiana now knew she had been unlucky. She had already been at once the most attractive and the most voluptuous girl in the tent, and she had been required to submit to rape, not only by the captain, a young woman who had in any event disliked her because of her English ancestry and aristocratic background – not that *she* had ever known any aristocracy – but by all the other girls in the tent. Even those who had not wished to participate had been forced to do so, as part of the apparently necessary "hazing" of the new girl.

Then there had been the boys in the adjoining camp. They had all wanted to get into the action, and a good many of the girls had been happy to accommodate them, even if pregnancy meant an abortion and then a labour company, which did not bear thinking about. Tatiana had at least been allowed to make her own decisions here, and had fought off all advances. While she had told no one, not even her mother, what had happened, she had vowed she would never return to another summer camp. But of course she had had no choice when the next year had come round. But this time she had been the tent leader – unusual at 17 but everyone knew her mother was a friend of the Party Chairman – and her tent had been a happy one. The girls had actually laughed.

Thus there had been a queue to get into her tent. This year, in fact, she was captain of the entire woman's camp. So if she could only accommodate 20 in her tent, who were envied by the rest, she could to a large extent control what happened in the rest of the camp. She wanted them all to laugh, this year. This year, too, she had nothing to fear from the boys, who had learned to have a healthy respect for her strength and her determination to use it. Summer camp had become a place to be happy, far happier than she could ever be at home, knowing that Stepfather was coming in every evening. As for Sophie Shermetska, she was having the best of all introductions to camp; there was no need to make an exception of her.

Tatiana stood beside the flag as it was lowered for the evening of 21 June. On the other side of the flagpole there stood Anatole Savin, captain of the boy's camp. Anatole was a good-looking boy of 19. Had Tatiana been the least interested in males she would have chosen him above any of the others. But he was, in any event, not a possibility for her – he was both shorter and more slightly built. Nonetheless they smiled at each other as the flag came down. "Good night, Comrade," Tatiana said.

"Good night, Comrade," Anatole replied.

Tatiana saluted – he was, technically, her superior – and then marched off to her girls. Everyone was just packing it in and retiring – it was already well past ten o'clock. She stood in the tent doorway while her subordinates tucked themselves in beneath their blankets, then put on her cotton nightdress and went back to the doorway for a last look at the night. In the distance she heard the piercing whistle of a train; the camp was not far from the Berlin-Moscow railway line, and that was undoubtedly the express, travelling from one capital to the other.

Tatiana wondered if she would ever travel from Moscow to Berlin by express train. That was an aspect of a future of which she had no idea. The Party would decide. She turned down the tent lamp, joined in the chorus of goodnights, and slept soundly, knowing that she would awake at the first light, which would be not long past three. But she was awakened before that, by the greatest sound she had ever heard.

Chapter 2

The Storm

Everyone in the tent woke at once. "Aircraft!" shouted Natasha Renkova. They gathered in the doorway to the tent, then spilled out into the utter darkness of the pre-dawn. The sky above them was black, but yet filled with sound.

"Thousands of them," whispered Sophie Shermetska, taking off her glasses to polish them in the hope of seeing better.

Tatiana just stared up into the darkness. The planes were undoubtedly flying from west to east. That could only mean they were coming from Germany, and going . . .? All the tents were emptied now, a milling mass of some hundred nightgown-clad girls, twittering like birds. Then there were new sounds, from the west, dull, distant explosions. They stared in that direction, and saw little bursts of flame dotting the horizon. Someone screamed. "Stop that!" Tatiana snapped. "Get dressed. All of you. Get dressed!"

The girls scattered back to their tents. Tatiana led the rush back to hers, dragged on her clothes, duty wear of heavy drawers and skirt and blouse, ankle-length socks, tough shoes. She crammed her sidecap on her head, and heard her name being shouted. She went outside and found Anatole and several other of the boys, half-dressed, clearly terrified. "What is happening, Tatiana?" Anatole asked, as if she had the answer to everything.

"We are being attacked."

"But by whom?"

"It can only be the Germans."

"What are you going to do?"

"I am going into town to see Comrade Markowitza."

Comrade Markowitza, as Camp Commandant, should have been sleeping out here with them, but she had a lover in Brest-Litovsk. "I will come with you," Anatole said.

"And me," Natasha Renkova said.

"And me." The chorus ran through the girls who were hastily re-assembling.

"You cannot all come," Tatiana told them. "You must not panic. Now—"

"There is a car!" Sophie Shermetska shouted.

"And the lights in Brest-Litovsk have gone out!" shouted someone else.

Tatiana looked west. The glow of the town had indeed disappeared, but beyond them the flaring lights and the rumbling explosions continued. Close at hand a car was bumping its way towards the camp. She and Anatole went to meet it as it slewed to a halt. Beside the driver was Commandant Verina Markowitza. She was a rather gaunt woman in her late 30s and was wearing a greatcoat over a nightgown, and, incongruously, army boots. Her head was bare, lank black hair flopping about her cheeks. "You must abandon this camp," she told the two young people.

"But what is happening, Comrade Commandant?" Anatole asked.

"The Germans have crossed the border in great strength. Oh, they will be hurled back," Verina Markowitza asserted. "But there may well be fighting close to here. You will go to the railway station in the village, and from there you will be evacuated."

"Can we not stay and fight?" Tatiana asked.

"Do not be a silly girl. You have no weapons. Get yourselves packed up and march to the railway station. I will meet you there. Hurry now."

Tatiana felt like saying if you will give us the weapons we will fight; she felt utterly outraged that something like this could be happening to Russia, without warning, from a nation with whom she was virtually allied. But she decided against it: Verina Markowitza had a short fuse, and carried a cane at all times, even now; her fuse was clearly shorter than usual this morning. Instead she wondered what would happen to her stepbrother Feodor. He was actually in Berlin! "Right," she told the girls. "Pack your bags. Then dismantle the camp. Fall in! We have to march to the railway station."

The nearest railway station was in a village several miles east of Brest-Litovsk; it was also three miles away from the camp, but it was where they had disembarked the previous week. The girls packed their haversacks and backpacks, took down the tents and loaded them into the handcarts, and lined up; Tatiana also had them load as much food as they had – mainly stale bread and sausage – into the carts: she had no idea when they would be able to obtain any more. By now it was growing light, and the flashes were less conspicuous. On the other hand, they could now make out huge columns of smoke rising above the town and beyond, and the noise was definitely louder. Overhead the planes still flew east.

The boys had now fallen in as well, beside them, and as they marched off, Anatole came to walk beside Tatiana. "Are you afraid?" he asked.

"Of course I am not afraid," she replied, by no means sure that was the truth. But she felt more excited, almost breathless.

"I suppose I will be taken into the Army when we get back to Moscow," Anatole said, gloomily.

"We will all be taken into the Army when we get back to Moscow. Hurry! There's the train."

They could see it quite clearly, steaming up the track, but they still had a mile to go. Some of the girls began to run, abandoning the handcarts. Tatiana let them get on with it; she knew they weren't going to make it. And by the time they staggered into the station yard the train was merely a puff of smoke in the distance. The people in the village hadn't even bothered to go on to the platform. But they were packing up preparatory to moving out. "Where are you going?" Tatiana asked.

"Into the Marshes," a man said. "Fritz won't find us in there."

Tatiana thought that was incredibly defeatist talk, and now some of the girls began to weep and throw themselves on the ground. Some of the boys began to cry, too. Even Anatole looked close to tears, asking, "What are we going to do?"

"Wait," Tatiana told him. She was more concerned that the station appeared to have been entirely abandoned; even the stationmaster had disappeared.

She summoned some of the less distraught boys and girls and had them bring the handcarts into the station yard. The village was by now as empty as the station, the people streaming to the east, carrying their bundles and accompanied by their dogs, chickens and pigs. "People?" Natasha Renkova said, looking to the west.

"Soldiers," Anatole said.

They had once been soldiers, Tatiana thought. They had discarded their weapons and were streaming through the cornfields towards the east. Some came close enough to the station to see the young people, whereupon they came even closer. They gazed at the girls and licked thir lips. "What are you running away from, Comrades?" Tatiana asked.

One, a stocky little man who wore a sergeant's stripes, pointed west. "The Germans. Haven't you heard?"

"You are a coward," Tatiana told him. "Where is your rifle?"

"Why, you little bitch—" he moved towards her.

Tatiana picked up one of the iron tent uprights. "You are wrong, Comrade Sergeant," she said. "I am a big bitch, and if you come a step closer, I will brain you."

He hesitated. "Leave them to the Germans, Sergeant,"

one of the men said. "Raping this lot will hold them up a while."

Still the sergeant hesitated. "What do you have in those carts?" he demanded.

"Our belongings," Tatiana told him.

"We'll just have a look."

He moved forward, and Tatiana again raised her iron bar; she was not going to let these louts make off with their scanty food supply without fighting for it. And by now her determination had aroused the others. Anatole led several of the boys to stand beside her. "Let's go, Sergeant," urged the private. "Before the Germans get here."

"They're coming," the sergeant said. "If you want to survive, you'd better come along with us. But I give the orders."

"Get lost," Tatiana told him.

He gave her a stiff middle finger then he and his men hurried off, making for the distant trees. "Don't you think we should've gone with them?" Sophie Shermetska asked anxiously.

"Into the swamp? They'll all die before the Germans get at them," Tatiana said. "We were told to wait here." She was happy to have orders she could obey.

Now it was broad daylight, and they were surrounded by the sounds of battle. Above their heads the planes continued to fly east, but lower down there were other aircraft, Russians, attempting to combat the aerial invasion. The young people stared at the planes, wheeling and diving, soaring and spitting red, at the vapour trails and at machines plunging from the sky beneath plumes of dark smoke, to shatter themselves in the earth. But all the aircraft falling from the sky seemed to be Russian. When they looked west, they continued to see flashes of light and clouds of smoke. There was an enormous battle going on only a few miles away: Brest-Litovsk was a fortress. "I bet we could pick up some rifles over there," said Gregory Asimov, pointing at the fields over which they had come in the dark. "I saw some of those fellows throwing them away."

"Then we would be combatants and shot by the Germans," Anatole objected. "Isn't that right, Tatiana?"

Tatiana bit her lip. How she would love to pick up a rifle. But she didn't want to be shot. Then to her great relief she saw a car bouncing along the track beside the railway line. "Comrade Markowitza!"

Girls and boys crowded around the car. "The train went by, Comrade Commandant," Anatole said.

"It never even stopped," said Sophie Shermetska, starting to cry all over again.

"Be quiet!" Commandant Markowitza commanded. "There will be another train in a few minutes. They are evacuating the town." Even as she spoke, they heard the wail of a siren. "Line up!" Commandant Markowitza ordered. "Prepare to board!"

The girls and boys hastily got into line, Tatiana at one end, Anatole at the other. Now they could see the train, hurtling towards them. There were people everywhere, even sitting or lying on top of the coaches; it occurred to Tatiana that it was going to be a terrible squeeze. But there was not going to be a squeeze at all. The train raced at the station without slowing. The girls started to surge forward, and Tatiana had to drag them back from the edge of the platform. The train did not stop and the people on the roofs and at the windows shouted at the young people, but their words were lost in the rush of wind. "Swine!" Commandant Markowitza threw her sidecap on the ground and stamped on it.

Several of the girls started weeping again. "Will there be another train, Comrade Commandant?" Tatiana inquired.

Comrade Markowitza glared at her.

"I am very thirsty," Natasha Renkova said.

"And hungry," someone else put in.

"There is a well in the station yard," Anatole ventured.

"May we drink the water from the well, Comrade Commandant?" Tatiana asked.

"Oh, do what you like!" Markowitza picked up her sidecap and slapped it against her thighs.

The boys used a bucket to pull up the water, and then knelt shoulder to shoulder with the girls, scooping it up with their hands. Tatiana wondered how clean it was, but she was as thirsty as any of them. Even Markowitza had a drink, then she surveyed them, hand on hips. "We will breakfast, then we will march into Brest-Litovsk," she announced.

Breakfast consisted of the bread and sausage. As they ate, the young people looked at each other, then beyond the trees fringing the station yard. The noise of firing was now very close, and over the town there was a vast pall of smoke. "Would it not be better to walk the other way?" Tatiana asked.

Markowitza glared at her, and the hand holding the cane twitched. Tatiana braced herself, but before Markowitza could hit her one of the boys shouted, "Tanks!"

They all turned to look where he was pointing and saw, coming out of the north, roughly from where they had been camped, an avalanche of steel monsters, heading straight for them, huge plumes of red dust rising behind them into the still air. "They will tell us what to do," Anatole said.

Markowitza glared at him in turn. But Tatiana was gazing at the tanks, and the pennons which were now becoming visible. "Those are German tanks," she said.

The girls gave a great wail of terror, and closed ranks as if ordered to do so, shoulder to shoulder. The boys did the same. "Quick!" Markowitza commanded. "Into the waiting room."

"It's locked," Gregory Asimov objected.

"Then break down the door!"

Does she really think 200 of us are going to fit into one waiting room? Tatiana wondered. And anyway, what protection will thin wooden walls offer us against tanks? But the boys were already smashing the glass panes in the door, reaching through to release the bolt. Then they led the rush into the room, the girls pushing and shoving to get past them.

Tatiana stepped away from them, and watched the tanks. Two of the huge iron monsters had stopped in a cloud of dust, not a hundred yards from the station. The others had continued on their way, wheeling to follow the railway track back into Brest-Litovsk from the rear. She stared at the two tanks, watched the guns slowly traversing to point directly at the station, straight at her. I am about to die, she thought. I am going to be blown into little bits. She was paralysed with the knowledge.

Then the hatches of the tanks were thrown up and leather-helmeted heads appeared. The girls and boys behind Tatiana, stopping their struggle to get into the waiting room, also stared at the tanks. Markowitza came forward to stand beside Tatiana. The man in the hatch of the first tank climbed out and dropped to the ground. Above him the muzzle of the gun continued to glare at them, and now another head appeared in the hatchway. The man came towards them, taking off his helmet as he did so. He did not look at all hostile, had a pleasant face, and was smiling. "You are our prisoners," he announced in Russian. "Lay down your arms."

"We have no arms," Tatiana explained. Markowitza made an inarticulate sound, furious at being upstaged.

"What are you doing here?" the German officer asked, looking over all of them and realising that only the Commandant could be over 20.

"We were in our summer camp," Tatiana said.

"You are the Commandant?"

"I am the Commandant," Markowitza declared.

"Then I make you responsible for these children. You will remain here until told where to go. Understood?"

"We will remain here," Markowitza agreed.

"Please, sir," Natasha said. "May we have some food?" There had not really been enough to go round.

"I have no food," the captain said. "When our ground forces get to you there will be food. It will not be long."

He rejoined his tank, and the two vehicles roared off to rejoin the battle. "We must hurry," Tatiana said.

Markowitza stared at her from under arched eyebrows. "Hurry, where?"

"Well . . . into the Marshes, I suppose." They had to accept the inevitable, however distasteful it might be. "They will hardly follow us there."

"I told the officer we would remain here," Markowitza declared. "We have surrendered."

"There may be some food in the houses," Natasha suggested. "Those people cannot have taken it all."

"That would be stealing," Markowitza said, severely. "Are you thieves?"

Tatiana felt like stamping her foot; the silly woman should realise that if they didn't take anything they could find, the Germans certainly would.

The boys also had some food in their carts, and they managed to have a frugal meal. Anatole sat next to Tatiana. "What are we going to do?"

"I think we should leave this place and try to reach the Marshes."

"But Markowitza has said no. She would punish us."

"She'd find it a bit difficult to punish us if we all went," Tatiana pointed out. Anatole chewed his lip in indecision.

Markowitza stood above them. "People are coming," she said, "Line up, and look your best."

Tatiana sighed. They had lost the right to make a decision. She called her girls into line, and they watched the columns of grey-clad soldiers who had bypassed Brest-Litovsk and were tramping across the fields. But instinctively she knew that the soldiers were less important than the cars approaching along the track from Brest-Litovsk. From the lead car there flew the swastika.

* * *

There were four cars, with four men in each. Three of the men in the first car were officers, very smartly dressed in black uniforms and high-peaked caps; they wore sparkling little badges – only when they came close did Tatiana see that the badges were those of the death's head. The rest of the men also wore black, but were less ornately dressed. They were however each armed with a Maschinenpistole 40, the Schmeisser sub-machine-gun, and these were presented at the young people as the black-clad soldiers fanned out to either side of the car.

Tatiana felt her stomach roll as the officers approached. Never had she seen such brutal faces, or such lustful ones as they looked over the girls, quite a few of whom were extremely pretty. But all three, having looked, brought their gazes back to Tatiana. None of the other girls had her beauty. She had an almost irresistible urge to turn and run as fast as her legs would carry her. But she knew that would mean a bullet in the back. The first officer addressed Markowitza in Russian. "You are in charge of these people?"

Markowitza stood to attention. "Yes, Comrade Major."

The officer stepped up close to her and slashed his gloved hand across her mouth. Markowitza staggered, and blood flew from her cut lip. She stared at the officer. Nothing like that had happened to her since she had become a Party member. A ripple of fear went up and down the line of boys and girls. "I am not your comrade, woman," he said. "I am your conqueror. You will address me as Herr Major."

Markowitza licked blood. "Yes . . . Herr Major."

"Now, you are the Camp Commandant? Then you are a commissar?"

"No, Herr Major."

"Do not lie to me, woman!"

"I am not lying, Herr Major. Of course, I have every hope of becoming a commissar, but . . ."

"That is sufficient! You are under arrest."

Markowitza's jaw sagged, as two of the soldiers came forward. She had still not made up her mind what to do, or say, when they grasped her arms, pushing Tatiana out of the way to do so. Then she reacted instinctively, trying to shrug herself free. Instantly the soldiers threw her to the ground, and before she could catch her breath one of them had kicked her in the buttocks. Markowitza gave a shout of mingled pain and outrage, and tried to get up, whereupon the other soldier kicked her in the thigh, and she fell again, rolling, arms flung wide, panting, skirt disarranged. The girls shuddered. One of the soldiers stood astride her and placed the muzzle of his sub-machine-gun on her breast while he snapped at her in German. "He is telling you to get up," the major said.

Still panting, Markowitza cautiously pushed herself out from beneath the German's legs and stood up. She was trembling, her cap had come off, her clothes were coated in dust, and to Tatiana's consternation, a tear escaped her left eye and trickled down her cheek. Markowitza, she with the cane, weeping? But she had also lost her cane. Now she gasped again as one of the soldiers jabbed her in the ribs with his gun, and she staggered towards the cars. "Now," the major said, surveying the rest of them. "Are there any Jews here?"

The girls glanced at each other. There were, in fact, several Jews among both the girls and the boys, but they all suspected that they would be arrested and beaten if found out. They could not help looking past the major at the Commandant, who had been taken down to the last of the cars and was being thrown to and fro between six of the men, Tatiana realised, while she was stripped of her clothing. Again she felt sick. The major walked up and down in front of them. "Well?"

Tatiana drew a deep breath. "There are no Jews, Herr Major."

The major paused in front of her; she found she was holding her breath, and had to let it out, very slowly. "Well," he said, "Anyone can see that you are not a Jew, even if you are a liar. But it would be a shame to ruin such a beautiful creature." He looked along the row of girls. "That one!"

There was another ripple through the ranks, but the sub-machine-guns were aimed at them, and no one dared move. One of the soldiers seized the girl at whom the major had pointed and dragged her from the ranks. Her name was Constantina Reykjava and she was a slight girl, only 16 years old. This was her first summer camp and Tatiana had found her a bit of a problem because of her homesickness and her terror of the open air. She had been weeping nearly all morning, and her eyes were red and swollen, which no doubt was one of the reasons the major had chosen her. "Now," he said, when she was brought in front of him. "What is your name, little girl?"

Constantina's teeth chattered. "Constantina Reykjava, Herr Major."

"And you are afraid of me. But there is nothing for you to be afraid of. Not unless you make me angry. You are not going to make me angry, are you?"

"No, Herr Major," Constantina muttered.

"That is very sensible of you. Turn round, Constantina." Constantina hesitated, and then obeyed. Tatiana could see that every muscle in the girl's body was tensed as she anticipated an assault. "Look at these girls, and the boys, Constantina," the major invited. "And tell me which ones are Jews." Constantine opened her mouth, and found herself staring at Tatiana. Hastily she closed it again. "Come along, girl," the major said.

"There are no Jews here, Herr Major," Constantina said, her voice little more than a whisper.

The major thrust his hands into Constantina's hair, long and wispy, mouse-brown, and pulled her head back; Constantina's sidecap fell off. "You are lying, Constantina," he grunted. Constantina gave a little whimper. Now all the girls and boys were looking at her instead of Markowitza, who had in any event disappeared behind the last car. So had two of the soldiers, who were no doubt raping her, Tatiana supposed. Now it would be Constantina's turn. But she was not going to be so lucky. "Very well," the major said. "Now you have made me angry, Constantina."

He gave an order, and four of the soldiers seized the shivering girl. Two held her arms while two more grasped her ankles and lifted her from the ground. They then laid her across the bonnet of the first car, continuing to hold her wrists and ankles, two on each side of the bonnet. It was now late morning and the sun was overhead, shining fiercely. The metal of the bonnet was hot, and Constantina gasped in discomfort, a gasp which became a scream as another soldier threw up her skirt and pulled down her drawers. White buttocks gleamed in the sunlight, and the major signalled one of the junior officers, who took from the back of the car a thin cane. This he showed to Constantina, who stopped screaming to burst into tears.

Once again the watching young people rippled with apprehension. Fifteen men, Tatiana thought, dominating more than a hundred. But they had the guns! At the first stroke of the cane Constantina's head jerked; she was so taken aback by the pain that she even stopped crying. But by the second she was weeping and screaming incoherently, straining against the four pairs of hands which held her spreadeagled across the bonnet, while the cane slashed again and again into the no longer white flesh. One of the girls gave a sigh and fainted; Natasha and Tatiana held her up – they had to presume that for anyone to fall down would involve her also in a beating.

After the twelfth stroke the major signalled his junior to stop. By then Constantina's buttocks were a bloody mess. The hands released her, and she slid off the bonnet, whimpering. Her knees gave way and she collapsed to the ground, but hastily tried to push herself up as her torn buttocks came into contact with the earth. The major nudged her with his foot. "Now," he said. "Are you ready to point out the Jews to me?" Constantina panted, and two of the soldiers held her arms to lift her to her feet. When her knees gave way, they held her between them; her drawers remained about her ankles but at least her skirt had fallen into place. "Come along now," the major said.

Constantina's head was drooping and he put his hand beneath her chin to raise it up. "If you do not tell me now," he said. "You will have to have another 12 strokes. I should think another 12 will scar you for life." Constantina cast Tatiana an agonised look. But Tatiana knew she was lost.

It was probably the humiliation as much as the pain. She closed her eyes. She did not wish to look upon the utter disintegration of a human being. "All you have to do is point," the major was saying.

Constantina was apparently pointing, because Tatiana could hear a great deal of rustling, sounds of despair, around her. Someone shouted, "Tatiana!" but she kept her eyes shut. She was their leader, their mentor, their certain refuge in time of trouble. And she was doing nothing to help them. She could do nothing to help them, save die herself.

"That is very good, Constantina," the major was saying, and Tatiana opening her eyes, saw that some two dozen of both sexes had been pulled from the ranks, and were standing in a group, looking forlornly at their fellows. Now it was Constantina who had her eyes shut. "Now," the major said to the rest of them. "Fall in. You are young soldiers of the Soviet Union, eh? Well, as of now you have been transferred. You are now young labourers for the Greater Reich. Come on, come on, fall in!"

The girls and boys obeyed; they were used to this kind of command. Tatiana turned to see them obey, and gasped as someone touched her on the shoulder. She swung back again, found a soldier standing to each side of her. It was painful to draw breath, she was suddenly so terrified. But she was not Jewish! The major had recognised that.

"What is your name, Fraulein?" the major asked.

Tatiana licked her lips. "I am Tatiana Gosykinya."

The major looked her up and down, as if seeing her for the first time. But he had been looking at her from the very beginning. Now he stretched out his hand and squeezed her left breast. It was a brutal gesture, with no suggestion of tenderness, or even lust, but merely to ascertain that there was flesh beneath the bulge in her blouse, and perhaps also to make her realise that she was entirely at his mercy. Tatiana gasped and instinctively raised her hand, only to have her wrist caught by one of the soldiers.

"Do you know what would have happened to you had you struck me?" the major asked. Tatiana panted. Now he squeezed the other breast. "We would have these off for a start. Secure her wrists," he said. Tatiana's arms were pulled behind her back and her wrists were bound. "That one," the major said, pointing.

Natasha Renkova was pushed forward, and her wrists also bound behind her back. The major felt her breasts as well. Natasha's face contorted with embarrassment.

"And that one." Sophie Shermetska was similarly treated; predictably, she burst into tears. The major smiled at them. "You three will not have to work for the Reich, with your hands. You can work on your backs."

He jerked his head and they were thrust forward, made to enter one of the cars and sit on the back seat, awkwardly and uncomfortably with their wrists bound behind them. Tatiana turned her head as the rest were marched off. Anatole caught her eye and gave a little shrug of the shoulders. There was still some spirit left.

The approach to Brest-Litovsk was littered with corpses, men lying in ungainly postures, already stiff. Few of them had rifles, and Tatiana realised they were men who had tried to run away, like those earlier men, more fortunate, at least in the short run, in having made the decision to abandon the struggle immediately. But they were Russian soldiers! There had been supposedly thousands of them, tens of thousands, hundreds of thousands. And they had run away at the first shock of battle!

Some had fought, and been defeated; the approach to the town was also littered with burned-out tanks, shattered by the inexorable panzers; there were even one or two crashed planes. But there was hardly any indication of German casualties. Closer to the town were the living who had not had the time to run, a huge mass of men herded together by the conquerors. They too did not have rifles.

But the battle still raged, for the citadel continued to hold out. German bombers swooped overhead, dropping their deadly cargoes, and German mortars pounded the old stone fortress from close range; both sent clouds of dust high into the sky from the crumbling stonework. But there were cracks of rifles from amidst the rubble, and the few guns and machine-guns still possessed by the defenders spat fire at their assailants. The town itself burned. Although it was midday, the smoke clouds made it seem like night, and the stench, composed of a hundred and one sources, but principally the sweetish odour of burning flesh, was nauseating, seeming to redouble the intense heat. Here and there German soldiers were picking through the wreckage, occasionally dragging people out of shattered houses, civilians as well as soldiers. Every so often there would be a shot. Sophie wept quietly. Natasha shuddered constantly. Tatiana sat rigid, staring at the guard, who stared back, grinning.

At last, some relief from the heat and the stench. They had emerged on the far side of the town where there was a prosperous-looking dacha, clearly belonging to the local Party boss. Here the swastika flag had already been run up the flagpole, and sentries were posted at the door. There were also several other officers, some, judging by their insignia, of quite high rank. They spoke in German, with the major, and there was some gesticulating and pointing. Tatiana became aware of a fresh noise overlying that of the burning town and the firing from the fortress, and looked to where the road crossed the frontier, perhaps a mile away; she caught her breath as she saw the immense amount of armour which was proceeding up the road, the truckloads of soldiers following them, intent on enlarging and exploiting their initial victory.

Now the officers' conversation obviously turned to the three girls, as their guard gestured them out of the car and the officers came across to inspect them. One very senior officer – Tatiana reckoned he was a general – with white hair and quiet features, was clearly disapproving. But a majority of the others were grinning and apparently pleased to see the prisoners. There was some argument, then the general snapped his fingers and another staff car appeared from round the corner of the house. He got into this, followed by one of the junior officers, who looked regretful at having to leave, and they drove out of the yard. The rest of the officers exchanged laughing comments, and the major turned to the three girls. "Inside."

Tatiana led them into the house, which had survived very well. Certainly no one had tried to defend it; the few cracked windowpanes had been caused by distant blast rather than bullets or bombs. "Upstairs," the major commanded. Tatiana led the way up the stairs. "There is the bathroom," the major said. "Use it. Take a shower. Use soap."

At some stage during the afternoon they were fed sausages and vodka. Sophie had stopped crying; she had taken off her glasses and ate with a wolfish anxiety. They were all very hungry. Tatiana ate more slowly, and tried to drink as little as possible, although the men kept forcing vodka on her. If only she could tell what they were saying. They seemed good-humoured enough, and they were rapidly getting drunk. But when they were tired of playing with their toys, would they just shoot them?

The major had been absent. Now he returned, and began giving orders. Reluctantly the men began to dress, staggering about the place, while the major lambasted them with his tongue.

"Please, sir," Natasha ventured. "May we leave now?"

Every head turned to stare at her, even if presumably the rest of the German officers did not understand what she had said. The major grinned at her. "Where would you like to go, little girl?" because Natasha, even naked and bruised, still looked like a little girl. She bit her lip.

"You stay here," the major said. "There'll be other friends wanting to have a chat with you. Like me!" He gave a guffaw. "You haven't serviced me, yet. I'll be back later. A couple of hours. Then I'll have you all to myself."

He gave more orders in German, while Tatiana tensed her mind while forcing her body to remained relaxed. She was as bruised and battered and humiliated as the other two. Her vagina felt as if it had been attacked with red hot pokers; her breasts and buttocks ached. So did her scalp, from the number of times a man in the throws of orgasm had twined his fingers in her hair. Her lip was cut, but she did not know when that had happened.

More important than any of these, however, was the damage done to her brain, her personality. Or *was* it damage? Might it not be an awakening, a realisation that she had reached a watershed in her life. Whatever had happened to her before today, she had never doubted that she would emerge unscathed, and in triumph. Because she was Jennie Gosykinya's daughter, because she was a Bolugayevska, because Uncle Josef had dandled her on his knee. Now it was up to her to survive. Which meant, first of all, escaping from this sexual hell. And if they were going to be left alone . . .

The officers were dressed and filing out. But one was staying. He had put on his pants but not his tunic, and now sat in a chair by the door. He had also put on his outer belt, from which there hung a revolver holster. "Fritz will keep an eye on you," the major said. "Until I come back. I have told him, should you misbehave, to shoot one of you in the belly. That is a very painful way to die, so I would advise you not to misbehave, I shall return later." He stood above Tatiana, fingered her nipple. "Then I will have you all to myself, Tatiana Gosykinya."

The door closed. Tatiana remained lying on the bed. Sophie was sitting on the floor, hugging her knees. She had stopped crying; perhaps there were only so many tears any one person could shed. Natasha lay on her stomach across the bed; for all that she had suffered, she still could not bring herself to face any man while she had no clothes on. She was close enough to touch. But not to speak to; the German officer was watching them, or, rather, watching Natasha'a buttocks – he seemed to find them fascinating. But that was surely to their advantage.

Tatiana tried to make herself think, plan. The thought of a bullet ripping her stomach apart was paralysing. Nor could she risk inflicting such a fate upon either of the others. Yet they would never have a better opportunity. Three against one. So he had the gun. The odds were still better than at the railway station. And here, she was sure, Natasha and Sophie would follow her lead. She got off the bed. Instantly, Fritz asked her a question. "Bathroom. Oh . . . Badezimmer?" she said.

He nodded. Tatiana went into the bathroom. For these few moments she was out of his sight. She opened the cupboard above the basin, found a razor, not, unfortunately, the sort used by her stepfather and stepbrother – appropriately known as a cut throat – but one of the new-fashioned "safety" types, where the razor itself was a small rectangular piece of thin steel, held in a cartridge case. The blade itself was still a lethal weapon, obviously very sharp on each side. But it would require getting to very close quarters – and there was no way she could conceal it about her naked body. Except . . . there was also a little tin of plaster dressings.

Tongue between her teeth, stomach rolling at the thought she might cut herself in such a place, she placed the blade on the inside of her thigh, as high as possible, and then added a strip of plaster to hold it in place. If Fritz were actually to fuck her with the blade there he would probably not only ruin her prospects for life, but his own as well.

She went back into the bedroom. Nothing had changed. She looked at the window. Whatever happened in here, they could not risk attempting to escape until dark. But that was only an hour off. As was the major's return. The whole thing had to be worked out very carefully, because the chance would be gone if the major came back before the guard was dealt with. The plan would also fail if the major were to return with friends. But he had suggested that he wanted her all to himself.

She lay on the bed again. Neither of the other girls moved. Tatiana suspected they had both received such shocks to their system they were in almost catatonic states. But she would need them, when the time came. The evening drifted by. The noise outside hardly abated. Guns and machine-guns still boomed and rattled from the fortress. Rifles still cracked as the Germans shot somebody they did not like the look of. Planes still flew overhead, even if there were no more dogfights. Trucks, tanks and guns still rumbled in the distance as the German war machine continued to roll into Russia. She almost dosed off.

Fritz stirred, went to the table and poured himself a glass of vodka. Tatiana looked at the window. It still glowed with light, but now the sun was definitely drooping into the west. She got up, went to the table as well. Fritz turned aggressively, and his hand dropped to his revolver butt. "Food," Tatiana said. "We wish to eat." She touched the leftovers from lunch. He shrugged, and sat down again. No doubt he was looking forward to a solid dinner once he was relieved. Tatiana shook Natasha. "Natasha, wake up. We must eat."

"I am not hungry," Natasha muttered.

"You must eat." Tatiana virtually dragged her off the bed, jerking her upright so violently that she came into her arms, their heads banging together. "Wake up," she whispered "And do what I tell you, without hesitation." Natasha goggled at her. Tatiana pushed her towards the table, went round the bed, and pulled Sophie to her feet.

"Leave me alone," Sophie moaned. "I want to die!"

"Then die in a good cause," Tatiana told her. "Go and eat. And do what I tell you." She dragged Sophie to the table. All three of the girls took something to eat, while Fritz sat down again, with his glass of vodka. Tatiana left the table and stood in front of him. He stared at her naked pubes as she said: "Would you like me to suck your cock?" In the same sentence, and without altering her tone, she added, "Both of you come here." Fritz looked from one to the other, his hand as ever dropping to the pistol butt. But then he relaxed as Tatiana knelt between his legs and unbuttoned his breeches. "Get his belt," she said.

Natasha obeyed. Again there was an initial resistance, but then he again relaxed although, as she slipped the buckle free, he drew the revolver and left it lying on his thigh, holding it there as Tatiana eased his breeches down around his ankles, and then his drawers. He was staring at her all the time, and she had to make him look away. "Kiss him," she told Sophie.

Sophie hesitated, then put her arms round Fritz's neck. He tried to push her away with his free hand, but with no great determination, as Tatiana now had him in her mouth. While she sucked, and while his face was hidden in Sophie's curls, Tatiana reached between her legs and pulled the razor free. Still without moving her lips, she brought it up. Natasha saw what she was doing, and her eyes widened. But she was now fully prepared to play her part. She slid her hand up Fritz's right arm and then down again in a caressing gesture, but as she came down she turned the hand holding the gun over. The fingers slightly tensed, and Tatiana sank the razor blade into the underside of his wrist, at the same time biting his penis as hard as she could. She felt pain as the upper edge of the blade cut into her finger, and her mouth filled with blood as she was hurled backwards by his knees. But even as he did that, Natasha, still holding the heavy belt, had crashed the buckle down on his hand with all her force. The grip, already loosened by the shock of the bleeding artery, relaxed entirely and the gun fell to the floor.

Sophie stopped kissing him, but she still had her arms round his neck, and now she threw all her strength against him. The chair teetered for a moment and then fell over. Tatiana thought the crash would have been heard throughout the building, but there could be no stopping now. Fritz's head had struck the floor. He was not unconscious, but definitely dazed, and blood was pumping from both his cut wrist and his half-severed penis. Natasha picked up the gun and levelled it, but Tatiana shook her head violently. They seemed to have gotten away with the falling chair – no doubt interpreted as Fritz amusing himself – but a shot would definitely bring somebody up the stairs.

The two girls watched her as she pulled the covers from the bed and put them over Fritz's face. Then they joined her in pressing the material down across his mouth and nose. He made a feeble effort to resist them as he regained his senses, but blood continued to pour from the wounds and he very rapidly subsided. They held the cloth in place until all movement beneath them ceased. By then the floor and carpet were soaked with blood, and they were covered in it themselves. "Shower," Tatiana said. "Quickly."

It was growing quite dark and she had no idea how much time they had. In fact, they were drying themselves when they heard feet on the stairs. "Shit!" Natasha gasped.

Tatiana darted across the room, beckoning them to follow her. She picked up the chair and stood against the wall, pointing at Natasha to stand facing the door. Her heart was pounding. This was it. If there was more than one. . . . The door swung inwards. As the light was not on the room was quite gloomy, but the major could see Natasha facing him, and grinned as he stepped inside. He was alone. But he was already pausing, and frowning, as he smelt the blood, and felt the damp beneath his feet.

Tatiana cast a hasty glance at the landing, saw that it was empty, and swung the chair with all her force. It crashed into the back of the major's head, sent him stumbling to his knees and then on his face. Fortunately, by then he had reached Natasha, and she went down under him with a little shriek, breaking the noise of his fall. Tatiana had closed the door in the same movement as she had swung the chair, and now she stepped above the major, and as he sought to rise, reaching for his pistol as he did so, she struck him again. The chair splintered, and she struck him again. This time it entirely disintegrated, but the major was almost out, lying on top of the panting Natasha and groaning.

Tatiana drew his pistol, reversed it, and struck him as hard as she could on the back of the head with the butt. He gave no sound and his head dropped as blood flew. Tatiana pushed him on to his back, and fetched the clothes from Fritz's face. The girls joined her to suffocate the major. "What are we going to do?" Natasha asked.

"Have another shower to get rid of the blood," Tatiana told her. "Then we'll get dressed, and when it's dark we'll drop out of the window."

"If they catch us, now—" Sophie muttered.

"They will skin us alive, at the very least," Tatiana told her. "So we had better make sure they don't catch us, eh? There are no Germans in the Marshes."

Chapter 3

The Swamp

"What do you reckon?" Joseph Cromb asked his wife.

Priscilla studied the newspaper. "I would say that bastard Stalin is getting just what he deserves."

"The British have said they will help the Soviets in every possible way," Joseph ventured.

"Churchill said that? He hates the Communists."

"Not, apparently, worse than he hates the Nazis. Roosevelt has also offered all possible help."

Priscilla looked at him. "I don't understand. Wouldn't it be for the benefit of everyone if we just let Hitler and Stalin slug it out? Obliterate each other?"

"If that were going to happen, yes," Joseph said. "Unfortunately, according to these reports, the Germans have utterly shattered the Russian frontier defences. They claim to have taken nearly 300,000 prisoners, 2,000 tanks, and nearly 2,000 guns. The Soviet air force has apparently been shot out of the sky. If all that is true, it has to be one of the greatest victories ever recorded. Another one like that, and the Soviet State could disintegrate."

"And good riddance."

"Emotionally, yes," Joseph agreed. "Realistically, it would be a disaster of the first magnitude. It would leave Hitler master of the entire old world save Africa, and the way things are going there's every prospect of him getting that too. Certainly India would fall. He would have won the war, even if Britain managed to hold out. She'd become merely an offshore island, slowly starving. Whereas, if Russia can be encouraged to fight and fight and fight, to hold on until the winter anyway, Mr Hitler might find that it is he who has over rearched himself."

"Now, whose point of view is that, *really*?" Priscilla asked.

"Well . . . the State Department."

Priscilla gazed at him for several seconds. "The answer is no," she said at last. "No, no, no! I cannot see how you could even want to."

Joseph sat beside her, held her hand. "Just listen for a moment, dearest girl. The State Department, this country, is going to help Russia even Bolshevik Russia for the reasons I have just given you. That is a fact, and nothing you or I can do will change it. The object of helping the Soviets is the defeat of Hitler. To do that, to help Russia properly, they need to send people there who speak and read fluent Russian and who will therefore be able accurately both to understand what they are saying and any written documents that may be presented. If any member of the mission also has first-hand knowledge of both the country and the regime, so much the better. Now, I am probably the best qualified person in America on both those counts."

"Joseph, you are wanted in Soviet Russia as an escaped political prisoner!"

"The State Department is making it absolutely clear that all charges against me have to be dropped."

"Can they protect you against Stalin's hit men?"

"They can hold him responsible for my safety. And they are going to do that. Anyway, right this minute Stalin wants our help more than he wants any personal revenge against me for having bust his system open."

"And you are willing to forget the fact that he had his goons torture you and mistreat you for ten years? You have the least Jewish point of view of any Jew I have ever met."

"I believe there is a time and a place for everything. Right now our business is to fight against Hitler. He is a far more serious enemy of the Jews than Stalin is. Let me give you an idea of how important this mission is: it's being headed by Hopkins himself." Harry Hopkins was perhaps Franklin Roosevelt's closest political associate, even if he held no department or cabinet post, was not even a member of the Senate or the House of Representatives.

"And of course, you are hoping to see Jennie again. Do you suppose you will recognise her, after all of these years?"

"I have every intention of seeing Jennie again," Joseph said. "This is the chance of a lifetime."

Priscilla sighed. But she knew that behind her husband's quiet demeanour there was a mind of immense resolution; had there not been, he would not have had the strength to survive those ten years in the gulag archipelago. She played her last trump. "And what will you tell Sonia?"

"I will ask Sonia to forgive me," Joseph said.

"I know it's asking a great deal," said the President of the Foundation. "But I believe this appeal is being circulated throughout the medical fraternity. They're pretty desperate over there, so anyone who is both qualified and can speak good Russian is worth his weight in gold. And I want you to be absolutely sure of one thing, Dr Bolugayevski: your work in Russia will count towards seniority here in Boston. Every day of it."

He paused, a trifle anxiously, as Alex Bolugayevski appeared to be considering. But Alex's mind had been made up almost the moment the President had begun to speak. He had been brought up to hate the Bolshevik regime, which had killed his father, murdered his half-brother, and, so far as he knew, his half-sister, raped his mother, sequestered his lands and his inheritance, and made him a fugitive. But he had not been brought up to hate Russia. That would have been impossible, even if he remembered very little of it – he had been born there. He had always intended to return, one day, without quite knowing when that would be possible. To be given the opportunity to return now, and in total safety . . . and to help in the fight against Hitler! Alex had no Jewish blood, but his stepfather was Jewish. Besides, here was adventure on a scale he had never supposed would come his way.

"Would you like to think it over?" the President inquired.

"Not necessary, sir," Alex said. "I will certainly volunteer."

How to tell Mother, there was the problem, he thought, as he completed his rounds and returned to his office. He took off his coat and sat behind the desk, stroking his chin. She would go spare! As for Joe. There was a tap on the door, and Elaine came in. "Hi!" Apart from when on duty together, they hadn't seen too much of each other over the past year. Now . . . he frowned. She was looking a little breathless, as well as defiant, as she closed the door. "Are you going to Russia?"

"I've volunteered, as a member of the medical team, yes. Seems they need all the doctors they can get."

"I've volunteered as well," Elaine said.

Alex raised his eyebrows. "I think it is a necessary qualification that the entire team should speak fluent Russian."

"I speak fluent Russian," Elaine said, in Russian.

"Good God!"

"I've been taking lessons, all this year," she said.

"Are you psychic?"

"I did it, because . . . I wanted to do it. I told you, I love everything about Russia. This is my chance to see it at first hand."

"You're not exactly going as a tourist!"

"So? I'll be doing just what I'm doing here, only in more exotic, and exciting surroundings."

Alex considered, and decided against reminding her that tending men who have been shattered in battle is likely to be slightly more traumatic than tending heart patients or premature deliveries, or that her surroundings were unlikely to be quite as aseptic or as well backed-up, both with staff and medicine, as in Boston. "Well, then," he said. "Congratulations!"

She was as handsome as ever. Why had he dropped her? Because he had realised that she was not going to fit in to the Bolugayevski ambience. He did not deny that she loved everything about Russia, that perhaps she was excited by and interested in everything Bolugayevski, but she was essentially a woman of 1941, and the Bolugayevskis were essentially a family firmly rooted in 1841, or certainly 1914.

He had felt her presence would be disruptive for all of them. But did that mean he was never going to marry, unless by chance he came across some other exiled Russian princess? That was an absurdity. In any event, marriage did not come into it. He was going to adventure. And she wanted to come along. And she was the most attractive girl he knew. "As we're going to be companions in war," he said. "Dinner?"

"Where?" she asked, cautiously.

He grinned. "At a neat little restaurant down by the harbour."

"I'm on duty tonight."

"Well, then, tomorrow."

They sat at a candle-lit table, and ate Maine lobster. "Tell me what I'm going to," Elaine said.

"Would you believe that I have no idea? I can't remember it."

"But your mother must have told you about it?"

"Often and often and often. Trouble is, Mom's memory has only two colours. One is very rosy, and definitely no longer has any reality. The other is utterly black, and I have no idea how accurate it is. I do know they're a pretty unholy bunch over there. Maybe even my cousin."

"You have a cousin still in Russia?"

"At least one. My stepfather's sister."

"Then she's not really a cousin."

"She is. You see, my stepfather is actually the son of my mother's cousin."

"Excuse me?" she said, totally confused.

He grinned. "It's a fact. Inquire into the history of a Russian princely family, like any royal family, and you come up with some fairly incestuous situations."

"I'll have to work all that out. Do you think when we, oops, I meant, you, get to Russia, you'll be able to see this cousin?"

"I certainly intend to try. But if you like, you can meet her too."

"That'd be swell. Gee, I am so *excited* . . ." Again they gazed at each other. Then she licked her lips, "I guess we'd better call it a night."

"And back you go to your two room-mates."

Another flicker of her tongue. "They're not there, tonight."

Priscilla Cromb stared at her only son for several seconds. Then she asked, with surprising calmness, "Has everyone in this God-forsaken world gone mad?"

"There's nothing dangerous about it, Mom!" Alex protested.

"Even if your name is Bolugayevski? Don't tell me: you have a guarantee of your safety. At least from the Russians."

"Why, yes. Absolutely." He frowned at her. "How did you know that?"

"Your stepfather has one too."

"Joe? Joe's going to Russia?"

"Yes," Priscilla said, grimly.

"Oh, boy! That's tremendous!"

"For you, I am sure."

"Oh, Mom." He dropped to his knees beside her chair. "It won't be for long. And it's something I just have to do. Can you understand that?"

She gazed at him for several seconds, then kissed him. "Yes. I understand that. But for God's sake take care, my darling."

He kissed her back. "I'll take care of Joe, too."

"Well," Alex said. "Last night in the old home town. And no duty. You never told me what your folks said about your volunteering."

"They're not too happy."

"Yeah," he said. They were on the sidewalk now, and he faced her. The summer was well advanced and the first leaf had just come down, wisping on to the pavement. "About us . . ."

She anticipated his mood. "We can't make any long-term plans now, Alex."

"Do you think there is any chance of us being sent to the same hospital?"

"Would you like that? Maybe we could twist a couple of arms. Would you like me to cook you dinner?"

"For four?"

"I'll send the others out." Elaine's nose wrinkled. "Again."

"Is there no news at all?" Jennie asked.

Ivan Ligachev put his arm round her shoulders. She seemed to have aged ten years in the past two months, but they had all aged ten years in the past two months, and those with relatives caught up in the fighting had aged the most. "Not since that first day. Brest-Litovsk and its environs were overrun in the very first attack. Now it is lost behind a veil of silence. And terror."

"Didn't *you* learn anything?" Jennie looked at her stepson, imploringly.

Feodor Ivanovich shook his head. "We were sent off the very first day."

"But you were not ill-treated in any way?"

"Well, no, Mother. They couldn't risk that, or we might not have let their embassy people go."

Jennie sighed. Tatiana was all that she had to hang on to, from the past. And the thought of her lying dead, raped and murdered by the invaders . . . perhaps worse, since the Germans had released the news that she had killed a German officer; she might have been tortured to death . . .

Feodor looked at his father above his stepmother's head. Owing to de-briefings and the delays consequent upon the huge upheaval which was overtaking Russia since the German invasion, this was actually his first visit to his father's apartment in Moscow since the start of the war. He had not in any event liked what he had seen; the city was clearly packing up and preparing to move as the German advance inexorably continued. Now he did not know whether he should add to his stepmother's trauma by telling her that he had met her cousin, long supposed dead, in Berlin, and clearly a prominent member of the triumphant Nazi hordes. But Ivan shook his head. Obviously he considered that his wife had sufficient to cope with, for the moment.

"She is very upset," Ivan confessed to his master. "Well, Tatiana is the great love of her life. Was, at any rate. And now she is a wanted criminal, accused of having murdered two German officers."

Josef Stalin slowly filled his pipe, as he was inclined to do in moments of stress. He had done a lot of pipe smoking recently. Obviously the fate of one young woman, when the entire Soviet state seemed to be falling apart, was irrelevant, however fond he might be of both Tatiana and her mother. From the position of head of state of a huge country it might be necessary to deal with the destruction of millions of people at a time – something he had done, in his time, with utter ruthlessness – but he knew that all life eventually came down to personalities; to the willingness of one individual, perhaps, to sacrifice himself for the State. He did not of course include himself in this reckoning: he *was* the State. Ligachev waited, anxiously; he knew better than to interrupt his master while he was filling his pipe. The first puff of smoke rose reassuringly above the walrus moustache. "What is the news from Sorge?"

His question took Ligachev by surprise, as he had still been thinking about Tatiana. Richard Sorge was the head of the Soviet spy system in Japan. "He assures us that the Japanese have no intention of going to war with us, in partnership with Germany, even if they do have an alliance. The Japanese have their hands full with the situation in China, and Sorge feels that if they intend to take any advantage of the present weakness of the Western Powers it will be at the expense of Great Britain and the Netherlands, in South-East Asia."

Stalin rose from his desk and walked to the enormous map of the world that filled one entire wall of his office. Now that the pipe was well alight, he could clasp both hands behind his back, as he liked; this helped to conceal his withered left arm. "Will that not involve the United States?"

"The Japanese do not appear to think so, Comrade Chairman. And Sorge agrees with them. He believes that Roosevelt is indulging in mere sabre rattling. The fact is, that while Roosevelt would like to join Britain in this war, and there can be no doubt that his position has been strengthened by his election victory last November, the vast majority of the population of the United States has no desire to become involved in a European war. And he cannot go to war without the consent of Congress. In any event, having America remain neutral is to our advantage, while they are willing to supply us with Lend-Lease materiel. Were they to enter the war, they could not possibly help us militarily, and they would then need their surplus materiel for themselves."

"How reliable is Sorge?" Stalin asked over his shoulder.

"Absolutely. One hundred per cent."

"Very well. Issue orders to pull two of every three divisions out of Mongolia and eastern Siberia, and move them west. This must be done as rapidly as possible."

Ligachev gulped. "With respect, Comrade Chairman, that is taking an enormous risk."

"You have just promised me that the Japanese will not invade us."

"Yes, but if the troops are withdrawn they might change their minds."

"I do not believe the Japanese are people who change their minds easily, even were we to announce these troop movements, which we will not. It will take them a while to find out. In any event, Sorge's outline of events makes sense. What are the Japanese going to obtain by invading Siberia? Chilblains. But by moving south, while the democracies are helpless, they can obtain rubber and tin, and above all, oil. I am prepared to back Sorge's judgement."

"I still think it is an enormous risk," Ligachev grumbled.

"Perhaps, but it is also a very necessary one. Look at the map! One army swallowed up on the frontier. Another swallowed up at Kiev. And now one swallowed up at Smolensk. These are not defeats, Ivan Ivanovich, they are catastrophes undoubtedly brought about by treachery. Clearly I did not shoot enough officers when we had that clean-out in 1937."

Ligachev swallowed. He was well aware that there were those saying the catastrophes had occurred simply *because* there were no competent officers left alive since the purge of 1937. This was like the campaign against Finland all over again, save that instead of suffering horrendous casualties – and failing – in their attempt to invade another country, the Red Army was suffering horrendous casualties – and again failing – in attempting to defend its own country from invasion. "We need every man we can spare west of Moscow." Stalin tapped the industrial area south of the city. "I want all of this plant moved, east of the Urals. It must be done now. It must be completed before the Germans get here."

"But that may only be a matter of weeks, Comrade Chairman. To move all of that plant will take months."

"It must be done in weeks, Ivan Ivanovich. The fewer weeks the better. Put all the old people and the intellectuals who have managed to dodge the armed services to work. Put the women to work as well. And the children, if necessary. Shoot the backsliders. Have it done."

Ligachev licked his lips. "Where is it to go?"

Stalin again studied the map. "It must be where there are adequate rail connections." He punched the map with his finger. "There, and there, and there." Ivan peered over his shoulder at the map. Some of the places chosen were hundreds of miles into Siberia, and winter was coming in. He wondered just how many more lives would have to be sacrificed to shift all of that heavy plant beyond the Urals. But he knew Stalin had no interest in lives, except in so far as the virtually inxhaustible human resources possessed by Russia were its principal asset.

Stalin returned to his desk and sat down. "Now let us consider your stepdaughter. Or at least the situation out there. The Germans claim to have utterly destroyed the Belorussian Front. Well, we can hardly argue with them on that. But there is no army in history, recent history, anyway, that has been *utterly* destroyed. So approximately 300,000 men surrendered, the spineless swine. Going on the casualty figures I have here, that leaves very nearly 100,000 unaccounted for. The Germans are claiming 75,000 Russian dead. Again, we are not in a position to argue with them on that. But that still leaves over 20,000 missing. Even if there has been some poor arithmetic, there has still got to be a sizeable number of men who were not killed and did not surrender. Now, Ivan Ivanovich, what do you think has happened to those men, not to mention Tatiana and her friends?"

"I suppose they have sneaked off to their homes and are pretending to be civilians."

"If that were true, do you not suppose Tatiana would have sneaked off to *her* home?"

"I think Tatiana is dead," Ligachev said, gloomily.

"If the Germans had got her they would have said so."

"She could just have died in a ditch somewhere. I have not suggested this to Jennie, of course, but it is the most likely thing."

"I should be very sorry to think that," Stalin said. "I think she is alive. In any event, I am convinced that there is a large number of people, men, women and soldiers, situated behind the German lines in the vicinity of the Pripet Marshes, or in the Marshes themselves. We know the Germans have not ventured in there. The Germans require roads, or at least surfaces firm enough to take their tanks and heavy guns. Not even our organised troops can venture into the Marshes. Anyone in there is safe."

"From the Germans, maybe, but not from starvation and disease," Ligachev said, more gloomily yet.

"Ivan Ivanovich, you are in a defeatist mood. I do not like that. There are people in those Marshes, people who are doing nothing when they could be fighting for the Motherland. The main German invasion route lies over the road running past Brest-Litovsk, and just north of the Marshes. A dedicated and enterprising body of guerillas could disrupt the German lines of communication."

"They'd be hanged if they were captured."

"Then they would have died for the Motherland."

"Do you really think a few attacks on that road and railway is going to halt the Germans, Comrade Chairman?"

"Halt them, no. Delay them, yes. It is not just a matter of holding them until we can deploy our Mongolians. There is also the weather to be considered. We are now into September. Next month the rain will start, and that will delay them further. Another two months and the snow will start to fall. Another month, and it will start to freeze. These Fritzes know nothing of a Russian winter. It defeated Charles XII of Sweden in 1707. It defeated Napoleon in 1812. It will defeat Adolf Hitler in 1941. I am certain of it. What we have to do is make sure he does not get so far, before the winter, that he cannot be driven back."

Ligachev continued to be concerned with minutiae. "Even supposing there are people in the Marshes, people able and willing to fight, how may we contact them? They are not likely to have radio sets, or the electric current to use them."

"We will fly in trained commanders, to organise them."

"Fly them in? To the Pripet Marshes?"

"Well, of course, they will have to be dropped by parachute."

"The Germans have total air supremacy in that region." Over all western Russia, he could have added.

"So it will be risky, even costly. But if we send up enough, small, single-engined aircraft, capable of flying near the ground, each carrying one or two specially picked men, or women, some must get through." Back to the expendability factor. But Stalin had a carrot on the end of his stick. "They will carry an order from me, Ivan Ivanovich, creating Tatiana Gosykinya Commissar for the Pripet, and Commander of Partisan Group One. Will that not please Jennie?"

"Tatiana is only 18 years old," Ligachev protested.

"Is that important? This is going to be a young people's war. And she has already shown that she is prepared to kill Germans, which is something not all of our soldiers seem capable of. We shall make Tatiana Gosykinya a Heroine of the Soviet Union, a human beacon for all other young Russians to look up to. We will give her a name, Ivan Ivanovich – The Red Maiden!" He chuckled. "So perhaps she is no longer a maiden. But it will attract everyone. The Red Maiden! But of course she will have to have someone to command *her*, at least behind the scenes. By tomorrow evening, send me a list of suitable personnel you have selected for parachuting into the Pripet, Ivan Ivanovich." He stroked his moustache. "And do you know whose name I would like to see on that list? Feodor Ivanovich."

"But he is my only son."

"As Tatiana is Jennie's only daughter. As is one of my sons serving in the air force, an even more dangerous assignment, at the present time. We are all in this together, Ivan Ivanovich. There is great danger for us all in this war. But there is also great glory to be gained, for those chosen to lead."

"Yes, Comrade Chairman." Ligachev hesitated.

"Is there anything else? You have a lot to do, Ivan Ivanovich. And it must all be done, quickly."

"I have here the list supplied by the American Embassy of the volunteer medical staff who are arriving in a couple of months. I have also a list of the members of the American mission, arriving in a couple of weeks, to discuss with us our requirements as regards materiel."

Stalin leaned back in his chair. "Ivan Ivanovich, do you suppose I can possibly be interested, or have the time to be interested, in the names of a bunch of doctors, or a group of accountants?"

"There are two names on the list which may be of interest to you, Comrade Chairman."

Stalin frowned. "Speak!"

"Included in the mission is the name of Joseph Cromb."

"Cromb?" Stalin chuckled. "You must admit the man has nerve."

"This man has defied you, and the Soviet State, for fifteen years, Comrade Chairman. He has denounced our prison system."

"No one seems to have believed him very much."

"He is under sentence of death, Josef. Now, to get the

mission here at all, we have had to issue a blanket safe conduct. However, when we did that we did not suspect that Cromb would be so bold as to take advantage of it."

"Having issued such a safe conduct, we must abide by it. These people are our friends, at the moment."

"That is why I say, an accident . . ."

"Ivan Ivanovich, in many ways you are a primitive. Should Joseph Cromb come to Russia, a man under sentence of death by the Soviet State but granted a safe conduct, and promptly meet with an accident, do you not suppose the world will understand that he was really executed? No, no, I think we will leave Mr Cromb alone for the time being. After all, is he not now working for us?"

Then he smiled. "In fact, I think we could do very well out of this, Ivan Ivanovich. I think we should roll out the red carpet for Mr Cromb. He has spent the last half-dozen years denigrating us. The world knows this. We will show the world that the Soviet State does not bear grudges. We will welcome Mr Cromb as one of ours. Yes, indeed, that will go down very well with the Americans."

"Joseph Cromb will wish to see his sister."

"Well, why not? I do not see any harm can come of it. And you, Ivan Ivanovich, will be a charming host at all times. The man is now your brother-in-law."

Ligachev snorted. "And the other one?"

"What other one?"

"Included in the list of medical personnel rushing to our assistance in one Alexei Bolugayevski."

Stalin's frown returned. "Who is this?"

"Alexei Bolugayevski is entitled to call himself the Prince of Bolugayen. He is the son of the Princess Priscilla and the late Prince Alexei. He is half-brother of the late Prince Colin, and he is stepson of Joseph Cromb."

"And he is returning to Russia? The arrogance of these people amazes me!"

"He also has a safe conduct," Ligachev said. "Are we to

roll out the red carpet for him as well? Am I to welcome him in my home, too?"

"Why not? But he is coming as a doctor, you say? We shall welcome him as an ally. How old is this young man?"

"He would be in his middle twenties, I suppose."

"And he is the son of a dashing soldier, and a romantically minded, headstrong mother. I remember the Princess Priscilla well." Stalin stroked his moustache reminiscently. "And undoubtedly he has been brought up to believe that he is a prince. Is he married?"

"That I cannot say. But I doubt it. I do not think a young married man would have been accepted for this mission."

"Then he is the very last Bolugayevski. Oh, indeed, Ivan Ivanovich, welcome this apparition from the past! Treat him well. Entertain him. Inflame his mind with the great deeds of his ancestors, deeds which he should certainly seek to emulate. Especially against the traditional foe, the Germans."

"It is expressly stated in the contract we have with these doctors that they are not to be exposed to actual combat, Comrade Chairman."

Stalin smiled. "But who are we to oppose the patriotic spirit of a true Russian prince, even if he is an American citizen? In any event, Ivan Ivanovich, at the rate the Germans are advancing, it is quite impossible to determine that what appears a safe area one day may not be a battleground the next. Such things are out of our hands, are they not?"

"Listen," Anatole said.

Tatiana raised herself and looked up through the trees, which obscured the sky. But not entirely. The aircraft was flying very low, circling over the morass beneath it and seeing nothing but the swamp, surely, but yet hoping for just a glimpse of life. The planes came fairly often, certainly four days a week. But they had never found anything on which to drop their bombs. Sometimes they dropped them anyway, blasting the foliage from a dozen trees or so. They had never hit anyone. The fugitives had learned to keep absolutely still and conceal their weapons while the aircraft were overhead. Not that they had many weapons. But even a knife, much less a rifle, might give off a gleam to be seen by eager eyes in the sky.

The aircraft noise died, and the birds could again be heard chirping away. Fewer birds now than a month ago; most had already left for the south. Lucky birds!

Anatole pulled on his trousers, then checked his fishing line. There was not much else to do in the Marshes than fish and hunt – there was a remarkable amount of wild life – and have sex. How odd, Tatiana thought, that four months ago I was a virgin, and looked forward to being one on my wedding night. How one's ideas on life could change!

The escape from the German officers' house had been far easier than they had dared hope. They had dropped from the bedroom window, into darkness, any noise drowned by the sounds of revelry from within, where that first tremendous victory was still being celebrated. Once in the town, amid the flames and the wreckage, they had been virtually safe. The citadel had still been holding out and the noise was tremendous. Everyone was in a state of high excitement. The Germans had imposed a curfew but few people knew of it, and although the conquerors were inclined to shoot at anyone they did not like the look of, that did not include three pretty girls. Tatiana had commanded Natasha and Sophie to submit to further rape and manhandling, as she had done herself, while carefully making sure none of their molesters realised they were armed with the two pistols they had taken from the dead officers.

Eventually they had escaped even the town and the soldiers. By then the early June dawn was already breaking, and on their way to the Marshes they had to crawl and hide. Fortunately, the dawn of the second day of the invasion had brought discipline back to the Germans; the conquerors of Brest-Litovsk had been required to resume their advance behind the main bodies which were already on their way to Smolensk. Brest-Litovsk had been left to the administrative troops, with a skeleton force to besiege the garrison until it could be bombed into surrender. The SS remained, required to seek out and eliminate all those regarded as undesirables by the Third Reich; these consisted mainly of Jews and commissars. And by the morning they had entered the bedroom at the officers mess and thus were now also on the hunt for the three girls. They were by dawn sufficiently far out of town not to know what was going on behind them, but Tatiana had no doubt a search was being carried out. They dared not risk exposure, and so found themselves a hiding place in an irrigation ditch between two cornfields, about a mile south of the railroad, where they spent the day huddled against each other covered by branches and leaves.

From a comfort point of view it was a relief that the ditch was dry, but before the day was finished they wished it had had a little water. They also had nothing to eat. But they were not tempted to go looking for either food or water as all around them roared and crashed the German war machine. There were men close by all day, inspecting and guarding and in places repairing the railway line, but so efficiently did they work that by evening those men were several miles to the east.

More terrifying were the tanks which came roaring out of the west, straight across the cornfields. On more than one occasion the huge monsters rolled right over the three girls, huddled in the bottom of their ditch, sufficiently narrow that there was no great risk of the tanks actually crushing them. It was none the less terrifying, and Tatiana had to hold Sophie's mouth to prevent her from screaming. They had resumed their journey once it was dark, which was not until well after nine that night. By then they had been so hungry they had even risked approaching the railway line to steal discarded scraps left by the German engineers, while when they came to an almost dry stream they lay on their bellies and licked the water out of the mud cracks. Only two days ago, Tatiana remembered, she had worried about drinking unboiled water from a well!

It had taken them four days to reach the Marshes, hiding by day and crawling by night, drinking water wherever they could find it, eating whatever came to hand, which included uncooked corn husks, discarded food, and, to their great joy, the remnants of a larder in a farmhouse they reached on the third day. The tanks had rolled through and over the farmhouse, but they had not stopped to investigate what might have been left behind, and buried in the debris had been a whole smoked gammon! By now the main German force had moved on. The road was still in constant use, but that was several miles to the north. The railroad was also very busy, but traffic moved along this at such speed it presented no dangers to the fugitives, while in addition the troops being carried forward were new men, who had not stopped in Brest-Litovsk, and knew nothing of what had happened there. One day, the three girls incautiously exposed themselves when in sight of the line, and the men on the train cheered and cat-called rather than shot at them.

But those who remained were setting about their grim task with brutal efficiency. On only their second day, when they had regained the vicinity of the railway station where they had been arrested, the girls came across what was obviously a mass grave. And from the few bits of clothing which remained attached to branches or half buried in the earth, they could not doubt it was the final resting place of those of their companions denounced by Constantina, as well, no doubt, as Commandant Markowitza. The thought that those innocents had been forced to strip naked, then dig their own grave, and then kneel, to be shot into it, was more horrifying than their own ordeal.

"What is going to become of us?" Natasha had asked.

"We are going to die," Tatiana told her brutally. "But not until we have killed a whole lot of Germans."

On the fourth day they were at last alone. The railway line curved away to the north, and before them were the thickly clustered trees of the Marshes. They were in it before they quite realised it, Sophie sinking to her knees in a sudden bog and all three of them becoming covered in mud before they had managed to drag her out and gain some relatively firm ground. Then they had looked around themselves in consternation. They were all city-dwellers, their experience of the countryside consisting of this fortnight every year. For Sophie, this was only her first year, and even for Tatiana, it was but her third. In addition, their relationship with the countryside had always been strictly controlled by camp perimeters and camp activities, by rules and regulations. Creepy-crawlies and odd noises in the night were shared between the 20 girls in each tent, and thereby alleviated.

Now they were in a world of trees and bushes and water. And sounds, from the cries of the birds to the odd distant splash. All unfamiliar, and all basically sinister when they did not know what was causing them. "It's a lost world," Natasha whispered.

"In which we have to survive until our soldiers come back," Tatiana had told her. Sophie burst into tears. "Pull yourselves together," Tatiana said. "We must move on."

"Where?" Nastasha asked.

"Further into the swamp. We are too close to the Germans here."

Natasha shuddered. "I'm hungry," Sophie complained. They had eaten the last of the ham that morning.

"Well, maybe we'll find some food," Tatiana said. "We certainly aren't going to die of thirst."

She made them get up and struggle on, trying to keep to the firmer ground, but being forced from time to time to wade through water which sometimes came up to their waists, while once Tatiana, who was leading, stepped into a deeper than usual hole and disappeared, having to be dragged back out spluttering by the other two. Following that they collapsed panting, on the next dry ground, promptly to be discovered by a cloud of mosquitoes.

Sophie lay on her back, slapping and scratching, staring up at the trees, and a bird perched on a branch, staring down at her. "Couldn't we use one of the guns, and shoot it?" she asked.

Tatiana drew the Luger, checked that there was a bullet in the chamber, and levelled it, holding it in both hands. Even so it swung to and fro alarmingly; hungry and exhausted, she was not at her best. She forced herself to concentrate, tensed all her muscles, aware that Natasha and Sophie were staring at her, willing her to succeed. She drew a deep breath, had the bird in her sights, and squeezed the trigger.

The noise was sharp put penetrative. The bird flapped its wings and lazily flew away. "Shit!" Tatiana commented, and gazed at the man who had suddenly appeared, on another little knoll, perhaps 50 yards away. Then she saw another, and another. And then the flutter of a skirt. Natasha and Sophie had stood up also, and moved closer to Tatiana, seeking her protection. Natasha had also drawn her gun. "Put it away," Tatiana muttered, and thrust her own pistol into her waistband; these people had to be their only chance of survival.

"I remember you," said the figure in a tattered uniform, his sergeant's stripes just visible on his torn sleeve.

"And I remember you, Comrade Sergeant," Tatiana said. "I remember you, running away."

"Ha!" snorted the sergeant. If he had thrown away his rifle in his haste to escape the battle for Brest-Litovsk, he had found himself a weapon since, and with his beard, his bandolier, and his tattered clothing looked as typical a bandit as Tatiana could ever have imagined. "And I suppose you have not run away?"

"We are running away," Tatiana said. "But we have

brought our weapons with us." She showed him the Luger, and pointed to the pistol in Natasha's belt. "And we have killed Germans."

"You children?" asked another man, contemptuously.

"We killed two German officers," Natasha said.

The men looked from one to the other, incredulously. "Well," the sergeant said. "Hand over those guns."

"Why?" Tatiana said. "We took them, in battle."

"I am in command here," the sergeant said. "I am Sergeant Shatrav. You must obey me."

"Will you feed us?" Sophie asked.

"As long as you obey me," Shatrav said.

Obeying Shatrav had not been a difficult matter: he gave very few orders. Initially, what he wanted to do most was get between Tatiana's legs, and she did not disobey his command to come to him. She didn't have a choice. For the rest, the little group of refugees concentrated on existing. They were working their way through the livestock the villagers had brought with them, but they also caught fish and snared birds and the occasional boar; they did not attempt to shoot them – quite apart from the noise, for causing which the girls were roundly slated, they had a very limited supply of bullets, a dozen rifles and half a dozen pistols amongst some 60 men and women.

It seemed an inconsequential existence to Tatiana. "What happens when the snow comes?" she asked. It was already raining most days.

"We wait for the spring," Shatrav told her.

"Will we not starve or freeze to death?"

"Some of us," he agreed, making it quite plain that he did not plan such a fate for himself. Or for her, if she continued to please him.

"I think we should get out of here while we can," she said.

"And go where? We are completely surrounded by

Germans, north, south, east and west. Our armies have been destroyed. For all I know, they already have Moscow, are already at the Urals. The only place they haven't occupied are these marshes. So this is the only safe place there is."

Tatiana couldn't believe that the Germans had overrun all of European Russia in four months. But she had no evidence that they hadn't. "If we have been so badly defeated, then we are lost anyway," she argued. "We can't live here for the rest of our lives, swamp creatures!"

"Why not?" Shatrav inquired.

There was no immediate answer to that. And Tatiana very rapidly discovered that none of the other fugitives was particularly anxious to leave the safety of the narshes; that went even for Natasha and Sophie, who were just glad to be with friends, among whom, to their delight, they found two of their camping comrades; Anatole and Gregory. "We escaped from work detail," Anatole explained. "It wasn't difficult."

Gregory giggled. "They said that if any of us tried to escape, they'd shoot three of those left behind."

"What has happened to Constantina?" Natasha asked. One of the Jewish girls denounced had been a special friend.

"Oh, she is very popular with the Germans. She has her own quarters. Well, they couldn't let her share our barracks. She'd have been lynched."

"So I don't suppose they were going to shoot *her* if you escaped," Natasha remarked.

"But you left anyway," Tatiana remarked.

"Well . . . the Germans also told us they were going to work us all till we dropped dead. Except for some of the girls. They took them for whores."

"So we thought we'd take our chances," Anatole said. "We told the others to come with us, but they were too scared."

"So I guess some of them got shot," Gregory said.

Tatiana didn't feel she could condemn them for sacrificing their comrades. They seemed to be in a survival of the fittest situation in any event. And she was actually very glad to see Anatole, her own age in contrast to the soldiers. Anatole seemed so much cleaner, and vastly less experienced, while she felt as if she had had a lifetime's experience over the past four months. Thus she seduced him, and as it was a rare autumnal fine day they lay on the hummock in the sunshine listening to the plane circling overhead. "Are we going to die?" he asked, nuzzling her breasts. All men liked to nuzzle Tatiana's breasts; she supposed she was the ultimate earth goddess.

"Of course," she said. "But not for a few weeks yet."

The following day the rain began in earnest, a sullen downpour which cascaded from the trees and soaked even the dry earth, while the water levels began to rise almost visibly. The fugitives sat, soaked and shivering because the rain was quite chill. "Surely we can create some kind of shelter?" Tatiana asked.

"Not worth the trouble," Shatrav said. "The rain'll stop, eventually. You object to being clean?"

Tatiana could have throttled him.

It was three weeks later that they heard the aircraft – at night. It was the first night in that period that it hadn't rained, but there still seemed to be water everywhere. Shatrav sat up. "What the hell—?" The plane was flying very low.

The fugitives were all awake now, peering up into the darkness. "Look!" Anatole had very keen eyes, and he was pointing. They all stared, and some could make out the two pale patches in the gloom, floating down to the trees. "Parachutes!"

"Germans!" They had all heard how the Germans had launched parachutists against Holland and Belgium the previous year, or against Crete only a couple of months before the invasion. "They're coming to get us," one of the women shouted.

"Scatter!" Shatrav bellowed.

"Be quiet!" Tatiana snapped. "There are only two parachutes." They stared into the sky and realised she was right. The noise of the plane engines was now fading, to the east. "Those are our own people," Tatiana said. "Come to find us."

They scrambled through the bushes and the water, making for where the parachutes had disappeared in the trees. "We must call out," Tatiana said.

"It could be a trap," Shatrav objected.

"If it is a trap then we are finished anyway." She cupped her hands about her mouth. "Who is there?" she called into the darkness. "We are Russian soldiers. Who is there?"

There was no reply, and they went on for a while. Then Tatiana tried calling again. This time a voice came back to them, from surprisingly close at hand. "Give us your names!"

Tatiana glanced at Shatrav, but he was too terrified to risk his name. "I am Tatiana Gosykinya," she said.

"Tattie!" Feodor Ligachev appeared from the bushes.

Chapter 4

The Partisans

"Feodor!" Tatiana shouted, splashing through the water to embrace her stepbrother. "Oh, Feodor. It is so good to see you."

He kissed her, several times. "It is so good to see you too! This is Olga Kaminskaya."

Tatiana peered into the darkness. Like Feodor, Olga Kaminskaya wore uniform – trousers instead of a skirt – and was armed with both revolver and sub-machine-gun, as well as a long-bladed knife. They both had heavy packs on their backs. As far as Tatiana could make out Olga was handsome enough, in a coldfeatured fashion, and was tall and well built, with long tawny hair curling out from beneath her sidecap. "Greetings, Comrade Gosykinya," she remarked.

"Who are these people?" Shatrav demanded, endeavouring to regain control of the situation.

"I am Captain Feodor Ligachev," Feodor informed him. "Sent to make contact with the partisans of the Pripet." The fugitives looked at each other. Partisans of the Pripet? "Lieutenant Kaminskaya is my aide."

"Have you come to lead us out of here, Comrade Captain?" Sophie asked.

"I have come to teach you how to kill Germans and blow up their trains," Feodor said. "Under the direction of your commissar."

Shatrav snorted. "I have commanded here since 22 June, Comrade Captain. Kill Germans? Blow up their trains? We have a dozen rifles between us, and not 50 rounds of ammunition. We have no explosives. This is a dream."

"You will have everything you require," Feodor told him. "We were sent to make sure that you were here." He nodded at Kaminskaya's pack. "We have a radio set. I have but to send a message, and the necessary materiel will be dropped by parachute. How many of you are there?"

"Sixty. But a third of us are women."

"Women can fight as well as men," Feodor said, equably.

"Comrade Kaminskaya, we need arms and munitions for 100 people in here. More will certainly join us when we are proved to exist and be successful. We also require emergency rations for that number to see us through the winter, and we will certainly need a medical team. Get that off right away." The woman nodded, laid her pack on the ground, and took out the radio. The fugitives watched her in amazement.

"Now, Sergeant Shatrav," Feodor said. "There is one thing about which you, and all of your people, must be quite clear. You no longer command here. The command goes to your commissar," Feodor went on. "Comrade Gosykinya."

There was a moment of silence, broken only by the muttering of Kaminskaya into her mouthpiece. Shatrav found his voice. "Comrade Gosykinya is an eighteen-year-old girl."

"She has killed Germans, which is more than any of you have done," Feodor pointed out. "As of this moment, she is your commanding officer, with powers of life and death over every one of you." He looked from face to face to make sure they all understood.

Tatiana could not believe her ears, while at the same time knowing a growing feeling of exultation. Uncle Josef had come through! Shatrav still did not look convinced, although he understood that he had to obey the captain's directive, at least as long as the captain was present. "We await your command, Comrade Commissar," he said, with more than a hint of mockery in his voice.

Everyone was looking at her, including Feodor. He had given her power. Now she had to exercise it. "How soon will our guns and munitions reach us?" she asked.

Feodor turned to Kaminskaya, who put away her earphones. "Immediately following the next heavy rainstorm, which will keep German fighters out of the sky. This is forecast for the night after tomorrow."

"Right," Tatiana said. "Then we return to the camp. Walk with me, Comrade Captain."

He fell in beside her, while the rest of the fugitives followed, led by Kaminskaya. "Can you handle it?"

"I think so. When I believe it!"

"I'll help you believe it."

She glanced at him. "You mean you're staying?"

He grinned. "There's no way out of here, Tattie. We're completely surrounded."

"We knew that. But why me, Feodor? As Shatrav said, I'm only eighteen years old."

"Propaganda value," Feodor explained. "The Germans publicised what you did, because it gave them an excuse to execute as many people as they wanted. And they have done that."

"Shit!" Tatiana muttered.

"What's done is done. Now we have to turn that to our advantage. They reckon you're dead by now, as they have heard nothing more of you and have not been able to find you. So you are going to rise up out of the swamp, very much alive, and carry the fight to them."

"Sixty people?"

"There'll be more. We reckon there are several thousand deserters in these swamps, or nearby. They'll come in when they have something to come in for. This is a great opportunity for you, Tattie. They are calling you the Red Maiden. Handle it right and you'll be a Heroine of the Soviet Union. With your connections, you'll be big in the Party."

"And when the Germans come in after us?"

"That would have to be a very large operation, Tattie. Right now, I don't think they're prepared to spare the men or the time. They're hoping to capture Moscow by the first snow, which will be any day now."

"You mean they haven't captured Moscow yet?"

"We don't intend that they should. I said that they're hoping."

They splashed through the mud for some seconds. Then Tatiana asked. "Is Mother all right?"

"Mother is fine."

"Well," she said, "this is it."

They straggled on to the little island they used as a camp. It was just getting light. Feodor placed his hands on his hips and looked around him. Kaminskaya's nose wrinkled in contempt. "Winter will be here in another month," Feodor said in a low voice. "You can't exist in the open air, in winter."

"I've always said that," Tatiana agreed. "But they wouldn't work."

"Well, you are the boss now."

Tatiana glanced at him, then at the fugitives, most of whom had flung themselves onto the sodden ground on reaching the camp; they considered they had had their exercise for the day.

She drew a deep breath.

"Right," she said. "Everyone to work. We commence building shelters right now." They stared at her. "I have given an order," Tatiana said.

Anatole and Gregory scrambled to their feet. Natasha and Sophie followed their example. No one else moved. "Up!" Tatiana said.

Shatrav sat up. "We have been through this before, Comrade Commissar," he said. "There are no materials. There is no way we can build any adequate shelter. There is—"

"There are trees that can be cut down," Tatiana broke in: "We have an axe."

"One axe," someone grumbled.

"It will do; you can take turns at using it. Do not cut the trees together; that may be noticed from the air. Cut them over a widely spaced area."

"And how to we get them here?" asked someone else.

"You drag them, Comrade."

"That will be an immense task," objected another one.

"Nevertheless, it can and must be done. Now. Get moving!"

Still they looked at her. No one moved. Tatiana looked at Feodor and Kaminskaya. They would back her, she knew. But they would not tell her what to do, or she would never gain authority over these people, many of whom were grinning at her. To them she was just a girl who had come to them for refuge. Well, they had given her that refuge, but they had exacted a price, certainly the men. She did not like any of them, save for the two boys, and, of course, Natasha and Sophie. In fact, she realised that she hated them. But she was being required to lead them to almost certain death for the sake of the Motherland. Well, then, she thought, let hatred feed upon hatred. But she would command.

"Give me your pistol, Comrade Ligachev," she said.

Feodor drew his pistol, and presented it to her, butt first. She wrapped her fingers round it and faced the reclining people. "What do you think you are going to do with that, Tatiana?" asked one of the men with a grin.

"Make an example of you, Comrade!" she said, levelling the revolver and squeezing the trigger. The sound echoed through the trees. The man had only been 20 ft away from Tatiana, and the bullet had struck him in the face. Blood, flesh and bone exploded from his head. His shocked companions scrambled to their feet and found themselves looking not only at Tatiana's pistol, but at the levelled guns of Feodor and Kaminskaya. "Now," Tatiana said. "Get to work."

* * *

The swamp became a hive of activity as the fugitives got busy. Within a week four substantial huts had been built, two on the main island, and two on neighbouring hummocks. They were the most primitive constructions, no more than logs of wood bound together, their interstices packed with mud which contantly had to be renewed as it continued to rain every day. "They're not going to keep out much," Tatiana said.

"Yes they will," Feodor insisted. "When it starts to freeze, that mud will freeze too. Those huts will be like igloos."

"But we won't be able to light any fires."

"They don't have fires in igloos. They rely on body warmth."

"How does that fit in with our instructions?" she asked. For Feodor had brought with him a booklet of more than 400 pages, entitled "The Partisan's Guide". It had been hurriedly and badly printed, but contained a list of instructions for the partisans to follow in their daily lives. There were instructions on how to attack and destroy the enemy, blow up his trains, disrupt his life. There were lists of very sensible precautions they were required to take. There was first-aid information and emergency advice, such as how to exist in the snow and which species of moss and bark were edible should they run out of food. Someone had obviously thought the whole thing through very carefully.

There was also a command that there were to be no pregnancies. Pregnant women were a liability, and were to be shot. Tatiana hadn't felt she could accept that, and could only pray the question would never arise. But for all she knew any or all of the women, herself included, could be pregnant right then; the uncivilised life and poor diets had made them all irregular, and as they had only been in the swamp four months and hardly taken off all their clothes at any time during that period, no one would have had the time to swell as yet, at least obviously. "Do not Eskimoes in igloos sleep naked?"

"That doesn't mean they spend all their time fucking," Feodor pointed out.

After Feodor and Kaminskaya's arrival the rain fell heavily the next day and into the night, and there were no German aircraft. Then, as had been promised, the rain stopped soon after midnight, and an hour later the Russian planes were overhead, and parachutes came drifting down to festoon the trees. The fugitives – they were now almost prepared to call themselves partisans – revelled in the guns and pistols, the ammunition and grenades, the blankets, but above all in the food, the bars of chocolate and the tins of cured meat, tea and, even more, the casks of vodka: Tatiana, Feodor and Kaminskaya had a difficult task in stopping them drinking themselves silly there and then. Only the medical team did not arrive, although there was a message promising that it would not be long delayed; meanwhile there was medical equipment for them to use as necessary.

Some of the equipment was lost in the swamp, some smashed on landing, but enough was recovered intact to give Tatiana a well-armed fighting force – although she did not as yet know if they would fight. But now they were to be trained to do so. Feodor made them take two hours off every day from their building and food-gathering labours to drill and learn words of command. Even the women were drilled, and gradually some sense of unity, even of esprit de corps, began to creep into their ranks. "Now we need to do something to make us truly comrades," he said.

"You will have to instruct me, Comrade Captain."

"The Comrade Captain and I are leaving the camp for a few days," Tatiana told the group. "We are making a reconnaissance before we undertake any offensive action."

"If the Germans find out we are here," Gregory said, "will they not come into the swamp after us?"

"That will make them easier to kill," Feodor pointed out.

"In our absence," Tatiana told them, "Lieutenant Kaminskaya will command." There was no argument about that; Tatiana reckoned that everyone was afraid of Olga Kaminskaya, with her cold looks and precise actions. Certainly none of the men had attempted advances.

She and Feodor humped their packs and set off. Although this was intended only as a reconnaissance they both carried machine-guns as well as pistols and knives and, of course, grenades. As ammunition was not to be wasted Tatiana had allowed herself only one brief practice with the sub-machine-gun, but it was not a precision weapon. It was now the beginning of November, and the weather was very cold; indeed, they had barely lost sight of the camp when snowflakes drifted through the trees. "This swamp will be frozen within a fortnight," Feodor remarked.

Tatiana slapped her gloved hands together. There had been enough warm clothing dropped for the entire group, and in her quilted sheepskin jacket, known as a *polushubki*, and thick trousers, worn over thick thermal longjohns, her felt boots, *valenki*, and fur hat with ear-flaps, her fur-lined gloves, she felt warm enough even if her face was cold. But winter was always a threat. And now in more ways than one. "Will that not make it easier for the Germans to get at us?" she asked.

"Not really. We will be more exposed to their aircraft because the trees will be stripped bare by the frosts, but there will never be ice thick enough in here to support tanks or heavy vehicles. And we will see them coming the more easily, as well. It is a pity, but I suppose only you and I know how to ski," he remarked. They had always spent every spare winter moment in the Lenin Hills north of Moscow, with Jennie and Ligachev.

"Do you not think any of the others will have learned?"

"Kaminskaya, I should think."

"Well," she said. "We don't have any skis, anyway."
He grinned. "We can always have them dropped."

The next day they reached the fringe of trees marking the boundary of the marsh. By now it had stopped snowing, it was very cold, yet Feodor clambered up a tree to gain an extra few feet of visibility across the fields to the railway track; they had been moving north-west, and this was actually the position where the Marshes and the railway were closest. More important, a stream meandered out of the marsh at this point. It was not very deep, but it had created its own little gully over the centuries. This too was only a few feet deep, but it needed to be crossed by a bridge, both for the railway and, farther to the north-west, by the road.

"So," Feodor said to Tatiana, waiting below. "The railway is still in constant use, as is the road. Obviously it is the railway we must aim at. The bridge is its most vulnerable place. Just to the west of it there is a siding. Yes, if we blow the bridge and immobilise the siding . . ."

"How well is it guarded?" she asked.

"That is what we have to find out tonight" He climbed down the tree.

They sat together and ate cold canned food while they waited for sunset, which was early at this time of year, and with heavy cloud building to the west it became dark even earlier. "Are you afraid?" Feodor asked.

"I would like a drink of vodka."

He shook his head. "Vodka when we come back. A moment's carelessness could cost us both our lives." He glanced at her. "You know what they will do to you if the catch you?"

"No," she said. "I do not want to know. They can surprise me – if they can catch me."

* * *

When it was properly dark they left the shelter of the trees and moved across the fields towards the railroad. The distance was about three miles, but as it had started to snow again they were reasonably well hidden in their white jackets and trousers, especially as the corn had not been harvested, and grew in wild profusion in places 5 ft high. It was still slow progress, for the ground even outside the swamp had in many places turned to bog, and it was exhausting work. At least the snow meant there were no German patrols about. But, then, the Germans had no reason to send out patrols at all, much less on such a filthy night; the front had moved on several hundred miles, and no doubt they knew there were some escaped Red soldiers hiding in the Marshes, but such fugitives had never been any kind of a threat.

It was ten o'clock before Tatiana and Feodor reached about a quarter of a mile from the railroad. From here they could see that the Germans had constructed a guard-post just to the west of the bridge, a hut in which a lantern glowed. It was impossible to be certain how many men were inside, but two were on duty by the bridge, stamping their feet and slapping their gloved hands together. Feodor and Tatiana waited and watched, while steadily growing colder. The sentries and their companions had obviously lit a fire earlier for it still glowed to one side of the hut. At midnight the guard was changed. Tatiana was so cold she wanted to leave, but Feodor insisted on waiting another two hours, and at two the guard was changed again. By then the fire had burned out. "Eight men and a sergeant," Feodor said.

Even as this change was made, they watched a laden train rumble by, passing another going west and empty, waiting in the siding. Through their glasses, Feodor and Tatiana watched it and the soldiers, who had re-made the fire, and several were sitting round it; they patrolled the line in twos, up as far as the bridge and back. "Should we not try at another place?" Tatiana asked, rubbing her lips against the cold.

"We must do the maximum damage," he told her. "Just blowing up a stretch of line will cause a delay of only a few hours. Blowing up the bridge will disrupt the line for a couple of days."

"We must risk our lives for a couple of days?"

"That is the maximum we can hope for. A couple of days here, a couple of days there . . . it all adds up, and winter is just about upon us. Come on!"

They cautiously made their way back to the swamp. It was well past midnight before they regained the trees, and then it was another couple of hours walk through the mud and the slush to a place dry enough to be both safe and reasonably comfortable. Tatiana fell to her knees. She was exhausted. It was far colder than the previous night, although it was not yet snowing.

"We cannot stay here," Feodor said. "We will freeze."

Tatiana took off her pack. "I must have some rest. And you too." She unrolled her sleeping bag. "We will keep each other warm."

He considered for a moment, then discarded his own pack. "Get in," he said. Tatiana slithered into her bag until she was up to her neck.

Feodor then extracted his own sleeping bag, and using it as well as the two packs propped together created a shelter for their heads. Then he inserted himself into her bag, wriggling down the length of her body until he also was enclosed to his neck. He then reached up and arranged their blankets to close up any openings above them. Lastly he arranged their weapons beneath the shelter, beside their heads, so that they would not freeze and be instantly to hand if required. Finally he brought his arms into the sleeping bag, felt in his pocket and produced the flask of vodka. Tatiana took a swig, felt the warmth of the liquor tracing its way down her chest to her stomach, gave it back to him, for him to drink in turn. "Just the one each, I think," he said, and restored the flask to his pocket.

"We would create more warmth if we could take off our

clothes," Tatiana murmured, suddenly aroused for the first time in four months.

He grinned. "We will be warm enough."

Tatiana kissed him on the mouth. He did not resist her. While she kissed him she took off her heavy gloves and touched his cheek. "Are my hands cold?"

"They are warmer than your lips," he confessed.

"Let me warm them more." She reached down and unbuckled his heavy outer belt. Then she could release the buttons on his winter trousers, and reach through to his inner belt. This too she released, before unbuttoning his uniform trousers. Beyond this was his winter underwear, a woollen combination set. But it had a fly and this too she unbuttoned, to thrust both hands inside and hold him. Now he in turn was feeling his way through her several layers of clothing; she was in fact dressed exactly as he was. A few seconds later his hands were between her legs. "Body warmth," she whispered, kissing him again. "With no risk of pregnancy."

"We will need twenty personnel," Tatiana told the assembled partisans. She and Feodor had discussed their requirements on the walk back to the camp. As always, Tatiana left all the planning to him; he was the soldier. But it was her business to lead. "I would prefer all the group to be volunteers," she went on.

Immediately, as she had known would be the case, Anatole and Gregory, Natasha and Sophie, stood up. "Are you going to be shamed by schoolchildren?" Tatiana asked. Several more of the men and two other of the women joined her. "Sergeant Shatrav?" Tatiana inquired.

Shatrav hesitated, then he also got up. "I suppose we are all going to get killed," he remarked.

"We are all going to kill Germans, you mean," she told him.

* * *

As before, Kaminskaya was left behind in charge of the camp. Two days later they were in position, and it was now that Tatiana outlined the plan Feodor had formulated. She did not like the plan, because it involved separation from Feodor, even if only for a couple of hours. Even more she disliked it because although she, as leader, had felt called upon to volunteer for the most dangerous part of the mission, he had not objected. But she had not argued against it; he would know best. "We will advance in two groups," she said. "Sixteen in the assault group, four in the detonater group. I will command the assault group, Captain Ligachev the detonater group. He and I have synchronised our watches. When we are in position, and the appointed time has arrived, we will eliminate the guards. Remember, the guard hut is to be undamaged, or at least, no more than is necessary. That is why we are not using grenades. From the point of view of the next train through, nothing must have happened. Once we have accomplished our purpose, the group will fall back, except for Comrade Savin and myself. We will use German uniforms and appear to be on guard duty. We will rejoin you as soon as possible but you are not to wait for us."

"You will be killed. We will all be killed," Shatrav grumbled.

"If we are killed, we will have died fighting for the Motherland," Tatiana told him. "But be sure about one thing: if any man, or woman—" her gaze swept them all before coming back to rest on Shatrav – "fails to do his or her duty, or shows any cowardice in the face of the enemy, I will kill him or her myself. Do not doubt this. It must be clearly understood, too, that any wounded who cannot regain the swamp under their own power will be abandoned. They will hand over their weapons, save for their revolver." Once again she swept their faces. "I would strongly recommend that anyone who is too badly wounded to regain the swamp should kill themselves before the Germans can capture him, or her."

* * *

They ate a brief supper, then they discarded their packs, to be picked up when they returned. "We need to leave someone here," Feodor said, "both to guard our gear and to guide us back to it. Choose."

Tatiana's emotions told her to select Sophie, who was too young, and despite her experiences, too basically innocent to be involved in something like this. But her instincts told her that that might turn out badly: Sophie was so frightened that if left alone she might well run away. Natasha was desperate to fight.

"Gregory," she said.

"Me?" the boy cried. "I wish to go with you."

"You will be fulfilling a far more important task by remaining here," Feodor told him. "You are our base. Without you, we are all at grave risk."

They made their way across the snow-covered field. When they were within a quarter of a mile of the bridge, the two parties separated. "Good luck," Feodor said, squeezing Tatiana's hand.

"And to you, Comrade," Tatiana said. Now she was on a killing high, the adrenalin racing through her arteries. She was going to war, properly, for the first time.

She studied the guard-post through her glasses. As with four nights ago, the Germans had lit a fire beside the hut, and there were five men crouched around it. Two more were stamping up and down the line by the bridge. That meant, if Feodor's calculations had been correct, that there would be two more actually inside the hut.

"Shatrav," she whispered. "Take three people and approach the guards on the bridge. Get to within point-blank range, but do not fire until I do. This is very important. No one must fire a shot until we are all ready. My first shot will be the signal."

Shatrav nodded, beckoned two of the men and one of the women, and crawled away into the darkness. "Romashov," she turned to the next most senior soldier. "Your eight people will shoot the men sitting round the fire. Again, you will wait for my first shot. And remember not to shoot at us!"

"Yes, Comrade Commissar," Romashov said.

"Anatole, you and Natasha and Surkov will come with me."

"I wish to come with you too," Sophie protested.

"You will stay with Romashov," Tatiana told her. "Don't worry, we are all in this battle together." She crawled away into the darkness, her three companions behind her. "Keep your weapons slung until it is time," she told them. There was no wind and the slightest sound might alert the soldiers.

It took them more than 15 minutes to gain a position some hundred yards west of the guard post. Then they crossed the railway line and crawled back along it, slowly approaching the guard hut. Beyond that, one of the soldiers rose from around the fire and moved towards the line, unbuttoning his flies as he did so. Tatiana flapped her hand to warn her companions to go down and remain still until he had finished, but as she did so a shot rang out. Instantly the Germans scattered from around the fire, drawing their pistols.

"Shit!" Tatiana said. But there was no further point in concealment. She levelled her gun and squeezed the trigger, even as firing became general from the other Russians. Tatiana reached her feet and ran to the hut. A man had just emerged in the doorway, holding a rifle. He fell to another burst of fire, then she felt a tremendous jolt, and found herself lying in the snow.

Natasha knelt beside her. "Tattie!" she screamed. "Tattie!"

"Get the hut!" Tattie snapped. Anatole and Surkov were already there, firing into the interior.

The shooting stopped; it had lasted less than a minute. Tatiana tried to sit up, and fell over again; the bullet was lodged somewhere in her body, she was sure, but she felt no pain at the moment; she was still suffering from shock. Shatrav stood above her. "Is it bad?"

"I don't know. Report."

"Six Germans dead, three wounded."

"Shoot them," Tatiana said. "Ours?"

"You are our only casualty, Comrade Commissar."

"Very good. Take command, Sergeant. Pull our people out, and return to the swamp."

Shatrav nodded. "We will make a litter to carry you, Comrade Commissar."

Tatiana raised her head. "My orders were that wounded had to fend for themselves. If I can get back, I will. But you must not wait for me."

Shatrav grinned. "I am going to disobey your orders, Comrade Commissar. You are our commander, and we have gained a victory."

Tatiana submitted; she had no desire to be left on her own in the snow, and she certainly didn't wish to be abandoned to the Germans. But she had intended to be one of the fake guards, and this was now prevented. Anatole had already volunteered, and Romashov agreed to stay with him. The dead Germans were examined, and the two whose clothing was least bloodstained were stripped of their uniforms, which Anatole and Romashov put on. Neither was a good fit, but they were not going to be examined closely. Then the lamp in the hut was relit, and the corpses dragged out of sight. By now Natasha and Shatrav and the other women had delved into Tatiana's clothing in search of her wound. They found it in her lower right ribs.

"There is at least one broken rib," the woman Christina said. Her gaunt features and raw-boned body hardly went with such a delicate name. "But you were lucky, Comrade Commissar; all this thick clothing took the velocity from the bullet, otherwise it might have gone right through you." She actually removed the lead with her fingers, while Tatiana gulped vodka. Then Christina bound it up and Tatiana's clothes were replaced.

It was so cold that she actually felt very little pain; that would come later. “All set?” Shatrav had taken command. Anatole and Romashov nodded, faces grim. In the distance they could hear the wail of the train whistle as it approached Brest-Litovsk. “Then let us get out of here,” Shatrav said.

A litter had been made from discarded German rifles and greatcoats, and on this Tatiana was laid. She suspected she would have done better to walk, for the improvised mattress was uncomfortable, and the four men carrying her could not help but trip and stumble or slip from time to time. Now they could see the train, coming ever closer; so contemptuous were the Germans of anything the Russians might be capable of that the carriages blazed with light. “Get down,” Tatiana said. They were still a mile from the trees, and could be picked out by keen eyes.

The group sank into the snow, and Tatiana raised herself on her elbow to watch. The train roared up to the bridge. Tatiana peered into the gloom, but could not make out Feodor and his people; they would of course be in the gully carved by the stream. Nor could she make out Anatole and Romashov, but she could see the light glowing in the hut, and clearly the train drivers were happy with that, for the train never slowed as it approached the bridge. But the train itself . . .

“The glasses!” she snapped. “Where are my glasses?” Shatrav handed her the binoculars, and she hastily focussed them as the train hurtled closer. “Oh, shit!” she muttered.

It was a troop train; every carriage, and there were at least twelve, was laden with men. But there was nothing she could do about aborting the attack; they had not considered such a possibility, and had agreed no signals for it. Equally, she was not sure Feodor would consider it, even had he known the catastrophe that was waiting to happen.

The train roared at the bridge, and then reached it. As it so did so, with perfect timing, Feodor fired his charge. There was a huge explosion. The night sky was seared with red. The watchers could see the train lifted from the track and hurled to one side. The first carriage behind it plunged into the gully with a scream of tortured metal. The second and third carriages were also derailed, coming off the track and falling over with huge crumps of noise, scattering men to and fro. But the nine carriages behind remained upright, and from them flooded men, forming ranks in obedience to the barked commands, opening fire into the darkness. They didn't know what they were shooting at, but they were blanketing each side of the wrecked train with bullets.

"Quick!" Shatrav said. "Back to the trees!"

"Anatole," Tatiana said. "Romashov!"

"We cannot help them, Comrade Commissar," Shatrav said. "They knew the risks they were taking." Tatiana bit her lip, but she knew he was right, and now her broken rib was starting to throb. She let her head droop, as she was taken into the trees.

The Germans continued to fire for another 15 minutes, then the noise slowly died. The partisans crouched close to the tree fringe, having located the glow of Gregory's flashlight and regained their gear. He wanted to know what had happened, and looked close to tears when he was told that his friend was almost certainly dead. But what of Feodor, Tatiana wondered, as the pain steadily increased. "How long do we wait?" Shatrav asked. "If we are still here at daybreak the Germans may well come after us."

"We wait until Captain Ligachev joins us," Tatiana told him.

He looked as if he would like to argue, but then wandered off to join his friends. Natasha sat beside the stretcher. "Would you like some vodka?" She held the flask to Tatiana's lips.

"Where is Sophie?" Tatiana asked.

"She is here. Somewhere."

"Thank God for that! Listen."

The Germans had stopped firing now, and the night was

still. They could not hear what might be happening two miles away. But closer at hand there was sound, and then the glow of a light. "It is Captain Ligachev," Shatrav said, hurrying forward.

"Respond," Tatiana commanded. "How many?"

"All of them." Gregory was excited.

The four figures appeared out of the snow. "That was well done, Comrade Captain," Shatrav said. "It was a splendid explosion."

Feodor looked over their faces. "Where is the Commissar?"

"I am here," Tatiana said. He knelt beside her. "Thank God you are all right," she said. "I was so worried."

"As I was for you. Where are you hurt?"

"I have a broken rib. But they would not leave me."

"Then I thank God for that," he said.

"Anatole and Romashov?"

"They are dead."

"I should be also, but they would not obey instructions and abandon me."

"They love you," he said. "But who disobeyed you first, and fired the first shot?"

Tatiana had forgotten that. "It was the girl, Sophie," Shatrav said. "She was very frightened."

There was a scuffle at the back of the group standing round Tatiana. Sophie had tried to run away, but had been seized by two of the women and brought forward. "Did you fire the shot?" Feodor asked.

Sophie bit her lip. "I . . . I didn't mean to. I was shaking. And my gun went off." She looked from face to face. "No harm came of it."

"No harm?" Feodor asked. "Because of you the Commissar might have been killed." Tatiana opened her mouth, and then closed it again. She could indeed have been killed. But there was a more important issue at stake. Feodor spelled it out: "You disobeyed an order in the presence of the enemy. You are condemned to death."

"No!" Sophie gasped. "You cannot! Please!" She turned to Tatiana. "We are friends!" Tatiana glanced at Feodor, whose face was stony. But his eyes were warning her not to interfere. They were all in this together. Their survival depended on being able to trust each other, absolutely. She had shot a man for not obeying her command instantly. The group respected and feared her for that, and no doubt that respect and fear had caused them to save her life tonight. To show favouritism, even to an old friend, would destroy all that trust.

Sophie saw Tatiana's expression harden, and turned to Natasha. "Natasha," she begged. "For the love of God!"

Natasha bit her lip. The group watched as Sophie was stripped of her winter tunic and breeches, her fur-lined boots. Sophie made no effort to resist them, merely trembled, her trembles turning to shudders as the cold got to her. "There must be no noise," Feodor said. "Use the swamp."

Shatrav beckoned three of the men and they grasped Sophie's arms. Sophie opened her mouth to scream, and Shatrav hit her in the stomach. Sophie gasped. A few moments later they heard the splashes, and another dreadful gurgle, and then watched Shatrav and his men returning through the trees.

"Let's move out," Feodor said. "We want to be well away from here come sunrise."

Part Two

Those Who Would Fight

Whither depart the souls of the brave that die in the battle,
Die in the lost, lost fight, for the cause that perishes with them?

Arthur Hugh Clough, *The Bothie of Tober-na-Vuolich*

Chapter 5

The Waiting

"We have never met," Ivan Ligachev said. "But I am your brother-in-law. Welcome to Moscow."

Joseph Cromb allowed his hand to be shaken. He knew enough about the Soviet Union to understand that nothing was exactly as it appeared. The fact that he had never met Ligachev before did not mean that back in 1925 this man had not played a part in arresting him, torturing him, and sentencing him to a lifetime in prison. And while he knew that Ligachev was indeed now married to Jennie, Jennie's previous husband was the man who had carried out that not-to-be-forgotten arrest. Yet he was telling the truth when he said, "It is good to be here."

"You are satisfied with the hotel?" Ligachev asked, anxiously.

"I think we all are." Joseph went to the window of his room to look down at the street and the pouring rain. Moscow actually revealed very little evidence of being a capital in imminent danger of attack, or of having suffered air attack at all. There had been a few damaged buildings, and no doubt there were actually a lot more; the low cloud and the rain helped to conceal a lot. On the other hand, he had observed at the railway station that people – mainly women and children – were definitely leaving the city, although in a very orderly fashion: only those with special permits could find places on the trains. "How long do we stay here?" he asked.

"As long as is necessary," Ligachev assured him.

"Won't the Germans have something to say about that? The last communiqué had them two hundred miles from the city."

"In the rain and the mud, two hundred miles is a long way, Mr Cromb. And soon the rain and mud will turn to snow and ice."

"Your confidence is inspiring. So, what have you got arranged for us?"

"Well, there is a full programme of meetings of course, including one with Comrade Stalin. It is obviously most important that we receive all the assistance your government can provide, just as quickly as possible."

"Yes," Joseph agreed, somewhat cautiously. One thing had been made perfectly clear to the delegation before it had left Washington: under no circumstances did the State Department intend to ship any materiel if there was the slightest chance of it being surrendered to the Germans in the event of a Soviet collapse.

"But the meetings do not start until tomorrow," Ligachev said. "For today, will you not come home with me and see Jennie? I know she would like that."

Joseph was extremely nervous as he was escorted in the elevator up to Ligachev's first-floor apartment, which was situated in a large and opulent eleven-storey building known as 'Government House', on the Moscow River embankment. The lower floor housed shops, a clinic, a cinema and even a branch of the Kremlin Restaurant, and he had no doubt that the apartment would be considerably above the average. But what was he going to meet inside?

It was actually 19 years since he had last seen his half-sister. In the autumn of 1922 she had fled from England, where, although her father was American and her mother less English than Russian, she had been educated as an Englishwoman. She had then been 16, and theoretically as far removed from the wild excesses of her Bolugayevski cousins as it had been possible to imagine. But always had she been Patricia Bolugayevska's daughter, and Patricia had been always less a Bolugayevska than a Russian, a wild spirit who had dabbled in anarchy and terrorism and indeed revolt. Patricia had been savagely punished for her transgressions against Tsarist Russia, but she had survived, and prospered . . . and remained a revolutionary at heart. Jennie had inherited all of that.

Remarkably, Joseph thought, he had not. Oh, he undoubtedly had a wildly romantic streak running through his character, which had got him into sufficient trouble in his time, but his outlook had more often been tempered by the characteristics inherited from the father he had never known, Joseph Fine, from actually having been born in Siberian exile, from being educated in the sober New England and English values of his stepfather Duncan Cromb and above all by his experiences.

He had not known sufficient of his half-sister, that was his problem. They had been separated by war during her early teens, and when he had returned she had already developed a deeply private persona into which neither Priscilla nor himself had been prepared to delve too deeply. That she would elope with a handsome Bolshevik agent had taken them both by surprise, where they should have expected it and taken steps to combat and end the relationship before it could develop. Since then, silence. Joseph's visit to Russia in an attempt to find her and persuade her to return to the West with him had cost him 12 years in the gulag archipelago. In all that time, so far as either he or Priscilla knew, Jennie had made no attempt to find out what had happened to him, or indeed to contact the rest of the family. Now she wanted to see him. Just like that! All the past was to be forgotten. But was that not why he was here? In every sense?

* * *

"We have not too much time," Ligachev told him. "The bombers normally come at eleven. Very regular people, the Germans." He opened the door of the apartment, stood back to allow Joseph to enter. Jennie stood just inside the door, facing it; the building, and the apartment, might be up-market by Moscow standards, but the walls were still paper thin and she had heard the steps on the stairs.

Joseph realised he might have been looking at his mother, the last time he had seen her, in the spring of 1917, just before he had embarked for France, and just before she had galloped off to her death in Revolutionary Russia. Patricia had been 39 then; Jennie was only 35, but she looked older. There was no grey as yet in her curling auburn hair, but there were stress lines in her face and around her eyes. She was also somewhat more slim than her mother had ever been, although she remained a true Bolugayevska, tall and strongly built and voluptuous, even in a somewhat shapeless dress. He wondered what she saw, as she took stock of him. Grey hair, certainly, and he was only 43, But apart from that, he felt no great signs of hardship or privation. Well, he had had several years to recover.

"Joe!" she said, and came forward. He took her in his arms, held her close.

"Champagne!" Ligachev said, uncorking a bottle. "That is what the Bolugayevskis always drink, is it not?"

"When we can get it," Joseph agreed.

Jennie was still holding his arm. "Are you all right?" she asked.

"Fit as a fiddle! And you?"

"Yes." But her answer wasn't entirely convincing, as she herself understood. She released Joseph to take a glass of champagne. "We have so much to talk about," she said, looking at her husband.

"Then I will leave you," Ligachev said. "Perhaps you will join me for lunch. Jennie will know where." He closed the door behind himself.

"He always eats the Georgian food at the Aragvi," Jennie explained.

"Seems a nice, relaxed kind of guy, your husband," Joseph said. "I didn't realise places like the Aragvi – Moscow's most famous restaurant – were still open."

"Moscow is trying to be normal. As is Ivan. He has his tensions. We all do. Please sit down." She did so herself, and he sat opposite her, taking in the furnishings as he did so. He could have been in the small downtown apartment of any lower middle-class American family. But these people were Soviet aristocracy.

"Nice place," he commented.

"Well, Ivan is a close associate of Uncle Josef."

"Excuse me?"

"Our great leader, Josef Stalin."

"Ah! Yes, I sort of gathered that. So was Andrei Gosykin, was he not?"

A cloud passed across Jennie's face, and she got up to refill their glasses. "If you knew how much those days haunt me." She stood in front of him. "Joe, I did not know what had happened to you, I swear it. I did not know that Gosykin was a professional killer, until it was too late. I wrote you, but I never got any replies. I know now that it was because Gosykin never mailed any of my letters. But I did not know it then. I just thought the family had discarded me."

"As they thought you had discarded them. If that is the truth . . ."

"It is the truth, Joe. I swear it!"

"Then we all need to do a great deal of apologising," Joseph said.

"I would like that very much. I would like to be your sister again. Especially now that you have come to help us in our great patriotic fight against the Nazis."

He found her carefully framed words, so obviously placed in her mind by the Party propaganda machine, disturbing. "We will do what we can," he said. "But there is one thing that still puzzles me: why did you stay in Russia, after you learned the truth about Gosykin?"

Jennie frowned. "Where was I to go? This is my home."

"Well, do you not think England, or America, is more your home?"

"Of course it is not. I am Russian."

Jennie actually only had a drop of Russian blood in her veins, through her grandmother: the mainstream was Scottish. "But the regime . . ."

"Our regime is better, and less corrupt, than any in the West."

"What of all the millions of people Stalin has had slaughtered? The great purges, of only four years ago, the . . ."

"Joseph, you are spouting Western propaganda," Jennie said severely. "Massacres? What massacres? Some people who attempted revolution against the government were killed. Does that not always happen in revolutions? The purges were of traitors and elements hostile to the government. Believe me, Uncle Joe hated what he had to do. But the good of the nation comes first. He knew there was this war coming, and he had to prepare for it, first of all by rooting out all the traitors in our midst."

If Stalin knew this war was coming, Joseph thought, he has gone about preparing for it in a very odd way. But he decided against saying it, which might provoke a quarrel – she obviously worshipped Stalin, but then, amazingly, so did so many Russians, he had discovered on his journey here, via the Arctic Sea and Murmansk. He chose to soften the subject. "I was told you had a daughter."

"Tatiana, yes." Jennie's eyes shone with pride.

"By Gosykin?"

"Yes. She is Andrei's child." She went to a small table, picked up the framed photograph and gave it to him. "That was taken this spring. Just before she went away on summer camp."

The photograph was redolent of regimented severity. The

girl wore a khaki sidecap, khaki blouse and skirt; it ended at her knees. But he did not doubt she would be wearing khaki stockings and severe brown shoes. The face fitted the uniform, in its solemn severity. But it was undoubtedly a beautiful face, the somewhat large regularity of Jennie's features sharpened by those of Gosykin himself. There was little hair visible, but Joseph got the impression that it was dark – the photo was in black and white. "She is very attractive. Is she in Moscow?"

"Tatiana is in the Pripet Marshes," Jennie said.

Joseph raised his head sharply. "But that is behind the German lines!"

"Yes. She was in summer camp close to Brest-Litovsk when the Nazis invaded. She was trapped there."

"My God! Are you not worried? Do you know if she is still alive?"

"We know she is alive," Jennie said. "And she is killing Germans. She killed two German officers who tried to rape her. Now she has been joined by her brother . . ."

"You have a son?"

"No, no. This is Ivan's son. He is a splendid fellow. He is a captain in the Army, and he volunteered to join his sister and her people in the Marshes. It is he who radioed the news that she is alive. And do you know what, Joe? She has been made a commissar, in command of that group of partisans."

"But do you realise how dangerous that is? Do you know what will happen to her if she is caught?"

Jennie's lips tightened, for a moment. Then she smiled. "She will not be caught." Her head turned, "There is the air-raid siren. We must hurry."

Her calmness was reassuring; Joseph had never been in an air raid before. It was, in fact, several years since he had been under fire. Now he followed her down the stairs and into the cellar beneath the apartment building, looking at the insubstantial walls as he did so. "Is this place supposed to withstand a bomb?" he asked.

"Not a direct hit, no," Jennie conceded.

"Or even one near by, I would have said."

She shrugged. "We are all in the front line now, Joe." The cellar was already crowded, but as all the people sheltering lived in the block they were all well-to-do and well-behaved, seating themselves quietly on blankets, in groups and showing no great curiosity at the stranger accompanying Jennie; Joseph took after his Jewish father rather than his Russian mother, certainly in looks, and there was nothing to indicate that they were half-brother and sister. "This is our place," Jennie said.

People were seated or standing all around them, but the spot she had indicated was vacant. "You mean you all have your own places?"

"Of course. This is Galina Shermetska." Joseph's head jerked up. The woman was short and plump, with crisp Tatar features and raven black hair. Jennie frowned at his reaction. "Do you know her?"

Galina Shermetska was looking him up and down. "I have never met you, Comrade," she remarked.

"No, you have not," Joseph agreed. "It is just that I knew a Galina once. Briefly."

"Galina lives in the flat above mine," Jennie explained. "We are the best of friends. Galina, this is my brother Joseph."

"Ah!" Galina said. "The American who writes bad things about the Soviet Union."

"An American who is here to help us," Jennie said.

Galina smiled. "In that case, Comrade, welcome to Moscow!"

The raid lasted half an hour. It was nerve-racking, because although they could hear the rapid fire of the Soviet anti-aircraft guns, there did not seem to be much in the way of air defence, and the bombs dropped all around them with unending intensity. Yet when they emerged into the rain it was difficult to determine how much damage had been done. Certainly as soon as the German planes departed Gorki Street was as busy as ever, and Aragvi, where Jennie and Joseph joined Ivan for lunch, was packed to the door. Joseph understood that places like Aragvi were only open to Party members and foreigners with hard currency to spend, but certainly at this level there was no shortage of anything, from caviar to champagne. "You will not believe this," Ivan said, "but the Germans are only fifty miles away. Do you know, they have captured Mozhaisk? When they got there the tram from Moscow had just arrived."

"Then may we expect them here for dinner?" Jennie asked.

"I do not think so," Ivan said. "We are counter-attacking."

It was amazing how calm everyone seemed to be, and not only at official levels either; that very day a call went out for a volunteer unit, a sort of Home Guard, to be raised to assist the soldiers in defending the city, and within a week 12,000 men had come forward. The difficulty was arming them. From the point of view of Joseph and the American delegation it was all very unreal. Although they stood every chance of being killed by a German bomb, they were basically in no danger should the Germans actually capture the city: the last thing the Nazis would dare risk would be antagonising the United States by deliberately harming any of its envoys.

Business continued as if there was no threat. They spent every day with officials from the various Soviet ministries, and were subjected to lengthy harangues; once they were even lectured by Stalin himself – this was the first time Joseph had ever laid eyes on the man he now knew had been responsible for locking him away, in atrocious conditions, for 12 years. But now was not the time for thoughts of vengeance, this would only be possible after the defeat of Hitler, if that was going to happen, Joseph thought. Stalin was in upbeat mood, reminding his audience of how Kutusov had beaten Napoleon, and Peter the Great defeated Charles XII of Sweden, both great soldiers who had appeared to have Russia at their mercy. "To compare Hitler or any of his generals with Napoleon or Charles is to make a bad joke," the Premier declared. But the Germans were there, and coming closer, and for all the confidence exuded by the Soviet leader, it was difficult to determine the source of that confidence. He admitted they were short of all the material of war. That was why the Americans were there. But what the Russians were asking for was aid on an unimaginable scale.

This led to a certain amount of dissension within the American camp. The military men, basing their professional opinions upon known facts, on the sheer magnitude of the German advance taken together with the enormous casualties in both men and materiel sustained by the Russians, were unanimous in their view that the Russians would probably not last the year. The civilians, headed by Hopkins, were impressed by the determination shown by Stalin and his leading henchmen, not to mention the people of Moscow themselves, and felt that, sufficiently encouraged, the Russians might well keep on fighting indefinitely.

Joseph's personal feelings were ambivalent. He invariably met Jennie and Ivan for lunch, and sometimes he visited them in the evenings as well, although this time was eaten into by the various social functions the Americans were required to attend. Quite amazingly, although the Bolshoi was closed, its reserve section, the Filiale, was still performing on Pushkin Street in the Operetta Theatre – it was even possible, on occasion, to watch Lepeshinskaya dance – while the cinemas, not to mention the Cocktail Hall on Gorki Street, were always packed.

It was an amazing, upsidedown society – there were days when one could suppose one heard the guns, now firing within 50 miles – and Joseph almost wished Alexei could be here to share the experience of being in at what might well turn out to be the end of the Soviet World. Of course the regime appeared determined to fight on and seemed prepared to back their words with deeds. In an amazing feat of physical and mental endurance much of the heavy industrial base on which the army depended for its sustenance had been moved, brick by brick and machine tool by machine tool, across the Urals and into Siberia. But Joseph knew there was a limit to how much people could take, as opposed to governments, which were able to have a larger and longer overall view.

Moscow was Russia's Holy City, even if such words as holy were officially not part of the Communist vocabulary, and if it fell, as seemed extremely likely, and the Germans as a consequence overran all of European Russia to those Urals – they had already taken Kiev in the south and overrun the Donbas, and the old family home of Bolugayen, in their drive to the Caucasus oilfields, and seemed on the verge of taking Leningrad in the north – again as seemed extremely likely, he did not think the Soviet system as it was understood in the West would survive. It might be able to do so in Asia, but that would be a kind of reincarnation of the old Tatar empires, ruled from places like Karakorum.

"We are now coming into Sverdlovsk," announced the smooth young man who was acting as guide and interpreter for the medical party. "Here we will disembark."

"But we haven't got to the Urals, yet," Elaine Mitchell complained.

"This is as far as you go," Sviatoslav – which was all they knew him by – explained. "Most of you."

"We're in their hands," Dr Haggard said. "But say, look at this." They crowded round him to peer through the window. The snow was clouding down quite thickly, but through the white haze they could make out a huge factory complex. "I didn't know you guys had factories out here," Haggard remarked.

Sviatoslav appeared to preen himself. "Three months ago, there was no factory here. That factory was moved, brick by brick, from nearby Moscow to protect it from the Germans."

"You saying you moved that factory in three months?" George Allcott demanded. "Bullshit!"

"The factory was moved in *two* months," Sviatoslav stated, without taking offence. Perhaps he did not understand the swearword, Alex thought, holding on to Elaine as the train came to a halt with much thumping and jolting. If there had been scattered moments on the voyage from San Francisco to Vladivostock, there had been none at all on the train journey from Vladivostock across Siberia, when every compartment had held at least four people too many, even for sleeping. They had had to be content with secret smiles.

"Sverdlovsk," Sviatoslav told the doctors as they disembarked into the most bitter cold any of them had ever known, a paralysing chill which immediately ate through their heavy coats and even their boots and thermal underwear, "was once known as Ekaterinburg. That means, Catherine's City. It was named after the Empress Catherine."

"Do you think we could have a hot bath?" Elaine asked. None of them had bathed throughout the journey from Vladivostock.

"Of course." He led them out of the station and on to the snow-packed street; their heavy gear was being unloaded for them. People hurried to and fro, but cast them scarcely a glance. Partly, Elaine was sure, this was because of the cold. But it was also partly because, she guessed, there had been so many comings and goings and general upheavals over the past few months that a few more strange faces were not relevant. "It was here in the then Ekaterinberg," Sviatoslav went on, "that Nicholas Romanov and his family were executed by orders of the Ural Soviet, in July 1918." He pointed. "That is the house in which they were imprisoned.

They were shot in the cellar beneath the house. Would you like to look at it? You can still see the blood."

"After we've had a hot bath," Elaine told him.

A government minister made them a speech filled with bombastic references to the might and greatness of the Soviet Union, with praise of the immense talents of Josef Stalin, and with dismissive contempt of the Germans and their claims. As the German claims, both as regards losses inflicted on the Russians and territory conquered from the Russians, were in the main accepted as true by the West, the doctors found themselves wondering how much else of what they were being told had to be lies.

Elaine was inclined to put it in the same class as the Romanovs' blood. Serology was one of the subjects she had specialised in, and she hadn't needed any samples to deduce that the blood on the bullet-marked wall of the cellar where the murders had been committed was not 23 years old, or even 23 weeks. She might just have accepted 23 days, that is if it was human blood at all!

Now she had some difficulty in keeping awake; they had been given baths, and then fed an enormous meal of mainly vegetables, but they had been so hungry it didn't matter, while they had all been required to drink at least a jug of vodka. Following which had come the tour of the infamous house, and now this unending lecture. She was in any event in a dreamlike state. Rather like that first night she had visited the Bolugayevski home in Boston. The only time she had visited their home. That had been like stepping through Lewis Carroll's mirror, not into a backwards world, but one which had long ago ceased to exist.

Now she had taken another step into living history. This was the here and now, but everything she had encountered; the seemingly endless forest that had stretched most of the way across Siberia to the enormous lake they had crossed by ferry; to the very ancient steamtrain in which they had travelled to their arrival in this city in which a tsar and his family had been murdered, actually during her lifetime; the free-standing porcelain bathtub and the maid who simply would not go away; the great four-poster bed; the intense warmth of the hotel – and then to compare it with the intense cold outside – made her feel she had somehow drifted back through the ages, without quite understanding how.

But Alex was here with her, and Alex was reality. She caught his eye and smiled at him, and he waggled his eyebrows. They were apparently coming to the important part of the speech. Elaine sat up and listened. The interpreter was reading off a list of cities, and she gathered they were about to be split up and sent, in twos and threes, to these destinations. Desperately she looked at Alex. Alex was on his feet. "Will none of us be sent to Moscow?"

"Moscow is a combat area," the interpreter explained. "You are not required to work in combat areas. This has been agreed."

"Can we not volunteer for such service?"

"Well . . ." the interpreter held a muttered conversation with the minister. "It would be very gratifying were you to do so," the interpreter said.

"Then I volunteer," Alex said.

"It must be understood that you are doing this of your own free will," the interpreter said. "You will sign a paper, eh? An indemnity."

"Surely," Alex agreed.

Elaine stood up. "I volunteer, too."

The interpreter stared at her in consternation, while the minister said, "It is not possible for us to accept a woman volunteer."

"Why not?" Elaine asked. "You have regiments of women soldiers, do you not? You have Russian women working in the hospitals in Moscow. I volunteer. I insist on volunteering."

* * *

It took Alex and Elaine another three days to reach Moscow, which made them the more grateful for the break they had had in Sverdlovsk, as once again there was no opportunity for bathing or even changing their clothes. The train was even more crowded than the trans-Siberian, and this time mainly with Siberian troops, hardy Mongols who until recently had been manning the line of the Amur to defend Russia from attack by the Japanese. Although, a couple of years ago, there had been pitched battles between the two sides, a recurrence of open hostility had now apparently been ruled out by the Kremlin, and these little, blunt-featured fellows were looking forward to having a crack at the Germans. They were also extremely macho, and found travelling in an overcrowded compartment in the company of a pretty girl a distinct pleasure. Alex reckoned Elaine was actually in more danger of being raped on the train than from any itinerant German. But she merely smiled and rejected all advances in the politest but firmest possible way.

In any event, even the Mongolian soldiers had more on their minds than sex. As they crossed the Urals the evidence of the enormous struggle going on in front of them, and soon all around them, became more and more unmistakeable. They looked at huge columns of refugees attempting to make their way east through the snow, presumably along roads, although these were invisible beneath the blanket of white which overlay the country several feet deep. Elaine thought them the most pitiful objects she had ever seen, because they were all either very old, of both sexes, or very young – anyone able to bear a gun or operate a lathe was fully employed. They drove carts or dragged and pushed cars where the animals were missing, each cart piled high with household goods, or they trudged along, with little bundles draped over their shoulders. "What do they live on?" Elaine asked.

"Whatever they can find," the guard told her.

"In this weather? Where do they sleep?"

"On the road."

Again she said, "In this weather? Don't they freeze?"

"Regularly."

"And nobody cares?"

"We are fighting a war, Comrade Doctor. Those people are the least valuable of our assets."

Elaine felt physically sick. But she could not stop staring at the refugees. Also moving along these roads, in the other direction, there were masses of troops, tanks and trucks, and the unfortunate people were constantly being pushed out of the way. The nearness of war was also evident in the bombers which came over every day, seeking the columns, seeking the trains, soiling the snow with freshly turned black earth and newly spilled red blood. Once bombs actually struck the line in front of the train, and the two Americans watched in awe as everyone on board worked all night to replace the broken track. "Can you imagine anything like this ever happening in the States?" Elaine asked.

"It did happen," Alex pointed out. "Only eighty years ago."

By the time they reached Moscow they were hearing the sound of the guns as well; the Germans were very close to the city. Alex had never been to Moscow. Born during the Great War, far to the south on Bolugayen, he had never had the opportunity before his mother had fled with himself and his half-sister Anna, by ship from Sevastopol to England. Actually, Mom had never been to Moscow either, but Joseph had, even if his memories were not happy ones. But Alex had read everything he could obtain on both the city and its history; he was disappointed to find how different it was to what he had expected. Partly this was a result of the snow, which has a tendency to make all cities look alike. But the snow at least hid the bomb damage, even if it made movement more than usually difficult, as it was impossible to tell where the craters were. The Kremlin, however, seemed undamaged, and St Basil's Cathedral was as awe-inspiring as expected, and could be gawped at even if Alex did not suppose he and Elaine would be allowed inside.

It was when they reached their assigned hospital that they realised what it was like to be in the middle of a real shooting war. They were welcomed by the Russian registrar, assigned quarters, widely separated, and told to report for duty in 15 minutes. Within half-an-hour Alex found himself supervising a nurse who was stripping away the torn and filthy clothing of a man who not an hour before had been shot in the chest. This was fortunate, as he had already lost a lot of blood. But the entire ward was filled with recently wounded men, so over-crowded that they were lying on the floors or two to a bed. The nurse was watching him; she was in early middle-age, had strong features, and contemptuous eyes.

"Right," he said. "Let's get to work. Where do I wash up?" She raised her eyebrows. "My hands," he explained, wringing them. "I cannot deal with this man until I have washed my hands."

The eyes grew more contemptuous yet. "There is no water available at this moment, Comrade Doctor. The supply in this area has been cut by a bomb. If you do not attend to this man, he will die. If your hands have germs on them, he may still die, but at least he will have had a chance." It occurred to Alex that he might have to rethink his ideas on medicine.

It was three days before he managed to see Elaine; all the medical staff were working 15-hour shifts with only the shortest breaks for food, and it was the merest chance that on this occasion they happened to find themselves in the Russian equivalent of a cafeteria together. "What do you reckon?" he asked.

"No one had ever again better complain to me about conditions at Boston General," she said.

"Amen!"

"I lost one this morning," she said, sipping her borsch; there wasn't much nourishment in the beetroot soup but it was certainly hot. "I was virtually holding his lung in my hand when it just stopped working. Shit! I've never lost one before. I mean, me, personally. There's always been somebody senior. God!"

"He doesn't exist around here. That's official."

Elaine gave a twisted smile. "I don't think He'd want to be involved in this, anyway."

It was another fortnight before Alex got to see his stepfather. He had managed to send a message that he was there to Joseph soon after arriving, but it took time for them both to be able to spare the time to meet. Joseph took him to lunch at Aragvi. "Some place," Alex commented. "You know, Joe, there's two different worlds here, operating side by side."

"Only two, you reckon?" Joseph asked.

"Point taken. Can you tell me exactly what is happening?"

"We could be at the turning point of this war. The fact is, the Germans really ought to have taken Moscow before winter set in. That they didn't is largely their own fault. It would appear that they reckoned this battle was won, and diverted a large number of their forces to a drive through the south for the Caucasus; they'd like to get their hands on the oil down there. But they should've cleaned up here first. They're now bogged down in the snow and the ice."

"But they're still there," Alex pointed out.

"Sure. But things are changing – the Russian way – all the time. They have some new mortars, called *katyushas*, which are very effective, and perhaps more important, very noisy. German prisoners speak of the devastating effect on morale these screamers are having. Then they are moving large numbers of Siberian troops to the western front."

Alex nodded. "I saw some of them on the train. But fresh

foot soldiers aren't going to be the answer, surely. Maybe the panzers are bogged down, but so are the Russian tanks. And the Germans still have total superiority in the air."

"All true. But the Russians now have a third and most important ally of all, the very weather that is holding things up. Again, reverting to those prisoners they have taken, the poor bastards are wearing what is by Russian standards summer clothing. Some of them don't even have overcoats; none of them has thermal underwear. A lot of them are suffering from severe frostbite. Another month, and the Russians reckon they'll be too cold to move, much less fight."

"You honestly think Russia can make it?"

"Yes, I do."

"What about Leningrad? Isn't that about to fall?"

"I wouldn't bet on that, either. They appear to be prepared to fight to the last man, woman, or child. And you can't blame them, if half the stories of what the Germans have been doing behind their lines are true."

"And you reckon they are?"

"I don't know, Alex. I do know that the Russians believe the stories. Did you know you have a cousin fighting with the Partisans? Commanding a unit, no less."

"I didn't know I had a cousin in the Russian army."

"She's not in the Army. She's a partisan."

"Did you say *she*?"

"Yes. A girl of eighteen, believe it or not. This is really a nation at war," Joseph pointed out. "She's Jennie's daughter. Would you like to meet Jennie?"

"Very much." Alex hesitated, "There's someone else who would like to meet her, too. Elaine Mitchell."

Joseph frowned. "The name is familiar. Do I know her?"

"I brought her to dinner, last November."

"Good God! And she's here with you? In Russia?"

"She's a doctor, like me. And as you have just pointed out, this is a war in which women have quite as much place as men."

"Russian women," Joseph argued. "You . . . ah . . . planning anything?"

"We're going steady," Alex said. "But I know she'd love to meet Jennie."

Climbing the stairs to the apartment Elaine felt quite as nervous as she had when entering the Cromb House in Boston. Even more than on that occasion she felt that she was not dressed for the part, or fully psychologically prepared. It was almost the first afternoon she had had off since arriving in Moscow, and she was desperately tired. She had managed to keep a clean dress for an occasion like this, but it was fearfully crushed. She had also managed to wash her hair, and indeed have a bath, but she still thought she smelt of disinfectant and death. Alex as always was encouraging, and squeezed her hand as the door swung in and they were greeted by Jennie. Elaine was impressed. Jennie was so very obviously a Bolugayevska, and yet she was also so obviously a devoted Communist. But she seemed delighted to see her cousin, and his girlfriend. "It is so strange," she said. "That so many of the family should be here, at this time."

"We are here, *because* of this time," Joseph pointed out.

Elaine could not help staring at the photograph of the girl in the semi-military uniform. "That is my daughter Tatiana," Jennie said, proudly.

"Alex has told me of her," Elaine said. "You must be very worried for her."

"Well, I am very proud of her. She is killing Germans."

"But out there, in a swamp, in the dead of winter . . ."

"I know it is hard," Jennie said. "But she will manage. Ah, here is Galina, come to join us for tea. Galina's daughter, Sophie, is serving with Tatiana, in the Pripet."

Elaine could not imagine that she could calmly serve tea to guests if her daughter was fighting and freezing in a swamp. Thank God she didn't have a daughter! The door opened.

"Ivan Ivanovich!" Jennie exclaimed. "I am so glad you

could make it. This is my cousin Alex, and a friend of his, Dr Mitchell."

Ivan scarcely gave the young people a glance. His face was glowing, his whole being redolent of excitement. "You have not heard the news!"

Everyone turned towards him. "We have gained a victory!" Galina said.

"No! We have not gained a victory. But we have gained an ally! The United States is in the war. With us!"

Chapter 6

The Task

The train pulled into the Tiergarten, the doors opened. But Alexander von Holzbach hesitated for several seconds before stepping out into the crisp January night air, because it would be stepping into another world. The one he had left a week ago had been hell, rising out of the pit to spread itself across the surface of the globe. In the one he had just arrived in even the temperature belonged in another world. Berlin was about three degrees below zero Centigrade, he reckoned. Once he would have thought that cold! Berlin was a glow of light. There was a black-out law – British bombers came often enough – but there was always sufficient warning of them when they crossed Belgium and Holland to enable the sirens to be sounded hours before they reached the city. Until that happened, the Berliners could enjoy themselves, with the enthusiasm that was essentially Berliner.

Officials saluted the major as he hurried from the station and sought a cab. Everyone was happily excited. Christmas was recent enough to be remembered, and they lived in the best of all possible worlds, at the centre of an empire that stretched from the English Channel and the Mediterranean to halfway across European Russia. Only Napoleon Bonaparte had ever held so much in the palm of his hand at one moment. No one seemed prepared to remember that Napoleon had held that much for less than a year.

As for the Americans, the German declaration of war had been the principal topic of conversation on the train; it had aroused even more opinions, pro and con, than Hitler's decision personally to take over operational command of all German armed forces. Again, no one had seemed to question why it had been necessary to declare war on the United States at all. The American quarrel was with Japan, who had so treacherously attacked her. Japan's alliance with Germany contained no mutual assistance clauses. In fact Alexander, who was a close friend of a good many generals and senior Party officials, was pretty sure that no one in Germany had suspected, much less been informed, that the simultaneous attacks on Pearl Harbor, the Philippines, and Malaysia had even been planned, much less reached the stage of execution.

But within hours Hitler had carelessly declared war on the greatest industrial power in the world. No matter that the Americans seemed a very long way away, that their armed forces were regarded as something of a joke, or that before they could interfere in Europe they needed to defeat Japan, or in order to do that they needed a fleet which they no longer possessed. The declaration had introduced, quite unnecessarily, a new set of parameters within which the war was being fought. With America in the War, Allied military strength had to grow, where German military strength had to diminish, unless Russia could be knocked out sooner than later. Alexander wondered if he was the only man in the German army who doubted that was possible.

Alexander's apartment was on the first floor of a block only just off the Unter den Linden. As there had been many stories of how Berlin had been bombed he approached it with some apprehension, although he had seen little damage on his way from the station. And to his great relief the building was untouched. Not even, so far as he could see, a pane of glass broken. He paid the fare and carried his bag into the entry hall. The concierge gaped at him as if he were a ghost. "Major von Holzbach?"

"Do I not look like him, Franz?"

"Oh, yes, Major. Oh, yes. Ah . . . welcome back!"

"I assume my wife is at home?"

"Oh, yes, Herr Major! Oh, yes!"

"Good."

He went to the stairs, aware of being more sexually aroused than for a long time. It did not pay to become sexually aroused in Russia, although Russian girls were available, either as prisoners or in the army-controlled brothels. But one never knew with a Russian girl when she would commit suicide by killing, or at least maiming, her partner. Besides, however much they had been washed and checked for disease, one could never be sure that Russian girls did not have lice. Alexander felt that sex should be a time for mutual enjoyment, and mutual satisfaction, and above all, mutual cleanliness. A glance over his shoulder as he went up the stairs, through the open door of the concierge's office, revealed that Franz was on the phone. Well, in this new Germany where everyone spied on everyone else, he no doubt had a duty to report every arrival or departure in his apartment building, even the owner of one of the apartments. It was not something Alexander supposed would bother him.

He climbed the stairs, inserted the key in the lock, and it opened for him. Anna stood there, arms outstretched.

"Alexander!" she screamed. Alexander was surprised, and not only by her apparent clairvoyance in knowing it was him at the door before he had opened it. It was only nine o'clock at night, yet she was in a dressing gown, and as he set down his bag and took her in his arms, he realised that she must have just got out of bed; she was as warm as toast and had that sensuous feel. He kissed her mouth. "Oh, Alexander," she said. "It is so good to have your back! I have been so worried. I had hoped you would be home for Christmas. But no matter, what is Christmas?" She appeared to be in a highly nervous state.

Alexander squeezed her. "It is so good to be back, I can tell you."

"Champagne!" she said, freeing herself and hurrying for the cold box. "I always keep one on ice, for this occasion."

"Why were you in bed? You are not sick?" He took the bottle from her and removed the cork while she held out the two flutes.

"No, no! But what else is there to do?"

He brushed her glass with his. "And I was afraid you would be out."

"Out where?"

He shrugged. "Dancing with some handsome man? Or at least at the pictures."

"Would you have been cross if I had been dancing with some handsome man?"

"Of course! I would probably have shot him, and beaten you."

She peered at him, as if uncertain that he was joking. Then she asked, "Have you eaten?"

"Nothing that could really be called food."

"Then let me prepare some supper."

"I'm more hungry for you," he said.

She even smelt of sex; he had an idea that one reason she might have gone to bed early was because she had been masturbating. But she was as responsive as ever, although the moment he had climaxed she was out of bed and putting on her dressing gown before hurrying into the kitchen. "How long have you got?" she asked over her shoulder.

"A week."

"Oh, how marvellous! Will we be in Moscow in a week?"

He gave a grim laugh, and got out of bed himself. "No."

She refilled their glasses, frowning at him. "Everyone here says that the Russians are beaten."

"Everyone here is so stuffed with propaganda they cannot tell the difference between white and black."

She set sausage and bread and lettuce on the table. "Then tell me the truth."

"The truth!" He drank some champagne. "The truth is that we are fighting a war for which we are quite unprepared." We were supposed to reach Moscow before the winter. No one gave any thought to the fact that before winter comes to Russia, there are always a couple of months of heavy rain. We were issued with maps, showing us all the great metalled roads which led directly to Red Square. Do you realise that there is perhaps one metalled road in all Russia? The rest, however they may be shown on maps, are mere tracks. No doubt they are planned as roads, but they have not yet been built. A few inches of rain and they become mud rivers. You should see a column of panzers ploughing through the mud at one mile an hour, if that. It would make you laugh if it wasn't so tragic."

"But you are within fifty miles, so it is said. One more push . . ."

"What are we supposed to push with? We have been within fifty miles of Moscow for weeks, in places, and have advanced not a step. Now that the rain has stopped, it has frozen. Can you imagine temperatures of forty below? It paralyses the brain. Do you realise that to start our tanks we have to light fires under the engines, for more than an hour? That our guns won't fire? That we have to saw our food into chunks to be melted? Do you know that I have seen a hundred men, with mules, trying to drag a field gun out of the ice in which it has been frozen?"

"But at least you have the hundred men and the mules," Anna suggested, dismayed by his pessimism.

"Ha! What do you think happened? We eventually pulled the gun free, But not its carriage as well. That remained firmly stuck, and will stay there until the thaw. But the worst thing of all is the effect the cold has on the men. They were not prepared for it, psychologically. They are not equipped for it, physically. They are losing toes and fingers and ears faster than you use that ersatz stuff they call coffee."

"My darling!" She put her arms round his neck and hugged him. "You are feeling depressed. A week in Berlin will restore your spirits. Remember that winter is only a season. It will end, in a couple of months, and then our armies will resume their advance, and I will meet you, as we arranged, in Moscow. I am so looking forward to that."

Alexander stood inside the doorway of the huge office and saluted, "Heil Hitler!"

"As you say, Holzbach. Sit down." Alexander crossed the room and sat, to attention, in the chair before the desk. He had only met Reinhard Heydrich half-a-dozen times before, and every time he had been more impressed, or perhaps, he thought, obsessed, by the cold good looks of the man, and the even colder clarity of vision of what he sought from life and for Germany. "What do you think of the situation?" Heydrich asked.

"I think it stinks, with respect."

Heydrich smiled. Alexander von Holzbach was a man who always spoke his mind. But he was also a man who got results. "There have been mistakes," he agreed. "On the other hand, it should all be brought to a successful conclusion, once the weather improves. These Russian counter-attacks are no more than pin-pricks. Their claims to have recaptured territory is pure propaganda; the Fuehrer has forbidden any withdrawals."

Alexander decided not to comment upon that; Heydrich had obviously been listening to the same handouts from Goebbels's propaganda department as had Anna. "However," Heydrich went on, "there can be no doubt that the Russians are tougher than we supposed, and that an immense effort is required to bring them down before any American influence can be imposed upon the war. This goes from the highest to the lowest, or the seemingly least important. As for example, are you aware that something like ten per cent of our army is tied down coping with the partisans behind our lines? Or that at least ten per cent of our materiel is sabotaged or destroyed by these partisans before it can reach our forces at the front?"

Alexander had already encountered bands of partisans, behind the Moscow front; every German soldier had done so. "I do not understand why they cannot be dealt with in the ordinary way," he remarked.

"My dear Holzbach, these people are not human. They are Slavs. That is a sub-species akin to the Neanderthals. They are brutish, unfeeling. They lack all sentiment. Announce that we will shoot a hundred people for every attack on our trains, they still attack the trains. So we shoot them. Nobody seems to care. Not even the hundred, one feels. It is becoming quite a problem." He got up and walked to the huge map of Russia on the wall. "And the biggest problem is here." He tapped the Pripet Marshes. "It is estimated that there are several thousand Russian soldiers and partisans hiding in these marshes. They are split up into several groups, but they are all nuisances." He grinned. "Of course, it is always possible to hope that they will all freeze this winter. Or starve. But we cannot assume this is going to happen. What is going to have to happen is that someone is going to have to go into those marshes and destroy these vermin. This has to be done, without fail, the moment the weather improves."

"You are giving me this assignment, Herr General?"

"Yes. With promotion to colonel."

"I am flattered. Would I be speaking out of turn if I said that I would rather fight Russian soldiers than Russian civilians?"

"I am sure you would, Holzbach. Although, as I have said, there are quite a few soldiers mixed in with these partisans.

However, it is a necessary task, and it is one which has to be carried out by someone who has no doubt where his duty lies. I know you are one of those men. We are not talking about straightforward fighting here. We are talking about extermination, by any means possible. *They* are using every means possible, I can tell you. Do you know what happened only a week ago? These wretched people came from their lair and took prisoner a patrol of eight men and a sergeant. Well, you or I might suppose those fools should have fought to the death rather than surrender. But surrender they did when they realised they were outnumbered and surrounded. We found them three days later, stripped naked."

Alexander nodded. "And castrated?"

"No. They had not been harmed in any way," Heydrich said. "But they had been tied up, together, and water had been poured over them. A great deal of water. Presumably this water had once been ice which had been melted over a fire, because the temperature was twenty degrees below freezing. In any event, this water very rapidly turned back into ice. So what we found was a kind of ice sculpture," Heydrich said. "Nine naked men, leaning against each other, frozen solid. I can tell you, it was not very good for morale. We must retaliate in kind. If they want atrocities, they will have atrocities. Does this bother you?"

"I do not like the idea of waging war in such a barbaric manner."

"War is barbarism, Holzbach."

"I understand that. I will make an example of these people, if I have to."

"There is another reason why I am giving you this assignment, Holzbach," Heydrich said. "Does the name Tatiana Gosykinya mean anything to you?"

Alexander frowned. "Tatiana Gosykinya is the daughter of Andrei Gosykin and Jennie Cromb."

"Correct. And Andrei Gosykin?"

"Murdered my wife's brother."

"Absolutely."

"This Tatiana murdered a German officer, did she not?"

"Two German officers, Holzbach."

"And then disappeared, and is no doubt dead."

"Well, she did disappear, yes. For a while we thought she *was* dead. But she wasn't dead, she was in the Pripet. And now the Russians are making a lot of propaganda noises about how she is a commissar, and a leader of the Partisans."

Alexander's frown deepened. "This girl cannot be more than nineteen."

"I understand she is eighteen. That does not mean she cannot be a mass-murderess. She is Gosykin's daughter, and if I remember the details of his trial, he was accused of killing several million people during Stalin's collectivisation programme. Oh, he was undoubtedly acting on Stalin's orders, even if Stalin eventually shot him for it. But he still killed those people. As for this child being a commissar, that is pure propaganda. But it is propaganda we intend to use in return. Your prime duty is to capture this Red Maiden, as she is called, and execute her as barbarously as possible with all the publicity you can manage. Let me know when you have accomplished her capture, and I will provide you with a film crew to record her last moments, moments in which she will be revealed for what she is, a snivelling, murdering, frightened little girl. You have no problem with this?"

"It will be a pleasure to avenge my brother-in-law, Herr General. I but wish to know my resources."

"There is an SS regiment in Pinsk, with a company in Brest-Litovsk. You will make your headquarters in Brest-Litovsk. You have carte blanche to employ as many of its people as you need, and to call on reinforcements from Pinsk if need be. I will give you a letter to General von Blasewitz, informing him of your mission and requesting him to give you all the assistance possible."

Alexander saluted. "Heil Hitler!"

Heydrich acknowledged the salute. "I will wish you Godspeed, Colonel von Holzbach. Carry out this mission speedily and efficiently, and you will command that regiment yourself."

"You did not mention that other matter to Major von Holzbach, Herr General?" inquired von Buelow, the adjutant.

"You mean that his wife has been seeing other men?" Heydrich stroked his chin.

"She had a man with her when von Holzbach arrived in Berlin, Herr General."

"And managed to get rid of him?"

"The *concierge* is in her pay, Herr General. He must have got word up to her, and that building has an interior fire staircase."

"That is very sad," Heydrich said. "Holzbach will go far, if he survives. And presumably his wife will rise as well, even if she is a two-timing bitch. But I am not about to interfere in the domestic life of a man to whom I have just given a very important mission. He needs to concentrate on his job."

Buelow cleared his throat. "It is our business, Herr General, to keep files upon all important Party members, and their wives."

"And I am sure you have done so most efficiently, Buelow. But I have just said, I wish Frau von Holzbach's file locked away, at least for the time being."

"Maintaining a file does not only imply surveillance, Herr General. It implies investigation, of the subject's background and ancestry."

Heydrich leaned back in his chair. "You will be telling me next that Anna von Holzbach is a Jew."

"That is exactly what I am telling you, Herr General."

"My dear Buelow, I doubt you would find a more obvious Aryan in all Germany. Frau von Holzbach is the daughter of the late Prince Alexei Bolugayevski of Bolugayen. And the late Prince of Bolugayen was actually the son of an Englishman, or rather, a Scot, named Colin MacLain, and his English wife, Jennifer Cromb. Her ancestry is impeccable."

"I was thinking of Frau von Holzbach's mother."

"An American lady, also, as I understand it, a descendant of this Colin MacLain, and therefore actually English. Or rather, Scottish, I suppose. So you have obtained some evidence of incest in the recent past. My dear Buelow, without incest, all of the noble families in Europe, not to mention the royals, would have died out long ago."

"With respect, Herr General, Frau von Holzbach was born in 1908. The Princess Dowager Bolugayevska was born in 1894, and was married to the Prince in 1912. Before this marriage," Buelow went on, "Prince Bolugayevski had been married to a certain Sonia Cohen, a Jewess."

"My God!" Heydrich remarked. "You are certain of this?"

Buelow tapped his file. "It is all here, Herr General. This Sonia Cohen is alive and living in New York at this time. Not only is she a Jewess, but she was the long-term mistress of Leon Trotsky, who was murdered in 1940."

"Give me that file," Heydrich said. Buelow passed it across the desk, watched his superior lock it in the safe which stood beside his chair. "Who else knows about this?" Heydrich asked.

"Only the people who researched it for me."

"How many?"

"Two men and a woman."

"Have them transferred to active service units in Russia."

Buelow goggled at his superior. "I am not criticising you, Buelow," Heydrich said. "Indeed, I congratulate you on your efficiency and thoroughness. But you have just handed me a political timebomb. Quite apart from not wishing to distract Major von Holzbach from his duties at this time, are you not aware that his wife moves in the highest circles? That she has been entertained by the Fuehrer himself?"

"But if we do nothing, Herr General, will she not continue to be entertained by the Fuehrer?"

"Certainly. And we will do something, at the right time. But for the moment, I wish nothing done, and I wish no one outside of this room to know of it. Do you understand me, Buelow?"

Buelow gulped. If he did not like the idea of sitting on such a political timebomb, as his boss had put it, he was far more afraid of his boss himself. "I understand, Herr General."

"A colonel!" Anna said over supper. "Soon to be a general!" Her eyes shone.

"It is a beastly, unpleasant task," Alexander said. "But it will have its compensations." He told her about Tatiana.

"Gosykin's daughter?" She jumped up and down. "Can I come with you, Alexander? I should so love to see Gosykin's daughter executed. You're going to be based in Brest-Litovsk. For Heaven's sake, that's hundreds of miles behind the front. You said I could join you in Moscow. Well, if we can't be in Moscow together, surely we can be in Brest-Litovsk!"

"A letter from Joseph!" Priscilla swept into the drawing-room, waving the sheets of paper. She gave almost a squeal of joy. "Listen to this! Hopkins' mission is returning home. But they are leaving a permanent secretariat in Russia. In Moscow, at least for the time being. And Joseph is to be its deputy head. Isn't that marvellous?"

"You mean he's staying there?"

"For the duration of the war. And he says I can join him, if I wish. If I wish! Well, actually, I asked if I could, a couple of months ago, and he said no. Now, he's changed his mind. Oh, to return to Russia, and on the up. And we'll all be together. Oh . . .!" she handed Sonia the last sheet and stood up. "There's so much to be done." Sonia bit her lip. Priscilla looked down at her. "Oh, Sonia! Listen, you can come too."

"Do you think it is possible?"

"All things are possible, right now. They need us, Sonia. Leave it with me. I'll organise it. But, you'll have to promise: no thoughts of getting at Stalin!"

"What do you think we should do?" Alex asked his stepfather.

The initial impact of America being at war had worn off, and it was time to consider the future. But he was so busy that this Sunday in Febuary was the first opportunity he had had to discuss the situation with Joseph. "You know I'm staying for a while? Until the end, as a matter of fact."

"Yes, but you're doing a job almost no one else can do."

"Yours is pretty vital too," Joseph pointed out. "Russia really isn't too well off for good doctors, right now."

"And what about the US Army?"

"I don't think they'll go short. There's also the point that if you opt to leave, and set the whole thing in motion today, which is not possible, you still won't get out of Russia for several months. If you join up it'll be several months more before you'll be considered sufficiently trained to be sent into a combat zone. We could be talking of more than a year. That seems to me to be a long time to be totally out of commission, as it were, at a time like this."

"You think I should stay."

"I do. I should point out that our entry into the war does not in any way affect your position. Your work here is still going to count towards your seniority when you get back home. Maybe more than if you served with the US Army and came out with a specified rank."

"I wasn't really thinking about that," Alex said.

"It still needs to be thought about. There's something

else I should tell you: your mother is coming out to join me."

"Mom is coming, here? To Moscow?"

"That's right."

"Isn't that going to be very dangerous?"

"Yes. But Priscilla is not an easy woman to dissuade. It won't be actually dangerous her being here. I mean, apart from the bombers. But getting here . . ."

"And you can't absolutely forbid it?"

Joseph gave him an old-fashioned look. "I have never risked trying to forbid your mother to do anything, Alex. Therefore I am still in one piece. In any event, going by her letter, she has already obtained State Department permission and visas and what have you. She's probably already left. Certainly she'll have left by the time I can get a letter back to the States."

"And you'd like her to be here. Well, then," Alex said. "I stay, and look forward to welcoming Mom."

"Good," Joseph said. "I know your mother will love to see you, and *in situ*, as it were. What is that attractive girl-friend of yours going to do?"

"Whatever I do, I imagine."

"You going to marry her?" Joseph asked.

"I don't think either of us have made up our minds about that, yet."

Joseph raised his eyebrows. "Not even while sharing this great adventure?"

"Well, we're not actually doing a lot of sharing, right now. We're both too damned busy, and when we do happen to have time off together, well, we're both sleeping in a very crowded barracks. I mean, separately, of course: she's in a women's barracks and I'm in a man's."

"I did realise that."

"So . . . I was wondering, the next time we do happen to be off duty together, well . . ."

"You'd like to use this hotel room."

"That would be great."

"You are a lucky young devil," Joseph said. "But still a devil."

"I am a Bolugayevski," Alex pointed out.

"This is very disappointing," Josef Stalin remarked, looking over the report on his desk. "The Germans are trumpeting that they have caught and hanged Gurianov, publicly, and now Solntsev. Those are two of our best partisan commanders. And what have we got to show for it? A few destroyed trains. A few enemy outposts attacked. A few Germans killed . . ."

"Gurianov's people killed well over five hundred Germans," Ivan Ligachev pointed out.

"Is that so? Verify it, Ivan Ivanovich, and if it is true have him made a Hero of the Soviet Union. But these others . . ." Stalin gesticulated at the map of Belorussia. "They have done nothing. What about Tatiana and Feodor in the Pripet? Group One, we have called it. There has been not a word for over a month."

Ivan nodded, sadly. "I very much fear they may have been taken by the Germans."

"They have not been taken by the Germans, Ivan Ivanovich, for the very simple reason that the Germans would have said so. They have made this great publicity fuss about capturing and executing Gurianov. They have made a great fuss about the public hanging of Zoya Kosmodemianskaya, after having virtually tortured her to death. Do you not suppose they would have made a similar loud noise about capturing Tatiana Gosykinya?"

"But in the Marshes, in the dead of winter . . . they may just have perished. Jennie is very depressed."

"Ha! Is there a woman in Russia who has not lost a loved one? And she does not even know that Tatiana is dead. I do not think she is. And even if she is, that entire group cannot have died. There are survivors, skulking. Have someone reach them, Ivan Ivanovich. Tell them we want to see action, results. Tatiana is sitting on a vital part of the German lines of communication. So she has blown up one train. Tell her there must be others."

Ivan swallowed again. "I will see what can be done, Comrade Chairman."

"No, no," Stalin said. "Do it!"

"They will need to be re-equipped."

"Then re-equip them. But have it done. Now!"

"Now, Comrade Chairman." Ivan stood up, and checked as Stalin raised his head.

"How is your brother-in-law getting on?"

"He seems to be entirely on our side. At this moment."

"You know he is staying on as part of their permanent mission in Moscow?"

"Yes. Jennie is pleased about that. Do *you* know that his wife is coming to join him?"

Stalin leaned back in his chair. "Priscilla Bolugayevska is returning to Russia?"

"She is Priscilla Cromb now, Comrade Chairman. Yes. Her visa has been applied for by the State Department. I can of course refuse it . . ."

Priscilla Bolugayevska, Stalin thought. He had only met the erstwhile Princess Dowager of Bolugayen once, and then briefly, but he had never forgotten her. He did not suppose any man meeting Priscilla Bolugayevska could ever forget her. Had he not been in the middle of sorting out all that treachery—. Of course, that had been several years ago. Priscilla would be getting on for 50 now, but even so, he had no doubt she would be worth meeting again. "This means that all three members of that cursed family will be in Moscow together," Ivan remarked.

Yes, indeed, Stalin thought. And the presence of her only son, were he in trouble or danger, might again bring Priscilla to his door. He would not pass up such an opportunity again. "Tell me about this so-called prince? I remember we considered the possibilities were he to be in Moscow when it was overrun by the Germans. Well, we both know that is not going to happen."

"They will try again in the spring," Ivan said gloomily.

"And we will be more ready for them in the spring. But I do not think that will be their main effort, in the spring. We already know that they have drawn off a large number of troops for the south. They are going to go for the oilfields of the Caucasus, Ivan Ivanovich. And we are going to have to stop them. However, let us discuss these partisans. I think it would be an act of great patriotism if the erstwhile Prince Bolugayevski were to serve with them."

"Alex Bolugayevski is an American. By the terms of the agreement under which these people came here, he cannot be sent into a combat zone."

"Ivan Ivanovich, haven't we been through all of this before? He volunteered to serve in Moscow, did he not? I am sure, if he knew the full facts, if he knew, for example, that his long-lost cousin Tatiana is fighting for her life in the Pripet, he would wish to be at her side."

"He already knows that. And Tatiana may be his cousin, but he has never laid eyes on her."

"Such a lovely girl. Show him a photograph. Get these things done, Ivan Ivanovich. There is a time for everything, and now is the time to get rid of this upstart with the least comment." He smiled. "Before his mother gets here."

"It will not be easy to get him to do this," Ivan said.

"If I thought it would be easy, I would give the task to someone else, Ivan Ivanovich."

Ivan stroked his chin. "But there may be a way . . . through his girlfriend."

Stalin raised his eyebrows. "He has a girlfriend, already? Clearly he is not being worked hard enough."

"She came with him. She is also an American."

"Hm. But that rather negates any influence Tatiana may have. I mean, as regards sex."

"I do not think that is important, Comrade Chairman. This woman of Bolugayevski's is, from the reports I have received, a romantic who dreams of great accomplishments for Russia. Oh, no doubt it is Tsarist Russia she dreams of, thanks to Bolugayevski, but then we are all together now, are we not!" He hesitated, nervously, as Stalin commenced to fill his pipe. "I believe we may be able to set this woman up," Ivan went on. "And where she goes, Bolugayevski will surely follow."

"What is it you say in America?" asked the young man. "Another day, another dollar?"

Elaine was surprised, but she smiled. Igor Dorzhenski was an incredibly handsome young man. His features were lean and hungry, his eyes deep and intense, his body slender but powerful. On and off, they had worked together for the past four months, but this was the first time he had shown any interest in her. Well, she supposed everyone in the hospital knew she was Alex's girl, but it was nonetheless gratifying to be noticed. "I didn't know you knew anything about American customs or sayings," she remarked.

"I am very interested in America. I read books on it."

"Do you?" She was even more surprised.

"I am going to go there, after the war."

"Will they let you?"

"Of course. Why should they not?"

"I can't imagine why not," Elaine confessed. Actually she couldn't, save that she had been brought up to believe that the Soviet government was essentially a totalitarian state.

"But first," Igor said dreamily, "there is the war to be won."

"Absolutely." Because it would be won, she knew, now that America was in it, even if at the moment there was no sign of the Russians winning their own war.

"And to win a war," Igor went on, "one must be prepared to take risks, make sacrifices. I shall be leaving the hospital next week."

"You can't possibly be called up? You're a doctor!"

"No, no, no call-up. I have . . . this must be a secret, between you and me. I should not be telling anyone."

Elaine felt quite breathless. "I shall not tell anyone," she promised.

"I have volunteered to work with the partisans."

Elaine frowned. "Isn't that terribly dangerous?"

"All war is dangerous. And it will be adventure, open air living, killing Germans, better than existing in this stinking hellhole waiting for a bomb to fall on us."

He was revealing a point of view she longed to share. "I wish I could go with you."

"Well, why not? A large percentage of the partisans are women, and I am sure they would prefer to have a woman doctor. In fact, where I am going the group is commanded by a woman. A relative of your boyfriend. Tatiana Gosykinya."

"She's in the Pripet Marshes, isn't she?"

"Probably the safest of all partisan groups. The Germans can't get in at them, you see. At least, not without waging a vast campaign, and they haven't the time to do that, now."

Elaine licked her lips. Of course she couldn't possibly go without Alex, and she was sure he wouldn't go for it. But it sounded such a delicious adventure. "But how would you get in, that far behind the German lines?"

"We'd be dropped by parachute."

"I've never made a parachute jump."

"They'd teach you. I'm having lessons next week."

"But you said you were leaving next week."

"Well, I only have to make the one jump. As long as they teach me how to do that, there is no problem. Now," he said, glancing right and left, but for the moment they were alone in the corridor. "I shall kiss you goodbye, in case I do not have the opportunity again." Elaine was left even more breathless.

* * *

"You have about the most accommodating stepfather in the world," Elaine said, as Alex unlocked the door of Joseph's hotel room.

"I would say it is because he likes you." Alex locked the door again behind him. "He would like us to get married. After this is over, of course."

"I'm sure that's sensible. I wish we knew when it was going to be over."

"Not for a while yet." He poured them each a glass of vodka.

"Does this aid or retard sex?" she asked.

"I should think one would lower our inhibitions." He sat beside her, kissed her. "It's been so long I'm not sure I remember what to do."

She kissed him back. "What time is your stepdad coming back?"

"Not for hours. There's no need to hurry. We can pretend we are an old married couple." But the vodka *had* lowered their inhibitions, and it was half-an-hour later before they felt like lying peacefully beside each other, like an old married couple. "You've heard about poor Dorzhenski?" Alex asked.

"What about Dorzhenski?" Faithful to her word, Elaine had not mentioned anything about Igor's having volunteered to serve with the partisans, although she had been dying to discuss it. But if he had told Alex . . .

"He's had the most absurd accident," Alex said. "Fell down a flight of stairs in the men's barracks, and broke his ankle."

Elaine sat up, pushing hair from her eyes. "You're not serious?"

"I am. He's very upset about it."

"Well, so would I be, if I'd broken my ankle."

"It's not just that. Seems he was going on some special mission. Now that's lost. I don't know what it was all about."

Elaine licked her lips. "I do."

* * *

Spring in the Pripet was marked by noise; the cracking of the ice. Winter was an abnormally quiet time, except when gale-force winds whipped blizzards through the gaunt trees. For the rest, there were no birds to sing, no fish to splash. And very little human movement.

It was not that the partisans were too cold to operate, although even in their *polushubki* and their *telogreiki*, their *valenki* and their fur hats, their thermal underwear and thick socks, they existed in a constant state of near freezing which made their sleeping bags more attractive than trekking across country. It was not even that they were on reduced rations throughout the cold months – which made the cold harder to bear – or that their weapons also had a tendency to freeze up. It was mainly because the winter left them too exposed. Even at night, and wearing white, they showed up against the white landscape unless moving very slowly and carefully . . . and since the incident with the patrol the Germans had kept their distances. Thus it had been a restful time, and as the batteries for Olga's radio had run down, and the replacements dropped had been lost, they were even cut off from orders or criticisms from their superiors.

Tatiana had used her time as well as she could in constant training, but both she and Feodor had to devote a great deal of their time to the maintenance of morale. Even before the radio had given out the overall picture had been grim. If the Germans had apparently been held for the time being, they were still in places within 50 miles of Moscow, and most good judges seemed to realise that they had been checked less by the Russian resistance than by the Russian weather. But spring was coming. Since the radio silence, there was no indication that things were improving, from a Russian point of view. The railway bridge had been repaired, and was now very heavily guarded, while trains continued to rumble to the east with monotonous regularity. The partisans had had to range farther afield, and accomplished very little. The massacre of the German patrol had been about their greatest coup, and however gratifying and amusing had it been to watch the naked men freezing to death and listen to their pleas for mercy through blue lips and chattering teeth, no one could imagine that murdering nine men was going to make any difference to the German war machine.

Tatiana was keenly aware of her failure to do as much as might have been hoped, and she was determined to recommence a campaign of terror as soon as the weather improved. She felt that despite all the hardship, the casualties, the uncertainty, she had a good team under her. It only numbered 57 now, and that included some new recruits, escapees from Brest-Litovsk. But one of these had been Valya Malevicha, the widow of a doctor who had been shot by the Germans for aiding a Jew to escape. Valya was as anxious to avenge her husband's death as anyone, but she was more valuable for her medical knowledge than her fighting skill; although not qualified, she had assisted her husband in his surgery and at his operating table, and even more important, she had managed to bring some of his equipment, and a few drugs, with her.

Both Shatrav and Feodor grumbled that more people should have joined them, but Tatiana considered this failure to attract larger numbers of recruits was actually a blessing in disguise. As rations for 100 for three months had also been dropped at the commencement of winter, it really meant that she had virtually two sets of rations for every person. Additionally, every remaining member of her band was now a tough and trained commando, adept in using all of his or her weapons, inured to hardship, and totally subservient to the demands of their youthful commissar. She had also been able to use the excuse of shortage of numbers to have Valya Malevicha perform abortions upon the five women who had become pregnant rather than execute them.

In acting thus she knew she was breaking the rules, and would thus be subject herself to condemnation and death when the war was over. She could only hope that by the time that happened her people would have become so loyal to her they would not denounce her; or that by her deeds she would have become a Heroine of the Soviet Union, and be able to rise above the odd disobedience of orders. What disturbed her was that while Feodor had not attempted to countermand any of her orders, she had been able to tell by the look in his eyes that he clearly disapproved. Of course he was both her step-brother and her lover, but even more than that he was a dedicated believer in the rule of Soviet authority.

She was closer friends now with Valya. Valya was very knowledgeable about the German activities in Brest-Litovsk, at least before she had fled following her husband's arrest. She was a small, surprisingly petite woman, with short, crisp yellow hair and matching features, who almost disappeared without trace into her winter woollies. But despite her personal tragedy she retained a sense of humour and a lively mind. She had told Tatiana that the Germans in Brest-Litovsk were in an entirely relaxed frame of mind. They had been agitated by the blowing up of the railway bridge back in the autumn, and even more so by the murder of their patrol just before Christmas. But in the couple of months since then they had determined that this particular band of partisans had either broken up, gone away, or died. "Then they are vulnerable," Tatiana said, standing on the edge of the trees and peering out across the snow. A train chugged by on the track two miles away, but there was no other movement to be seen.

"It is a very long way away," Valya pointed out.

Tatiana nodded. "But if we can do it and get away with it, it would be a triumph."

Chapter 7

The Masters

"Let me get this straight," Joseph said, looking from face to face. "You have sent my stepson and his woman friend into the Pripet Marshes? Several hundred miles behind German lines?"

"We did not *send* them," Ivan Ligachev protested. "They volunteered. That group of partisans needs a medical team. We had one all lined up to go, and then its leader had an accident and broke his ankle. We were seeking a replacement when Mr Bolugayevski and Miss Mitchell volunteered. We thought it was a splendid gesture."

"The terms of the agreement were that none of our people should be sent into a war zone."

"Oh, come now, Joseph, all of Russia is a war zone. European Russia, certainly."

"And to do it without informing me . . ."

"These operations are necessarily secret. They have to be."

"If they are taken by the Germans, they will be tortured and executed!"

"My Tatiana has been there for more than six months," Jennie said quietly.

"I am sure that is one of the reasons Alexei volunteered," Ivan said eagerly. "To be with his cousin."

"He has never met his cousin," Joseph said.

"He has been here, and seen her photograph," Ivan pointed out. But he took Elaine with him, Joseph thought. Oh, the crazy young fool, who couldn't make up his mind whether he was Russian or American, or even which Russia he was fighting for. Only that he had to fight. And what was he going to tell Priscilla, who was coming to Moscow to be with her son?

As with the arrival of Feodor and Olga, it was not possible for the partisans to locate the drops until it was daylight, which was eight o'clock the next morning. Then they went out in several bands, to cover as wide an area as possible, while keeping in sight of each other. It was Gregory's group that sighted the first chute, lying on a hummock of land. There was another close by, but this was on an ice-covered stretch of marsh; the container had smashed the ice and was half in and half out of the water beneath. Gregory whistled to summon the rest. His people were already opening the first container. "Food!" Natasha said. "Tins of food, chocolate, coffee, milk. Tremendous!"

"So we will have a feast," Tatiana said, panting up to them, her breath coagulating into ice crystals before the scarf she had wound round her face. "Let's get that one."

"The ice is not thick enough to bear a man's weight," Gregory pointed out.

"Then we must drag it ashore. Break a branch from that tree."

This was done, and after several efforts by Gregory, with three men forming a back-up, the first holding him round the waist, the branch was lodged in a fold of the chute and pulled ashore. Then it was just a matter of dragging in the container, which was very heavy, and because it had struck the brittle ice rather than solid ground it had not split open. Gregory and Shatrav prised up the lid. "Grenades," Shatrav said. "Machine-guns! Ammunition."

Now, Tatiana thought, we can really carry out an offensive!

"And what are these?" Natasha asked, taking out one of the strange objects.

"Anti-tank rockets," Shatrav told her. "But there is no launcher."

"People!" Olga said.

They turned, their weapons thrust forward, to see three people coming through the trees towards them. Two were men, carrying another container between them. The third was a woman, from her long dark hair, although she was dressed as a man. Surprisingly, Tatiana thought, only one of the men was armed, not the woman. The elder of the two men – Tatiana reckoned he was in his forties, with a pock-marked, stern face – looked over the ragged band. "You must be Tatiana Gosykinya," he remarked.

"I am Commissar Gosykinya," Tatiana said, not wishing him to be under any misapprehension. She was more interested in the reaction of the two younger people to her name. The man was in his middle or late twenties, she estimated, big and strong and good-looking, with yellow hair: there was something vaguely familiar about his features, although she could not think where they might have met. The woman was about the same age, also tall and handsome, although somewhat slightly built. But both of them had definitely heard her name before.

"I am Colonel Peter Gerasimov," the elder man said. "I have come to take command of this group."

Feodor and Tatiana exchanged frowns. "I am the Commissar," Tatiana said.

"But I have been placed over you," Gerasimov said, equably. "I have a letter of instruction from State Secretary Ligachev."

"Show this letter to me."

"When we have found somewhere slightly warmer than this," Gerasimov said. "There is also this gear to be transported." He tapped the container he and the young man had been carrying. "Medical supplies, and a special present. I will show you later."

Tatiana was still trying to digest the fact that she had been superseded in command on the orders of her own stepfather! "And who are these people?" she inquired.

"Medical staff," Gerasimov told her. "This is Dr Alexei Bolugayevski, and Dr Elaine Mitchell. They are Americans, come to Russia to serve with us against the Germans."

"Did you say Alexei Bolugayevski?" Tatiana asked.

Alexei grinned as he came forward to embrace her. "I am your cousin."

"You have made yourselves very comfortable here," Gerasimov observed, sitting before the fire between the twin row of huts.

In the food container there had been several well-wrapped bottles of vodka, and the partisans were busily getting drunk. Even Tatiana had felt like a drink; she supposed she needed one to find her way through this sudden morass of unexpected developments. Now she sat beside the man who, apparently, had the power to have her arrested, or even shot! Ligachev's doing! She passed the letter of instruction to Feodor. She wished she had had the opportunity to discuss the situation with him, but that had not yet arisen. She looked across the fire at Alexei Bolugayevski, sitting between Valya and the American woman, but who spent most of his time staring at her, which was not going unnoticed by his fellow doctor. Tatiana presumed they slept together. It would have been odd had they not.

"I wish you to be very clear about one thing," Gerasimov said. "I have not come here to discipline you, Comrade Commissar, or to reduce your rank."

"It is a very strange thing for a Commissar to be outranked by an army officer," Feodor commented.

"These are strange times. It is the wish of our great leader that the partisans in the Pripet show more activity.

There has been very little activity over the past few months."

"It has been all we could do to keep ourselves alive over the past few months, Comrade."

"Nonetheless, other groups, and many farther north than this, have operated throughout the winter. Your work here has been disappointing. So has your lack of communication with Moscow."

"The batteries for our radio have gone flat." Olga was seated with the command party.

"I have brought you new batteries, and more will be dropped regularly. You must report on a regular basis." He gave another of his slightly sour grins. "But you must have something to report. That is why it is necessary for you to make things happen."

"I understand this," Tatiana said. "I have already formed an initial plan." She outlined what she had in mind. Gerasimov stroked his chin as he listened.

"That would be a splendid coup," he said when she had finished. "To carry the war right into the heart of the city . . . but it may be costly."

"We are prepared for that." But she could not resist adding, "Will you lead us, Comrade Colonel?"

"That would be pointless, you know the terrain and I do not." He watched her lip curl in contempt, and grinned. "But I shall accompany you, certainly, and serve under your command, Comrade Commissar. As I said, I have been sent here to make sure you fight, not to tell you *how* to fight." He pointed to the bazooka, which was his 'present' to them. "You will need me to fire that."

"I hope you do not feel that we are muscling in on your territory," Alexei said to Valya. "Moscow was not aware that this group already had a doctor."

"I am not a doctor," Valya explained. "My husband was a doctor, and I assisted him."

"And your husband isn't here now?" Elaine asked.

"My husband is dead. He was murdered by the Germans."

Elaine looked at Alex for help. "I am sure he will be avenged," Alex said.

"That is our intention, yes," Valya said.

Tatiana came round the fire. "Walk with me, cousin," she said. Alex hastily scrambled to his feet.

Elaine watched them go into the trees. "She's very beautiful," she remarked. "I suppose she's killed a lot of Germans?"

"Yes," Valya agreed.

Elaine licked her lips and hastily dried them again on her sleeve, before they froze. "Have you? Killed a lot of Germans, I mean?"

"I have not killed any Germans yet," Valya said. "I have been the medical officer. But now that you are here, I expect to begin killing Germans."

"Oh! You mean we're not required to kill any?"

"Only in self-defence," Valya said.

"Oh!" Elaine said again. Colonel Gerasimov had talked about nothing else but killing Germans on the flight from Moscow. While it had never in her life occurred to Elaine that she might ever have to kill anyone. But they were all in it now. All the boys she had grown up with, and who would not have hurt a fly save on the football field, were now in uniform and being taught how to kill, and then being sent out to kill. She supposed she was the lucky one. Only in self-defence! She was not sure she could kill anyone, even in self-defence.

"So," Tatiana said. "You are the only surviving son of the late Prince Bolugayevski. That must mean that you claim the title for yourself." Ice crunched beneath their feet as they walked through the trees, away from the huts, and their breaths clouded before their faces. Yet was it warmer today than yesterday, and the noise of the ice breaking in the swamp was almost continuous, as if the entire surface of the earth was cracking.

"In my more romantic moments," Alex confessed.

She glanced at him. "It would not be good for my people to know of these romantic moments. What are you doing in Russia at all?"

Alex explained.

"And you have stayed, even though America is now in the War?" said Tatiana.

"We felt we were doing an essential job here in Russia."

"We? You and this woman? Is she your woman?"

"We have an understanding," Alex said, carefully.

Tatiana appraised him for some seconds. Then she said, "We are engaged in a serious business. It is not a joke, an adventure, a game of cowboys and Indians. Do you understand this?"

"I have spent the last four months working in a hospital in Moscow. We both have. We are not quite wet behind the ears."

"You have been involved in a clean war. This is a dirty war."

"Is there such a thing as a clean war?"

She shrugged. "Maybe all wars are dirty. But there are degrees of dirt. This is the bottom line. You must not be taken alive. Even more, your woman must not be taken alive. You understand this?"

Alex swallowed. "Yes."

"I am telling you this, not only for your own sakes, but for the sakes of all of us. We have very strict rules. When we go into action, the wounded who cannot make it to the swamp by themselves must be destroyed."

"That is barbarous! What a word. Destroyed!"

"Nevertheless, it is a rule which must be obeyed. Anyone failing to obey it will be executed himself, or herself. As our medical officers, you will be principally responsible for implementing this rule."

"You mean you cannot trust your own people? You are afraid that if they are captured and interrogated by the Germans they will lead them to your camp."

Tatiana snorted. "Interrogated! What civilised words you use. Yes, Comrade Cousin. I am afraid that we will be betrayed by any prisoners we lose. Not because I do not trust them, but because the truth will be tortured out of them, very slowly, and very painfully. After that they will die anyway. Therefore we, you, would be committing an act of mercy by making sure that that does not happen. There can be no argument about this."

He remembered that Tatiana was just 19 years old. "And if the wounded person is you, Comrade Commissar?"

"The same rules apply. As they would to you, Alexei. Now, would you like to sleep with me, tonight?"

"Not tonight, if you do not mind."

He slept with Elaine, who was equally in a state of some shock. Which increased as he repeated his conversation. "Jesus!" she said. "What a way to live! As if they were animals."

"They are animals. And we must be animals, too, if we are to survive. It was your idea to come here," he reminded her.

"Sure. Maybe I did think it would be like cowboys and Indians." She smiled into his ear. "But if you read the history books and get behind the John Wayne glamour, that was a pretty dirty business too. We're sure going to have something to tell our grandchildren."

"Supposing we have any. Elaine, I want you to remain behind when we carry out this raid that Tatiana's planning."

"I came here to work and fight, not skulk in a bush."

"Do you suppose I could possibly shoot you if you got hit and couldn't walk?"

"Do you think I could shoot you? We'd both be shot by Tatiana. At least we'd go together."

They lay in silence for a few minutes. Alex didn't know

how the rest of the group were getting on. There were another ten couples in this hut with them – although neither Tatiana nor her step-brother were among them – but as the place was reminiscent of the interior of an icebox there had been no temptation for either Elaine or himself to take off a stitch of clothing, nor was there any indication that anyone else had done so. If the chill kept down the odours the stillness only emphasised the grunts and snores and farts of the other inmates. It occurred to him that this must be what it was like in prison – save that in the worst prison there were seldom more than four to a cell.

"Now," Tatiana told her people, who were gathered round the fire. "It is a matter of crossing something like twenty miles of open country, entering the town, committing as much mayhem as possible, specifically with regard to the German headquarters and the railway marshalling yard and their communications, which means the electricity generating plant, and regaining the Marshes again. However, the first thing that needs to be done is a thorough reconnaissance. Valya has volunteered to lead this reconnaissance, as she knows Brest-Litovsk well. Natasha and I will accompany her. We will be gone for two days. In my absence, Colonel Gerasimov will command."

"Why are you only taking women on this reconnaissance?" Shatrav inquired.

"For the reason that if we are taken, we will most probably be raped and beaten and then released. If a man were to be taken, he would be assumed to be a partisan and immediately taken into custody."

"But are you not known in Brest-Litovsk?" asked someone else. "And Natasha."

Tatiana smiled, grimly. "Anyone who knew us in Brest-Litovsk is long dead," she assured them.

* * *

"This is a terrible country," Anna von Holzbach grumbled, peering from the window of the train as it rumbled across the plain east of Warsaw. The winter snows were definitely melting now, and they seemed to be travelling through a vast black bog. "There are no features to it. No mountains. Hardly a hill!"

"Nevertheless," Alexander said, looking up from his papers. "It is some of the most fertile land in Europe. All that black earth, just waiting to be sown and then harvested. It really is too good for the Poles. Well it is no longer theirs, to be sure. But the same goes for Belorussia and the Ukraine. There is enough arable land in these few hundred square kilometres to feed us for the duration of the Reich. A thousand years!"

"When do we get to Brest-Litovsk?"

He looked at his watch. "In half-an-hour."

Anna put on her hat. She was excited returning to Russia after all these years, and as a conqueror! The train clanked into the station. Anna stood at the window to look out. She knew that Brest had been the scene of fierce fighting the previous summer, that the citadel had held out for a month. Well, that was easy to tell from the shell-torn ruins of the fortress. The Germans had not bothered to rebuild it, they had no use for such things as forts. Their secret was their mobility, and their unceasing onward movement.

Little had been done to repair the town either, apart from such buildings as the conquerors had appropriated for their own. One of which would now be her home for the rest of this year, Anna supposed. She did not imagine it would take Alexander more than a year to destroy a few partisans.

A group of officers waited on the platform to welcome the new SS Colonel and his wife. Salutes and handshakes were exchanged, and there was a young woman to present a bouquet to Anna. "How nice," she said. "I did not know there were German girls in Brest-Litovsk."

"There are several, fulfilling official duties," explained

Captain Clausen. "But this girl is Russian." Anna raised her eyebrows. "Do not be alarmed," Clausen said. "She is one of our people, now. Her name is Constantina."

"Constantina," Anna said. "How quaint."

"Constantina will be your maid," Clausen said.

Anna wasn't really sure she wanted a Russian as a maid, but she could hardly expect to have a German maid in Brest-Litovsk, where it was very important that the Germans projected the master-race image. So she said, "I am sure she will do very well, Captain," and got into the car beside Alexander.

"So, tell me about these partisans, Captain," Alexander said, as they were driven through the city. Close at hand the damage was more severe than it had appeared from the train, but what Anna found more disconcerting than the broken windows and cracked plaster was the emptiness of the streets; there were people about, but they moved furtively, as if afraid they would be at any moment thrust from the pavements – many indeed walked in the gutters anyway, however deep the muddy water.

"We have seen or heard nothing of the partisans since last November, Herr Colonel," Clausen said. "Since that unfortunate incident of the patrol."

"But they are still there, I presume? You are not telling me I have come all this way for nothing?"

"Only time will tell, Herr Colonel. They could well all have frozen to death. It must have been very hard for them in that swamp during the winter."

"Well," Alexander said. "We will just have to go into the swamp and find out, Clausen."

The captain did not look happy at that prospect, but fortunately they had now reached the Colonel's residence, a comfortable villa set outside the town. "This was once the dacha of the local commissar," Clausen said, as he ushered Anna into the downstairs hall. "You are not superstitious, I hope, Frau von Holzbach?"

"Not in the least. What have I got to be superstitious about?"

"There was a double murder here, last summer. Three Russian girls were brought here for interrogation, and, through carelessness on the part of the commanding SS officer, they managed to make their escape, killing two officers on the way." He led the way up the stairs. "I am afraid the murders took place in this room; it is the master bedroom."

"I have heard of that case," Alexander said. "Was not the leader of these three succubi a woman called Tatiana Gosykinya?"

"That is quite correct, Herr Colonel."

"And she is the one who is now the leader of this group of partisans?"

"Well, that is possible, Herr Colonel. They used her name when they were active last year, and the Russians have used it as propaganda. But, as far as I am aware, she is only a girl. And as we have not heard of her for several months, she is certainly dead."

"It is she I have been sent here to deal with," Alexander said.

Before the onset of the Russian winter there is the Russian autumn, during which it rains nearly all day. At the end of the Russian winter there comes the Russian spring, in which it does rain all day. Anna was given ample cause to remember this during her first week in Brest-Litovsk. The rain teemed down, and the roads of the town, which had not been adequately repaired from the bombardment of the previous summer, soon became a mass of water-filled potholes into which men and vehicles could disappear without trace. Even driving between them in broad daylight was a hazardous and uncomfortable business, while it was quite impossible to keep dry, even inside the house, because of the continual damp. But Anna hated being cooped up inside the house anyway. She had not been lying when she had told Clausen that she wasn't superstitious, but the place definitely had an air of gloom about it. Besides, she was lonely, with Alexander gone all day to the military headquarters in the centre of town, studying maps and making plans to invade the Pripet the moment the weather improved. In Russia, she reflected, one was always waiting for the weather to improve.

She went out every day, usually accompanied by Constantina, to visit the market, although there was very little to buy. However, after nearly a year of German occupation, one or two shops had re-opened, operated by German entrepreneurs who had moved in and commandeered the premises, and quite often these had some goods in from Germany. She had just emerged from one of these places, Constantina at her side carrying the bag containing her purchase of new shoes, when the maid gave a squeak of alarm and dropped the bag. "You silly little bitch!" Anna snapped. The sidewalk was an inch deep in mud.

"There, madam! There!" Constantina was pointing, and shaking.

"What on earth are you gabbling about? Pick up those shoes."

Constantina ignored the command. "One of *them*, madam. One of the women from the Marshes. I saw her!"

Anna frowned and looked across the street. Opposite where they were standing was a side street, which was now empty, although there had been three people there a moment earlier. A German policeman hurried up. "Is there something the matter, Frau von Holzbach?"

"Tell him," Anna commanded.

Constantina was shaking. "I saw one of the women from the Marshes," she said. "One of the women who murdered Major Fraenckel. I saw her."

"How can you be sure?" the policeman asked.

"We were friends once. We were in camp together when the war started."

"And you so willingly betray her?" Anna asked. Constantina burst into tears. By now Anna's car, which had been parked farther down the street, had come up. "Get in," Anna told Constantina. She turned to the policeman: "You had better go down there and see what you can find." The policeman saluted, and looked for some support; he wasn't that keen on following a murderess into the back streets of the town. "Take us home," Anna instructed the driver. "Now tell me what this is all about," she commanded Constantina. "You were friends, and now you are enemies. How did this happen?"

"We were in camp together," Constantina sobbed. "In June of last year. Then the Germans came, and we were captured. They wanted to know which of us were Jews, but Tatiana who was our camp leader would not tell them, so . . ." tears rolled down her cheeks . . . "they took me and beat me until I pointed out the Jews. Then they made me one of their servants. But Natasha, the girl I saw just now, and Tatiana . . . the way they stared at me. They have come to murder me. I know they have!"

"Well, we may not let her do that," Anna said. "What happened to the Jews you denounced?"

Constantine wiped her eyes on her sleeve, "They were shot. They were made to dig their own grave. One big hole in the ground. Then they were made to strip naked. Then they were made to stand on the edge of the hole and shot. Commandant Markowitza was with them. Their bodies fell into the pit and the earth was thrown in on top of them. Not all of them were killed outright. Some were still crying out when the earth was thrown on top of them." She shuddered. "It was terrible!"

Anna felt like shuddering herself. But she could not, in front of this girl. "And the others? Those who were not Jews? Did they all escape into the Marshes?"

Constantina shook her head. "They were sent off to labour camp."

"But you were kept here?"

"If I had gone with them they would have murdered me."

Anna listened to Alexander's feet on the steps. "Were you in any danger?" he demanded.

"Perhaps, according to Constantina."

"Well, we will get the bitch, and make her squeal, I can promise you that."

"I'm sure you will. Leave us, Constantina." The maid scurried from the room. "She has just been telling me a ghastly story." Anna repeated what Constantina had said. "Is that all true?"

Alexander went to the sideboard and poured himself a glass of schnapps. He held up the bottle, but Anna shook her head. "Yes," he said. "It is all true."

"Schoolchildren!"

"May I remind you, my dearest girl, that it was you who insisted on coming into a war zone. We are fighting for our very existence, here,"

"I thought we attacked *them*?"

"We did, because we need the space they are occupying for ourselves. You must understand that: you have read 'Mein Kampf'. Now that we are at war, it is a continual matter of hard decisions. The Jews and the commissars are our enemies. They are fanatical opponents of the Reich. If we do not destroy them, they will destroy us." Anna sat down. There was a kind of ghastly logic about what he was saying. "They are in exactly the same category as those people in the Marshes. Sworn to defy us to the end. I have been sent here to defeat them. And to defeat them means to kill them. Every last one. I thought you wanted that."

Now Anna did shudder. "But was it necessary to make those children undress?"

"War is a sufficiently wasteful business in its essentials. It is the policy of the Eisengruppen to reduce the waste as much as possible. The clothes worn by these people, any jewellery or accessories they may have, can be recycled for use by Germans."

"What an obscene thought! Why stop at their clothes? Why not re-cycle, as you put it, their hair and the gold in the teeth?"

Alexander finished his drink and refilled the glass. "We are already doing that." She stared at him in horror. "Athough not in the case of these schoolchildren. I am sorry you find this hard to accept, Anna. But as I have said, we are creating an empire which will last a thousand years. An empire which will be populated by Germans. Any non-German elements, and particularly any Slav elements, are disposable. Right now we need their labour. Thus we are only dealing with the Jews and the commissars at the moment. But we will eventually deal with the entire population."

"I feel quite sick," Anna said.

The phone rang. "We have made an arrest, Herr Colonel," Clausen said. "Will you come down?"

"Yes. Do nothing till I get there," Alexander said.

"It would be helpful if you could bring the girl Constantina with you, Herr Colonel. She identified the woman in the first place."

"I will do that." Alexander hung up. "Constantina!" he called. "You will come with me to SS Headquarters." He glanced at Anna. "Do you wish to come too?"

Anna swallowed. But she wanted to see her husband at work. To *know* him, in a way she could never hope to do in bed.

Chapter 8

The Attack

Once Tatiana and her two aides had left on their reconnaissance, Gerasimov ordered the doctors to carry out a careful examination of all the members of the group, Alex and Elaine undertook the task with considerable misgivings, not least because none of the partisans had removed anything but the most essential clothing since the previous autumn. "What they really need," Alex told the colonel, "is a good hot bath. All of them."

"And where do you suppose they are going to obtain that?" Gerasimov inquired.

"Well, failing that, a good cold bath. It really is a miracle that there has been no outbreak of typhus. We can thank the cold for that. But once the weather warms up, as it is doing . . ."

Gerasimov nodded. "We shall have that done the moment the Commissar returns. Now tell me about their general health."

"Well," Elaine said. "Not one of them has been on a proper diet these last six months. There are traces of scurvy and a lot of their gums are in poor shape. Also, although we don't have the equipment for proper testing, I think there could be some incidences of TB before too long. What these people are really suffering from is exposure."

"Can they all fight? By that I mean, can they all take part in the coming raid?"

Elaine looked at Alex "Most of them."

"Which are the ones who cannot?"

"Why is it important?" Elaine asked.

Gerasimov gave one of his grim smiles. "It is important, to you, because I, your commanding officer, have asked a question which must be answered."

"No matter how many of us go on the raid," Alex said, "it will be necessary to leave a few people here, to mind the camp."

"And any of our people are capable of doing that?"

"In our opinion, yes."

"Very well. Remember that you are responsible for your opinion, doctor." He walked away.

"Jesus!" Elaine muttered. "Are you thinking what I am thinking?"

"That he will not maintain any useless mouths? Yes. I think you are probably right."

"And suppose he said, 'So-and-so is too old or decrepit to fight, get rid of him,' what would you do?"

"Elaine, we are soldiers fighting in the dirtiest of wars, and doing the dirtiest of jobs. All we can do is obey orders."

"Seems to me we both took an oath, once. Or was that in another existence?"

"We took an oath to save life wherever possible. But if there is only food and shelter for 60 people, and we have 61, well . . ."

"That is positively obscene," Elaine said. She got up and walked away from him, half expecting him to follow and attempt to explain himself. But he didn't.

What is happening to us? she wondered, as she walked through the trees, away from the encampment. It had all been a glorious escapade, enshrined in the same glorious adventure that Russia had always been, for her. The discomforts of the journey had been nothing more than adventure. Even the ghastly conditions in the Moscow hospital had been an aspect of it life, and death, in the raw. But they had still been governed by ethics. She had not supposed anything could ever change that, and if any of the stories which had been circulating about the behaviour of the Germans were true, well then, they were to be pitied for having so abandoned the tenets of humanity. Thus coming here had been a continuation of the adventure. And if they had both been shocked by the conditions in the Marshes, the attitudes, it had still not been something to affect them. They remained doctors. They would save life wherever they could, even in these stark surroundings.

But now Alex could contemplate taking life, from their point of view innocent life, and certainly not in self-defence, simply because he might be ordered to do so. Had he changed that much? Or had he changed at all, and was only now revealing his true self? His Russian self, his innately savage self. He was the man who, up to five minutes ago at least, she had been going to marry. She heard a footstep and turned, sharply, but it was Olga Kaminskaya, armed to the teeth as usual. "Running away, Comrade?" Olga asked.

"Don't you sometimes wish you could?" Elaine asked. "Don't you wish you could snap your fingers, and be somewhere else?"

"It is not good to think like that," Olga said. "That way lies madness. Look, that pond is free of ice."

Elaine turned to look as directed. "I'll bet it's still pretty cold."

"Oh, nearly freezing," Olga agreed, and began taking off her weapons. "The Colonel says you think we all need a bath."

"Don't you?" Elaine asked. "But that is another dream, and you tell me we must not dream."

"I am going to bathe," Olga said, continuing to undress. "Look." She had put her hand in her pocket and now she produced a cake of soap. "I have saved this, all winter." Although it was not at that moment raining, and the sun was attempting to peep through the clouds and even penetrate the trees, it remained very cold; Olga's entire body was tumescent as she removed the last of her clothes. Elaine had been struck with the almost feline grace and power of the woman when she had examined her. But that had been clinical. Out here in the woods Olga was beautiful, especially as she had freed her black hair and was shaking it loose round her shoulders. "Brrr," she said, passing her hands lightly over her breasts. "Do you not also need a bath?"

"I had one last week, before leaving Moscow. If you don't mind, I'll let the weather warm up a bit."

Olga carefully pocketed her soap; it was quite dry again, its softness coagulated in the cold. "That is a shame," she remarked. "If you would bathe, we could make love together. It is better than with a man." She giggled. "There is no risk of pregnancy."

Elaine had never been so embarrassed in her life. Such suggestions were not made in Concord, Mass., or Boston either, for that matter, even among three young women who had shared a somewhat small flat. "Listen!" Olga said. "People!" Elaine felt utterly relieved as she peered into the trees and the two figures staggering towards them. "It is Tatiana," Olga said. "That is good. But . . ." she also stared at the two women. "Where is Valya?"

The entire group sat or stood around the fire, while Tatiana and Natasha ate hot food and drank vodka. They were both still in a state of some shock, and what they had to say put most of their companions into shock as well. "We did not know Constantina was still in Brest-Litovsk," Natasha said.

"We did not know she was still *alive*," Tatiana said. "We thought that someone would have strangled her by now. Or that she would have been sent off to Germany. But she was there, bold as brass . . ."

"So well-dressed. So prosperous," Natasha said.

"Standing on the pavement beside a German officer's wife," Tatiana said. "Staring at us."

"She recognised me," Natasha said.

"I think she was terrified," Tatiana said. "She started shouting and screaming and pointing . . ." Our commissar, Elaine thought, unable to suppress her contempt. Reduced to a frightened little girl.

"But you got away," Gerasimov prompted.

"We ran. We knew we had to hide until dark, but they came after us. We hid, and then we were seen again. I don't think they knew it was us; they were just looking for three women. We decided we would just walk away from them. But they called on us to halt, so we ran." She flushed, and glanced at the colonel. "I suppose that was very foolish of us."

"Very," he agreed.

"Then Valya slipped and fell." Natasha took up the tale. "We stopped and looked back. The Germans were very close, and she shouted, 'Help me!'"

"Then why did you not?" Olga inquired.

"I tried," Tatiana said. "I fired at her. But I missed. Then I saw her draw her own gun, but before she could use it the Germans were upon her."

"There was nothing more we could do," Natasha said. "We had to get away."

"And you succeeded," Gerasimov remarked, contemptuously. "Leaving your comrade in their hands."

"There was nothing more we could *do*!" Natasha shouted.

Tatiana looked at Feodor, who sighed. "Well, as she will certainly tell them our plans, this operation is off. We shall have to think of some other way of striking at them."

"What makes you so sure she will tell them our plan?" Elaine demanded. "She struck me as being a very brave, determined woman."

"Comrade," Olga said, pityingly. "Valya is no longer a woman. She is a *thing*, so overwhelmed with pain and self-disgust she will wish only to be dead. But she cannot be dead, until she has told them what they wish. So she must exist in agony, until she tells them what they wish.

There is no possibility of resisting the sort of torture they can inflict."

Elaine bit her lip and glanced at Alex. But his face was determinedly impassive. "Well, there it is," Gerasimov said. "The meeting is ended."

"No," Tatiana said, her voice low. "The meeting is ended when I say so. I am the Commissar." The partisans exchanged glances. "Valya is dead," Tatiana said. "And before she died, she will have told the Germans . . . what? That we were reconnoitering the town with the view to attacking them. She did not know what we were going to attack, or how, or when, because I did not tell her. I have told no one, save Colonel Gerasimov and Captain Ligachev. So there is no need for us to abandon our plans. And now we have Valya to avenge, as well."

"That is madness," Shatrav grumbled, as usual. "If they know we mean to attack them, they will double their guards, their alertness."

"They may well do that, but they will think like you, Comrade Shatrav. They will think that we have abandoned our plan, because we know they will expect us. Well, we shall confirm their conclusion. We will divide our forces. Forty determined men and women can do as well as sixty; it is only a matter of degree. Captain Ligachev, you will take twenty comrades and proceed north to the railway line and the bridge. Exactly where we attacked last year. At a moment to be arranged you will assault the guard-post."

"With twenty men?" Feodor asked in dismay. "That is now virtually a fort, with a garrison of at least fifty."

"It has machine-guns," someone said.

"And a mortar," Shatrav put in for good measure.

"That is because it remains their most vulnerable position in this vicinity," Tatiana pointed out. "When I say assault, I do not mean you must carry it by the charge. You will open fire on it with everything you have. Colonel Gerasimov, you will accompany them with your rocket-launcher and fire rockets into the post."

"While you do what?" Gerasimov demanded.

"I will lead the larger force to the outskirts of Brest-Litovsk. The Germans will be alarmed by the attack on the railway bridge, and will despatch reinforcements to the post, especially as they will be convinced that we have entirely changed our plans since their capture of Valya. Once they have done that, we will have no trouble in entering the town."

"You are basing your entire plan upon an assumption of what the Germans will do," Gerasimov objected.

"Well?" Tatiana demanded. "Is that not what every general has done since time began? The successful ones are those who made the accurate assumptions." She looked round their faces. "It is dangerous, but so is any assault."

"It could work," Feodor said.

"It *will* work," Tatiana insisted. "The operation will take place on Saturday night; there is no moon and, hopefully, there will be cloud cover. But I will select the teams now. Olga, you will come with me, as will Natasha; she knows the layout of the city. You will also come with me, Gregory. Shatrav will accompany Captain Ligachev." She went through the entire group, selecting each man or woman by name. Six, three men and three women, the oldest, were chosen to remain. "But not in the camp," Tatiana told them. "You must be prepared to give covering fire to Captain Ligachev's group, in the first instance. And then to us."

Bebrikov, who would command, nodded with grim determination.

"That leaves only the medics," Feodor said.

"They are of no use to us on the operation," Tatiana said.

"Of course we can be of use," Alex protested.

"Can you shoot straight? Have you ever shot at a man?" Tatiana demanded.

"Well . . . no. But you are sure to suffer casualties."

"You know our rule about casualties, Comrade Cousin.

You will be needed, here, to care for those who make it back."

"That kind of puts us in our place," Elaine remarked. They stood together at the fringe of trees, looking out across the abandoned cornfields. It was the first time they had been alone together in several days, and Elaine was very grateful that Alex had elected to walk with her. She had in fact been rather unnerved by Olga's proposal, even if it hadn't been repeated: that was because Olga had been preoccupied since Tatiana's return. As she had been warned that sexual relationships within the group were on a casual basis, she had anticipated some heterosexual advances – but as there had been none she had relaxed, assuming that everyone understood she was Alex's girl. Now she had to come to grips with the fact that sexual relationships were even more casual than she had supposed, and by no means as orthodox.

It was hardly something she could discuss with Alex, simply because she had no idea what his reaction might be. They seemed to have been gradually growing apart since their arrival in Russia, certainly since they had entered the Marshes. But now they were on their own again, rejected by the main group, simply because they were not professional killers. Back to the Hippocratic Oath. "I have to admit," she said, "that I didn't think she was up to taking decisions like that. Not after the state she was in when she first came back. Do you think they'll make it?"

"Some of them," he said. She glanced at him, and he flushed. She knew he was thinking of Tatiana, and not in the least because she was group leader. What bothered her was that it might not even be because she was his cousin. "People!" he said.

They both instinctively dropped to their knees, and then to their stomachs; the snow had all gone, but the ground remained wet and soggy, as were the fields. But it was not actually raining at the moment, and slowly rumbling and splashing towards them were four tanks, two lorries, and two command cars, bouncing across the uneven ground. "It's an attack!" Elaine whispered.

"Get back and alert the others!" Alex said.

"While you do what?"

He grinned. "No heroics. I'm just going to keep an eye on them. If they start to come in, I'll run, believe me."

Elaine hesitated, but it made military sense to keep the Germans under surveillance. She crawled away from him for some 50 yards until she was out of sight of the enemy through the tree screen, then she rose to her feet and ran over the uneven ground, stumbling in and out of puddles, ignoring the cold and wet discomfort.

"Hey! What are you doing?" It was Shatrav.

"Germans!" she panted. "Coming into the swamp. Alex has stayed behind, watching them."

Shatrav produced his whistle, and blew a prolonged blast. "If this is some kind of joke—" he warned.

"Come back with me, and I'll show you."

He preferred to wait until he was joined by the officers and another dozen partisans. "Coming into the swamp?" Gerasimov demanded. "It makes no sense. Their vehicles can never get in here until the ground dries."

"It may well be a reconnaissance to determine just what strength we possess," Tatiana said. "Olga, you will return to the camp and put it in a state of defence. Two blasts on the whistle means we are falling back on you, and will defend the camp. Three blasts means we are scattering into the woods and not offering resistance. Now, show me these Germans, Dr Mitchell."

Again Elaine had to admire the way someone so young could take command of a situation. She set off back through the trees, but had not yet regained the fringe when they encountered Alex. "Where is the enemy?" Tatiana demanded.

"They have withdrawn."

"Do you mean they came twenty miles just to have a look, and then went away again?"

"No," Alex said. His face was grey. "Come."

He led them back through the trees until they could see the fields, and the large wooden cross that had been erected some hundred yards away. "Shit!" Feodor muttered.

Tatiana levelled her glasses. "It is Valya," she confirmed. "What is left of her." Gerasimov took the glasses to see for himself.

"We must help her!" Elaine used Alex's glasses to study the naked body which had been nailed to the cross, at wrist and shoulder, groin and through each thigh; where Valya had once had breasts were bloody wounds, and there were scorch marks around her hairless groin.

"Help her?" Feodor's voice was thick.

"Well . . . at least we must give her a decent burial."

"Do you not suppose they have snipers posted overlooking her?" Tatiana asked. "They are just waiting for us to leave shelter and go to her."

"You can't just leave her there to rot," Elaine protested.

"She is doing no one any harm," Tatiana told her.

Alex licked his lips. "Will you still go ahead with your plan?"

"Of course," Tatiana said. "But we will delay it for three weeks, until the next moonless period. By then they will have ceased overlooking Valya." She looked from face to face. "And now we have a good reason to kill Germans, eh?"

"It is more than a fortnight, now, Herr Colonel," Captain Clausen said. "And there has been no movement from inside the swamp."

"And the woman?" Alexander asked.

"She still hangs there, mainly by her bones, now. She has been attacked by birds. Once the weather really warms up they will soon have her picked clean."

"Well, as I have no doubt there *are* people skulking in

that bog, we shall leave her there as a warning. But I agree that you may pull your people out. However, I still intend to launch a sweep through that forest as soon as this abysmal rain stops and the ground has had time to harden."

"Yes, Herr Colonel," Clausen agreed doubtfully. He felt that this operation could only be unpleasant and would cost men, in return for perhaps half-a-dozen living scarecrows captured to be tortured to death like the woman. That did not appear a businesslike exchange.

"So, I would like a complete plan of action on my desk tomorrow morning," Alexander said. "Especially in relation to the men available, and the best possible maps of the Pripet. You will refer Major Pritwitz to me should he cause any trouble. We must have his men, and I will need a back-up from Pinsk as well."

"Of course, Herr Colonel. But, with respect, there are no maps available of the Pripet."

"None were captured from the garrison?"

"I do not think the garrison had any, either."

"Damnation! And that woman gave us no information?"

"We asked her about the people in there, not the nature of the marsh, Herr Colonel."

"And she told us not more than sixty, but armed and dangerous. Well, that is certainly not a force to be afraid of. But there must be some people in this godforsaken place who know their way into the Marshes. Find one, Clausen. More than one would be better. Offer them whatever you have to, but we will need guides."

"I will see what can be done, Herr Colonel."

"Tomorrow morning," Alexander ordered, and left the office. He felt a glow of pleasant anticipation. He was an intelligent, thinking man, to a degree introspective, and spent a good deal of time examining himself and his motives. These last were simple enough: he intended to rise in the hierarchy of the Party. He already knew he was one of Heydrich's protégés. Heydrich liked his people to be cold and ruthless, unbending and, remarkably, fair. Fair, that is, to the Nazi principles and their approach to every subject. Humanity did not come into it. But humanity was inescapable . . . or inhumanity. Alexander found one of the most interesting aspects of his own character, and the characters of those with whom he worked and whom he commanded, was the way over the past few years their humanity had grown, and changed, into an *in*humanity that would have been terrifying had it not been both necessary and inescapable.

He remembered being terrified when he had knelt beside the dead body of his friend Colin Bolugayevski. As hardly more than a boy he had witnessed some very grim sights during the Great Civil War, when he had fought beside Count Colin – as he had then been – against the Reds. But that had become a distant memory during the relatively civilised years in Paris, and memories of the war, whether the Great War or the Russian Civil War, had been shared with so many people. His return to Germany with Anna had reawakened his fears. But he had become one of the elite mainly because of Hitler's interest in his wife. He had never begrudged that, had then, as now, sought only advancement. The difference was that then he had not known what would be entailed. Working for Hitler, or, more precisely, for Roehm and then Himmler and Heydrich, had taught him the true meaning of personal violence. The first time he had been required to beat a man's face into a bloody pulp he had vomited in sheer disgust. But that had passed, and soon he had been enjoying what he had to do, the sense of power that surged through his arteries with every blow.

The first time he had been required to step up to a man, put the muzzle of his revolver against the nape of his neck, and squeeze the trigger, he had felt less revolted, although still disturbed. When he had been required to carry out an interrogation, he had not been sure he would be able to do it. Then, when he had stood above the naked, bound, and abjectly terrified young man who was to be his victim, his sense of power had grown, combined now with lust. He could do anything he liked to that helpless body, vent every terrible desire he had always endeavoured to keep suppressed, deep in his soul.

His experiences outside Moscow had given him a new insight into what could be accomplished, and equally, into his own deepest recesses of inhumanity and lust. Of course it had to be a carefully controlled inhumanity. He was a German officer, at all times required to be dignified and unemotional, no matter what passions might be raging inside. He flattered himself that he had never betrayed himself in the slightest to his subordinates, which was why he was so highly thought of by his superiors.

But that pose had been easy to maintain where his victims were bearded, lice-ridden, basically unintelligent human beings. They had convinced him that the Fuehrer had been correct in his judgement of the Russians. Valya Malevicha had been something different. Not only had she been by far the most attractive woman ever to fall into his hands, but she had been intelligent and quick-witted, well educated and intellectually alert. Destroying her had been the most horribly exciting event of his life, made more enjoyable by the fact that she understood what he was telling her, what he would do to her. She understood that he was going to kill her at the end of it, in the most painful and humiliating method he could devise. It had been a treat to watch her mentally preparing herself to do battle. And a bigger treat to watch the collapse of her defences, one after the other. It had been better than having sex with her. Out of it had come a passionate desire to achieve the same relationship with this Tatiana Bolugayevska-Gosykinya, the young woman Valya Malevicha had named as the leader of the 'partisans', as she had called them, a woman of both beauty and determination, Valya had claimed. A woman who was actually only a girl. A woman who was his cousin by marriage. A woman he had never seen, but with whom he felt the closest affinity. A woman after whom he lusted, with all the inhumanity that had developed in his character.

The command car drew to a halt, and the bodyguard, who accompanied Alexander everywhere since it had been discovered how easily the partisans could penetrate the town, leapt out, opened his door for him and saluted. Alexander touched the brim of his cap with his swagger stick and went inside, the door of the house being opened for him by Constantina. Constantina had been like a cat on hot bricks ever since she had recognised one of the women partisans. From her point of view the Gestapo had captured the wrong woman. She lived in terror of assassination, hated to leave the Colonel's house. Now she took his cap and stick, cloak and gloves. "The mistress is upstairs, Herr Colonel," she said in her usual half whisper.

Alexander nodded, went to the sideboard, and poured himself a glass of schnapps, taken in a single gulp. It was not that he felt safer when inside his own house. Quite the reverse. He took a deep breath and climbed the stairs. His fear of his wife had grown over the past fortnight. When he had permitted her to stay for the preliminary examination of the Russian woman, he had sought at last to gain a psychological advantage over her. He was the hardened, inhuman interrogator; what was going to happen to Valya Malevicha had happened to several dozen people under his eyes and on his instruction. Nothing that could now happen could possibly affect him.

Anna, for all her early adventures, had lived a sheltered life. It had been almost a gentile life since he had risen in the Party hierarchy. She had never seen a human being tortured to death. And he had the evidence of how upset she had been when she had learned of the execution of the Jewish schoolchildren. He had expected her to rush from the room in horror, had anticipated hurrying behind her to comfort her and assure her that these things were necessary for victory, and in doing that proving his own mental as much as physical strength, to gain a victory of his own.

Instead she had sat, gazing at the woman, not even wincing when Valya had screamed her heart out and her throat dry. Anna had insisted upon attending every session, and it had taken Valya three days to die. And every minute of those three days had been savoured by his wife; there had been times when he had almost suspected she would have liked to join in the interrogation herself.

Alexander opened the bedroom door and went in. Anna had clearly recently bathed, and sat at her dressing table, wearing only her camiknickers, carefully etching her eyebrows. She spent a great deal of time every day over her make-up, and as a result invariably looked immaculate. He stooped to kiss the nape of her neck, and she reached behind herself to slide her hand over his trousers. The discovery that she was perhaps a greater sadist than he had made her inexhaustibly randy, where before he had always felt she had regarded sex as a wife's duty rather than a pleasure to be enjoyed. So perhaps he had gained something after all. Save that he no longer had the least desire to have sex with *her*. "Tell me," she said, "shall I wear the red or the blue?"

"Is it important?" He released her and took off his belts.

Anna swivelled on her stool. "Have you forgotten? We are going out to dinner with the General."

"Damn!" He had forgotten, and was not pleased to be reminded. General von Blasewitz maintained his headquarters in Pinsk, some 60 miles to the east, and on the south side of the Marshes, but whenever he visited Brest-Litovsk he insisted upon entertaining his senior officers and their wives to dinner, whether or not he actually liked them. He certainly did not like Colonel von Holzbach. Blasewitz was an old-fashioned Prussian Junker, who had been decorated in the First World War. A career soldier, dedicated to the greatness of Germany, he had accepted the Nazi takeover of the government, and then the armed services, as representing the will of the people. But he made it very clear that the more he saw of this government the less he liked it. He had no objection to going to war with Russia – like most Germans he feared Russia more than anything else – but he believed wars should be fought between armies, not peoples.

He regarded the Gestapo and the SS, with their instructions to deal as harshly as possible with their enemies, as excrescences. He had to work with them, but he did not make any bones about loathing them. Thus while he beamed as he kissed Anna's hand, and remarked, "Ah, Frau von Holzbach, you grow more beautiful every time we meet," he merely gave Alexander an icy stare. "I understand you have a matter you wish to discuss with me, Colonel."

"Indeed, Herr General. A most important matter. Shall we say tomorrow?"

"It will have to be early. I am leaving at noon."

"I shall be here at seven, Herr General." They played an elaborate game. But it was a game Alexander knew he was certain to win: he had Heydrich's instructions in his pocket, and not even Blasewitz would dare go against Heydrich's written requirements.

As she had expected, Anna was seated on the General's right hand at dinner. There was a Frau Blasewitz, and like many of the senior German officers, now that this part of Russia was so securely in their hands the General had installed her in Pinsk. But he never took her on his tours of inspection, certainly not when they included Brest-Litovsk, and Anna von Holzbach.

He had made his first advance on his first visit three months ago, and she had smiled flirtatiously, but allowed nothing further. He had come on stronger on his second visit a month ago, and she had dropped her napkin at dinner, so that, in gallantly retrieving it, he had been able to run his hand the entire length of her leg from her ankle to her thigh; as her skirt had been slit to above her knee, he hadn't done too badly, and had clearly spent the rest of the night suffering from acute indigestion. Then again she had called a halt. But tonight he would be seeking something more. And why not, she wondered? She did not find him an especially attractive man – but he *was* a general. And recently Alexander had not been the most loving of husbands. He seemed preoccupied so much of the time.

On the other hand, how would he react? He was obviously quite unaware of the lovers she had taken in Berlin during his absences. But there was no way she could sleep with the General without the whole of Brest-Litovsk knowing about it. However, the General clearly had a plan. "What I really enjoy," he announced, "is an after dinner game of chess. Do you play chess, Frau von Holzbach?" He had, of course, asked her this on the occasion of their first meeting, so he was taking no risk.

"I adore chess, Herr General," she said.

"I wonder if you would give me a game? I have played most of these fellows. I know all their moves too well."

"Well . . ." Anna glanced at Alexander with assumed docility.

"By all means give General von Blasewitz a game, my dear," Alexander said. "But if you do not mind, Herr General, I shall retire. Chess bores me, and we have an early day tomorrow, do we not?"

"Ha! ha!" Blasewitz laughed. "Yes, indeed. But I am used to long nights. The responsibilities of command, you know. Do not worry, Colonel, I shall have your wife delivered home safely as soon as our game is finished."

"I am sure of it, Herr General." Alexander clicked his heels and said goodnight to the other officers, leaving Anna in a very uncertain frame of mind. He had to know why she was staying, and yet he had raised not the slightest objection. Perhaps he was waiting for her to come home and would then beat her. She rather thought she might enjoy that.

But there was no turning back now. The other officers

were also saying goodnight and filing from the room. "I shall need my car to send Frau von Holzbach home," the General told his adjutant. "In about an hour's time."

"It will be ready, Herr General."

The door closed and they were alone. "Will our game really only take an hour, Herr General?" Anna inquired.

"I am an impatient man." He got up and opened the door leading off the dining room, which Anna saw led directly into a bedroom. It looked a very comfortable bedroom, with a fourposter bed, but she did like her affairs to contain a medicum of romance. Then as she preceded him into the bedroom the telephone jangled. "God damn it to hell!" Blasewitz snapped, and picked it up. "I said I was not to be disturbed!" he bellowed into the mouthpiece.

Anna could not hear what was being said on the other end of the line, but she could tell someone was shouting. At the General? She watched his face slowly turning red. "Are you drunk?" he bawled. More shouting. "Then turn out the garrison," Blasewitz snapped. "Yes, you will command them, Pritwitz! Haste, now. I wish these scum destroyed." He banged the receiver onto its hook, and glared at Anna. "Was not your husband sent here to deal with these so-called partisans?" he demanded.

"Why, yes, Herr General. I know he is planning . . ."

"Planning!" roared the General.

"He has to wait until the weather improves, you see . . ."

"By God!" Blasewitz shouted. "*They* are not waiting for the weather! They are attacking the bridge." He picked up the phone again, thumping on the handle. "Get me Colonel von Holzbach!" Someone apparently protested, because his voice again rose to a bellow. "I don't care what time it is, you fool! Get me the Colonel. Now!"

"We will use your bed, Constantina," Alexander told the maid. "I do not think my wife would like to think of me fucking you in her bed, eh?" Constantina trembled. She had supposed being promoted to be the maid of the SS Colonel's wife would have lifted her above the raping she had suffered time and again when working for junior officers. But she had no intention of refusing the Colonel, to be beaten. She climbed the stairs ahead of him, unbuttoning her blouse as she did so. She only wanted it over and done with. But before he had time to touch her, although she knew he was immediately behind her, the phone jangled.

"Who is it at this hour?" Alexander called down the stairs; his batman, Carl, was in the kitchen.

Carl had already answered it. Now he came to the doorway and looked up the stairs. "It is General von Blasewitz, Herr Colonel."

"What?" Alexander ran down the stairs. Something must have happened with Anna. But what? He grabbed the phone. "Yes, Herr General?" He listened to what Blasewitz had to say. "Yes, Herr General. Yes. Right away." He hung up. He did not believe it. The partisans, not more than 60 of them the woman Valya had said, attacking a fortified post? That was madness. Or was it a trick by Blasewitz to get him out of Brest-Litovsk? But he had to go. "Fetch my clothes, you stupid bitch!" he bawled at Constantina, who was peering down the stairs.

"Oh, get dressed and go home," Blasewitz said. "My entire night is ruined."

What about mine? Anna wanted to ask. For an hour and a half they had rolled and wrestled, sweated and exhausted themselves, absolutely to no point. She pulled on her clothes, dragged back her hair.

"Oh, do not look so disconsolate," Blasewitz said. "There will be another time. When your husband has dealt with these partisans, eh?"

When he may not be in such an accommodating mood, Anna thought. "Suppose he gets himself killed?" she asked.

"Why should he do that?"

"Have you not sent him out to the bridge?"

"That is no reason for him to be killed. Men like Holzbach are great survivors." He was dressing himself now. "I suppose I had better see what is happening myself." He accompanied her down the stairs. Two adjutants and the chauffeur were waiting in the hall. "What is the news?"

"Only that there is a severe engagement at the bridge, Herr General. The enemy are using a bazooka. But we are holding them."

"Holding them?" Blasewitz demanded. "I wish them destroyed. We will take Frau von Holzbach home, Willi," he told his driver. "Then we will go out and see for ourselves what is happening." Willi clicked his heels and opened the door. As he did so, something came through it, flung hard. "What the devil is that?" Blasewitz exclaimed.

"Grenade!" shouted one of the adjutants.

There was a huge explosion.

Chapter 9

The Destruction

Tatiana's grenade was the signal for the operation to begin. She had divided her people into eight groups of five, each with a designated target. Hers was the German Headquarters building, and this she now charged, hurling her second grenade as she did so, while her companions opened fire with their sub-machine-guns. She ran up the steps through the clouds of smoke, burst into the hallway. The chauffeur had taken the first grenade in the chest and would have been unrecognisable by his mother. The second grenade had passed over him and exploded between the two adjutants. They were both dead. Lying at the foot of the stairs was a man in the uniform of a general. He seemed to be suffering more from shock than any physical injuries. Tatiana levelled her sub-machine-gun and shot him through the head.

By now her companions had also entered the hall, their guns cutting down the three men who were emerging from the communications room. "Get in there and destroy all their equipment," Tatiana commanded, and saw the woman.

She was tall and very blonde; the ultimate Aryan. She was lying on her side, arms and legs drawn up. There were cuts on her back where her gown had been ripped apart by the blast, but she was obviously alive; she was shaking with fear, Tatiana dug her fingers into the thick yellow hair and pulled the head back. She frowned; there was something very familiar about the features. Even about the eyes, wide and staring at her. But Tatiana could not imagine ever having met her before, as she was definitely a German. She threw the head away from her, and the woman collapsed again, hugging herself.

Tatiana ran up the stairs, opened doors and cupboards. But there was no one up here. She went down the stairs again. Shots and explosions, screams and shouts were coming from all around her. "Torch it," she said. Her companions began making a heap of papers and material on the floor. Tatiana nudged Anna with the toe of her boot. "You had better get out of here, or you will burn."

She spoke Russian, as she knew no German, but surprisingly the woman seemed to understand her. She raised her head, staring at her.

"Get out," Tatiana snapped again, kicking her towards the door. Then the fire was lit, and she led her men down the outer steps; Anna had disappeared into the darkness. Someone shot at them from a corner, and they returned fire. Then there was a huge explosion from a few blocks away; Olga's detonation squad had carried out their assault on the electricity generating building. Instantly the town was plunged into darkness, save for the glare from the fires, while the noise seemed to increase. "Let's go," Tatiana said. Now the noise was overwhelmed by the roaring blaze of the power station, which quite dwarfed the burning headquarters building. But from the barracks there still came the rattle of small arms fire. Gregory was in command here, and a few minutes later Tatiana had joined him. They continued firing while the other groups came out of the darkness. Natasha's group was the last to arrive; she had been sent out of town against the villa where they had been held by the German officers the previous year. "Well?" Tatiana demanded.

"It is on fire."

"Were there any SS men there?"

"Not one," Natasha said. "I think they must all have gone up to the bridge. But look what I did find." The shivering Constantina was dragged forward.

"Well, Colonel," Major Pritwitz said. "I do not see what all the excitement is about."

Alexander's car had just arrived at a position about a mile south of the bridge and the post. Here the main body of reinforcements sent up from Brest-Litovsk had disembarked from their trucks and been deployed to either side of the railway track. The fort itself was lost in the gloom, but it was still clearly in German hands. And the attackers . . . "Where are they?" Alexander demanded.

"They seem to have withdrawn," Pritwitz said. "Well, if that is the worst they can do, I do not see why you are bothering to go into the swamp after them, Colonel." Alexander frowned into the darkness. He had never regarded the Russians with the contempt felt by so many of his fellow officers, and to him it was incredible that the partisans should have issued from their marsh, with all the attendant risk – not least that of confirming they were there at all – simply to engage in a long-range gun battle, which had damaged absolutely nothing, and then melted away into the darkness again. "I think we shall all go home to bed," Pritwitz said, and turned. "My God!" he said.

Alexander turned too, and saw the enormous glow on the south-west horizon. "That is Brest-Litovsk," Pritwitz gasped.

"Major, bring your men back," Alexander snapped. "As fast as you can." He ran to his car. "Drive, goddammit!"

He stared at the flames as they bumped over the uneven track back to town, while a hundred thoughts tumbled through his brain. The principal one was that he had been outwitted. So, of course, had Blasewitz, but he wasn't interested in

Blasewitz now. He had been sent here to destroy a nest of partisans, and the partisans had all but destroyed him! But there remained revenge. He had never been so angry in his life.

The streets of the town were packed with people, Russian civilians and German soldiers, scurrying to and fro, attempting to put out the flames, which had spread from the generating plant to the neighbouring houses. Other quarters were on fire, and dead bodies still littered the ground. Alexander directed his driver to Headquarters, but progress was slow because of the clogged streets as people, recognising the command car, clustered round it shouting and screaming. Then he saw the burned-out building. Here too flames had spread to either side, and the street was a mass of glowing rubble.

"Alexander!"

Alexander leapt out of the car at the scream, and Anna staggered towards him, half-naked and bloodied. Alexander held her close, deducing from both her bedraggled appearance and her smell that she must have been lying in a gutter. "What happened?"

"It was terrible! Grenades! Then they came into the house, and shot the General in cold blood. I was just leaving to go home. Oh, Alexander . . ."

"Take Frau von Holzbach home," Alexander snapped to his driver. She was not doing any good for the morale of the soldiers who were accumulating. "Tell Constantina to put her to bed with a sedative."

"But Alexander . . ."

"I will be with you in a little while," Alexander assured her. The car drove off, while he contemplated the burned-out wreckage of the Headquarters building. But there was obviously nothing to be retrieved from there, and if Blasewitz was dead, he was in command. For the time being all their main communications had been wiped out, but there remained radio contact with Pinsk. This had to be by means of batteries as electric power were gone, but he managed to get through and explain what had happened, putting the entire blame on Blasewitz's decision to over-react to the attack on the railway bridge. But assuring General Hassler, Blasewitz's second-in-command, that he was in control of events and would take care of the situation.

"But I need some assistance," he said. "Do you not have a parachute regiment training in your area? Yes, Herr General, I know it would be better to wait until the weather improves, but we must make an example of these people, now! Thank you. No, no tanks. Tanks are useless in that swamp. Tomorrow at dawn? Not before then? That is more than twenty-four hours! I see. Yes, that will be capital; twenty miles in. But it would be of great assistance if there could be an air strike as soon as possible. This morning. Yes, Herr General; I intend to have them all."

By now Pritwitz and his men had returned, and Alexander set them to restoring order. "Get your engineers working on repairing the electrics," he said. "That is top priority."

"Surely avenging this mess is top priority," Pritwitz objected.

"It will be avenged. But communications come first. While that is being done, assemble all the Russian residents of the town in the square. I will be back in an hour."

He called for a car and drove out of the town, but did not have to go very far. The villa that had been his home for the past few months was a burned out wreck. "Where is my wife?" he demanded of his chauffeur.

The chauffeur licked his lips, nervously. "Here, Herr Colonel."

Alexander got down and walked across to the other car. Anna was huddled on the floor in the back. The chauffeur had thoughtfully wrapped her in a blanket, and she had hugged this around her. But she still shivered. "Anna," Alexander said. "It is I, Alexander. you are safe now. There is no longer any need to be afraid."

"Safe?" she whispered. "Safe! How can any of us be safe, in this country? I want to go home, Alexander!"

Alexander frowned at her. "It was your idea to come," he pointed out.

"I want to go home!" Her voice rose an octave.

"Listen," he said. "I am going to avenge what has happened. I am going to capture this cousin of yours, and crucify her while she is still alive. Don't you want to see that?"

"It was her," Anna muttered. "I recognised her. It was Tatiana Gosykinya. I think she recognised me, too, but she was in too much of a hurry to follow it up. It was her!" she suddenly shouted. "She threw the grenades. And she shot the general! Just like that. Boom boom! Just like that. She's going to come again! I want to go home, before she comes again!"

Alexander raised his head to look at the two drivers. After all these years of maintaining and indeed increasing his dignity before his men, he was being betrayed by the terror of his wife. But he was also curious. "You say you recognised her? Tell me what she looks like. Is she tall and blonde, like you?"

"No," Anna said. "Oh, she is tall. but her hair is black. Gosykin's hair."

"And her face?"

"Oh, she is beautiful! But it is a cold beauty."

"And she looks like a Bolugayevska?"

"She looks like a devil," Anna said. "She is going to kill me, Alexander. I know she is. I want to go home."

Alexander considered pointing out that if Tatiana Gosykinya had intended to kill her, she would have done so. But suddenly all he wished to do was be rid of her, to clear the decks, as it were, before he had Tatiana stretched naked before him. "All right," he said. "I am going to take you somewhere for the night, where you can be warm and change your clothing. Then tomorrow I'll send you back to Berlin."

"Change my clothing," she muttered, and raised her head. "It's all in there. All gone! Burned up, with Constantina."

Constantina, he thought. Burned up. There was a shame.

"I'll find you some clothes for tonight," he promised her. "Then when you get back to Berlin, all your other clothes will be waiting for you, in the apartment. Come along, now." He took her to the mayor's house, gave instructions.

"Don't leave me, Alexander," she begged.

"I must. I have a lot to do."

"But you'll come with me back to Berlin, tomorrow."

"No," he told her. "Not until I have finished here." He drove to the town square, where several hundred people had been assembled. Most had been up anyway, aroused by the raid, and were at least half-dressed. But they were still bewildered as well as, now, terrified. "Clausen, you will take out every tenth person from that crowd."

"You mean, every tenth man, Herr Colonel?"

"I mean every tenth person, man, woman or child."

Clausen gulped. "Yes, Herr Colonel."

"Major Pritwitz, I want the maximum number of men you consider available made ready to move out. You will leave an adequate garrison, but I do not anticipate any further aggressive action by the partisans at this time. Every man will carry a week's rations, and a hundred rounds of ammunition. Every company will be accompanied by a machine-gun section."

"You are going after those people?" Pritwitz was aghast.

"I am going to wipe them from the face of the earth."

"But we have no tanks! At least let us wait for some tanks."

"Tanks will be of absolutely no use in that marsh," Alexander told him. "This is a job for infantrymen. If you are afraid, you may remain here in command. I will lead the assault. We move out at dawn." Which was now only an hour away.

* * *

It was first light long before the partisans regained the Marshes; they had abandoned the commandeered cars as each one had got stuck in various mini-swamps that existed in the cornfields. The last of the vehicles was left on the edge of the trees. But there had been no pursuit. "They are shocked silly," Gregory declared.

"Tatiana!" Feodor folded her in his arms for a hug and a kiss. "An absolute triumph."

They had suffered only three casualties. Even Gerasimov wanted to hug and kiss her, while the two American doctors gazed at her with admiring eyes. Alex came forward with outstretched hand, to take hers, and Elaine followed his lead. The others who had remained behind stood around with their mouths open. "It has been a triumph for all of us," Tatiana said. "Especially for Olga." Olga gave an appreciative smile. "Now we must anticipate a counter-attack," Tatiana said.

"If they come into these swamps, we will destroy them," Gerasimov declared.

"That depends how resolute they are," Tatiana said. "Now, quickly, Bebrikov, you and your people prepare a meal. Christina, you and your women collect up all the food and clothing and divide it into six equal parts. Secure each part for moving out. Gerasimov, have you any rockets left?"

"Half a dozen."

"Take them to the edge of the wood, in case they have tanks. We saw none in Brest-Litovsk, but they may have been hidden away. I will join you in a minute. The rest of you, eat and rest. Sleep, if you can."

"We are going to fight them, Tatiana?" Gregory asked.

"Yes. But how we fight them depends on circumstances. So, rest. I will follow Gerasimov. I will send back to inform you what we plan to do."

"I will come with you," Feodor said.

"And what of us?" Alex asked. "So far we haven't had much work."

"Arm yourselves," Tatiana told him. "You are going to

have to fight, whether you like it or not. And then you will have work." She hurried back through the trees.

"I've never fired a gun in my life," Elaine said.

"This is a sub-machine-gun," Olga said, handing her the weapon. "It has a safety-catch, see? Leave the catch on until you intend to shoot. Then flip it off, level the gun and squeeze the trigger. It fires nine hundred bullets a minute but also one at a time. You do not have to be a markswoman for this." Elaine took the gun, gingerly.

"What about you?" Olga asked Alex.

As a Prince of Bolugayen, he had been taught to shoot from an early age. "I'll have one of those."

She gave him the gun. "Now here, . . ." she held out two strings of grenades. "I suppose you have never used these, either?"

"It's not actually a hobby in Boston."

"Listen. When you need to use it, pull the pin. This thing here. Then count up to four, and then throw it."

Elaine took the grenades even more gingerly than she had taken the sub-machine-gun. "Can't I just throw it without counting to four?" She didn't see herself calmly standing there with a live explosive in her hand.

"No, because if you throw it right away, the person you are throwing it at will pick it up and throw it back, and you will be the one killed. After the count of four he no longer has the time to do that."

"Oh," Elaine said, feeling vaguely sick.

Alex slung his grenades from his belt. "Where do you want us?"

"I think you had better stick close to me," Olga said. "And I am going to join Tatiana."

They made their way back through the trees to the fringe of the marsh, where Tatiana and her command were installed. It had not rained during the night, but now there was a steady drizzle, which limited visibility to little over a hundred yards. "Well," Tatiana said. "We will have to use our ears instead."

They listened, but for more than an hour heard nothing. It was nearly noon, and the rain mist had taken on a yellow hue to suggest there was a sun up there, somewhere.

"Planes," Feodor said.

"They had to be expected," Tatiana said. "Now, no one is to move. Lie down and lie still. You will be just as safe doing that as running about." She hoped those back at the village, Christina and Bebrikov, would have the sense to do the same.

They could not see the aircraft, but they could tell the were flying quite low. Then there came the first *crumps* of the bombs slicing through the trees and hitting the earth. Elaine lay on her face with her hands over her head. She had never been under fire before, this close; the air raids in Moscow had always seemed somewhat remote, and besides, even when there had been an emergency going on and they had been unable to go down to the shelters, the mere fact of having stone walls around one gave an impression of protection. Out in the open she felt intensely vulnerable. The raid only lasted about half-an-hour. In that time a large number of bombs were dropped, but few of them on the fringe of the marsh, and there were no casualties among the advance guard. Then the noise of the planes dwindled, and they could hear other noises, engines, and people. "Talkative lot," Feodor commented.

"Probably trying to keep up their spirits," Gerasimov suggested.

"Those are Russian voices," Tatiana said.

They stared into the rain mist, hands tight around their weapons, and saw the people emerge into view, more than a hundred of them, Elaine estimated, some of them still wearing nightclothes, shivering in the damp, exhausted by their long march from the town; several had to be held up by their companions. "What are they?" she whispered.

"Hostages," Olga replied, lying beside her.

Elaine licked her lips as she saw, appearing behind the people, the ranks of grey-clad soldiers, and the command cars. "No tanks," Gerasimov said, with satisfaction.

But a lot of men, Tatiana thought; and if they did not have tanks, they had an awful lot of machine-guns, and even one or two small mortars. "Nobody move, nobody shoot," she said.

The partisans waited, watching one of the command cars, which drove right up to immediately behind the Russian civilians, who were staring less at the forest than at the cross and the hanging skeleton of Valya Malevicha. "Listen to me, in there," blared the loudspeaker on the command car. "I know some of you are still there. This is Colonel von Holzbach speaking. I am giving you a chance to surrender. Surrender now, and you will be treated as prisoners of war. Refuse to surrender, and I will shoot these people in front of you. These people are your own kith and kin. You will watch them die. And when they are dead, we will come into the marsh after you, and exterminate you like the rats you are. None of you will survive. You have thirty minutes to come out with your hands in the air. Thirty minutes."

"Shithead!" Tatiana muttered.

"That man is the one I told you of, married to your cousin," Feodor said, "I met them both in Berlin."

"Then it was she last night," Tatiana said. "My God, I held her hair in my hands."

"And you did not kill her?"

"I saw that her face was vaguely familiar, but I had so much on my mind it didn't really register."

"That is a pity," Feodor remarked. "Well, we may be able to get her husband, anyway."

"You mean you're not even going to consider surrender?" Elaine was appalled. "You're just going to lie here and watch your own kith and kin shot?"

"There are none of *our* kith and kin in that lot," Olga said.

"But they are still Russians!" Elaine begged. "And the

German officer said we would be treated as prisoners of war."

"You mean we would be treated like dog-shit," Shatrav growled.

"Anyway," Olga said. "We have a job to do – staying alive. Those people are useless mouths."

Elaine would have tried again, but Alex put his hand on her arm, and shook his head. Angrily she threw it away, but she realised there was nothing she could do. She had jumped, quite literally, with both feet into hell. Willingly!

Tatiana had been using her binoculars. "There are about a thousand of them," she said. "We cannot possibly hope to fight such a number, face to face up. Thus it is better that we do not even try. Pass the word to fall back on the camp. There is to be no shooting. Under no circumstances must we reveal our whereabouts or our numbers. They will get tired of looking for us, soon enough."

"How far back will we go, Comrade Commissar?" someone asked.

"Why, as far as we have to."

"And the traitor?" Natasha asked. She wanted to have the executing of Constantina more than anyone.

"There will be time for the traitor," Tatiana assured her.

They had not gone more than a few hundred yards when they heard the rattle of machine-gun fire and the shrieks of the people being mown down. Elaine stumbled to her knees, but Olga and Alex took an arm each to urge her on.

The people in the camp were waiting for them, anxious for a fight, and were bitterly disappointed when Tatiana told them there would be no resistance. "We are going to break up into groups of ten," she said. "The food is already divided up, as are the blankets. Each group will have a radio, but these are not to be used except in emergency; the Germans will be listening on every possible frequency. Then we are going to fall back into the forest. As the Germans advance, we retreat. When they have had enough and retreat again, we will advance again."

"They will destroy our camp," someone said.

"Then we will merely build another camp when they have gone." There were to be six groups. Tatiana appointed Shatrav to lead one, Bebrikov another, Gerasimov another and Olga a fourth. Reluctantly, but knowing it had to be done, she gave the fifth group to Feodor. She would lead the sixth group. "Natasha, you will go with Olga."

"And her?" Natasha looked at Constantina, who had been made to sit on the ground, her hands tied behind her back.

"I will take her with me."

"Then I wish to come with you too," Natasha said.

"And I have said you will go with Olga. That is an order. Alex, you and Elaine will come in my group. You too, Gregory; I put you in charge of the prisoner. Now, let's move out." Natasha looked as if she would have argued some more, but then changed her mind when Olga held her arm. Tatiana knew all about Olga's sexual preferences; she hoped the lieutenant would keep Natasha's mind occupied. But what was she going to do with Constantina? Why, execute her, of course. As soon as her group was away from the rest.

Tatiana had given each group a compass direction in which to travel, so they would not get in each other's way. Now she led her people due east, away from the encampment. Following a compass course meant that they could not seek consistently dry land, but had to splash through the various morasses, sometimes as deep as their shoulders; they had to carry their weapons, the haversacks of food and blankets, and especially the radio, above their heads, an exhausting business.

Constantina, with her arms still bound behind her, was

in most danger of tripping and drowning, but Christina and Gregory held an arm each, both to hold her up and urge her along. Elaine was another who found the going very difficult, but Alex was always beside her to help her when necessary. "Oh, to be in Moscow, now that spring is here," he quipped.

She managed a smile. "Oh, to be anywhere but here," she muttered.

They had walked for an hour when Tatiana called a halt on a hummock of dry land. Now they were entirely on their own, surrounded by the silent trees. But when they listened, they could hear the rattle of automatic fire, well into the distance. "They have found one of the groups!" Gregory said.

"No, they have found the camp," Tatiana said. "They are wasting bullets."

"Will they not be able to follow our tracks?" Elaine asked.

"Yes. But we will keep ahead of them. These marshes stretch for a hundred miles. They can never catch up with us."

"How long do we cart this carrion?" Christina asked.

Tatiana sighed. "This is far enough."

Constantina looked from left to right. "No," she said. "Wait! Please . . ."

"You are accused of betraying twenty of your comrades to the SS as Jews," Tatiana said. "Do you accept your guilt?"

"I had to," Constantina panted. "You were there, Tatiana. You saw. They would have beaten me to death if I had not."

"So you caused twenty of your friends to be shot," Tatiana said. "You were there, Gregory. Do you support the charge?"

"She is guilty," Gregory said. "I was there."

"Then let me hear your votes," Tatiana said.

"Death," Christina said, without hesitation.

"Death," Gregory said.
"Death," the other Russians said.
Tatiana looked at Elaine and Alex. "You cannot be serious," Elaine said. "You said she would be properly tried."
"That has just happened," Tatiana explained.
"Without her even being allowed to offer a defence?"
"You heard her defence. She was afraid that if she did not denounce her comrades she would be beaten to death. So she caused the death of twenty of them."
"But . . ." Elaine looked at Alex. "You cannot let this happen. I mean, in cold blood . . ."
"I am saving her a lot of misery. If I had sent her off with one of the other groups she would be a long time dying," Tatiana said. "Will you vote, or not?"
Alex licked his lips. "She *is* guilty." he muttered in English.
"And you are just going to let them murder her?"
"I think the term is 'execute'."
"Well?" Tatiana demanded.
"Death," Alex said.
Tatiana smiled. "Thank you. And you, Elaine?"
"No," Elaine said. "I cannot agree."
Tatiana shrugged. "It does not matter. We have a majority. Gregory! You cannot use a gun."
Gregory nodded and stepped up to Constantina, drawing his knife as he did so.
"No," Constantina gasped. "No!" She threw back her head to utter a scream, but Christina caught her round the chin from behind and she could only gurgle. She tugged on her bonds and stamped her feet, but Gregory stood beside her and drew the knife across the exposed, pulsing throat. He put so much force into the slash that Constantina's neck was all but severed. Blood spurted out, and Christina hastily released her; Constantina hit the ground like a dropped sack. Gregory knelt and wiped the knife blade clean.
Elaine turned away and dropped to her knees to

vomit. "Move out," Tatiana said. The group recommenced its march.

Tatiana stood beside Elaine and kicked her in the thigh. "You had better come. The Germans will cut much more than your throat if they catch you." Between them, she and Alex pulled Elaine to her feet and set off after the others.

Tatiana supposed she should feel sorry for the two Americans; they had really got themselves into a situation quite outside of any experience they had ever supposed they might have. But then, she reflected, were we not all thrown into a situation we had never supposed we might have to endure, last summer? The difference was that she felt she and her people, even young girls like Natasha, had been more mentally tough than the Americans. Of course, some, like poor Sophie and Constantina, had not measured up to the strain, but they were the minority. Whereas, from what she had read and been told, all American youth was brought up to believe in the best of all possible worlds, where people who killed, or even robbed or committed sex crimes, were the great exceptions, to be shunned and locked away. To be dropped, literally, into the midst of a society where those aberrations were the norm, and needed to be practised to stay alive, must be traumatic, she understood.

She sat with her back against a tree, her sodden blanket drawn around her, and slept, heavily. She awoke with a start at the first light. A noise? "Planes!" Gregory had been sleeping close to her.

Tatiana rubbed sleep from her eyes. "The orders are the same as before. No one move."

The drone was coming closer. The group remained sitting or lying, staring up through the trees. But there were no explosions. "Those are not bombers," Christina said.

"They are just looking for us," Gregory suggested. Tatiana stood up, her heart suddenly pounding. They would not have sent so many planes on a reconnaissance. She shaded her eyes, for it had stopped raining and the sun was rising out of a clear sky, and gasped as she saw the myriad parachutes, drifting downwards, to the east. Gregory was also on his feet. "Oh, shit!" he muttered.

"What are we to do?" Christina asked. The others had also got up, as well as Elaine and Alex.

"Do you think the others have pulled out?" someone asked.

"Of course they have not pulled out," Tatiana snapped. "Or those paras would not be coming in."

"Then we are trapped, between two forces."

"We must fight, now," Gregory declared.

Sixty men and women, against Hitler's crack troops, Tatiana thought, both before and behind. "We must try to survive," she said.

Part Three

Those Who Would Conquer

> My name is Death; the last best friend am I.
>
> Robert Southey, *Carmen Nuptiale*.

Chapter 10

The Survivors

Ivan Ligachev laid the report on his master's desk. "They are making a meal of it," he said, gloomily.

"Again, they would, wouldn't they?"

Stalin studied the prints on the desk in turn. "We do not know these were partisans. They could be anybody."

"That body . . ." Ivan tapped the photograph, "is definitely the woman Natasha Renkova. Not only has she been identified by her own family, but the Germans have named her."

Stalin bent his head over the photograph. The girl was shown hanging by the neck, but her face was remarkably undistorted although she was naked from the waist up. "Barbaric!"

"They have named other captives, who we know were members of Group One. That is a photograph of Colonel Gerasimov hanging. There can be no doubt that their claims are substantially true: Group One has been wiped out. My son," Ivan said. "My stepdaughter. And the two young Americans! Jennie is quite distraught. As for Cromb . . ."

"Jennie has been distraught before," Stalin pointed out. "And as you say, as for Cromb . . . but isn't it time the Americans learned that war is not one big boys' adventure story? Anyway, I do not believe the Group has been wiped out, or that Feodor and Tatiana are dead. Or the Americans.

Look at this report, these photographs. Colonel Gerasimov! Leader of the Partisans! Natasha Renkova! Leader of the Partisans! The capture and execution of those two has been given the greatest possible publicity. Now, Ivan Ivanovich, do you not suppose that if they had captured and executed Tatiana Gosykinya, Heroine of the Soviet Union and true Leader of the Partisans, or Feodor Ligachev, son of a Chief Secretary of the State, they would have been given even greater publicity? As for capturing two Americans serving with the Partisans . . ."

"So perhaps they were not captured. That does not mean they are not dead. If they are alive, they would surely have called out on their radios."

"Ivan Ivanovich, you are rapidly becoming an old woman. They are alive. They are lying low because of the German presence. That they have not used their radios may be for any one of several reasons: they may have lost them, their batteries may be flat, or they may simply be afraid of giving away their positions. But the Germans cannot remain in the Marshes. Soon they will pull out, and Group One will have reconstituted itself."

"Then they will need assistance. Arms and ammunition. Food. Medical supplies."

"They will have to wait, and survive, until we have the time to help them. We have more important matters." He stood before the map. "I believe Hitler has abandoned his attempt to take Moscow by direct assault. Oh, his men are holding, but we are holding *them*. It is down here I do not like." He laid his hand on the Donbas and the lower reaches of the Volga. "He is shifting huge masses of men and materiel in that direction. That is where he is going to concentrate his big summer thrust. If he can get right through to the Caucasus oil fields, if he can secure the Volga, not only will he have gained a great victory, but it may then happen that we will be forced to abandon Moscow because retaining it will no longer have any meaning. The man is a considerable strategist. His weakness is that he attempts to do too much at the same time. Now we must stop him. Here. No matter what happens, he must be stopped *here*."

Ivan peered at the map. The city of Tsaritsyn, recently renamed Stalingrad, which was already under attack by the Germans, was certainly of some strategic importance in its position astride the Volga. He could not help but wonder if Stalin's determination to choose this as the southern city to be held no matter what the cost had to do with that change of name.

"I put this in your care, Ivan Ivanovich," Stalin said. "Whatever the garrison needs, it must have."

"I will see to it." Ivan hesitated. "Have I your permission to tell Cromb about your opinion on the Pripet?"

"Of course. We do not want him becoming depressed. Convince him that his stepson is still alive."

"It will certainly be necessary to do that," Ivan agreed. "His wife is in Archangel."

Stalin raised his eyebrows. "The Princess? Well, well! I look forward to seeing her again." He stroked his moustache. He was not normally a sexually motivated man. He could admire, and desire, beauty, but since this impotency matter had become a problem he preferred to sublimate himself in his work. *Had* preferred; equally had he always found it difficult to be friends with women. Or, indeed, with anyone he did not actually employ. He adored his children, but they did not adore him. They did not seem to understand that the often terrible things he had had to do, and of which they knew had been undertaken solely for the good of the country. They considered he had been responsible for the death of their mother. And now this latest personal catastrophe . . . his son Iakov had been taken prisoner by the Germans after crash-landing behind the enemy lines. The Germans had promptly offered to exchange him for a specified number of German officers who had fallen into Red hands, and he had refused. Thereupon the Germans had said they would treat Iakov Stalin as an ordinary Russian prisoner of war. If only a tenth of the rumours seeping back to Russia were true, that was virtually a death sentence. Because the Russians had never signed the Geneva Convention on the treatment of prisoners, no Russian prisoner had any rights, not even the right to live!

But how could he, head of the state, leader in the fight against the Nazi horror, seek to obtain the release of his own son when he could not obtain the release of the millions of other sons and brothers and fathers held by the enemy? His children could not understand this. Thus he felt estranged from his own family. But he was estranged from all those around him, those who knew of the frightful cost of collectivisation and the five-year plans he had forced through so ruthlessly.

Thus a comparative stranger, a so beautiful stranger, might provide a welcome relief. Of course Priscilla Bolugayevska-Cromb had every reason to hate him as much as anyone. When she had returned to Russia, not ten years ago, searching for her husband, she had believed what he had told her, that he had known nothing of Joseph Cromb, who had been murdered by rogue elements in the NKVD. Only after Cromb had escaped had she learned the truth. Yet she was coming back again, of her own free will! It seemed she was utterly fearless. "I should like to meet her again, Ivan Ivanovich," he said quietly. "The Princess."

"Of course, Josef. If you wish it. But there is a problem." Josef sighed. Where Ivan Ligachev was concerned, there was always a problem. "She has a companion travelling with her," Ivan said.

"I would expect her to. What is the problem?"

"This woman's name is Sonia Cohen. On her passport, and on her visa. On our files she is better known as Sonia Bolugayevska, although some have her down as Sonia Trotsky. Incorrectly. They were never married."

"That woman has returned to Russia? How?"

"As I have said before, Josef Vissarionovich, our people in Washington are so delighted to be *persona grata* with the Americans they are granting visas left right and centre. Along comes a woman who is obviously Jewish, has a Jewish name, and is also very elderly, for whom a visa is requested by the wife of one of the principal members of the American mission here, in order that this elderly Jewess may travel with her to rejoin her husband . . . you see how it is. Nobody bothered to check."

Stalin began to fill his pipe. "What do you suppose she wants?"

"As she undoubtedly knows who gave the order for Trotsky's execution, it is my opinion that we should not wait to find out, Josef Vissarionovich."

"How old is she, exactly?"

Ivan opened his file. "Sonia Cohen was born in 1877. She is sixty-five years old."

"Are you asking me to be afraid of a sixty-five-year-old woman?"

"If she is capable of crossing the Atlantic in time of war then she must still be capable of squeezing a trigger or detonating a bomb. You say you would like to see Priscilla Bolugayevska-Cromb? What if she comes accompanied by her 'companion'?"

"The woman would be searched before being allowed admittance."

"Searching is not always a complete protection. I am sorry, Josef Vissarionovich, but in my opinion the only certain protection is for this woman to meet with an accident before she ever gets to Moscow."

"And the Princess?"

"Well, how do we know she is not part of the plot."

"To assassinate me in revenge for the death of Trotsky?" Stalin said thoughtfully. "We shall see. But as I have explained, we cannot simply eliminate American citizens when we are so dependent upon them for the sinews of war. I will keep an eye on the situation. You may leave it with me, Ivan Ivanovich. I want you down at Stalingrad."

Ivan blanched. "You wish me to go down there, myself?"

"Yes. You have the authority to overrule timid army commanders, and to requisition whatever is required."

Ivan swallowed. "I will leave right away. But before I go, I feel I must inform Cromb that his wife and old friend are here."

"I wonder if you should, at this time." Stalin struck a match and puffed contentedly. "Does not this man Cromb constantly complain that we will not let him see what is actually going on at the front, how his Lend-Lease materiel is being used?"

"The Americans are always complaining," Ligachev said.

"I am speaking about Cromb. I think it is time for you to take him up on his requests. Show him exactly how we are defending the Motherland. If necessary to the last bullet. And the last man, of course."

Ivan licked his lips. "You expect me to go into the firing line?"

"Well, Ivan Ivanovich, you cannot ask Cromb to go by himself, now can you?"

"But I cannot do this until he has seen his wife. That is why she is coming to Russia."

"Ivan Ivanovich," Stalin said. "The matter is urgent. You are leaving Moscow tomorrow. Take Cromb with you. And in all the circumstances there is no necessity to tell him the Princess is actually in Russia. It would only cause distress. And when he returns it will be such a pleasant surprise for him. That is, if he does not get hit by a German bullet."

He watched Ivan gulp as he left the office. Ivan Ivanovich was not very bright, but he understood what he had been told to do, and he would do it, even where his brother-in-law was concerned. However, he could not be trusted with the other matter. Stalin summoned one of his secretaries. "I wish to speak with Comrade Beria," he said.

* * *

"Do you really think that is so?" Jennie asked, clinging to her husband's arm. "That Tatiana and Feodor could have survived?"

"And Sophie?" Galina had come down to see if there was any news. "Her name was never mentioned, either."

"Josef certainly seems to think so." Ivan looked at Joseph, who was also present.

"I hope to God he's right," Joseph said. "But the name of this SS colonel the Germans are publicising as the man who destroyed the partisans, Holzbach . . . I knew someone with that name once."

"You knew a Nazi?" Jennie was appalled.

"He wasn't a Nazi then. They hadn't been heard of. But he was a German, with a Russian mother. He and I fought together, briefly, for Denikin's White Army against the Reds. That was in 1919."

"I am sure that is an episode in your life you will wish to forget," Jennie said severely.

Joseph grinned. "I'm afraid not, Sis. It happens to be the episode of my life in which I met Priscilla. I have no intention of forgetting that."

"And you really think this may be the same man?" Ivan wished to defuse the incipient quarrel.

"Well, twenty-three years ago? Hardly likely. There has got to be more than one Holzbach in Germany."

"Don't you know what happened to yours?"

Joseph shook his head. "The last I saw of Holzbach was him riding off with Colin, to continue the fight."

"Colin survived. Up to a point," Ivan remarked.

Jennie flushed.

"Yes," Joseph said, thoughtfully. "In Paris. I suppose it is possible . . . In the present circumstances, I don't think this fellow's identity is relevant, Ivan. I think my people, and yours, need to be pulled out. They've done their bit."

"I understand how you feel, Joe," Ivan said, sympathetically. "But there is no way they *can* be pulled out; they are several hundred miles behind the German lines. Even supposing they could be found; we have lost radio contact with them. No, they will have to sit it out until our armies reconquer that territory."

"And when do you think that will be?" Joseph demanded. "Before this coming winter?"

"I'm afraid that will not be possible."

"And you expect them to survive the winter in that marsh?"

"They survived last winter," Jennie said.

"God! What is Priscilla going to say? What's the word on her arrival, anyway?"

Ivan turned his hands out. "There is no word. But I am sure she is on her way. However, we must continue the fight. And in this regard, I have the most tremendous news, Joseph. Listen to what you and I are going to do."

The band played as the train pulled into the station. Alexander stood to attention and gave the Nazi salute, Pritwitz and Clausen to either side. Heydrich stepped from the train and touched his cap with his stick. "Welcome to Brest-Litovsk, Herr General," Alexander said.

"I can only spare an hour." He led Alexander aside. "Berlin is disappointed in you, Holzbach, for not carrying out your mission with the degree of success we had anticipated."

"With respect, Herr General, what the Russians have called Group One has been liquidated. Those were my orders, and that is what I have accomplished."

"At the cost of one of our generals and a considerable additional loss of life. Also," Heydrich added, "your claim to have succeeded in your mission would appear to be slightly exaggerated. Where is the woman Tatiana Gosykinya? The one they call the Red Maiden."

Alexander gesticulated. "Somewhere in that bog. Dead."

"You have seen her body?"

"Had I seen her body, I would have had it hanged, dead or alive."

"Then you cannot be sure she is dead."

“Nothing has been seen or heard of her for the past three months.”

“Nothing was seen or heard of her for most of last winter, until she suddenly erupted into your midst. It is *her* body we wish to see hanging from a balcony in Brest-Litovsk, Holzbach, not that of her underlings. Your mission is not yet completed.”

Alexander swallowed. “And my promotion?”

Heydrich gave one of his cold smiles. “As I have just said, your mission has not yet been completed. Your future is in your own hands. However, I should warn you that you will no longer be working directly under my aegis. I have been promoted, in a manner of speaking. I am to go to Prague, where there has been some subversive activity, which I have to stamp out. I can tell you that I shall succeed in *my* mission.”

Alexander was not in the least interested in Heydrich’s mission. “Then who is to be my superior, Herr General?”

“You are to come under the direct command of Reichsfuehrer Himmler.” Alexander gulped. He had only met Himmler once, and had not liked him. “The Reichsfuehrer is taking a personal interest in the settlement of the outstanding problems in Belorussia and the Ukraine,” Heydrich went on. “As you know, Holzbach, we have plans to resettle these areas with Germans, but that cannot be done until the population has been entirely pacified. The Reichsfuehrer wishes this accomplished as rapidly as possible. Now I must return to Berlin. There is one more thing. Tell me about your wife.”

“I have had to send her home, Herr General. She happened to be in the Headquarters building, playing chess with General von Blasewitz, when the partisans attacked the town. The general was shot before her eyes. I’m afraid she became rather hysterical, and refused to be calmed.”

“Yes. A pity. May I give you a word of advice, Holzbach? Divorce her. I do not think her behaviour is fitting in the wife of a man who may yet rise high in the Party.”

Divorce her, Alexander thought. Yes, he wanted to do that. "But . . . what grounds do I have?"

"I will tell my adjutant to contact you," Heydrich said. "He has a file on your wife. He will be able to provide you with the necessary grounds." He smiled. "Do not look so concerned, Holzbach . . . Buelow has a file on you as well!"

As it was high summer it was already growing light when the aircraft touched down at an airstrip some miles outside the city. It was a military strip, and as the windows were blacked out the two women had no idea what to expect. In the event, there was very little to see; merely a scattering of buildings and widely dispersed aircraft, and several craters in the various runways.

"I'm glad I didn't see those before we landed," Sonia commented, as they were hurried across the tarmac, along with the other passengers, mainly military personnel.

"I imagine the pilot knew they were there," Priscilla said, pulling off her headscarf and shaking out her golden hair as they entered the very small Arrivals Hall. She had come equipped for a long stay, but she had been assured her heavy baggage was following by road and rail, travelling well to the east of the German positions outside Leningrad and north of Moscow. She wondered if she would ever see it again. But for the time being she was just happy to be here.

"Priscilla? Gosh, you haven't changed a bit." Priscilla, who had been looking for Joseph, gazed at the big, handsome woman with the grey-streaked auburn hair. But you have, she thought. It was 20 years since last she had seen her cousin, who was at the same time her sister-in-law. Searching for Joseph during her last visit to Russia in 1935, Stalin had offered her a meeting; Jennie's then husband, Andrei Gosykin, had just been condemned and shot for mass murder, and Stalin could not do too much for the visiting aristocrat – one of the men Gosykin was supposed to have murdered was Joseph Cromb. Priscilla had believed everything she had been told, something for which she had never forgiven herself, but she had not been able to bring herself to meet the widow of her husband's murderer, no matter how closely they might be related. Now that was history and yet she could not prevent the stiffness which overtook her as Jennie came forward for an embrace. "And Aunt Sonia!" Jennie said.

The two had also not met for nearly 20 years, since Trotsky had been degraded and banished from Moscow with his mistress. "You are looking well," Sonia said.

"Welcome back!" Jennie embraced her in turn, watched by interested officials, as they had been speaking English. "I have a car," Jennie said. "Is that all your stuff?"

"All we were allowed to bring," Priscilla said.

They were led out to the chauffeur-driven limousine. By now it was broad daylight, and they looked at green fields and low hills. There was little evidence that a major conflict was raging only a few miles away. "You will hear the guns, as we get closer," Jennie assured them.

"Where is Joseph?" Priscilla asked, as they joined the road – hardly more than a track – outside the airport.

"I'm afraid he is down in the south."

"You mean he's not here? But I sent him a message from Archangel, that we had arrived."

"Did you? It never got here. But I'm afraid communications are a bit chaotic at the moment."

"But, then how did you know to meet the plane?"

Jennie had been briefed; it did not bother her to lie to this woman, who she had never really liked. "The pilot called ahead on his radio." She smiled. "Got me out of bed. But there is nothing to worry about. Joseph is on a tour of inspection, with my husband Ivan. It is part of his job, you know, seeing what we need in military aid, and – what I think the Americans consider more important – seeing how their materiel is being used. They will soon be back."

"But Alexei is in Moscow?" Priscilla asked, anxiously. "He wrote to tell me that."

"Ah . . . yes, he was here," Jennie said. "But he has been transferred to another post, outside of the city."

"You mean I can't see him, either?"

"Not right this minute. I'm sorry." Now they were close to the city and could see evidence of the German bombardments. And as Jennie had promised, through the open windows of the car they could hear what sounded like a continuous rumble of thunder coming from the west. "It is really a stalemate out there," Jennie explained. "The Germans are making their main effort in the south."

"You said Joe was in the south. Do you mean he could be in danger?"

"Good heavens, no! He is with my Ivan." Jennie giggled. "Ivan never gets into danger."

Sonia gazed at the craters in the streets, the damaged buildings, some of them entirely collapsed. Nor were there many people to be seen. "Has the city been evacuated?" she asked.

"Well, partly. All non-essential mouths have been sent east. But the majority of the population is still here. You will not see them, because they are all working."

"And what work do you do?" Priscilla asked.

Jennie giggled again. "I am the wife of a senior Party Official."

She took them to the Metropole. This had sustained some bomb damage, but there were still flunkies to assist them out of the limousine and into the lobby. "Could be New York," Priscilla remarked. "Well, not quite!"

Two army officers saluted them as they went to the desk. Sonia stared at them in amazement. "They have epaulettes, and red tabs!"

"They are colonels," Jennie explained.

"In the Great Civil War, whenever an officer was captured with epaulettes, Trotsky had his men nail them to their shoulders."

Jennie gave a little shudder. "Those days are history. Oh, I know that down to the German invasion officers wore no proper insignia, but now Uncle Joe wants everyone to have a pride in the army, and the uniform." She gave one of her little giggles. "He has even allowed the churches to be re-opened, so that if they wish people can pray. It hasn't been popular with some of the hardliners in the Party, of course, but they can't do anything about it, and it is certainly popular with the soldiers and the people. Now, . . ." she was busily signing forms. "We have put you in Joe's room for the time being, Priscilla; we'll move you to a double when he gets back. Sonia is just along the corridor." She accompanied them upstairs with the porter. "I hope this is all right."

"It seems very comfortable." Priscilla opened the wardrobe and looked at Joe's clothes hanging there; the sight of them was reassuring.

"I know you'll want to bathe and change after your long journey," Jennie said.

"We were told that we should report our arrival to the Embassies," Sonia said. "I am travelling on a Mexican passport."

"We'll do that this afternoon. But first, Sonia, I would be very pleased if you would have lunch with me, at Aragvi."

"That would be very nice," Sonia said, but . . ." she looked at Priscilla.

"Oh, Priscilla will be busy. She has been invited to lunch, with Uncle Joe." Sonia's mouth opened, and Jennie misinterpreted her expression. "I'm afraid the invitation is for Priscilla only," she explained. "She and Uncle Joe are such old friends. But I am sure you will receive one, in due course."

Priscilla was actually very content that her first meeting with Stalin would be without Sonia; the situation was so terribly ambivalent. She had not expected to meet Stalin at all, except perhaps in passing, as it were, at an official reception. But to be invited to lunch on her first morning in Moscow . . . He had to know that she had learned the truth about him, that she knew he was a mass murderer on a scale even Hitler had not yet, to her knowledge, achieved. More importantly, she now knew how casually he had lied to her about Joseph. Equally, he would know that she had been the prime agent behind Joseph's eventual rescue and return to the States, to write those damning articles, which, sadly, so few people seemed prepared to believe.

But she was Priscilla Bolugayevska-Cromb. Was she going to fear an elderly dictator who had once been overwhelmed by her beauty? She had no doubt at all the real reason she was going to lunch in the Kremlin was that like all megalomaniacs, and even more those who manage to become dictators, Stalin envisaged that he could explain away anything he might in the past have done to her or about her. She would happily meet him on those grounds. But she was glad that Sonia would not be present. Even if she did not believe that her old friend would break her word, there was too much between Stalin and Trotsky's mistress for them ever to have a civilised meeting.

To her surprise they were to eat in his office, tête-a-tête. There was a secretary present, but she was hardly more than a part of the furniture; a table was set, for two, against the wall beneath the window. "Madame Cromb!" Stalin came round his desk to embrace her and kiss her on each cheek. "It is such a pleasure to welcome you back to Russia! Even at so difficult a time."

"It is actually a pleasure to be here, Monsieur Stalin." But she could not resist adding, "Quite a lot has changed since last I was here."

"What else is life, but change?" Stalin asked.

Champagne was served by a flunkey, and then the secretary bowed, and withdrew. "But you are winning your war," Priscilla said, allowing herself to be guided to a chair.

"With America's help, certainly. When the United States

is able to deploy its great power in Europe we will win it even quicker. But for the time being, we are indebted to men like your husband for his unstinting support."

He had given her an opening she could not resist. "A man you once condemned to a living death."

Stalin's eyes narrowed for just an instant. Then he said, "Do you still hold that against me?"

"Should I not? You lied to me."

"Those were difficult times. Shall we eat?" White-coated waiters were hurrying in with caviare followed by sucking pig. Russia might be hanging on by her bootstraps, but Stalin apparently had no intention of starving to death. "I should like you to forgive me, Priscilla," he said. "You do not mind if I call you Priscilla? And you must call me Josef," he went on, without waiting for her reply. He smiled. "It is a name I am sure you will find easy to remember. But of all people, I wish you to forgive me."

"I can't imagine why that is important to you."

"Because you are important to me."

My God, she thought, I am being flirted with by the head of the Soviet State. But she had her reputation for icy calmness under any circumstances to maintain. "Tell me why."

He made a gesture with his good hand. "This war will see many changes. It is already seeing many changes. One thing is certain, Soviet Russia will never be the same again. It might even be possible for you to consider it again as your home." He refilled her glass.

"My home in what way?" she asked, as casually as she could.

"I am sure you would find much to occupy yourself. Look at your cousin Jennie."

"You would offer my husband employment? Do you think he could possibly accept anything from you?"

She could tell he was growing angry; his ears were red. But he continued to disguise his emotions behind the urbanity of his huge moustache. "No doubt that is a question I shall have to put to Monsieur Cromb, in the course of time. Supposing, of course, he survives this war."

"I guess we are all in that position."

"He is perhaps more so than the rest of us," Stalin said.

Priscilla frowned. "Jennie says he is with Ivan."

"That is perfectly true."

"You mean you have sent my husband into a war zone."

"I have sent him where he wanted to go, Priscilla. I am sure he understood the risks. As I am sure your son understood the risks."

Priscilla caught her breath. "Where is Alexei?"

"Your son is a Russian. A misguided one, perhaps, but nonetheless a sincere patriot. He volunteered for work with the partisans. He wished to serve with his cousin Tatiana. We were flattered. Tatiana is a Heroine of the Soviet Union. One of our great leaders."

"You sent my son behind the German lines?" Priscilla was speaking in a low tone.

"As with your husband, I sent him where he wished to go. Sadly, there seems to have been some trouble in the Pripet. The Germans are claiming that Group One, that is the group under Tatiana's command, has been wiped out." Priscilla clasped both hands to her neck. "I consider this to be Nazi propaganda," Stalin said. "But there can be no doubt that Group One, after bringing off a great coup, has suffered a heavy defeat. Some of its commanding officers were certainly captured, and executed. After having been tortured, of course."

"Oh, my God!" Priscilla muttered.

"It is the German way, when dealing with irregulars," Stalin said. "But then it is their way when dealing with so many people. But you see, they have made no mention of the capture and execution of Tatiana, or of any Americans, and I have no doubt they would have found this a great propaganda ploy, so we may be sure it has not happened."

"But you do not know what *has* happened," Priscilla said. "They may be dead, for all you know."

"That is certainly possible. You may rest assured that we are doing all we can to find them. Remember that Tatiana Gosykinya is almost like a daughter to me. So we have a common interest in what is happening in the Pripet."

"And when you find them you will bring them out?"

"Well, we will see what needs to be done. We will have to see who wishes to be brought out. I am sure Tatiana will wish to remain and reconstitute the group. As for the Americans . . ."

"You keep saying 'Americans'. Is there another doctor with my son?"

"Oh, indeed! A young lady, of whom I understand he is rather fond."

Priscilla was frowning again. "You cannot mean Elaine Mitchell?"

"That is the name, certainly."

"You sent her to join a partisan group?"

"No, no, she volunteered. Like your son."

"They *must* be brought out, whether they wish to come or not."

"As I have said, we will have to see what can be done."

They gazed at each other, and he refilled her glass. "You are mad," Priscilla said. "Do you really think you can blackmail me into your bed with the lives of my husband and my son?"

He studied her for a few seconds; colour had flared into her cheeks, but now it was fading again. "In Russia, but more particularly here in the Kremlin, Priscilla, I can do anything I please."

Priscilla was surprised at how calm she felt, for all that her heart was pounding; that was mainly at the effrontery of the man. "Don't you think my husband and my son will wish to know what has happened to me?"

"As I have suggested, Priscilla, whether or not they are ever able to do so also depends on you."

He was overwhelming her with the sheer impossibility of resistance. But she was the Princess Dowager of Bolugayen. "Haven't you forgotten that I had a travelling companion?"

"Of course, the famous Sonia. She is certainly never going to leave Russia again."

Priscilla caught her breath. "Then Jennie led us into a trap?"

"No, no! She knows nothing of it. Jennie is not the sort of woman one can trust with a secret. But she will do and say whatever she is told to do or say, afterwards."

Priscilla pushed back her chair. "You really think you can just kidnap two, if you'll pardon me, well-known women, at whim?"

"It is my whim, Priscilla, if it comes to that. My whims are obeyed without question here in Russia. When someone needs to be arrested, he or she is merely tapped on the shoulder . . . and disappears. Everyone else looks the other way."

"My God!" Priscilla said. "You admit this?"

"Who are you going to tell? Or, for that matter, who is going to believe you? Will you take coffee? Or tea?"

Priscilla licked her lips. "Tea." Stalin rang a bell, and a waiter came in to remove their plates. Another poured the tea. Should I not call on them for assistance? Priscilla wondered. But they were their master's creatures. So was everyone in the Kremlin, as he had just spelled out for her. She had walked, with that supreme confidence which many regarded as arrogance, straight into the centre of his spider's web. She had wondered, when she had been in this same office eight years ago, if she had entered a trap . . . and had been treated almost like visiting royalty. Thus she had returned. But this time . . .

"Drink your tea," Stalin recommended. "And tell me why you are so angry. You are a woman, I am a man. We are both no longer in the first flush of youth, You, however, have retained almost all of your beauty. While I, sadly, have aged more than I should because of my many responsibilities. But have I grown repulsive to you?"

Priscilla finished her tea and set down the cup; her hand was perfectly steady. "I should like to leave now."

"And I should like you to stay for a while. As my guest, here in the Kremlin. I have had an apartment prepared for you. You will be very comfortable."

"You mean I am your prisoner."

"I mean you are my guest. I look forward to your becoming more than that, but I understand that you may need some time to think about it."

"That was very satisfying," Sonia remarked, sipping her coffee. "I shall have to revise my ideas on Russia at war. In the West we are constantly being told how very unpleasant it all is, how people are starving. And dying."

"Oh, they are," Jennie agreed.

"But not you. Not a member of the Party. Or that member's wife. Does this not bother you at all?"

"Well . . ." Jennie shrugged. "Those who have to shoulder the burden of leadership have got to be as mentally and physically fit as possible. Would you not agree?" She grinned. "You certainly felt that way once."

"Yes," Sonia said. "When I was a lot younger. Do you ever hear from Tatiana?"

A cloud crossed Jennie's face. "It is not possible. But Ivan says she is alive. I must believe that." Her expression brightened. "And she is killing Germans. She is a Heroine of the Soviet Union, for killing Germans."

"Is that so very important to you?"

"Of course! That is all that matters, at this time."

"When do you think Priscilla will return from the Kremlin?"

"Not till quite late I imagine. Uncle Joe likes long, leisurely lunches. What would you like to do with your afternoon?"

"I think, if you do not object, I would like to go to the Mexican Embassy first, then I shall return to the hotel, and rest until Priscilla returns. It has been an exhausting journey."

"Of course," Jennie said, sympathetically. "My car will take you." The two women walked to the door and were helped into their summer coats. Jennie studied the bill for some seconds before signing it.

"Will you not come with me?" Sonia asked.

"No. I have some shopping to do."

Sonia frowned; Jennie had suddenly become almost breathless.

"Then no doubt we shall see you later," Sonia said.

"Of course," Jennie said, more breathless still. "It has been a great pleasure, Sonia, meeting you again after all of these years."

Almost as if she doesn't *expect* to see me later, Sonia thought. She got into the back of the limousine, and the car moved away from the kerb. It turned a corner, and then pulled into the kerb again.

"This is not the embassy," Sonia remarked.

The driver made no reply, but each of the back doors opened simultaneously to allow two men to enter and sit on either side of her.

Chapter 11

Treachery

Deja vu! Sonia thought. Oh, *deja vu*! She had been arrested so many times, the first when she had been 18 years old. But that was 47 years ago, and was a distant nightmare. Not that her later arrests had been any more pleasant. But this simply could not be happening. She forced her voice to remain calm. "What do you want?" she asked.

"We wish you to come with us, Madame Bolugayevska," one of the men said.

"You have the wrong person," Sonia said. "My name is not Bolugayevska. It is Cohen. Here—" She opened her handbag. "I am a Mexican citizen. My passport."

The man did not even trouble to look at it. "In our records you are Bolugayevska, madam. Please do not make trouble."

"Look," she said, opening the passport to show him her visa. "I was granted permission to come to your country. I am also expected at both the American and Mexican Embassies." Oh, how she wished she had insisted upon checking in at the Embassy before having lunch. But Jennie . . . she had forgotten how enthusiastic a supporter of the Communist regime Jennie was.

"It is just down here," the man said. The car had turned into Lubyanka Square.

"Have you been here before?" the man asked. His companion had remained silent throughout the drive.

"No," Sonia said. What am I to do? she thought. Unlike Priscilla, I do not even have a husband waiting for me, and in time looking for me. She realised she was biting her lip to stop herself from screaming. Are you not afraid? she had asked Priscilla. But where was Priscilla?

"That is strange," the man said, as the car swung through an arched gateway; the gates were opened for them by armed guards. Beyond there was a courtyard, entirely surrounded by the high walls of the NKVD headquarters. "I was told you had been arrested before?"

"Yes," Sonia said. "By the Okhrana. But that was in Leningrad."

"We have several ex-Okhrana people working for us," the man said. Sonia wondered if he meant that to be reassuring.

The car stopped and it was indicated that she should get out. Here at least there was a difference; in strong contrast to her previous arrests, no one seemed very interested in her. Her escort showed her through a doorway into a corridor between offices, and then up a flight of stairs. As she recalled her youth, going up was not necessarily a good thing, but it was always better than going down. Another corridor, and then another door, opened for her by her more talkative escort. "The woman Bolugayevska," he announced. "Please enter."

Sonia drew a deep breath as she stepped into the room, and then let it go again in a rush of astounded terror. It was not that the room was identical with so many interrogation rooms in which she had found herself in the past, containing as it did a table and a chair, and nothing else at all. but the man rising from the chair, tall, bald, moon-faced, and wearing glasses . . . the most horrible moments of her life had been suffered at the hands of an almost identical man. But it couldn't be; her tormentor had been hanged, by Trotsky, in 1919. Anyway, Michaelis had worn a monocle; this man wore rimless glasses. "Has she been searched?" he asked.

"No, Comrade Commissar."

"Then do it," the man snapped. "She may be armed."

"I am not armed," Sonia gasped. But protesting, as always with these people, was a waste of time. Her arms were gripped and she was pushed forward and across the table while fingers explored her. Her skirt was thrown up and she felt hands on her thighs and between her legs. *Deja vu*! she told herself.

The hands left her. Sonia's knees had all but given way, and she had to hold on to the table to stand straight. But now she was angry as well as afraid. If they were going to destroy her, at last, she would go down with all her guns blazing. "Does it amuse you to assault helpless women?" she asked, loading her voice with as much contempt as she could.

The moon face merely gazed at her for some moments, then he indicated the chair. "You look distraught. Sit down, Madam Bolugayevska, before you fall down."

For a moment Sonia was too surprised to move. The last time she had been in this situation she had been forced to lie on the floor, to be assaulted. Slowly she moved round the desk and sat in the chair, aware that her escort had left, closing the door; she was alone with the moon face. "My name is Cohen," she muttered.

"I prefer Bolugayevska. You have been arrested before," he said. "Therefore you will understand that to search you was necessary."

"Of course," Sonia said. "But not to find any concealed weapon I might have been carrying. Merely to begin the breaking down of my ability to resist you. But as I *have* been arrested before, surely you must have known it was a waste of time, in my case. So we are back to your desire to assault helpless women. Even those old enough to have been your mother."

The lips parted in a brief smile. "That is an intriguing thought, Madam Bolugayevska. But I think we do understand each other. My name is Lavrenty Beria."

"I have heard of you. You are head of the Secret Police."

"That is a crude way of putting it. I am Commissar for Internal Security."

Sonia shrugged. "A weed by any other name . . ."

"You are being deliberately antagonistic. Do you not realise that you are in an extremely dangerous situation?"

"Tell me about it!"

He stood before the desk, raised his hand and ticked off the fingers. "You were the mistress of Trotsky. With him you were condemned to perpetual exile from the Soviet Union. You remained with him while he wrote a series of articles and even a book denigrating the regime of Premier Stalin; you probably contributed to his work. "You have a distinguished record, Madam Bolugayevska. You are now an associate of an arch anti-Communist, Priscilla Cromb, and in the company of this woman you have chosen to return to Russia."

"With a visa and safe conduct issued by your government."

"Issued by me, personally, Madam Bolugayevska. What I have given, I can also take away."

"I am expected at both the Mexican and American embassies." She was clutching at straws, but straws were all she had.

Beria nodded. "Unfortunately, they do not even know you are in Moscow. Or indeed, where you are. And you must realise that the disappearance of one elderly female, who is of no importance to anyone, is not really going to be followed up in these tumultuous times."

"If I am so unimportant, why am I under arrest?"

"Because it is possible that you may be important, to us, to me, if not to your embassies. I know that you were virtually standing beside Trotsky when he was assassinated. Did Mercador say anything?"

"Not to me. He was overpowered by the guards before he could say or do anything."

"But I would say that you have an idea who sent him. So, tell me why you returned to Russia."

"I came as a travelling companion to the Princess Bolugayevska."

"I do not believe you," Beria said. "You do realise that you are entirely in my power? That there is nothing I cannot do to you."

Sonia's nostrils flared as she inhaled. "I have been in this position before, Comrade, and I am still here."

"So, you have a great deal of courage," Beria said. "But you see, I already know why you have returned to Russia. It is to avenge your lover's death. Is that not so? It is to kill Premier Stalin. Is that not so?"

"With my bare hands?"

"I am sure you have determined a way. In any event, your room at the hotel is now being searched. I can tell you that Premier Stalin certainly supposes you have come to assassinate him. That is why you are here. That is why it is his wish that you just . . . disappear. He is a very nervous man, is our premier. He is so paranoid he is virtually psychotic. And you see, as I am his faithful servant, I have no choice but to make you disappear."

Sonia swallowed. "Just like that?"

Beria smiled. "Just like that, Madam Bolugayevska. But you know, people who disappear have a great potential asset – the effect they have when they reappear. That is unless, of course, one is so inadvertent as to kill them before they can do this. I do not think it would be such a good idea to kill a woman as famous, as experienced, and as vengeful as yourself, Madam Bolugayevska." He went to the door and opened it. The two men who had arrested her had been replaced by two women. "You will go with these comrades," Beria said. "Behave yourself, do not attempt to escape or anything stupid like that, and you will find that life can be quite pleasant."

Sonia could hardly believe her ears. But she knew she was not actually being released – and she was curious: for all his moon face, Beria seemed to be playing a very deep game. "And when Premier Stalin learns of the little subterfuge you are planning?"

"He will not learn of it, until I am ready. Premier

Stalin does not concern himself with what happens inside Lubyanka Street – or underneath it. That you have done as he wished, and disappeared, will make him pleased."

Sonia glanced at the two women, who waited, faces immobile.

"They are mine," Beria said. "They stand with me, or they fall with me. They know that."

"May I ask what has happened to the Princess?"

Beria shrugged. "You may ask. But I shall not tell you. I do not know."

The rain teemed down. It was heavy rain and in the swamp it was incredibly loud as it thumped on branches and trunks, splashing into the pools of water which were growing by the second. The seven people huddled beneath the minimal shelter of a larger-than-usual clump of trees; they could not prevent themselves from getting wet, but they had been wet for so long it did not matter. The long, hot days of summer were already a distant memory, though they were only a month in the past.

But that was because the memory was so horrifying. Throughout the dry period the Germans had scoured the Marshes, hunting, finding, capturing, and killing. The vast majority of the partisans had been killed or captured in that first week, trapped between the paratroopers and the advancing infantry. Among them had been both Gerasimov and Natasha. Elaine did not suppose any member of the Group had grieved very much for Gerasimov. But Natasha, so young, so attractive – Tatiana had wept when she had heard. And even after that initial success the Germans had kept on looking and destroying. Some of those captured had been tortured to death right there in the marsh; their screams still seemed to echo through the trees as their mutilated bodies rotted on the ground. Others had been taken off to Brest-Litovsk for questioning before their tortured bodies had also been dumped in the marsh.

"They are trying to terrify us into surrender," Tatiana had said.

But even the Germans had had to abandon their daily sweep when the rain had started. On the other hand, as the rain would be followed by the cold, they could reasonably anticipate that those few surviving partisans, lacking shelter and adequate food, would be frozen to death by next spring.

In the beginning, Tatiana had been inspiring in her confidence. "So, the Germans have won a small victory," she had told them. "It does not compare with what we achieved in Brest-Litovsk." And then, a fortnight later, "Moscow does not know what has been happening here, because we have been unable to call out. But they will find out soon enough, and then they will send help and replenishment." Then, another fortnight later, "Of course they know what has happened, but they will not attempt to replenish us until the weather changes and the Germans withdraw. To drop supplies to us now would be to risk them falling into the hands of the Germans."

They had all believed her, simply because most of the time they had been too frightened and exhausted to think for themselves. They had spent the summer crawling from one hiding place to the next, never sure when they would hear a challenge and the crackle of automatic fire. They had eaten their fish and their birds raw, because they had been afraid to light a fire. They had also, at Tatiana's insistence, followed the good book and eaten edible moss, bark and flowers, to provide a balanced diet. They had survived and, amazingly, so far not one of them had fallen sick. But pneumonia and hypothermia, perhaps scurvy even, were lurking in the wings; whatever their efforts they were all definitely undernourished.

And even Tatiana's confidence had begun to wane as autumn had set in and there was still no word from the outside world. Her real fear was that the High Command in Moscow might have believed the German propaganda that

Group One had been entirely destroyed, and that there was no point in attempting to contact them, much less drop food and munitions. She knew that lacking at least some boost to their food supply and tools to recreate some shelters for themselves – they had lost everything save their personal weapons in their flight – they were not going to survive the winter.

Thus she had made the decision to go to seek help from the other groups who she was certain were operating somewhere else in the vast recesses of the Pripet. She had taken her step-brother and lover with her and left Olga Kaminskaya in command. She had not said how long she would be away, but she had not yet returned, and the temperature was dropping every day.

So was morale. It had not been very high to begin with, but they had continued to be imbued with her spirit, even when she had warned them that she and Feodor might have a considerable search in front of them: the area involved was a matter of several hundred square miles of the most inhospitable country, including several large rivers, and they had no idea how close the next group might be, or how far the Germans might have penetrated.

"We may be weeks," Tatiana had said. "Have faith."

That had been four weeks ago. Now at last she had returned. She came through the trees, accompanied by several men and women. "Tatiana!" they shouted. "You have linked up?"

Tatiana stared at them as though they were strangers.

It was Elaine who asked the fatal question. "But where is Feodor?"

"Feodor is dead," Tatiana spat at her.

The Volga, in addition to being the longest river in Europe, had also, Joseph reflected, to be the busiest. This was because the Russians had not yet succeeded in building any intensive network of either roads or railways, so that their navigable rivers remained their main arteries for transport; the Volga was the superhighway of all Russia. Now it was packed with craft of every possible description, from sleek river-gunboats to rowboats, as well as paddle steamers that would not have been out of place on the Mississippi in the previous century.

He and Ivan travelled by government steam-launch, flying the hammer and sickle ensign, threading in and out of much larger vessels, being given water wherever and whenever they wanted it; everyone could see there was a commissar on board. They enjoyed every comfort, the food and wine were excellent, and when they tied up for the night at a station on the bank girls were brought on board to entertain them. Ivan took the fullest advantage of these perquisites, and was disappointed that Joseph did not appear to be interested, not even in his well-filled young secretary, a girl named Nadya, who he intimated was perfectly willing to share herself with the American. Joseph certainly had women on his mind, but they were not Government-employed whores: he was too concerned at the absence of any news from Priscilla. His last certain known fact about her was that she had left America, but exactly when or by what ship he had no idea – convoy sailings were naturally top secret. But the message from his brother-in-law James Cromb indicated that her departure had been well over a month ago. Since then, nothing. Her ship could have been torpedoed and she could be dead!

Ivan was reassuring. "Travel takes time in war," he said. "Look how long it is taking us to get down the Volga. Your wife will be waiting for you when you return."

Some 50 miles north of Stalingrad they were told the launch could go no farther. "The Germans have reached the river in places, Comrade Commissar," the Colonel who had greeted them on the bank told them. "It is too dangerous to proceed."

"They have not crossed?" Ivan was anxious.

"Not yet. But they have also penetrated the city; our men are steadily falling back."

"Are they authorised to do this?"

"They have no choice, Comrade Commissar. They are outnumbered at least two to one, and outgunned by an even higher ratio."

"Take me to your commanding officer," Ivan said.

This involved a long drive in an American Dodge truck, Joseph was interested to note. And with every mile the evidence of war – and defeat – became more obvious. Apart from the roars of the guns to the south-west, there were men on the move, some down the river bank, but others east. "Why are those men withdrawing?" Ivan demanded of the Colonel.

"They are exhausted, Comrade Commissar."

The general in command of the Stalingrad Front, Marshal Igor Sheremekov, was a tired-looking man with a nervous twitch who bristled when Ivan started asking questions. "Of course those men are exhausted! They have been trying to hold back the Germans now for three months. I need more men, Comrade Commissar. I need more guns. I need more shells, I need more bullets. Above all, I need more planes."

They were in an underground bunker, but could still hear the crump-crump of bombs dropping all around them; the Germans had total air superiority. "You have not said you need more tanks," Ivan said.

Sheremekov grimaced. "I would very much like some more tanks, Comrade Commissar. But as I cannot throw them against the Germans until I can cross the river in force, supposing that is ever going to be possible, they are at the bottom of my list of priorities." He indicated the map.

"You see that the Germans are on the Volga at Rynok in the north; they have been there since the twenty-third of August. They are also on the Volga at Kuperosnoye in the south; they have been there since the beginning of September. My principal task, as I see it, is to prevent them crossing the river and thus manoeuvering in our rear. We are managing to do this."

"You are wrong, Comrade General," Ivan said. "Your principal task, your only task, is to prevent Stalingrad from falling."

Sheremekov straightened. "I do not think that is possible. The Germans are already in the city."

Ivan continued to study the map. "I see that you still hold three bridgeheads: the one marked Gorokhov, the one marked Ludnikov, and the one marked as the Main Bridgehead."

"That is so, at this moment, Comrade Commissar. But we can only use them at night, and then it is highly dangerous."

"War is highly dangerous, Comrade Marshal. I have given you your orders. You must carry them out."

Sheremekov's lip curled, contemptuously. "I do not think you understand the situation, Comrade Commissar. Have you ever been under the sort of firepower the Germans can bring to bear?"

"No," Ivan said. "But I intend to see for myself what this fire power is. Who commands at the Main Bridgehead?"

"Vassily Chuikov. He is a hothead."

"That is what I want, hotheads," Ivan said. "Mr Cromb and I will go down there tonight, Comrade Marshal."

Ivan showed Joseph what he had written to transmit to Stalin. "You are recommending the dismissal of Sheremekov? Just like that?" Joseph attempted to think of any British or American state secretary, who possessed such power. Or who would dare exercise it in so ruthless a fashion.

"He is too defeatist. He does not believe the Germans can be beaten. We have to have a Front Commander who believes they *can* be beaten. Here."

"Who do you have in mind as a replacement?"

"I have no one in mind. It has to be Josef Vissarionovich's choice. He has told me what he wants done. I am telling him what he needs to do to have it done."

"Amen! Would you put in a personal message from me? I surely would like to know where Priscilla is, and what she is doing."

"Of course," Ivan said, and wrote some more.

Joseph realised that he was actually becoming quite fond of the fellow. He had disliked him on sight, because he was mentally conditioned to dislike all Communists on sight, certainly anyone who might have had anything to do with his imprisonment, and as Ivan was an intimate of Stalin's it seemed obvious that he would have been involved. But since arriving in Russia this time he had realised that the average Russian official changed his opinions whenever required to be part of the current Party outlook – for example Ivan and Jennie, having not been to church at all for 20 years, had recently become regular attenders at St Basil's simply because Stalin had indicated that it was now acceptable to pray for the survival of the Motherland, as long as the Germans were invading – and was nonetheless a genuine and even enthusiastic believer in whatever he was told had to be his mores of the moment. Ivan had been told to be friends with the American observer, and he was prepared to be as friendly as possible. Besides, he was obviously good to, and for, Jennie. While he was now revealing a side of his character Joseph had never suspected to exist, as in addition to recommending the immediate replacement of Sheremekov after a single meeting, he was listing with both expertise and panache the military requirements he considered necessary to hold Stalingrad.

"Get that off tonight," he told Nadya. "And do not let anyone know what is in it, or I will scar your plump little bottom." Nadya giggled enthusiastically and Ivan pinched the object of his desire. "When you have done that, come back here and I will scar it anyway, eh?"

So here comes another sleepless night, Joseph thought.

Not that he would have slept much anyway. They were perfectly secure in their bunker, but the German air raids continued all night, and the constant shaking of the earth would have kept anyone awake. But he was also excited. He had served with the British Army on the Western Front in 1917 and 1918 – and been awarded the Military Cross for gallantry – and he had briefly been a staff officer with Denikin's doomed army in the Great Civil War. But he knew this was warfare on an entirely different scale – even to Passchendaele. The difference was in the fire power. He recalled borrowing his batman's rifle to take potshots at German aircraft strafing the British positions during Ludendorff's great push in March 1918; what price a rifle against a Heinkel or a Messerschmidt!

Next morning they drove down to the command headquarters for the actual defence of the city. This was comparatively safe, as the rain had now set in with true Russian intensity, and accurate bombing was no longer practical. In another bunker they met General Chuikov. Here was a bluff, hearty, professional soldier rather than a Party appointee; thus he was still only a general while Sheremekov was a marshal. He grinned as he shook hands. "I have received a call from Front Headquarters," he said. "Warning me that a dragon is on the way, Comrade Commissar. A dragon who will require me to do the impossible."

"Your orders are to hold Stalingrad. No matter what."

Another quick grin. "That is not a practical order, Comrade Commissar. What you should have said is that I must hold the city to the last man. Very well, sir, I will do that. But to hold it, no matter what, is not possible, for the simple reason that very shortly I am going to run out of men."

"You will have more men," Ivan promised him. "You will have all the men you need."

"Then Stalingrad will not fall." Suddenly, and for the first time, Joseph realised that he was hearing the simple truth.

"I wish to visit the city itself," Ivan announced over lunch. As usual both the food and the vodka were of the best quality, no matter what might be happening only a few miles away.

Chuikov raised his eyebrows. "You understand that this is dangerous, Comrade Commissar? The Germans are actually in the city. No one knows for certain where they are at any moment, but they control most of it. Our people are defending mere pockets."

"Nevertheless, I must see one of these pockets for myself."

Chuikov shrugged. "Very well. I will arrange it for tonight." He looked at Joseph. "Are you going too, Mr Cromb?"

"You wished to look at some fighting for yourself, Joseph," Ivan pointed out.

"Why, so I did. Sure, I'll come with you, General."

Chuikov grinned. "Oh, I said I would arrange it. But I am not coming with you."

"You are afraid? To be with your own men?" Ivan was scandalised.

"If I were afraid, Comrade Commissar, I would not be here at all. But tell me this: do you have a replacement ready to step into my shoes and continue controlling and co-ordinating the defence if I am killed?"

"Of course I do not."

"Therefore you must permit me to exercise the greater courage of remaining at my headquarters, hopefully controlling events, until such a replacement is available."

"Touché," Joseph grinned, as Ivan looked utterly dumbfounded.

* * *

The night was ideal for their purpose: low cloud and a persistent drizzle. Without headlamps they drove to the river bank, but their driver seemed to know every inch of the rough track, as well as the various craters in it. Chuikov accompanied them as far as the water. From the east bank they looked across nearly half a mile to the city itself, perhaps a more fearsome sight in the darkness than it would have been in daylight. It burned in many places, the red glows melting into the rainmist to give an impression of a city in hell, and the gunfire, mostly small-arms, was continuous, punctuated by occasional shrieks or shouts that echoed through the night. "I assume all civilians have been evacuated?" Ivan inquired.

"All who could be," Chuikov said. "You will not find any alive."

Joseph noted that despite the real chill in the damp air, a portent of winter which could not be very far away, Ivan was sweating heavily. If he was as afraid as he appeared, then he was a very brave man for persisting with this surely unnecessary adventure. As for himself, he had already determined that the Lend-Lease equipment was being used to its best advantage . . . but he was not going to back out now. Besides, his sense of excitement, his anxiety to participate, was growing with every second. He might have been educated in England as an Englishman, he might have spent the past few years in the United States and become a naturalised American, and he might have spent the most horrible ten years of his life in prison in this country, but yet, this country was where he had been born, and where his mother and father had been born, and where both had died: no matter what, he was a Russian. And here were Russians engaged upon a defence which would surely become as famous as Hastings or Waterloo, as Bunker Hill or Gettysburg.

The river was in constant use; Chuikov took advantage of the conditions to ferry fresh men and munitions across to the city, and bring out those too badly wounded to continue fighting. There was, of course, no question of bringing out the dead. Joseph and Ivan were found seats in an inflatable dinghy, and paddled out into the darkness by their escort. "I cannot swim," Ivan confided. "If we are hit I will drown."

Joseph grinned. "I'll save you, old son!" Ivan gave him a very odd look.

Then they were at the other side and scrambling ashore, crawling over what had once been docks but were now rubbled heaps of stone, half in and half out of the fast-flowing water. Now they were actually in hell, rather than merely looking at it. Despite the drizzle the heat from the burning buildings was intense, while rising above even the smell of burning materials was the stench of decaying human flesh. A Colonel Vladimirov had accompanied them, and he now led them forward, over what must once have been one of the main streets of the city, but was now a shell-cratered rubble. In front of them, looming out of the gloom and silhouetted against the red haze beyond, were the frames of once high-rise buildings, their roofs long gone, their windows empty of either glass or frames, their walls seeming about to collapse. Ivan apparently had the same apprehension. "Do those often come down?" he asked Vladimirov.

"Regularly, Comrade Commissar," the Colonel grinned. They entered what had once been a department store, Joseph estimated, ducking low as a barrage of mortar bombs landed all about them. "They are not firing at us," Vladimirov hastily reassured them. "They are just firing."

Inside, the building was as great a shambles as without, what had once been orderly counters now a mass of splintered wood and glass, some even with the remains of the dry goods on display still visible, if equally torn and destroyed. Vladimirov led them down a flight of stairs into the basement, where they found some 50 men, lying or sitting, drinking vodka and chewing lumps of bread and sausage. "Captain Arkovski." Vladimirov gestured to the man who had risen at their entry.

The captain looked no different to any of his men. His clothes were filthy, his hat seemed matted to his hair, and he wore a stubble of beard. Nor did he seem the least impressed at being introduced to a commissar, much less an American hanger-on. "The situation is that the Jerries hold the far side of the street," he explained, having taken his visitors up to the sentry station, where half-a-dozen begrimed figures were standing guard, occasionally exchanging shots with the enemy, more, Joseph estimated, in a mutual communications exercise – "I am awake so don't try anything funny; are you awake?" – than because they actually saw a target.

"When will they attack?" Ivan asked.

The captain shrugged. "Who can say? They attacked this morning, but we threw them back. That is the eighteenth attack they have made across this street."

"And you have held them every time. That is very good," Ivan said admiringly.

Arkovski ignored the compliment. "When they first reached this street, nearly two months ago, they were hysterical. I think they thought the city was theirs. They actually dragged a piano out on to that pavement and one of them played it while the rest danced. I think they were drunk. They had this building, then. But we counter-attacked and drove them back out."

"And since then you have held on," Ivan said enthusiastically. "Tell me what it is you most need."

"What I most need, Comrade Commissar, is to take my men out of here for rest and recuperation. Certainly my wounded."

"What percentage of your strength are wounded?"

The captain grinned. "One hundred."

"And what percentage can still fire a gun?"

"One hundred."

"No withdrawal is possible," Ivan said. "What you will have is reinforcement. I am arranging this now. They will be here by dawn. But here you must stay until the Jerries are destroyed."

"And are the Jerries not also being reinforced, Comrade Commissar?"

"They will run out of men before you, Captain."

"It is to be hoped so, Comrade Commissar," Arkovski said. "But give me reinforcements, and I will cross the street and retake that building."

"It is time we were leaving," Colonel Vladimirov suggested.

"We will stay for the counter-attack," Ivan said.

The Russian officers looked as concerned as did Joseph. "If you do not leave now, Comrade Commissar," Vladimirov pointed out, "you will have to remain here all day tomorrow. You will not be able to cross the river until it is again dark."

"I have come here to understand the situation," Ivan declared. "To do that I must estimate the German capabilities as well as our own."

The two officers exchanged glances, clearly both of the opinion that they had enough to contend with without the presence of mad commissars. Joseph felt the same way, although he understood that Ivan was clearly following orders; he would have given a lot to know just what those orders were. But when Arkovski and Vladimirov both looked at him, he shrugged. "I'd like to have a look at what's going on as well," he lied.

"Then you had better be armed," Arkovski decided. Rifles were fetched, and Ivan and Joseph were given a quick lesson in how to use them.

"I must return to my duty," Vladimirov decided. "The boats will be ferrying men all night. So if you change your mind, before dawn, Comrade Commissar . . ."

"We shall return tomorrow night," Ivan said, and watched the Colonel retreat into the gloom. "Are all your senior officers this unwilling to face the enemy?" he asked Arkovski.

The captain grinned. "They have their job to do, Comrade Commissar, as I have mine. If I survive this, will I be promoted colonel?"

"You have my word on it," Ivan promised.

"Then please do not get yourself killed. How about you, American? Have you ever been in a battle before?"

"Several," Joseph told him.

"Is that a fact." The captain was sceptical. "Where?"

"I was in the British Army on the Western Front in France for two years in the Great War," Joseph said. And grinned in his turn. "And afterwards, I fought in the Great Civil War. On the White side."

"Then at least you know how to defend a lost position," Arkovski said. "I assume you gentlemen have dined?" Ivan nodded. "Then you will permit me to do the same." He led them back down into the vault.

If the garrison of the department store was a little short of food, there seemed no lack of vodka; Joseph estimated that at least half of the men sitting and lying around them were drunk. "Do you think that is a good idea?" he asked Arkovski.

The captain shrugged and took a drink himself. "It makes them fight. To live in hell, Comrade American, one needs to lose touch with reality."

They were all also, as the captain had said, wounded, or they would have been counted as wounded in any normal situation. But nicks and scratches meant nothing in Stalingrad, and the several badly wounded, men shot through the chest or with broken arms or legs, had been patched up as well as possible and still retained their rifles, occupying various defensive positions. There were even some dead, lying with rifles cradled in their arms; Joseph was reminded of 'Beau Geste'. But these dead had been around too long, and the cold had not yet set in sufficiently; they melded into the general stench.

To his surprise, he nodded off, and was awakened by a great deal of stealthy movement around him in the darkness. "The reinforcements have arrived," Ivan told him. "We are going to counter-attack across the street."

Joseph sat up, checked his rifle, ran his hand over his stubbled chin. The toilet was the ground beside one; everyone else was doing the same; this too melded into the general stench. Cups of vodka were passed round; there was no tea or coffee, as there was no means of heating water – had there been any water. "We do not have to go in the first wave," Ivan said. "We are not soldiers, eh?"

Joseph was not quite sure what they were, at that moment, and as earlier, he was again imbued with a desire to participate, to fight with these men. But he did not really wish to die with them to become an unknown and unburied corpse. Thus he willingly fell into the rear rank of the assault force. By now it was just starting to grow light, and Arkovski gave the order for his mortars to be fired. There were 12 of these; Joseph had not previously noticed them in the dark. Now they exploded together, and again and again as their gunners fed them with projectiles. The buildings on the far side of the street burst into flame and rubble. Arkovski was on his feet, armed with rifle and bayonet, waving his arm. His men shouted "Ourrah! Ourrah!" and followed him into a hail of machine-gun fire, which had several of them collapsing amid the stones.

"Let's go!" Ivan said, rising to his feet and crawling through the shattered back wall of the department store. Joseph scrambled beside him, following the last wave of Russian infantry. Several more men in front of him had fallen, but he was unaware of actually being shot at. Dimly he realised that Ivan had gone from in front of him, and checked, as he reached the street.

At that moment he felt a thud somewhere in his body. He spun round and fell, still grasping his rifle. The noise was tremendous, men screaming, weapons exploding, the whole now submerged beneath another very heavy shower of rain which came streaming down. Yet he could hear Ivan screaming. Joseph turned back to find him, saw his friend lying on his back some feet away. The main body of Russians was across the street now, firing their weapons, whooping and shrieking. They were ignoring those of their comrades who had fallen in their anxiety to secure their victory. But I am not a soldier, Joseph reminded himself.

He made to go to Ivan, and fell flat on his face; all power to move seemed to have been taken away from his legs. Yet he felt no pain. Then he realised it was still the shock of being hit; the pain would come soon enough. He dragged himself forward. "Ivan," he said. "Ivan!" he shouted.

Ivan did not move; he had stopped screaming. Joseph lay beside him, for how long he did not know. He thought he lost consciousness for a while, then he was aroused by the thump of boots about him. "He has lost a lot of blood," someone said.

"Well, patch him up as best you can," Arkovski said. "We will send him back across the river as soon as it is dark."

"Fucking amateurs!" said the first voice.

Joseph was inclined to agree with him, for now the pain was starting to strike, making him moan in agony. "Drink," Arkovski commanded, and held a glass of vodka to his lips.

Joseph drank, greedily. "The Commissar . . .?"

"Is dead. And you are badly wounded," Arkovski said. "But I do not think you will die. But tell me something, were you hit before, or after Commissar Ligachev?"

"At about the same moment, I think," Joseph said. "Is it important?"

"Probably not. It is just surprising. What I should have asked was, were you hit before or after you turned round to see what had happened to him?"

"Oh, before. I didn't know anything had happened to him until after I was hit. Is that important?"

"It is again, surprising," Arkovski said. "You see, you were shot in the back."

Chapter 12

The Animals

"Well, how is our patient today?" Joseph blinked at Chuikov. He was still not quite sure where he was; the previous few weeks had been lost in delirium, with only snatches of reality penetrating his consciousness. He had been aware principally of anxiety . . . but he could not relate the anxiety to reality. "I am told that you are now really on the mend," Chuikov said. "Is that not good news?"

"Where am I?"

"You are in one of our hospitals on the east bank of the river. It is quite safe here, you are underground and the Fritzes seem to be running out of aircraft. Or maybe the weather is just too bad for them to fly. In any event, we do not see so many of them about, now."

There was so much he wanted to ask. "Stalingrad?"

"We are holding, and they are making no progress. One has to say that they have the courage of fanaticism. They have poured an entire army into this battle and have not succeeded. Now winter is upon us. Any sane general would withdraw, regroup, and consider his next move. But not Paulus; he keeps edging forward here, being driven back there, and edging forward again. I suppose he is being told what to do by Hitler, just as we are being directed by Stalin. Neither is a military genius. It is the name of the city that makes it so important to our leaders. Half a million casualties, for a name."

Joseph wondered how such an outspoken man had got to be a general in this crazy world, and how much longer he would remain one. At least while he was fighting so brilliantly, presumably. "So you have achieved stalemate," he agreed. "But the Germans will still be there next spring."

"I do not think so," Chuikov said. "General Rokossovsky is preparing a counter-stroke now. If Comrade Ligachev never did anything else, he at least gave us a fighting commanding officer." He gave one of his so-attractive grins. "There you have all of our military secrets, Comrade American. And as soon as you are strong enough to travel I must arrange to have you sent home. I mean, at least to Moscow."

Joseph did not wish to return to Moscow, and a twice-widowed Jennie, and the uncertainty of Alex's fate. And to a consideration of what had actually happened to him. He had been shot in the back . . . and the only person behind him to his knowledge had been Ligachev. His friend! And Jennie's husband! It could of course had been an accident. But if not . . . there was nothing he could do to discover the truth until after the war, if then. And until then, he wanted to be here, at what was clearly the decisive battle of the war. And where, paradoxically, he would be far safer than in Moscow, if Ligachev's shot had *not* been an accident. But Priscilla? Chuikov might have been able to read his mind: "By the way, Comrade American, a message came for you while you were delirious. I assume it is in reply to a query of yours, but as it was contained in a larger message, I am afraid I read it."

"What did it say?" Joseph's voice was urgent.

"Simply that your wife, who I assume you were expecting to meet you in Moscow, has been delayed. The northern convoys have been very badly disrupted this last summer, and have suffered heavy casualties due to German action. Your wife has been advised that it would be better to wait until things improve before attempting so hazardous a journey."

"Then where is she?"

"I believe she is still in England, intending to come on as soon as it is practical." Joseph lay back with a sigh. Always the pragmatist, Priscilla. But thank God she was safe. "So," Chuikov said. "As soon as the doctors say you can travel, I will have transport arranged."

"I'd prefer to send a couple of messages. One is to my wife in London, advising her to remain there until she hears from me. The other is to my superior in Moscow, requesting permission to remain with you and oversee the battle for Stalingrad to the end."

Chuikov raised his eyebrows, and then smiled. "You will be welcome, Comrade American. And I will give you my assurance that you will not again be shot in the back."

"I am so terribly sorry," Stalin said. "He died most gallantly, leading a charge. Why he was leading a charge I cannot say. But there it is. Ivan Ivanovich was above all a patriot."

Jennie sat before his desk in the Kremlin. "But Joseph . . ."

"Was badly wounded. However, I believe he is making progress. Is that not splendid news?"

"Yes," Jennie muttered. "Will he be returning to Moscow?"

"When he is fit to travel, of course. Now, Jennie, here is some really splendid news. We have heard from Tatiana. She is alive and well. As I was certain was the case, she and a few of her associates survived the German assault on the Pripet, and she has made contact with another group, farther to the east. And the message says that Alexei Bolugayevski is also alive. Is that not splendid?"

"Oh, yes." Jennie was very close to tears. "And Feodor?"

"Sadly, no. Poor Ivan Ivanovich's family has been quite destroyed. But yours is well and thriving. And will thrive still more."

"You'll bring her out? Tatiana?" Jennie was not the least concerned about Alex Bolugayevski. "She has surely suffered enough, Josef. And now that Ivan is gone . . ."

"I cannot bring her out, even if I wished," Stalin explained. "Besides, she does not wish to come. She wishes to reconstitute her group and carry the war to the Germans. I think that is admirable. As soon as this Stalingrad business is cleared away, and that will not be long now, I am going to give her all the support I can. Your daughter is going to be one of the great heroines of this war, Jennie."

"Until she is also killed," Jennie said sadly.

"I do not think she will ever be killed. I think she has the gift of survival. And you will be proud of her. I can understand your feeling depressed. But think of the thousands, millions, of wives in Russia who have lost their loved ones. You must be brave! And as soon as you have spent a decent period mourning, we will find you another husband, eh?"

Jennie's head jerked. "No! I do not wish to marry again."

"You are depressed," Stalin repeated. "We will talk about it later."

"I will not marry again, Josef!"

Stalin smiled. "Of course you will not marry again, Jennie. Until, and unless, you wish to. Now go home and rest."

Jennie got up. "Am I allowed to ask what has happened to Priscilla and Sonia?"

Stalin's eyes became opaque. "They are no concern of yours."

Jennie hesitated, then left the room. Once she was safely away, Beria came in. "A crushed woman."

"She has been crushed for a long time," Stalin agreed.

"But you remain fond of her. I wonder you do not divorce your present wife and marry her yourself." Stalin filled his pipe, and Beria knew he did not wish to discuss the subject. "What *is* the situation with Joseph Cromb?" he asked. "I gather that Ligachev failed in his mission."

"Ivan Ivanovich was one of nature's failures," Stalin said.

"Considering Jennie, I would say he was even a failure as a husband."

"So, shall I send one of my people to complete the business?" Beria asked. "If Cromb is seriously ill in hospital, it should not be very difficult."

"I am inclined to leave things as they are, for the moment," Stalin said, striking a match and starting to puff. "I have had a communication from Rokossovsky. Here." He held it out. "Cromb appears to wish to stay and see the job finished, as he puts it. I think that is admirable. He may well stop a legitimate bullet. In any event, I wish him to be about, for a few weeks more at the least. He, above all others, will be the man to tell the world of the glory of Stalingrad."

Beria knew very well what his chief had in mind, and it was not the glory of Stalingrad. "As you wish. I agree, it would be most convenient if he were to stop a German bullet, or a German bomb. However, if you change your mind, you have but to say."

Stalin surveyed him through a cloud of smoke. He had never really liked Beria, although he had to admit the man was efficient. Perhaps that was what he most disliked about him, his efficiency – and his obvious ambition. These were characteristics he had himself possessed when he had been Beria's age. "I assume that other matter has been tidied away?"

"Of course, Comrade Chairman."

"And you have been through Ligachev's papers? Was there anything of interest in them?"

"Nothing," Beria said, and wondered if he had spoken a shade too quickly. "They contained mostly observations of people and events. Very dull. But then, as you have said, Comrade Chairman, he was a very dull man."

Stalin nodded. "Then we shall look forward to victory at Stalingrad."

Beria understood that he had been dismissed. He would dearly have liked to ask about that *other* matter, but he dared not. He clicked his heels and left the room.

*   *   *

Beria returned to Lubyanka Street. Here he felt at home, because here, everyone was *his* servant. He could command anyone of these healthy, handsome young women, and men, to do anything he required, and they would obey him without a moment's hesitation. He wondered at his own moderation. He so often felt like exceeding it. But he was going to have to rely on these people when the time came to seize power, and it could not be very long delayed – Josef Vissarionovich was well past 60, smoked and drank too much, and was impotent. That made him smile. Was the old devil hoping his ex-princess would restore his sexual youth? But the fact was that, on top of all of those debilitations, he had been subjected now for two years to enormous stress. For all his projection of external calm, it showed in his growing paranoia. No, he thought, it could not be so very long now, by those very laws of nature Stalin had so often chosen to disobey.

He went down to the secret inner courtyard of the prison complex, a prison within a prison. Here there were 12 sound-proofed cells. Once entered, one was entirely cut-off from the outside world, except insofar as the gaolers might enlighten one. In the centre of the quadrangle formed by the cells there was an open air exercise area. Here the prisoners were exercised, one at a time; as their cells had no windows, they had no means of knowing who was sharing their confinement with them. But they did know that the exercise area was actually open to the sky, even if that sky, peeping coyly between the high, windowless walls on either side, was at once small and far away. Only for half an hour in each day in summer was the sun visible in that sky; the inmates would beg their guards to allow their exercise period to be at noon. But in the depths of winter it did not matter; they were better off in their warm and comfortable cells.

Because the cells *were* warm, and comfortable. Beria

nodded to the duty guard, who unlocked the door of Number Seven. He looked at a bed, a table and two chairs, a toilet and washbasin, even a book case, well filled. This was because the people down here were not being prepared either for trial or execution, or for exile to the living death of the gulags. They were here because the world supposed them dead. They were here to be resurrected, as and when he considered it appropriate. To be effective at that time they needed to be in the best of health. It amused him to think that when Stalin finally got tired of trying to persuade Priscilla Bolugayevska-Cromb to be his mistress, he might require her to be liquidated. There was, in fact, nothing else that he would dare do with her. Then she would be given to him. To disappear, as and when he chose. He thought he might enjoy that.

But then, he enjoyed having Sonia down here. She sat at her table, reading a book. She looked up at his entry, but neither rose nor spoke. She had this unnerving habit of treating him, and indeed everyone inside Lubyanka, as her inferiors, regardless of the fact that they, certainly he, could snuff her out of existence with a snap of his fingers. But a woman who had survived Colonel Michaelis of the Okhrana, and then Radislav the butcher, and then Trotsky the terror, would presume that she knew everything a man could do to a woman, with the comforting reflection that she was alive where they were all dead. But surely she had also to be aware that he could do far worse things to her than merely rest a gun muzzle on the nape of her neck. Perhaps she thought her age protected her from his lust. He was surprised at himself, but he still found her attractive. But that was because of who and what she was more than any physical beauty she might have retained. And who and what she would be, one day. "Were you and Joseph Cromb ever lovers?" he asked.

She smiled. "Nearly." And then frowned. "He's not dead?"

Beria smiled in turn. "Nearly. Stalin issued his death

warrant, but that fool Ligachev got killed first. Jennie is desolated."

"No doubt she has been desolated before." Sonia had nothing going for Jennie, who no doubt at all had led her into this trap, or had certainly not warned her it was going to be sprung.

"Oh, indeed. To lose two husbands violently is traumatic. But at least she knows that this husband died gallantly, if ineptly."

"And Joseph?"

"Is in hospital. He was badly wounded, but he will recover. Does that thought please you?"

"Very much. Will I be allowed to see him?"

"I cannot say. But I have more important news for you. Do you know what happened to your daughter, Anna?"

Sonia's features stiffened. "She died, in 1923. She was murdered with her brother. My son. They were murdered by Andrei Gosykin, Jennie's first husband."

"Yours is a tangled family," Beria said sympathetically. "However, Anna did not die, in 1923. She disappeared."

"She disappeared, as you say. And was never heard of again."

"Which is not the same thing as being dead, as you should know. Suppose I told you that she was, and is, alive?" Now Sonia did stand up, involuntarily.

"It is true," Beria said. "I do not know what happened to her after her brother was murdered. But I do know that she finished up in Germany, married to a German named Holzbach, who happens to be a colonel in the Waffen SS." Sonia sat down again; she was breathless. "This information was contained in Ligachev's private papers. It was certainly known to his son."

"And Jennie?"

"That I cannot say. Did she give any indication of it when you met?"

Sonia shook her head. "We only had time for a brief lunch before I was arrested. Where is my daughter now?"

"We know that Holzbach is in command of the SS in Brest-Litovsk. It was he who liquidated Group One. Possibly his wife is with him."

"You are saying that my daughter is a Nazi?"

"Her husband certainly is. That is rather amusing, don't you think? *Your* daughter, a Jewess, married to a senior officer in the SS? A man who is going places, so they say."

"But . . ." Sonia bit her lip.

"Oh, indeed, the Nazis are obviously unaware of her ancestry. Even her immediate ancestry. According to Feodor Ligachev's notes she is blonde and beautiful, very Aryan in appearance,"

"Yes," Sonia muttered. "She took after her father."

"So, you see, it is an interesting situation. Would you like your daughter to be sent to a concentration camp? We understand life there can be quite severe."

"Of course I do not wish her harmed," Sonia said. "Please . . ." Again she bit her lip.

Beria smiled. "Do you know, I never expected to hear you say please, to me. Perhaps to anyone."

"I am asking for the life of my daughter."

"Even if she is a Nazi? Even if she would certainly have you shot, were you ever to meet? At least in Germany."

"She is my only living blood relative," Sonia said.

"And these things are important. Well, I shall not send Ligachev's dossier to the Germans. Unless I have to. And one must hope that I never have to."

They gazed at each other. "I am sixty-six years old," Sonia said.

"I assure you that you look much younger," Beria said.

"I have news of your husband," Stalin said.

Priscilla turned, sharply. She had been looking out of the window, watching the snowflakes clouding down. Apart from the fact that she was not free, she was living very comfortably in a splendidly appointed apartment. She had books, she could write letters – not that there was any hope of posting them. The only thing she lacked, physically, was a radio, and thus news of the world outside the Kremlin. And Stalin waited for her surrender.

Such a situation would have been incredible in London or New York, or any civilised Western country, where there was freedom of speech and thought, and more important, an investigative media. But this was Russia, where attitudes were still rooted in the Middle Ages, where despots still ruled, and did as they wished, caused people to disappear as they wished; and yet were restrained *by* their wishes. She had no doubt that she was constantly watched. She had not troubled to discover which of the mirrors were one-way, which of the fittings were bugged. If Stalin wanted to see, and hear, her most private moments there was nothing she could do to prevent it. But he still dreamed that one day she would come to him. "And of your son," he said. "Good news."

"They are in Moscow?"

"No. In war time it is very difficult to bring families together. But they are both alive and well. Up to a point, at any rate. I am afraid Joseph has been badly wounded . . ."

He had taken her by surprise. "My God! I must go to him! You must let me go to him . . ."

"Calm yourself. There is no need to be concerned. He was hit by a bullet."

"How can he have been hit by a bullet? He is not a combatant." She pointed at Stalin. "You had him shot."

"Had I had him shot, my dear Princess, he would be dead. He wished to see for himself conditions in our front line. So I agreed that he could go to Stalingrad, with Ivan Ligachev to look after him. One would have thought that Ligachev could keep him out of trouble. So what happens? Ligachev gets himself shot. And killed."

Priscilla was not the least bit interested in Ivan Ligachev, a man she had never met. "Will Joseph be all right?"

"I am told he will recover with proper care and attention. And proper instructions to his doctors, of course, that he should be given priority treatment. That he should not be neglected."

They stared at each other. "You are the foulest bastard who ever walked this earth," Priscilla said.

He pointed his finger towards her. "One day you will try my patience too far."

"I look forward to it," she said contemptuously.

His cheeks were suffused, but his voice remained even. "I have also news of your son. He is alive and well, and serving with the partisans in the Pripet. Would you not like to see your son again?"

"Only if I can do so with honour."

"What do you want?" His voice was almost a wail. "Are you not living in the most luxurious surroundings? Do you not have movies to watch and books to read? Have you not servants waiting on you, hand and foot? Do you not eat the best food and drink the best wine? What more *can* you want?"

"Apart from my freedom, I have what I want, Comrade Chairman. My honour. Nothing else is of the least importance."

He turned away from her and stamped to the door. She found she was holding her breath, because she had no idea what he was going to do next, whether he would carry out any of his threats. At the door he checked, and turned again. "Suppose I told you that I intend to leave this office and give orders that your husband is to be executed? What would you say to that?"

"I would say that you cannot have my husband executed, Premier Stalin, because your government gave him a safe conduct to come to Russia. You can, of course, have him murdered. You are good at having people murdered. But be sure the world will find you out." He slammed the door behind him, and Priscilla could allow herself to fall across her bed. Oddly, she had no desire to weep, even if she might just have sealed Joseph's death warrant. But she felt utterly exhausted.

The snow, clouding down, lying feet thick in places, gave even Stalingrad a beauty, as long as one could forget what the snow was hiding. But the Russian soldiers were happy; they knew the beast was mortally wounded. Now it was only a matter of waiting for it to lie down. The counter-offensive, mounted north and south of the city, had met with little opposition from the satellite forces protecting the Sixth Army's wings. These Rumanians, Hungarians and Italians, even less than the Germans, were not equipped for survival, much less combat, in sub-zero temperatures, and they lacked the ideological fanaticism of their German masters. They had crumbled away into defeat and surrender. Paulus had been surrounded.

Yet he fought on, commanded to do so by Hitler, buoyed by the promise of supply by air, by the knowledge that Germany's greatest general, Manstein, was leading a relief force. But even Manstein had been unable to break through the encircling Russian Fronts, and the Luftwaffe had been unable to supply a tenth of what the Sixth Army needed, in food and munitions, to survive. And still they fought on. "One day," Chuikov said, "my people will discover that no one has fired at them for twenty-four hours. Then they will advance, and they will find that there is not a single German left alive. Is that not a great tragedy? Those men were a splendid fighting force, and they have been allowed to rot." He grinned at Joseph, and then at the faces of the officers seated round the mess table, securely and warm underground. "So, let us drink to Christmas and victory. I think we may get drunk tonight, Comrade American."

The chunky little soldier had grown on Joseph day by day. As had the men of Stalingrad. He had not of course been allowed to return across the river to the actual fighting; he had not recovered sufficiently from his wound to do that, as yet, even supposing Chuikov, who had assumed a personal responsibility for him, would have permitted it. His only downside was that he had heard not a word from Priscilla.

Chuikov assured him that his letter had been sent. And undoubtedly he was being optimistic in expecting a reply in such a place and at such a time. At least he could feel sure she was safe. And it had been, nonetheless, an enthralling two months. Which was now soon to end.

Meanwhile, toasts. He had become used to the Russian way of spending an evening drinking endless toasts. But tonight he had some of his own. "I give you a multiple toast," he offered, swaying to and fro. "Eisenhower and Montgomery, Torch and El Alamein."

There was a moment's silence from the gathering of officers, then Chuikov gave a great shout of laughter. "And why not? They are at least fighting. Now, Comrade American, if they had fought those battles and won those victories in France instead of the desert, it might have mattered."

"That'll follow!" Joseph asserted.

"We shall see." Chuikov blinked at the little man who had just entered the officers' mess. "Who the devil are you?"

The newcomer was wearing a belted overcoat and a fur hat rather than uniform, and carried a briefcase. "I am Commissar Bruitzov," he announced.

"Come to see the end of the show, eh? Here, have a drink."

"I will not drink, thank you, Comrade General."

Chuikov leaned forward to peer at him. "Are you a Russian?"

"Well, of course I am a Russian."

"And you do not drink? At Christmas? You are a spy! He is a spy!" he bellowed. "Hang him!"

The officers staggered to their feet. "And you are drunk," Bruitzov said. "You are all drunk," he added, disparagingly.

"It is the curse of the Russian army. Of Russia itself. I did not say I do not drink. I said I will not drink now. I have an urgent despatch for you, General."

Chuikov waved his hand to postpone the hanging, at least for the moment. "Give it to me, Comrade Commissar."

Bruitzov tapped his briefcase. "In private."

"Then it can wait."

"It is most urgent that I give it to you now."

"Do you think he means to assassinate me?" Chuikov asked at large. "If he does, don't forget to hang him."

His subordinates shouted their enthusiasm for that idea, as the General followed Bruitzov from the room. "Will he not report you all to the high command?" Joseph asked Colonel Limski, Chuikov's adjutant.

"He can report us to whoever he wishes," Limski said, pouring vodka. "The days of the commissars are done, my friend. It is the army and the people who rule Russia now. For that, we can thank the Fritzes, eh?"

Joseph wondered if he was right.

When Chuikov returned, he looked relatively sober. But, then, it was always difficult to be sure when the General was actually drunk. "Where is our friend, Comrade General?" Limski inquired.

"Looking for a ride back to Moscow," Chuikov said. Limski looked at Joseph, raising his eyebrows. "How drunk are you, Comrade American?" Chuikov asked.

"No more drunk than you, Comrade General."

"Then come outside."

It was Joseph's turn to raise his eyebrows. "Do you mean to assassinate *me*, Comrade General?"

Chuikov led him into the office adjoining the mess hall. "Why does Comrade Stalin hate you?"

Joseph shrugged. "Because I escaped from the gulag, I suppose. And then told the world what it was like."

"Then why did you come back to Russia?"

"It is my homeland. I wished to help it. To help you. To win your war. I have a safe conduct, signed by Commissar Ligachev."

Chuikov snorted. "Who is now dead! When last you came to Russia you had a safe conduct, signed by Commissar Trotsky. Did that protect you?" Joseph rubbed the back of his head. He needed to think, and it was difficult with the vodka clouding his brain. "That man was sent here to kill you," Chuikov said.

"Just like that?"

"That is how things happen in Russia, Comrade American. A tap on the arm, and one is never seen again."

"Then why have you sent him back to Moscow?"

Chuikov grinned. "Because I am not having any friend of mine murdered, even by order of the state. You are my friend, Comrade American. I like you!"

"Will this not bring you a lot of trouble?"

"Not while we are winning. Not while *I* am winning. And I am doing that. Afterwards . . . Well, as I have said before, I believe there will be a new dawning in Russia. But for the time being, I strongly recommend that you stay with my headquarters. That is the only way I can guarantee your life. You wish to stay, in any event, do you not?"

"I do, yes. But I will have to square it with my superiors. Am I allowed to tell them why?"

Chuikov shrugged. "They will not believe you. They will think you are shell-shocked, or suffering from paranoia. It is a common Russian disease. But you and I will advance together, to victory, eh?"

Five weeks later, on 2 February 1943, Paulus surrendered what was left of his Sixth Army. The Battle of Stalingrad was over, and the German Army had suffered the greatest defeat in its history.

* * *

Anna von Holzbach looked up from the paper she had been given to read. "Do you expect me to believe this, Major von Buelow?"

"As it is true, yes, Frau von Holzbach," Buelow said. "Do you deny any of the charges?"

Anna snorted. "Of course I do. They are utterly false!"

"My dear Frau von Holzbach, the comings and goings from this apartment have been recorded by the concierge. He has admitted, in fact, aiding and abetting you in carrying on these clandestine visits. He records that you were 'entertaining' a gentleman friend just after new year last year, on the night your husband returned from the Russian Front, and telephoned you a warning so that your guest could make his escape by the fire-stairs. Can you really hope to deny that this happened?"

"That bastard!" Anna muttered.

"Your husband certainly believes it. When he was shown this evidence, he was appalled. But as a German officer, there was only one course he could take."

"And who showed him this so-called evidence, Herr Major?"

"I am afraid it was my distasteful duty to have to do so, Frau von Holzbach."

"Your duty!" Anna sneered. "So, now I am to be divorced. Just like that. Me! Do you think I can be discarded like a worn-out glove? I am a Russian countess. I am the daughter of a prince. I will deny these charges, Herr Major. I will denounce Franz as a liar and a Peeping Tom. And in the first place, I shall return to Brest-Litovsk and confront my husband."

"That will not be possible, Frau von Holzbach."

"I cannot visit my husband, if I wish?"

"Brest-Litovsk is a war zone, and can only be entered with a permit. You have no permit, nor will you be granted one."

"Well!" Anna bridled. "You persist in assuming that you can treat me like dirt, Herr Major. But as I have reminded you, I am not dirt. I shall take my case to the Fuehrer."

Buelow gave a gentle cough. "Have you seen the Fuehrer recently, Frau von Holzbach?"

"Well . . . no. He is a very busy man. I understand this. What with Stalingrad, and the Americans landing in North Africa, I understand how busy he is. But he will always help me. He has said so."

"I do not think the Fuehrer intends to receive you again, Frau von Holzbach. With your permission, I shall speak bluntly. Apart from your . . . peccadilloes," Buelow went on, "I have been forced to present other information to Reichsfuehrer Himmler. These regard your racial origins."

Anna gasped. But she was a fighter. "I am the daughter of Prince Alexei Bolugayevski of Bolugayen."

"Your mother was Sonia Cohen. Not only was this lady a Jew, but she was a well-known Communist, the mistress of Leon Trotsky, no less. She has also recently returned to Moscow, with the agreement and indeed one might say at the invitation of the Stalinist regime. Thus she is obviously still a Communist, and therefore by definition an enemy of the Reich."

"And she has denounced me?" Anna was aghast.

"I do not think she even knows that you are alive," Buelow said.

"Then how . . .?"

"It is our duty to know all there is to know about people," Buelow explained. "That we have not interfered before is because it was General Heydrich's decision not to do so, and thus interfere with Colonel von Holzbach's career. But now that General Heydrich is dead, I have felt obliged to turn over the files to Reichsfuehrer Himmler. The Reichsfuehrer is appalled. But, like General Heydrich, he is concerned with the effects on morale, and indeed, society, were this lamentable business to be made public. Thus I am empowered to make this offer to you, Frau von Holzbach. Accept the divorce and the settlement your husband is offering you. Do not contest it in any way. And then, live very quietly, and nothing more will be heard of the affair."

Her mother, Anna recalled, had been faced with such a situation, and such an ultimatum, by her father. Mother had acquiesced. But Mother had acquiesced in so many shameful things. Anna's chin came up. "And if I defy you?"

"Then you will be sent to a concentration camp."

"You would not dare! Do you not suppose I will tell the world of it?"

"The world, Frau von Holzbach, does not believe much of what comes out of our concentration camps. Half of the world does not even believe they exist. I hope you will be sensible. Now I must bid you good day." He saluted and left. The papers remained on the table where he had placed them. Anna stared at them for some seconds, then she picked them up, threw them to the floor and stamped on them.

"I do not think you will have any further trouble from the lady, Herr Colonel," Buelow said. "I have frightened her very badly, and she must now accept her lot. If she does not, well then, her lot could be a good deal worse."

"You said she would not be harmed," Alexander snapped.

"She has not been harmed, Herr Colonel. Nor will she be harmed, as long as she behaves herself."

"You'll take a glass of schnapps?"

"Thank you, Herr Colonel, that would be very nice." Buelow watched Alexander himself go to the sideboard and pour, although there was a secretary in the room, seated primly, knees crossed, in a chair in the corner. Her name, he gathered, was Jutta. And she was obviously a good deal more than a secretary. He assumed this not only because she looked at Holzbach from behind her horn-rimmed glasses with total possession, or because she had not been told to fetch the drinks and was accepting one from her boss as if entitled to it, but also because of her bulging white shirt front, on which her tie lay like a ski jump, and her contrastingly slim hips and slender legs, accentuated by the black skirt and stockings; any man separated from his wife who employed such a woman and did not take her to bed would need his head examined, or some other portion of his anatomy. She was not terribly pretty, her features being somewhat blunt, and the glasses were off-putting, but one could always take the glasses off, and then release the crisp yellow hair from its tightly restraining bun.

"When will the divorce be final?" Alexander asked.

"It is final now, if you wish it, Herr Colonel." There was a faint stirring from the settee. But Buelow did not suppose Holzbach was such a fool as to marry this girl. "There was a less personal matter the Reichsfuehrer wished me to discuss with you, Herr Colonel. You have heard the news?"

"It is not very good, is it," Alexander said. He did not really wish to think about the war situation right now. He wanted to sit down and think about Anna, about all those years, about the guilt which gnawed at his mind, day and night. The fear, too. "You are quite sure my wife will not be harmed in any way?"

"You no longer have a wife, Herr Colonel. But I have said that she will not be harmed, as long as she behaves herself. The news I was talking about is this Russian claim that the so-called Group One has been reconstituted, and is again led by the woman known as the Red Maiden, Tatiana Gosykinya."

"Pure propaganda!"

"You reported that this Gosykinya was dead."

"Because she was. Is. I liquidated that entire group."

"You are saying that the Russians are lying about this?"

"I am saying that it is pure propaganda."

"There have been no incidents in this vicinity?"

"There have been incidents, Herr Major, as you well know. But they have been isolated and of very little importance. I shoot ten hostages when one of my men is murdered."

"At that rate you will soon run out of hostages," Buelow suggested, slyly.

"I cannot be held responsible for individual acts of madness by these sub-humans," Alexander protested. "If, as you suggest, Herr Major, I run out of hostages, then I shall also have run out of would-be partisans. They are one and the same, at various times. Now I have a question for you to put to the Reichsfuehrer: why am I still stuck in this hole? I am a fighting soldier with a distinguished record. It seems to me, with what has happened at Stalingrad, that the Reich needs every fighting soldier it has to be at the front, fighting the Russian army, not shooting or hanging girls and boys out for a dare."

Buelow nodded. "I will report your request for a transfer, Herr Colonel. As to whether it will be successful . . . there was the matter of publicly exposing the body of this Red Maiden . . ."

"What am I supposed to do? Produce a bag of mouldering bones?"

"That would be better than nothing," Buelow agreed.

Elaine and Christina stood on the edge of the new encampment – created much farther into the swamp than the original camp, and thus more difficult of access by either friend or foe – and watched the partisans streaming through the trees. She and Christina were the only two left in the camp. Christina was regarded as too old, too weakly feminine, to take part in any raid. There were over a hundred of them now, men and women – or there had been more than a hundred when they had set off. Elaine found she was counting, at the same time as holding her breath. But there were at least a hundred people coming towards her. "Gregory!" She ran forward.

Gregory was starting to grow a beard now, although he too was not yet 20. He carried his weapons like the most experienced brigand. He grinned at her. "He's back there. He's all right."

"Was it successful?"

"Successful? We blew two bridges, destroyed a quarter of a mile of track."

She hugged him, looked past him, at Alex. He was clearly exhausted, but was walking quite freely. Elaine released Gregory, and ran to him. "A success!"

"Tremendous." He hugged and kissed her. He was on a high. They all were. "But we have work to do. There are wounded."

Several were being carried on litters. Long forgotten were the original, unacceptable requirements. Elaine led the way back into the camp, unrolled her bag, prepared her instruments. She was almost out of anaesthetic, and very short on antiseptic. But she was used to that now, to conditions she would unhesitatingly have rejected in Boston, or even in Moscow. "You should rest," she told Alex, and he knelt beside her.

"There are a good dozen," he said.

"She can manage," Tatiana said. "And she is right, your hand is not steady enough while you are this tired."

Elaine looked up. Tatiana certainly looked tired. But her face wore the savage delight of success. For her, life was the war and the blood of life was the killing of Germans. She had not ever, so far as Elaine knew, considered an end to this unearthly existence. "I believe I am to congratulate you, Comrade Commissar," she said.

"Congratulate me when this war is won, Comrade Doctor. Attend to this wound first."

Elaine gulped as Olga was laid on the ground before her. They had tended to avoid each other since that day by the pool of freezing water. Now Olga's face was twisting with pain, and her trousers were soaked in blood. "How bad is it?" Elaine asked.

"We are waiting for you to tell us," Tatiana pointed out. The partisans crowded round to watch as Elaine released Olga's belt and pulled down her trousers. Along with her anaesthetics and antiseptics, she had long abandoned any hope of privacy, for either herself or her patient; the partisans were fascinated by her work, partly sensually, partly ghoulishly, and partly because they knew that the next time it might be themselves lying there.

"Have you nothing to give her?" Tatiana asked.

"What I give her depends on what I have to do to her," Elaine said.

"Well, vodka, at any rate." Tatiana snapped her fingers, and Shatrav held the flask to Olga's lips; she gulped noisily.

Elaine removed the undergarments, and then the rough bandage which had helped to stem the bleeding, now she sighed with relief; the bullet had lodged in the fleshy part of the left thigh, but had not severed the artery. "Hold her," she said.

Willing hands grasped Olga's arms and legs; Tatiana herself held her thighs, her shoulder brushing Elaine's as the bullet was extracted. Olga screamed and attempted to writhe, but was helpless. Then she screamed again as Elaine poured raw antiseptic into the wound, then slowly subsided as Elaine re-bandaged the wound and pulled her clothes into place. "Will she live?" Tatiana asked.

"Hopefully. But she must rest for several days. She has lost a lot of blood."

"We must all rest for several days," Tatiana said. "Now these."

There was one other woman and eight men needing attention. Two of the men were seriously wounded. Elaine worked slowly and carefully, wondering what someone like Dr Haggard would say if he could watch her moving from patient to patient with blood-stained, unwashed hands? In fact, she wondered where Dr Haggard actually was, now? "I would like a drink of vodka," she said, when the task was completed.

"And you shall have one," Tatiana promised. "You are a very good surgeon, Comrade Doctor. When you have finished your work."

"You mean there's more?"

"A simple job." Tatiana waved her arm, and a man wearing a German uniform was forced forward by the eager partisans. He was a young man; Elaine would have said he was not out of his teens. His hair was yellow, his face not unhandsome but rendered ugly because of his fear. But as far as she could see at a glance, he was unhurt.

"What is the matter with him?" she asked.

"Nothing. We brought him back here to amuse ourselves. To amuse yourself, Comrade Doctor. Prepare him," Tatiana commanded.

The boy screamed in terror as he was thrown to the ground and his trousers and drawers pulled down to his knees. "Is he not well endowed?" Tatiana asked. "Now you can cut it, and them, off. Do not worry with anaesthetic. We wish to hear him scream."

Elaine drew a sharp breath. "I'm sorry," she said. "I'm here to heal, not kill."

Tatiana smiled. "He will not die from being castrated. He will die afterwards when we hang him. Now do it." She drew her revolver and presented the muzzle to Elaine's temple. "Do it or die. Then I will do it for you."

Chapter 13

The Prisoner

Elaine knelt in the shallow water and washed her hands again and again. There was movement all around her, but she was not aware of it. At least the dreadful screaming had stopped; the mutilated body was dangling from a tree. But the screaming would never stop for her. It would ring in her ears for the rest of her life, over and over again. Just as her hands would never be clean, no matter how often she washed them. Amazingly, she had not vomited. It was as if her guts were composed of cast iron.

What would she tell her grandchildren? "What did you do in the war, Grandma?"

"Not a lot. But I cut off a man's balls while he screamed and begged."

The only solution was not to have any grandchildren.

"Did you enjoy it?" Elaine half turned her head, then looked into the water again. It was not very clear water, but she could make out the form of the woman standing behind her. "You are too civilised," Tatiana said. "But I suppose that goes for all Americans. I would like to visit America, after the war."

"You'd find it kind of dull," Elaine muttered.

Tatiana smiled and knelt beside her. "I would never find it dull. I would visit you. Would you not have lots to show me, as I have had lots to show you, here in the swamp? And then, we would have so much to remember. Do you not suppose we might have a great deal more to remember?"

Elaine continued to stare at the water, and then felt Tatiana's fingers on her arm. She did not turn her head. "You may be the commissar, Tatiana, but so help me God, if you lay another finger on me I am going to kill you. Remember, you've taught me how to do it."

The fingers fell away and Tatiana stood up. "You are a silly woman," she remarked. "I feel very sorry for you."

That night Elaine slept alone; Alex had been summoned to the sleeping bag of the Commissar.

Alex panted and gasped his way to orgasm; but so did the woman. Woman! Tatiana was not yet 20, and he was all but 30. But when it came to sex, he was a child in her arms. Or, he reckoned, any other aspect of life – or death. Most importantly, death.

It was tempting to suppose that the awful events of the past two years had made her so. That she had been a sweet virgin of 18 when she had been so brutally raped by the Germans, seen her friends destroyed, and been forced to kill, herself, in order to survive. That in the process of surviving, and of being made into a national heroine by the Soviet propaganda machine, she had lost all humanity, in its higher sense, and had become nothing more than an animal, however intelligent, however ruthless, however feminine. Now she would suck him into that nether world she ruled so successfully. And there was no way he could resist her. She was his commanding officer. She was the queen, the goddess of the swamp, and of their lives. But there was no way he *wanted* to resist her. If he was captured by the Germans tomorrow, and a noose hung round his neck, he would face them with contempt, because he would think, What can you know of life and death, of love and desire, when you have never been held in Tatiana Gosykinya's arms?

But where did that leave Elaine? Poor, helpless Elaine, who

had willingly followed him – or had she not led him? – into this twilight existence, and was now as helpless as himself. His year in the swamp beside her, his understanding of her enormous depths of courage and resilience, and above all, his appreciation of the way in which she had kept herself aloof from the bestiality that had slowly overtaken all of them, had made him understand her true value. She might never have been a princess, but she was in every way worthy of being the wife of a prince. His wife. If they survived. And if she still wanted him!

So what do I do? Elaine wondered. I am sunk in the deepest pit of hell, with no way out. The next day Alex had tried to explain. "I should never have allowed you to come here," he said, seeking her out and leading her away from the group for some privacy.

"Did you know what it would be like?" she said.

"I had an idea. You know, I don't believe any human being is too far removed from the caveman. After all, it's only been a few hundred generations, and when you think how little physical change mankind has undergone in those generations, it's absurd to suppose he would have undergone a bigger mental change. So he's accumulated a lot of knowledge which he doesn't really know how to use, and he's developed a lot of fine ideas, which he can only really accept in the abstract. And inside he's still a caveman. Wars bring that out."

"Quite the philosopher!" Elaine said. "Was she good?"

"Do you really want me to answer that?"

"Yes," she said fiercely.

"She was . . . uninhibited. And hungry."

"I would say that sums her up. So, I guess . . ." she gave a little shrug.

"Because I was summoned to the bed of our queen? Because she is that, you know, Elaine. That can't make any difference to us."

"You reckon? You could've said no."

"And risk being sent on some kind of suicide mission because I'd put her back up?"

"She wanted me, first, you know," Elaine said. "And I said no." Alex stared at here in consternation.

"What's upsetting you?" Elaine asked. "That she wanted me at all, or that I refused her?"

"I would say the next time she comes at you, say yes."

"The idea gives you a kick, is that it?"

"Listen, Elaine, the name of this game is survival. Survival until it is all over. Until we can pick up the mainstream of our lives again. You and me, Elaine. Together."

"Alex," she said. "This isn't ever going to be all over. Not for us."

So what the hell? she thought. If you can't beat them, join them. But in her own way. Whatever plans Alex might have for their future, he was lost to her in their present; this was made abundantly clear as he spent almost every night with Tatiana. They still worked side by side on the wounded every day, but they spoke little.

So, if she wants a fight, she can have one, Elaine thought. Both of them. Carefully she renewed the dressing round Olga's thigh, having coated the wound with iodine. "You're about as good as new," she said.

Olga, as usual, had been watching her with that peculiar intentness of hers. They were not alone, but were to one side of the hut, and could not be overheard if they spoke quietly enough. "I am glad," she said. "I would not like to miss the next raid."

"Your leg will not be strong enough to take part in a raid for at least a month," Elaine told her. And reported that to Tatiana.

"That is a nuisance," Tatiana said, visiting the patient. "Well, Olga, you will just have to stay and command the camp, this time." She was planning another vast raid in quick succession to the last. "Hit the enemy while he's hurting," she declared. She now commanded 120 partisans, and they had all the guns and grenades and explosives they needed. They even had machine-guns. All partisan units had been commanded to increase their activities with the commencement of summer, for Russian intelligence had learned that the Germans were concentrating a vast panzer force south-east of Kiev, which could only mean an attempt to regain the ground, both physical and moral, that they had lost following the catastrophe of Stalingrad. Therefore the maximum disruption was required behind their lines.

Tatiana made her dispositions with her usual efficiency. And again as usual she left only the three women, Christina, Olga and Elaine, and the five wounded who had not yet sufficiently recovered, in the camp; Bebrikov had been killed. "We may be gone some time," she said. "But you may be sure we will achieve a great success." She gazed at Olga and Elaine. "Enjoy yourselves," she remarked.

Almost as if she knows what I have in mind, Elaine thought, knowing she was flushing with anticipated guilt. Alex was of course accompanying the Commissar. "I think she regards me as her private physician," he said when he came to say goodbye.

"She certainly regards you as her private something," Elaine agreed.

"I don't think now is the time for us to quarrel," he said, gently.

"I'm not quarrelling." She kissed his cheek. "Take care, you big oaf." She watched them tramp off through the trees.

"Are you going to have his child, after the war?" Olga asked.

"That was the idea, once."

"What changed your mind? Not because he is sleeping with Tatiana?"

"You wouldn't say that's a reason?"

"Every woman should have at least one child," Olga said.

"It does not really matter who the man slept with before – the mother that matters." Elaine looked at her in astonishment; she had never expected to hear that philosophy from Olga. Olga actually flushed, slightly. "Oh, I mean to do that. I wish to be a mother. But being married has nothing to do with what I really enjoy best."

"I guess it doesn't," Elaine said.

The two women gazed at each other. "Do you know, it is over a year since I first wanted you," Olga said.

"I know," Elaine said.

"But you did not want me."

"I guess . . . well, it's not something I have been brought up to."

"But now you wish to. To get your own back on Alexei and Tattie?"

She was too discerning. So there was no use in pretending. "I guess. But . . . also to, well . . . find out what it's like."

Olga smiled. "If you are not careful you might find yourself enjoying it."

"Well," Elaine said. "That's up to you, isn't it."

Olga felt in her pocket and produced her cake of soap. "You see, I have kept this especially for us. To share."

"They struck here, and here, and here, Herr Colonel." Clausen indicated the places on the map. "Four lengths of line torn up; the road detonated in two places."

"Casualties?" Alexander asked.

"We lost twenty-five men, with three missing. I very much fear they were captured by the partisans."

"And the partisans?"

"Lost seven dead. We took no prisoners."

"That is not a very good rate of exchange," Major Pritwitz commented.

"What is so infuriating is that we do not seem able to do anything about them," Clausen complained. "We thought we had wiped them out last year. But now they are back. They strike, and then disappear again into that morass. We shoot hostages, and it does no good. My men are suffering badly in morale, Herr Colonel. And with all the other news . . ."

Alexander knew what he meant. The total defeat of the German and Italian forces in North Africa, the invasion of Sicily, all the rumours about the coming invasion of France . . . and the steady withdrawal of German forces in Russia following the Stalingrad debacle. The last was what mattered most, because it was here in Russia that the war would be won or lost. But he still did not doubt that it would be won.

"One cannot expect unbroken success in war, Clausen," he said. "There have been setbacks. There will no doubt be others. But this summer should clarify the matter here. I can tell you in confidence that the Fuehrer is about to launch another huge invasion of European Russia, just over there, to regain all the ground we have lost because of the treachery of Paulus." He gestured at the map, at the country to the south-east of the Marshes. "He is assembling the greatest tank army in history, and he will knock the Red Army out of existence."

Pritwitz's expression remained sceptical; he had heard all this before. "So, it is a case of all German forces moving forward. I know we thought we had liquidated the partisans in the Pripet last year. We made a mistake. *I* made a mistake," Alexander added magnanimously. "But let us call that a reconnaissance in force. This summer we are going to do it right. Now we know what we are up against, and who we are up against. A few hundred scarecrows, nothing more. We have at our disposal four thousand men, and I have asked, and been given, the use of all of them. It is already summer. The rain has virtually ceased. We will give it another week for the ground to firm up, then we will sweep that marsh from one end to the next, slowly, step by step and bush by bush. We will slaughter every living human being that we find in there. We shall destroy these vermin, utterly and irrevocably. Major Pritwitz, I wish your dispositions on my desk tomorrow morning." Jutta clapped.

*   *   *

Alexander sat at his desk, studying the dispositions suggested by Pritwitz. He intended to lead this seek-and-destroy mission himself. Now it was simply a matter of allotting the subordinate commands. He looked up as the door opened. "Ah, Clausen. Now, I know I scheduled the advance into the Pripet for next week. But as I am sure that has been leaked, and probably to the partisans as well, I intend to bring it forward. We will commence tomorrow. You will instruct Major Pritwitz to put everyone on the alert, and give orders that anyone seen leaving the town is to be shot on sight." He leaned back in his chair, frowning. "What the devil is the matter with you?"

Clausen looked ready to explode. "They have struck again, Herr Colonel. There has been a massive raid on the line north of the Marshes. They have attacked a munitions train and blown it up, torn up the line for several miles. We have suffered heavy casualties."

"Bastards!" Alexander said.

"I have given orders for all operations to be suspended, and all available men to be mobilised and sent up the line."

"You have done *what*?" Alexander snarled.

"Well . . . they need help out there."

"Cannot you see, Clausen, that this is exactly what the partisans wish us to do? Their whole strategy is based on our reactions to their attacks. Our *over*-reactions, Clausen. On our rushing to and fro like chickens with our heads cut off. Well, this time we are not going to oblige them. Cancel your orders immediately, and reinstate the orders for tomorrow morning. We move out at dawn."

"But . . . there will be no one there!"

"That will be all to the good. We will scour the Marshes while they are scouring the countryside. We know they always return to their hideaway. Well, this time, when they do, they will find us waiting for them. We will make a slight change in our dispositions. I will take a thousand men into the Marshes from the west. You will take another thousand round to the north-west, and advance from there. Major Pritwitz will hold the remainder in reserve here. When the partisans return, and are engaged, Pritwitz will move up behind them. This time they will have no alternative but to retreat into open country. And once we have them in open country, we have them, Clausen. This time they will dance to our tune, not we to theirs."

Am I damned? Elaine wondered. Well, if I am, then hell is a pretty pleasant place. Because nothing physical had changed. She looked at the same trees, the same water, listened to the same swamp noises. This *was* hell, the hell into which she had so carelessly wandered. But for the moment it was populated by only one devil, and it was she who made it paradise.

She raised herself on her elbow to look down at her lover's sleeping face. Olga was quite remarkably beautiful. Because of the natural solemnity, almost grimness, of her features, this was not apparent to the casual glance. One had to get to know Olga, to see her smile or, better, to watch her in the throes of passion, to realise the beauty that lay beneath the mask of tragic foreboding. Olga certainly had that; she lived for the present because she evaluated the future in the most sombre colours. While her figure was perfection; that had been easy to tell on first acquaintance. And now both face and figure were hers. What an amazing thought! She had never felt that she possessed another human being. Certainly she had never *possessed* Alex. But for all of the two years she had been in the Pripet Olga had been searching, and perhaps for a long time before that. Now she had found what she wanted.

Elaine slid out from beneath the blanket and tip-toed to the door; in the summer heat she slept naked, as did Olga. In the far corner, Christina snuffled contentedly in her sleep.

Christina was a dear. She was well aware of the relationship that had sprung up between the lieutenant and the doctor, but it was not her business to criticise. Perhaps she envied them. They did not bother with setting a sentry; they knew the Germans could not get at them without making sufficient noise to alert them. Besides, the enemy would presently be fully occupied trying to catch up with Tatiana.

Elaine went outside and into the bushes, then returned and stood on the edge of the pond and stretched. It felt delightfully wanton to be standing naked in a forest. Had it not been for the wounded men in the hospital hut she thought she would not bother to dress at all, but live out this surely brief idyll to its fullest extent. But as the men were there . . . She turned back to the hut, then heard the sounds of someone coming through the swamp, not far away. One or at the most two. She reacted without hesitation, reached the hut in four strides, and armed herself with a sub-machine-gun. Both Olga and Christina awoke and did the same, without wasting the time to ask questions. A man emerged into the clearing; his clothes were torn, and he looked exhausted. "Stop right there!" Olga commanded.

The man checked, looking left and right, panting, trying to decide where the voice had come from. "Are there others?" Olga asked.

"No," he gasped. "There is only me."

Olga went outside, Elaine and Christina following. The man goggled at the two naked women. Christina was dressed; Christina was always dressed. "You are from Brest-Litovsk," Olga said. "What have you to tell us?"

The man licked his lips. "I am so thirsty . . ."

"There is water." Olga gestured at the pond. "You can have vodka when you have told us why you are here."

"The Germans are coming." The man lay down on the edge of the water and drank.

"Go on," Olga invited.

"They are coming next week. A week today. The entire garrison of Brest-Litovsk, commanded by Colonel von

Holzbach himself. He is going to sweep the entire marsh from end to end, if it takes him all summer. Inch by inch, until every partisan is killed or captured."

"How do you know this?"

"Their men sleep with our women. Orders were given that anyone trying to leave the town without a pass was to be shot on sight. Four of us tried. The other three were shot." He had finished slaking his thirst, and knelt, staring at them.

"Give him some vodka, Christina," Olga said, and went into the hut to dress.

Elaine followed, and also pulled on her clothes. "Do you believe him?"

"We can't afford not to. Listen, I will go after the group. I am strong enough now. They must be warned, and Tatiana must make her dispositions."

"Shouldn't I go?" Elaine asked.

Olga smiled. "Yes, you should. But can you? Would you be able to find them?"

Elaine sighed. "I suppose not."

"Besides, you are the doctor, not me. Do not worry. I will find them, and return, well within the week. Four days at the most. You stay here with Christina, and nurse those men."

"And this man?"

Olga gave another grin. "He can't go back. He will have to stay with you. Enjoy him."

She had to be joking! Peter Petrovich was a most unprepossessing character. However, he seemed anxious to please, and willing to work, which meant that she and Christina had less to do. Elaine decided to let him sleep in the hut with them that night, if only as some protection from the mosquitoes swarming out of the stagnant water. She had a curious sense of elation; Olga had left her in command. Christina certainly did not seem to mind, and it was the very first time she had been in control of events. Not that there were any events to control, or indeed any people apart from the old woman and the man and the five wounded. But it was a pleasant feeling.

She slept heavily, was up as usual at dawn to wash, standing on the edge of the water, as usual, enjoying the sunlight that was already piercing the foliage and listened to the distant roaring of engines.

Distant! Only a few miles, to the edge of the swamp. She dashed back inside and woke the others. "You said a week!" she shouted at Peter Petrovich.

"They said a week," he protested, following her outside.

"What are we to do?" Christina asked.

Elaine bit her lip. Now she could hear the beating of drums and the blowing of bugles; the Germans were conducting this as if it were a shoot. But to them it was, a shoot. She could think of nothing to do, save what they had done last year, and hope to be undiscovered. She could only hope that this early sweep might turn out to be a blessing in disguise, as the Germans would surely have come and gone before Tatiana and the main body returned. But what about the wounded? Three of them could move by now, and were leaving their hospital hut to discover what was happening. "Take everything you can carry," she told them. "And then scatter into the trees. Keep going east." They exchanged glances, and looked at their bandages. "I'm sorry," Elaine said. "There is nothing else we can do. When the Germans have gone, I'll be able to tend you again."

They nodded, with resignation, Christina with grim determination, Peter Petrovich with some delight; there was a great deal of useful materiel lying around the camp. Her command, Elaine thought. At the first crisis she was telling them all to fend for themselves. But there was nothing else to do. "What about us?" asked Vladimir. He was one of the two who were still too weak to move. Elaine bit her lip. They had to die. She had to kill them, because she was their commander. That was what Tatiana would have done. Or Olga. But could she do it? Vladimir saw her dilemma. "Leave us two grenades," he said. "One each. Please, Comrade Doctor."

Elaine was on the verge of tears. "I am so terribly sorry!"

Vladimir shrugged. "You have kept us alive longer than we had expected. Now you must hurry."

A fine commander, Elaine thought, taking orders from her own men. But now all she wanted to do was get far away. She filled a pack for herself with food, stuffed in as much of her medical supplies as she could, belted on a revolver with cartridges, and took a sub-machine-gun with two spare drums of ammunition. She could carry nothing more. "Well," she said to the others. "We'll see each other when this is over. Off you go."

The five of them, each even more heavily laden than herself, went into the trees, while she gave Vladimir and his companion a grenade each, and saluted them. Then she went outside and looked around. There were some explosives left, and presumably if she were a properly trained guerilla she would be able to set up some kind of a booby trap for when the Germans reached the camp, but she had no idea how to go about it. My command, she thought again. The briefest command in history. She listened to shots, and instinctively unslung her gun. But the shots had come from the west, and her people had gone east. The Germans were either firing at each other or an animal. But it was time to go.

She studied her compass, decided to head north-west, simply because that was the direction in which Olga had gone, yesterday. She made quite good progress, picking her way through the various ponds and bogs. Some birds were disturbed by her progress, but then all the birds were disturbed by the racket the Germans were creating; she did not suppose the Germans would know whether it was themselves or an enemy who was doing the disturbing. But she was carrying more weight than ever before in her life, and after a couple of hours, she needed to sit and rest. It was now mid-morning and quite hot, and very pleasant, with the sun streaming through the trees. But for the sense that she was being followed she thought she would be quite happy. Then she heard another shot, from quite close at hand – and it had come from the north of her.

She sat up, unslinging her gun. If that fool Peter Petrovich had lost his nerve . . . but he had gone to the east, not the north! She saw movement, and rolled into the shelter of the nearest bushes, watched a group of German soldiers coming through the trees. Oh, my God, she thought. Her heart seemed to slow. She had thought they were all behind her. But these must have come in from the north-west. There was quite a lot of noise behind her as well and she realised that she was trapped. But surely, if she just lay hidden, they would go away again. Then, above the cacophony, she heard the barking of the dogs.

Elaine had read of people's blood running cold, and dismissed it as novelists' hyperbole. But now she felt her entire body seeming to turn to ice, realised her teeth were chattering with fear, had to clamp her jaws together. What to do? Stand up, sub-machine-gun blazing, and go out like a heroine? But it was only worthwhile being a heroine if people knew about it. She wouldn't last a moment, and she would be left, a nameless rotting corpse in the swamp. And besides, she didn't want to die. Not now. Not when life was just beginning to promise again.

But if she lay there and were taken alive . . . could anything Tatiana and Olga had told her of the way the Germans treated their prisoners be true? She had the evidence of her own eyes that Valya had been crucified. But there was a glimmer of hope. Something Tatiana had let slip. "They treat us like shit because they think all Slavs are sub-human," she said. That was tragic, but she was not a Slav. Anyone could see that. The yelping of the dogs was coming closer. If she didn't do something, now, they would be upon her, tearing her to pieces. If she was going to die, she wanted it to be in one piece. Elaine drew a deep breath, laid the gun on the ground, and stood up.

She was seen immediately, and rifles turned towards her. "Kamerad!" she shouted. It was about the only German word she knew. She drew another deep breath, held her hands high above her head, and walked towards them.

They were chattering to each other, and now a sergeant stepped forward, staring at her as she came closer yet. Then he said a single word. She had no idea what it was, but it didn't sound the least friendly. "American," she said. "I am American. Also, I am a doctor."

He said the word again, and when she still didn't respond, made a gesture to his men. Before Elaine understood what was happening she had been seized by her arms and legs and thrown to the ground, to be pinned there on her face while other hands tore at her clothes and body. My God, she thought: I am being raped. Just like that. Breathless, she didn't know whether to scream or not, and then realised that, at least in this first instance, they were more intent upon searching her. Her belts and pack were pulled off, the contents of her pack scattered on the ground.

She spat earth from her mouth. "That's good medicine," she protested.

The sergeant appeared to resent her comment; he knelt beside her, thrust his fingers into her hair, and pushed her face into the earth, to and fro, as if he were squeezing half a lemon. She panted and choked on the dust, and then was able to spit it from her mouth and blow it from her nostrils as he released her and she could gasp for breath. Obviously speaking was impossible until she found someone who understood English. She made to push herself up, and he put his boot between her shoulder-blades and pushed her flat again. Once more she was winded, and now she felt hands on her waist belt, releasing it and pulling down her trousers. She couldn't stop herself screaming "No! You can't do this to me! I am not Russian. I am American!"

They rolled her on her back as they pulled her trousers

right off. "No!" she begged, and hated herself as the tears started from her eyes. "American," she moaned.

Someone was pulling off her boots, and she was naked from the waist down. She had a curious feeling that the whole area of her body between her navel and her knees, the exposed part, no longer belonged to her, and yet she could feel it as if it were swelling and about to burst. But the sergeant was also interested in her upper half, and was tearing open her blouse to expose her breasts. "Oh, God!" she gasped. "Oh, God!" she shrieked as men pulled her legs apart and one knelt between.

And her prayer was answered. By God? Or the devil? Her brain was filled with such screaming terror and disgust that she had not heard the words, but suddenly she was released, the men around her standing to attention. The man who had been going to have first go at her stood, absurd, with his pants about his ankles and a huge erection. Elaine blinked tears from her eyes and stared at an officer, crisply handsome in his black uniform and high-peaked cap. He was looking at her with some interest, and no evidence of pity. Well, she thought, if I am to be raped I would rather it was by an officer. Then he spoke, in Russian, "Where are your companions?"

Elaine sat up. There didn't seem a lot of point in trying to conceal her private parts, but she drew up her knees and hugged them. "I don't know. I am alone."

"Do not prevaricate with me, woman, or I shall give you back to my men. You are a partisan."

"I am an American doctor," Elaine said. "I have been caring for the partisan wounded, yes. But I am not one of them." Pray God, she thought, that he does not know about the man I emasculated.

"It is a nice day," he said, without warning, in English.

"It is too warm," she replied, also in English.

He stared at her, and then, deliberately, at her body. He carried a swagger stick, and this he now placed between her knees and forced her legs apart. She let them go. She felt quite weak, terribly aware of all the eyes staring at her, of all the lust with which she was surrounded. "You are filthy," the officer remarked. "You are covered in dust."

"That is because your men rolled me in it," she said.

"Dress yourself."

No one was going to help her, or stop looking at her. Elaine had to turn on to her knees to reach her clothing, and stand up to pull it on. She sat down again to lace up her boots. The captain gave orders in German and two men grasped her arms and pulled her up. Her hands were then taken behind her back and her wrists bound together. Then they urged her through the trees, to the west, away from their comrades, and the officer.

They walked and splashed their way for several hundred yards. Without the use of her arms for balance, Elaine stumbled several times, and would have fallen had they not caught her arms and held her up. Then they stopped, and looked over their shoulders. Their comrades had faded from sight, and they were quite alone. And although Elaine couldn't tell what they were saying, she knew they were talking about her. They are going to rape me, she thought. Oh, my God! And there was absolutely nothing she could do about it. Her knees gave way and she sank down while one of the men grinned at her. He was the one who wanted to do the raping. The other wasn't so sure, and had produced a whistle, with which he clearly meant to identify themselves to any of their comrades in the vicinity.

Now the argument grew quite heated, while Elaine knelt between them, scarce daring to breathe. Then the non-rapist apparently won the argument, for he gave a shrill blast on his whistle. But the other was not to be entirely denied, and he unbuttoned Elaine's blouse again to slide his hands inside and finger her breasts, drawing the nipples time and again across his palms. God, she thought, I'm going to be sick! Or have hysterics. Then he released her, and there was a crashing in the undergrowth, and more men appeared. At their head was a very distinguished-looking officer, a

Colonel from his uniform and his demeanour. He gazed at her, frowning, while the men did some explaining. "You say you are an American?" he asked in English.

"Yes," she said. "Please . . . I am a doctor."

He jerked his head, and the two men lifted her to her feet. Her blouse was still open, and once again she was terribly aware of being stared at.

"Come," the officer said.

She was led back to the encampment, showed the two corpses lying with their chests blown away. "You did this?" the Colonel asked.

"No. They did it to themselves. They did not wish to be captured. Do you think you could untie my wrists?" He seemed a very civilised man, both in his speech and his demeanour.

"Why not? I am sure you are too intelligent to attempt anything foolish." He nodded to one of his aides, and the ropes holding Elaine's wrists were cut. Eagerly she rubbed her hands together, wincing at the pins and needles. "Now, go into that hut," he commanded. Elaine obeyed. She had to go on believing that he was as much of a gentleman as he appeared. "I am Colonel von Holzbach," he told her, when they were inside, and alone. "I am in command of this area. And you are . . .?"

"Dr Elaine Mitchell." She was still rubbing her hands together.

"You understand that even medical personnel can be considered as combatants, certainly in circumstances such as these?"

Elaine licked her lips. "I understand that I can be treated as a prisoner of war."

He smiled. "There are no prisoners of war where partisans are concerned, Dr Mitchell. Undress."

Oh, Lord, she thought. Not again! "I have already been searched, Colonel von Holzbach."

"I know. I wish to look at you." Elaine bit her lip to fight back a rising sense of panic. Then she took off her clothes, pausing when she was down to her drawers. "Everything," he commanded. She sighed, and slid them down to her ankles before stepping out of them. "You are filthy," he said.

"Well, your men rolled me in the dust," she explained. She had to try to be rational about what was happening. She would go mad otherwise.

"I hate filthy women," Alexander told her. "Go outside and bathe."

"In front of all your men?"

"Are you ashamed of your body? It is a good body. Let them enjoy it, while they can."

Elaine swallowed. "You mean it's not going to be around all that long?"

"That depends, Dr Mitchell, on what you have to say to me. When you have bathed, and washed your hair."

Elaine drew a deep breath, and stepped out of the hut. What had happened earlier had been a kind of kaleidoscope of horror, an outburst of angry energy, both by her and her captors. But this was cold-blooded humiliation, governed by fear. She knew she was trembling as she walked down to the water. Only yesterday she had done exactly this, in all the glory of her confident young womanhood. Now she was a frightened creature, knowing only that she was facing utter catastrophe.

Her appearance drew the men. They clustered on the water's edge to watch her go in, watched her scoop the water over her body, then her hair. I could rob them all, she thought. I could push my head beneath the surface and start breathing as hard as I can. But they would not let her drown, and the thought of being resuscitated by these grinning louts was worse than having to bathe in front of them. She soaked for several minutes, then stood up, water dripping from the hair plastered to her shoulders, from her breasts and her pubes, rolling down her thighs, and walked away from them, through a double line of soldiers, and up the sloping ground to the huts. Alexander stood in the hut doorway, watching her. "That is much better," he said. "Now you like what you are, a very handsome woman. And you have made my men happy. Now, come and make me happy."

Elaine stepped into the hut, and he closed the door. She turned to face him, forcing her hands to remain at her side. "I am a prisoner of war," she said. "Under the Geneva Convention . . ."

"Do you want to make me angry?" he asked, and stood immediately in front of her. She kept her eyes on his face, even when he suddenly caressed her breast. "Yes, you are my prisoner. No, you have no rights at all, Dr Mitchell. I can cut these off, if I choose." He gave a little squeeze, and she involuntarily stepped back. "Or I can hold lighted matches between your legs. Or I can pull out all of your fingernails and toenails. Or I can have you flogged to death. I can do any or all of those things, and there is no one going to stop me. Do you understand?"

Elaine gasped. She couldn't be hearing this. "So now, tell me what I wish to know. Question, you are a member of the partisan organisation known as Group One, commanded by a certain Tatiana Gosykinya. Correct?"

"Yes," Elaine said. She was too frightened to lie, and besides, at this stage there was no point. When she lied, it had to be a good one.

"And she is presently away raiding our lines of communication. Why were you left behind, by yourself?"

"I was not by myself. I was left behind to care for the wounded. You saw two of them. The others could move, and I told them to scatter into the swamp."

"That is very good. Now, when do you expect this Group One to return?"

Elaine took a deep breath. "They are not going to return."

Alexander frowned. "Why not?"

Elaine licked her lips. "Orders from Moscow. All the

partisan groups in the Pripet are to amalgamate into one large group, to strike at . . ." if only she had a better idea of Russia. "To strike at Pinsk."

"You expect me to believe that? If they are not coming back, why were you left behind?"

"I told you, to care for the wounded. As soon as they were all able to move, I was to lead them east to the concentration."

Alexander studied her for several seconds, while her breasts heaved with apprehension. "I think you are lying," he said at last. "You certainly look like someone who is lying. On the other hand, you could be telling the truth. But there is an easy way to find out." He opened the door, spoke in German. "Go outside," he told Elaine.

She hesitated. "May I get dressed?"

He smiled at her. "That would be to ruin your clothes, Doctor."

Elaine gasped as two of the men seized her arms. She was almost becoming used to such manhandling, but this time she felt it was going to be a more serious matter than a few sexual frolics, or even rape itself. She was marched across the clearing, again watched by the entire command, and made to stand against a tree, facing it. Her arms were carried round the bole and tied together. The rough bark ate into her flesh and she squirmed with discomfort. "Now," Alexander said, "I am going to beat you till you bleed. Who knows, your screams may bring your comrades to your aid."

Behind her, Elaine heard the snap of a whip.

Chapter 14

The Victors

"It has been more than a week now, Herr Colonel," Clausen said. "And not a sign of them. Perhaps the American woman was telling the truth."

"Meanwhile," Pritwitz said – the two majors always endeavoured to see Alexander together, his temper was so uncertain – "my men are rotting in that swamp, being eaten alive by mosquitoes." Alexander continued to stare at the report which had just arrived on his desk. On the first day of the great battle being fought around Kursk, the Russians claimed to have destroyed more than 500 German panzers. That had to be propaganda nonsense. What was disturbing was that the OKW was making no very strong denials. There had obviously been a disaster. And Kursk was not all that far from the Pripet, in terms of Russian distances. If the Russians were to come rolling in here . . . It made his blood run cold. And OKW was obviously anticipating something like that. Double all strongpoint garrisons, the message ran. All positions must be held to the last man, until our next, decisive, counter-attack can be launched. *Next, decisive, counter-attack!* Launched with what arms? Worst of all had been the orders from the general in Pinsk to transfer half his command to that city, as being nearer the Russian advance. He felt physically sick. "What are your orders, Herr Colonel?" Pritwitz persisted. "We must either continue our original plan, and sweep right through the swamp, or we must pull out."

The subordinate officers knew nothing of what was happening in the east, nor could they; morale was low enough as it was. "As the partisans obviously know of our plans," Alexander said, "to resume our sweep might be to march into a trap. Pull your men out, Major. I will have fresh orders regarding our dispositions ready for you tomorrow."

Pritwitz hesitated in surprise; he had expected to be given the command to resume the advance. Then he clicked his heels and saluted. "Heil Hitler!" He left the room.

"What will you do with the woman, Herr Colonel?" Clausen inquired. Alexander stroked his chin. "I think, in all the circumstances, Herr Colonel," Clausen ventured, "that she should be disposed of, quickly and quietly. Not only is she an American, but she is intelligent and articulate. Were she to survive she could make a good deal of trouble." He hesitated. "I would take care of the matter for you, Herr Colonel."

Because you would like to get your hands on her, Alexander thought. "I will let you know what I decide," he told him, and got up. Clausen saluted in turn, and held the door for his chief. He knew where Alexander was going, waggled his eyebrows at Jutta, patient in the outer office. But Jutta was not concerned; she knew her boss-cum-lover better than anyone.

Alexander went down into the cellars to look at the woman. There were no cells down here, just a large room with a ceiling supported by thick pillars. It made an ideal torture chamber, and Clausen had managed to assemble an impressive collection of instruments, calculated to frighten the life out of anyone. Almost anyone. Alexander had had no doubt at all that Elaine Mitchell had been terrified when she had been brought down here, her back and buttocks still bleeding from her whipping in the forest. Now she was sitting on the floor, chained to one of the pillars. She was naked, but her body was surprisingly unmarked, apart from the slowly fading weals. That was because he had not been able to bring himself to mark her. Now, when she heard the footsteps, she pulled her knees the more tightly against her body, and turned away from him. She did not have to look at him to know who it was.

She was a most attractive woman, although by no means beautiful, and by no means voluptuous; her breasts were too small, her hips too narrow. Her legs were splendidly long, but they were too thin. And of course, she was clean, because he had her bathed every morning – it was simply a matter of turning the hose on her; the floor, in fact, was still wet now from her morning's immersion. But she was also a symbol of the hell that raged in both his mind and his body, all the time. When he had first seen her, he had been inflamed with the purest lust. Again, not because of her looks, especially; the woman Valya and the girl Natasha had both been far more generously endowed. It had been, and remained, the aura of her. He had been able to tell right away that she was more intelligent even than the woman Valya. She would *know* what was happening, she would *feel* in a way that a sub-human Slav never could. He had known that he was going to have the most gloriously ghastly experience of his life, tearing from this woman the secrets of the swamp. It had even occurred to him that he could torment such a finely-tuned mind without actually laying a finger on her, a kind of hors d'oeuvre. "Do you know what I am going to do to you?" he had asked her.

"No," she had replied. "Why do you not just do it?"

Then he had been unable to stop himself from touching her, stroking her, caressing her breasts, squeezing her buttocks before abruptly stepping away from her, both because of the expression of contempt in her eyes, and because of the men standing around, watching him. And Jutta.

Jutta understood. "Why do you not bring her up here," she had said in the privacy of their bedroom.

"And fuck her to your heart's content. It's what you want to do, isn't it? I'd make sure she didn't resist you."

But Jutta was only capable of understanding part of the problem. He had never yet raped a prisoner. He had had his chance when they had been alone in that hut in the forest together; perhaps his men even supposed he had done it, then. But he had not. And to bring Elaine Mitchell up to his bedroom would be as obvious to everyone as if he were to take her here in the cell. Well, then, torture her to his heart's content. He had done *that*, often enough, to other prisoners. He had personally supervised the destruction of Natasha Renkova, as a human being. His men expected it of him. Clausen had stood at his shoulder, holding the alligator clips which would send the electricity coursing through Elaine's body and her screams echoing through the building. But she had stared at him as he had taken the first clip, and the stare had reached right down into the recesses of his soul, where once he had been a gallant gentleman fighting for the tsar. "Let her think about it for a while," he had told Clausen.

That had been a week ago, and Clausen was more puzzled than ever. So was Jutta. So, best to end it, quickly and cleanly, he thought, as Clausen had recommended. This woman, this so civilised, intelligent woman, had recreated his past. But he could not admit that past. Therefore she would continue to torment him until she died. His hand rested on his revolver holster, and she turned to look at him. Once again he was impaled on that gaze. Why? Because she had not wept and screamed when he had had her flogged. She had revealed amazing courage, great fortitude. But surely she would weep and scream if he inflicted more pain on her now. Would that not break the spell, make her the victim instead of himself? "Go away," Elaine said in a low voice. "Kill me, or go away."

* * *

"There is no one there," Shatrav reported. "No one alive."

"It may be a trap," Alex argued.

As usual, the partisans all looked at Tatiana to see her reaction. Immediately Olga had joined them, she had commanded them to pull back into the Marshes some distance farther to the east, while she had sent messengers to the other groups warning them of the impending sweep. That had been a week ago. Then the day following Olga's appearance her scouts had reported seeing large bodies of Germans approaching and entering the swamp. "That swine Peter Petrovich has betrayed us," Olga had snarled.

"Or the Germans fooled him," Tatiana said. "We will just have to sit it out."

"But Elaine! I told her to wait for my return, with orders from you."

"One of us must warn her," Alex had said.

"You would be caught and executed," Tatiana said. "Elaine is a sensible girl. She will know the Germans are coming, and bring those of her people who can move to us. She will be here tomorrow."

But she had not come. And now . . . "You say there are no living left?" Olga demanded of Shatrav.

The sergeant had gallantly carried out a personal reconnaissance. "All strung up in a row, they were," Shatrav said. "Christina, some chap I don't know, and three of the wounded. The other two had had the sense to blow themselves up."

"Were they mutilated?" Tatiana asked.

"Of course."

"And the Germans?"

"Are pulling out. All of them."

"But where was Elaine?" Olga asked.

"She wasn't there. I reckon they must have taken her alive. Maybe it was what she told them has caused them to withdraw."

"Oh, Jesus!" Alex muttered.

"We have to get her out of there," Olga said.

"That is being stupid," Tatiana declared. "She is gone. She should have killed herself. There is nothing we can do about her now." She looked at Alex. "I am sorry. But you know the rules."

Alex's shoulders hunched. To think of Elaine being interrogated by the SS . . . Elaine, who had always refused to accept that this world of brutal death and destruction was anything more than a nightmare, now forced to accept this . . . "I will get her out," Olga said.

"How do you propose to do that?" Shatrav inquired.

"That is my business. I will go into Brest-Litovsk and get her out. I will also make sure the Germans stay out of the Marshes. I will just need some special equipment."

"I will come with you," Alex said.

Olga shook her head. "You would be a nuisance. One person can do this, if she knows what she is about. Two is too many."

"You are stark, raving mad," Tatiana said. "I absolutely forbid it."

"You can either give me permission to go, or shoot me," Olga said. "Because I am leaving, now."

"Colonel . . ." Hans the batman was stammering with excitement and anxiety. "Herr Colonel, there is someone . . .!"

Alexander was out of bed in a moment, pulling on a dressing gown. As he went to the door Jutta instinctively handed him his Luger pistol. Alexander pulled the door open. "What the devil is the matter with you?" he demanded.

"A woman, Herr Colonel. She demands to see you."

"Demands?" Alexander was already halfway down the steps. "Who is this woman?"

"Her name is Tatiana Gosykinya."

Alexander checked in consternation. "Is this your idea of a joke, Hans?"

"It is the truth, Herr Colonel."

The front door was opened, and Alexander had reached

the foot of the steps. Standing in the centre of the porch there was certainly a young woman who filled Anna's description of the Red Maiden – tall, handsome, and with a wealth of curling black hair. She did not have Bolugayevska features, but she obviously took after her murderous father. To either side of her there stood one of the guards, rifles levelled. "Has that woman been searched?" he demanded.

"No, Herr Colonel. She . . ."

"If they lay a finger on me, I will blow this house up," Olga said, and opened her coat. Tied to the belt round the waist of her tunic were a dozen sticks of dynamite, and the revolver she carried in her right hand, the hammer already cocked, was resting with its muzzle on one of them, so that the removal of her finger would fire the gun – and detonate the charges.

Alexander swallowed, and instinctively took a step back. "What do you want?" he asked.

"To speak with you, Herr Colonel. Will you not let me in?"

"If she means to blow herself up, Herr Colonel . . ." Hans said urgently.

"I am not going to blow myself up," Olga assured him. "Unless any attempt is made to arrest me. But do remember that if I am shot, even if I am killed outright, I will release this hammer, and then we will all get together in Kingdom Come." She smiled at them.

Alexander licked his lips. "Come in," he said, and retreated farther into the house. Olga followed him, and looked at the stairs, where Jutta waited, wrapped in a dressing gown. "Leave," Alexander said. "Get out."

"No, no," Olga said, "I think your mistress should stay. If you do have to go, would you not like her to be with you?"

"What do you want?" Alexander asked again, while Jutta sat heavily down on the steps. The guards remained standing in the doorway, looking for some instruction from their commander, and getting none: Alexander could not take his eyes from Olga.

"You have a prisoner," Olga said. "An American doctor, Elaine Mitchell. I wish her released."

"Just like that?" He was starting to get his nerve back. "If I refuse, are you going to blow us all up? That will not save your doctor. That will in fact seal her death warrant."

Olga took a sharp breath; she had at least learned that Elaine was still alive. "I understand that. I will offer you a bargain. Me for her." Alexander stared at her. "It is a very good bargain for you," Olga pointed out. "She is of no value to you. She knows nothing of my plans or even of the forces at my disposal. She is a doctor, nothing else. Nor is she actually guilty of fighting against you, of killing Germans. She has never accompanied me on any of our raids. She is just a doctor. Whereas I am the Red Maiden. Is it not I you have been waging war against, for the past year?"

"You are offering me your life, for hers? Why?"

"I am her lover."

"You . . .?" Alexander's mouth fell open in consternation.

Jutta gave a short laugh. "You must love her very much."

"I do."

Alexander licked his lips. "So, if I let her go, you will surrender yourself to me."

Olga smiled. "I am not exactly a fool, Herr Colonel. You will bring Dr Mitchell up from your cells, and you and I will drive her to the end of the road to the Marshes, and there she will be set free. Once she is free and has gone into the swamp, I will surrender myself."

"Now you are taking *me* for a fool," Alexander said. "What you mean is, you are trying to lead me into a trap. No doubt your people are waiting for me, on the edge of the marsh."

"My people are not waiting for you, Colonel. This is between you and me."

"You expect me to believe that?" But as he gazed at her, he did believe that. Then she must have another plan. "I see," he said. "But you are determined to commit suicide as soon as you regard your lover as safe, then you will blow yourself to bits, and me with you. I do not like that idea. So here is what we will do. I will release Dr Mitchell, and as you say, we will drive her out to the swamp and set her free. We will be accompanied by a force adequate to protect me from any treachery. However, we will stop before we reach the swamp, and you will take off that human bomb arrangement you are wearing. You may retain your revolver. I promise you, there will only be a driver and myself in the car, and my support will not be close enough to jump you, so you will still have the advantage. Then, the moment Dr Mitchell is safely into the trees, you will hand over your revolver, and we will return here."

"I could still shoot you, once Elaine is safe."

"Of course you could. But then my driver would shoot you. And he would be under instructions not to kill you, but to leave you well aware of what is happening to you. And it would be quite a lot! Whereas, if you fulfil your part of the bargain, I will promise you a quick, clean death. A bullet in the base of the head. The death I was planning for Dr Mitchell."

It was Olga's turn to lick her lips, and Alexander wondered if so young a woman had really considered the inevitable climax of her gallant little adventure. But he was aware of a growing excitement. All of his dreams were slowly coming true. And how insignificant was Elaine Mitchell beside this splendid creature. To think of her at his mercy . . . "You are crazy," Jutta said from the stairs. "She means to kill you, no matter what."

"I think we will be able to work something out," Alexander said.

"Olga?" Elaine peered at her friend. She was in any event totally bewildered at having been taken out of her chains in the middle of the night, given clothes to wear, and then taken to the Colonel's house. He has succumbed to his lust at last, she thought. And I have been defeated. For the past week she had existed in a naked world, naked in the flesh, naked in the mind. Her only certainty was that she must endeavour to maintain that initial advantage, defy him and all his minions to the end, and die when the time came with a smile on her lips. The nameless heroine, dying in a nameless cellar. But now, perhaps, she was going to be publicly executed. But there was Olga, smiling and confident. And Holzbach? And that hateful woman who looked at her as if she would devour her. "Has the war ended?" she asked.

"Not yet," Olga said.

"Then I don't understand."

"There is nothing to understand. I have negotiated your release, that is all."

"But . . ." Elaine looked from face to face.

"No questions," Olga said. "We must make haste."

It must be a trick, or I am dreaming, Elaine thought, as the car bumped over the rough track leading to the Marshes. She sat in the front, beside the driver, while Olga sat in the back with Holzbach. It was all so terribly civilised, so confusing, so unreal. And so terribly sinister. There was a panzer to either side of the road, and four trucks behind the command car, each filled with soldiers. But Olga seemed content. Elaine had been forbidden to turn her head, even to exchange a glance with Olga. Dear Olga, who had risked so much and was now actually pulling it off.

"Here will do," Holzbach said.

The car stopped, as did the trucks and the tanks. Elaine tensed, because the Pripet was still several miles away. And something was happening in the back seat, but she didn't know what. Then they were driving again, until even in the darkness the great trees began to loom in front of them. "This is the end of the road," Holzbach said, as the car came to a stop.

"Then you will get out here, Elaine," Olga said. "Go into the trees, find your way to where the others are. There are no soldiers left to fear."

"Elaine opened the door and got out. Now at last she could turn to look at them. "Aren't you coming?"

"Oh, indeed," Olga said. "But the Colonel and I have some unfinished business. Go into the trees and keep walking. I will join you in due course." Elaine looked at Holzbach. How she hated this man. And now, just to walk away from him after all the abuse that had been heaped on her . . .

"Go!" Olga said. Elaine turned and walked into the darkness.

"Your gun," Holzbach said.

"When she is safe," Olga said.

They waited. "You know," Holzbach said. "You are a very brave woman, Tatiana Gosykinya."

Olga shrugged. "I have had a good life. That woman is an innocent. She does not deserve to die in this quarrel."

"I am sure you are right," Holzbach said. "But still, for one so young as yourself . . . you are not yet 21, are you not? But you look much older. That no doubt is a result of your experiences."

Olga smiled; Elaine had disappeared. "It is a result of my age, Herr Colonel. I am not really Tatiana Gosykinya. My name is Olga Kaminskaya, and I am a lieutenant in the Red Army. And I am 29 not 20."

"You lied to me!"

"Well, I did not think you would be interested in exchanging a mere lieutenant for Elaine." Holzbach stared into the darkness. "You will never find her now," Olga said. "And the real Tatiana Gosykinya and her people *are* waiting for her; if you attempt to invade the Marshes in the dark you will suffer heavy casualties. So . . ." she reversed the gun and held it out.

Holzbach took it. "Never trust a woman," he remarked. "Do you know, Lieutenant Kaminskaya, I have said that so often, and yet here I am, allowing myself once again to be betrayed by one."

"I have not betrayed you," Olga said. "I misled you, perhaps. But I am ready to fulfil my part of the bargain. You may kill me whenever you choose."

"Whenever I choose," Holzbach said, and signalled his driver. "I do not think that will be for some time yet."

"We had a deal . . ."

"Based on a misapprehension on my part. My deal was with Tatiana Gosykinya. Now you also have to endure a misapprehension, my dear Lieutenant." Olga took a quick breath, and hurled herself at him, willing him to use the revolver. But the chauffeur had already got out of the car, and used his own gun to give her a blow on the back of the head which had her slumped half conscious in the bottom of the car. Before she could recover he had pulled her arms behind her back and handcuffed her wrists together. She gasped, and Holzbach dug his fingers into her hair, to drag her up and throw her on to the seat. "Take me home, Willi," he told the driver.

"Today, the war was won," Stalin announced.

Priscilla raised her head. "You said that after Stalingrad."

"After Stalingrad, the war could not be lost," Stalin explained. "After Kursk, it is definitely won. It would be won more quickly if your Americans and British would invade France. But even if they are afraid to do so, we no longer need them. Are you not pleased, Priscilla?"

"Is Joseph safe?"

"Oh, yes. He is safe. He seems to have been adopted by one of our generals."

"And you are more powerful than ever."

"As you are more beautiful. Come now, will you not celebrate our victory with me?"

"If it is my victory as well."

He shook his fist at her. "You are the most infuriating woman I have ever known. Do you know what I can . . ."

"Do to me? Have you not told me a hundred times! I think that is your biggest thrill, imagining what you can do to me. Telling me all your filthy dreams. But it still won't give you an erection, will it?"

He gazed at her, astonished to hear such perfect lips using such expressions. "Then surely you have nothing to fear from me."

"I do not fear anything from *you*, Comrade Stalin. But if you mean that I have nothing to fear from sharing your bed, you are mistaken. It is a matter of honour rather than fear. It is a masculine misconception that the entire sexual universe revolves around orgasm and ejaculation – if that does not happen, then nothing has happened. That is not correct. If I allowed you to touch a single part of my body, sexually, I would be dishonoured. And of course, so would you. But you long ago discarded any concepts of honour, did you not?"

She had to keep challenging him, rather as a lone traveller surrounded by wolves had to keep a fire burning between him and them all the time. It was the only way of keeping the beast out. But this time she suddenly realised she had gone too far, as the glare in his eyes suddenly overtook his entire face, so that he became convulsed with a mixture of lust and hatred. She stood up as he lunged at her, and tried to put the table between them, but he moved with surprising speed for a man of his bulk and age, caught her arm, and threw her across the table itself.

Temporarily winded, she tried to push herself up, and was seized by the nape of the neck and thrust down so hard she banged her face on the wood. Her skirt was already thrown up around her shoulders, and he was dragging on her knickers, pulling them down around her knees. She tried to kick, but that only enabled him to yank them right off. Freed for the moment of his grasp, she rolled off the table and on to the floor, striking it with a thud that again left her gasping for breath, and before she could recover he was on her again, once more throwing up her skirt, holding her legs apart as he knelt between, then putting one hand on her chest to hold her flat while he fumbled at his belt and buttons.

Desperately, Priscilla struck at him, while fighting back the urge to scream. She had not screamed when Rotislav the valet had done this to her 25 years before, and besides, a scream would only bring his creatures in to help him. This was a battle she had to fight, and win, on her own. But for a moment she thought she had lost, as his trousers slid down. She had been wrong in her assumption that he could not have an erection. Her arms were free, and she could strike at his face. But did she dare scratch the cheeks of probably the most omnipotent man in the world? She panted while she tried to come to a decision, and realised that the immediate crisis was past, and that she had, after all, won; he was already drooping, before he had even attempted entry.

She could only hope it was not a pyrrhic victory, as he threw himself on her, muttering into her ear as his moustache roamed over her face. She made herself lie still. He was not re-erecting, and had to know that. He rolled off her, turned his back on her, dressed himself. Still she lay absolutely still, even if she was unable to suppress her gasps for breath. Then he went to the door and left the apartment.

Priscilla lay still for several seconds before getting up in turn, and dressing herself. She ached in so many places she couldn't count them all. She went to the mirror on the wall and peered at it, not for the first time wondering if it was two-way glass and there was someone looking back at her. There was always a jug of vodka in the room, and she poured herself a glass, spilling a good deal of it as her hands were shaking. She could not imagine what might be going to happen next. She *dared* not imagine what might be going to happen next. Stalin was no philosopher. He had no ability to see life through other eyes, to understand, and therefore, to forgive. He was a monster, who had failed to impose his manhood on the object of his desire. She could expect only destruction.

She sat at her table and waited, as she had done for so long. She was tensed all the time, but even so she jumped when the door finally opened, standing up instinctively. She looked at a tall man with an utterly bald head, a great moon face, and rimless glasses. He wore uniform, and held himself stiffly. "My name is Lavrenty Beria," he announced. "I am Commissar for Internal Affairs."

Priscilla held her breath; that meant he was head of the secret police, the NKVD. "Am I under arrest?"

"It is the wish of Comrade Stalin that you leave this apartment and go to stay with your cousin Comrade Ligachevna, until arrangements can be made for you and your husband to leave the Soviet Union." Priscilla's knees gave way, and she sat down. "There are certain conditions attached," Beria went on, speaking in a complete monotone.

"I was sure there would be," Priscilla muttered.

Beria continued to look at a spot immediately above her head. "You will discuss your stay in the Kremlin with no one. Do not suppose that because you have left Russia we cannot find you and destroy you at will: remember what happened to Comrade Trotsky. I have no doubt that you will wish to tell your husband of your stay here, but should the slightest word of it reach any newspaper in the world, my people will seek you out and your husband, wherever you may be. Do you understand this?"

"I understand you," Priscilla said. The arrogance of these people, she thought, that they can just imprison someone for several months, subject her to threats of an horrendous nature, and then calmly let her go again with the warning not to talk about it! But then, as no one had appeared to believe Joseph's articles about life in the gulag, why should they not be arrogant?

Beria went to the door. "You have fifteen minutes to pack, then my people will come for you."

"And Monsieur Stalin?" she asked.

"Monsieur Stalin does not wish to see your face again," Beria told her.

"Why, Priscilla," Jennie said, and hugged her. "How very good to see you. Have you had a nice vacation?" They might have last seen each other only yesterday. "You are looking so well," Jennie said. "And isn't the news tremendous? They are calling it the greatest tank battle in history. And we have won it! The panzers are entirely wiped out. Now the war will be won. Tatiana will be coming home!"

And Alexei, Priscilla thought. Pray God he is still all right. And Joseph! "I should like to see Sonia," she said. "Is she at the hotel?"

"Sonia?" Jennie raised her eyebrows. "Sonia went back to the States some time ago."

"The greatest tank battle in history," Chuikov said proudly. Joseph could well believe that. For the past fortnight he had been an appalled spectator of a conflict which had staggered the imagination, as thousands of great steel-clad fighting vehicles had clashed, their guns spitting flame and lead, every so often exploding into blazing fire and smoke. Now they littered the fields, burned-out skeletons, in whose midst were other skeletons that had once been men. But there could be no doubt of the magnitude of the victory. For every destroyed Russian T34 tank there were some four German Panzers. And these were mostly Tigers, the giant tanks of the battlefield, yet unable to withstand the concentration and weight of the Russian fire.

Equally there could be no doubting that this was the beginning of the end of the German invasion of Russia. All the reports spoke of columns of German troops and their allies streaming west, no matter what directives they might have received from Hitler. The Russians now had almost total air superiority, and their planes could watch every German movement. "So where do we go from here?" he asked that night at dinner, where as always the vodka flowed and there was great good humour.

"Ah!" Chuikov said. "*We* continue the advance. Next stop, Germany, eh? But you, my friend, you go back to Moscow."

Joseph frowned. "Is that an instruction from Stalin?"

"It is an instruction from your wife, Comrade. She has finally arrived. Do you not wish to obey her?"

They clung to each other, while Jennie looked on benevolently. "I thought you would never make it," Joseph said.

"So did I," Priscilla answered, truthfully.

He held her at arms' length. "You look magnificent!"

"Which is more that can be said for you!"

"I am fully recovered," he assured her. "It's just a matter of *looking* well again."

The door of the apartment opened. "This is my friend, Galina Shermetska," Jennie said. "She lives upstairs."

"Mr Cromb I know," Galina said. "And you are the Princess. The reports of your beauty have not been exaggerated."

"Galina's daughter Sophie is serving with the partisans in the Pripet," Jennie explained. "With Tatiana. And Alex, of course."

"It is so long since we have heard from them," Galina said.

"You must be terribly worried," Priscilla ventured.

"They will be all right," Galina asserted. "They are with Tatiana."

Her confidence was touching. Priscilla wished she could feel the same way about Alex. But first, there was Joe to be savoured. "We have so much to tell each other," he said, when they were at last alone.

"I think it should wait until we are out of this foul country," Priscilla said. He raised his eyebrows in surprise. She made a moue. "Even the walls have ears, wouldn't you agree?"

"Can we go, without Alex?"

"I don't think we have any choice. Nor do I think our staying will help him, one way or the other."

"There are a whole lot of things I simply do not understand," Joseph confessed.

"Well, we're talking about Russia, right?" she asked.

The partisans crowded round the radio to listen to the news and their instructions. "Kiev," Shatrav said. "They are in Kiev." It was almost impossible to believe; Kiev was less than 250 miles away.

"The enemy is in full retreat," the voice said. "Now is the time for all true comrades to rise up and strike the beast, strike him so that he can never recover from the mauling he has received from the Red Army. Here are the instructions for the Partisan Groups. These instructions must be implemented as rapidly as possible. Groups One, Three and Four will amalgamate. Concentration centre will be map reference Seven A. I repeat, concentration centre will be map reference Seven A."

They looked at each other; no one in Group One needed to be told that map reference Seven A was in their section of the Pripet. "The commander of this unified force," the voice continued, "will be Number One. I repeat, the commander of this unified Group will be Number One."

All heads turned towards Tatiana. "Now you really are a general," Shatrav said, admiringly.

"Your target is reference Number Twelve," the voice said. "I repeat, your target is reference Number Twelve, and your instructions are Number Six, pending the arrival of Red Army units."

He went on to other instructions, while hands tore at the reference book. "Brest-Litovsk," Tatiana said. "We are to assault Brest-Litovsk. What is Number Six?"

"Take and hold," Alex said.

"Brest-Litovsk?" Shatrav studied the page. "We are to hold it?"

"Pending the arrival of Red Army units."

"Hold the town?" Shatrav scratched his chin.

The voice was still speaking. "Using Code Seven, transmit the day of your assault, and you will receive air support. I repeat . . ." Tatiana got up and walked away from them, staring into the trees. She was to be commander of three groups. Such had their numbers grown over the summer that she would have more than a thousand people under her command. But to take a town! And then hold it! They had virtually taken the town a year ago, with less than a hundred partisans. But they had never considered trying to hold it.

"Can we do it?" Alex asked, standing behind her.

She turned to face him. "Of course! We have been told to do so. But we shall make some plans of our own. I will work it out. You will help me. The first thing we need to do is utterly destroy the rail links, both east and west of the town, so it cannot be reinforced. Blocks must be erected on the road, as well, and all bridges must be blown. Bring the maps."

He had become her right-hand man since the deaths of Feodor and, they had to presume, Olga – although so far as they knew Olga had not been executed as her body had not been publicly displayed. "And Elaine?"

"Elaine will have to come with us, or remain by herself in the swamp. We will need every man and woman. But I would have supposed she would wish to come with us. Holzbach is still in command in Brest-Litovsk. I would have thought she would wish to be revenged on him for what he did to her."

"If only we knew what he did do to her," Alex muttered, without thinking.

"I would have supposed you at least would have found that out by now. If not it might be a good idea *to* find out now."

She was, as always, utterly confident. Alex did not suppose she in any way loved him, or even felt the slightest affection for him; Tatiana Gosykinya, above all the women he had ever encountered – or all the men, either – was totally amoral and ruthless. It was not that she was self-centered, or that she valued herself more highly than anyone else. If she did do that, on occasion, it was because she was required to lead, and she knew that only she could do the job. She was totally dedicated to the job, to the winning of the war, and, in her small part of the conflict, that meant the killing of Germans. He did not even suppose that when she tortured a man to death she enjoyed it, or even found it interesting, any more; it was simply her business to make war as hellish as possible – for the enemy. But she was also a woman, with a sexual drive as strong as her hatred. And he was her chosen mate, whatever his own feelings in the matter. Well, he would have had to be gay not to be overwhelmed with desire every time he crawled into her sleeping bag. But that did not mean he could not love another.

If only he knew, or could be the least sure, that he did love, that he *could*, any longer. More importantly, that Elaine could, any longer. She had refused to speak of her experiences at the hands of the Germans. Nor had she spoken of exactly how Olga had got her out, but she knew Olga had sacrificed her life. What else did she know? Although Olga had neither divulged her plan to them, nor given them any idea of the timescale involved, there had been the usual patrols along the edges of the Marshes, and one of these had found Elaine, wandering alone through the darkness. Tatiana and Alex had examined her together, realised that she had been beaten. But as far as Alex could discern, she had not been tortured in any other way. When they had asked her, she had merely gazed at them, her face closed and cold. It had remained that way.

"Do you think she is suffering a breakdown?" Tatiana asked.

Alex had no doubt that she was, but he wasn't going to say so, just in case Tatiana had it in mind that anyone suffering a breakdown might be an unnecessary mouth to feed. "She'll come round," he had said.

But Elaine remained as aloof as ever. She had always been a private person, quite astonishingly so in view of the utter intimacy in which the partisans had been forced to live for the past two years. But however much she might have to expose herself, or perform her necessaries in the company of several others of both sexes, she had never indulged in the banter that invariably accompanied such acts; it was as if from time to time she could take leave of her body, and while it remained there, her mind had soared to a plateau beyond the reach of other humans. Perhaps that ability had stood her in good stead when it had come to withstanding Nazi torture. Equally perhaps, was the possibility that her mind had had to escape once too often, and now could not return. Or did not wish to return. Alex suspected he was the only member of the Group who would even faintly be able to understand that.

He found her sitting on the banks of a pond, idly watching the fish that darted to and fro in the clear water. It was a marvellous day, with not a cloud in the sky and warm enough to take off one's jacket, as Elaine had done. She was, in fact, as pretty as a picture, with her hair loose and tumbling past her shoulders, and her rather solemn face relaxed. He sat beside her. "What do you think of the news?"

"I think it is tremendous," she said.

"We're all set to let rip. Elaine, you will have to come with us, this time."

"Yes," she said.

He was surprised. She had never wanted to before. "It'll be rough."

"I know." She turned her head. "Do you think Olga is still alive?"

"There's a chance. One feels that if they had executed her they would have done so publicly. But . . . it's been a month."

"You mean, if she has spent a month in that cellar then she is dead, to all intents and purposes." He bit his lip, and she touched his hand. "I only spent a week there."

"Do you want to talk about it?"

"Do you want me to?"

"It's just that, perhaps, if you did you might feel better."

"I have no feelings about it, Alex. And there is nothing to talk about. Nothing happened." Alex made no comment, but she could tell from his expression that he either didn't believe her or he felt her brain had closed down the memory.

"It's the truth," she said. "That man, Holzbach, is a psychiatric case. He wanted me, sexually. He came close to taking me, sexually. But he could not bring himself to do it. Then he wanted to hurt me, as he did the first day. But because I would not scream he could not do that again, either. So he would just come and look at me. He and his goons." She shuddered. "Just standing there, looking at me. Or playing a hose over me." She gave another shudder.

"Were you afraid?"

"Of course I was afraid. Every time he came I supposed he had made up his mind to kill me. But he didn't."

"And it doesn't appear as if he has killed Olga, either. So maybe we will be able to rescue her."

Elaine looked at him. "Do you understand about that? About her and me?"

"Yes. What I would like to know is where that leaves you and *me*?"

Elaine sighed. "I didn't love her, Alex. But when you went off with Tatiana . . . all right, you were summoned to do that. But that still left me out in the cold, right? So I was lonely, and miserable, and she was there, and, well,

I'm not quite as sexless as I appear. The problem was, is, I guess, that she genuinely loved me. And sacrificed herself for me."

He nodded. "So we'll get her back."

"And afterwards?"

He gazed at her for several seconds. Then he said, "Let's kill as many Nazis as possible, and rescue Olga. Then we can talk about afterwards."

Alexander von Holzbach leapt from his desk as the windows in his office rattled. The explosion had come from west of the town. Jutta had also started up, abandoning her typewriter with a squawk of alarm. Alexander peered out of the window to see a pall of smoke rising in the distance. Jutta stood beside him, grasping his arm, forgetful for the moment of the propriety she normally maintained when in the office. Alexander went to the door, threw it open. "Where is Major Clausen?" he bawled.

Clausen ran in a moment later. "The railway line has been blown up. A massive explosion. God knows how much HE they put into it."

"To the west?" The partisans had never operated on the Polish side of the border before.

Even as he spoke, there was another explosion, to the east. The two officers stared at each other in consternation, because there now came several other explosions. "The bridges!" Clausen gasped.

Jutta screamed. Alexander slapped her face. "Stop that!" She burst into tears, and sat on his desk. Alexander faced Clausen. "Get through to Pinsk. Tell them we are under attack. Tell them that we have been isolated by both rail and road, for the moment. Tell them that we need help." Particularly, he thought, he needed to have back those men Pinsk had drained off from his command, which had reduced his effectiveness to a dangerously low level. "And send me Pritwitz."

Pritwitz looked as confounded as anyone. Because Alexander had not showed them the top secret despatches he had been receiving, warning him of the utter catastrophe that had overtaken the German army farther to the east, of the necessity to prepare to defend Brest-Litovsk to the last man. "Pull yourself together, man," Alexander said. "We are under attack. Implement those dispositions I gave you for the defence of the town."

Pritwitz gulped, and hurried off; he was as aware as his chief that he did not have sufficient men for the task he had been given. Jutta's glasses has come off when Alexander had slapped her. Now she dried her face, picked them up from the floor and put them back on her nose. "If they get in here . . ."

"They are not going to get in here," he snapped. But just in case he strode into the outer office, where Clausen, red in the face, was spluttering into the phone.

"The lines have been cut, Herr Colonel."

"Send out a radio message. Then come with me. They would assault us, would they? We shall give them the best possible answer." Clausen swallowed, and stared at Jutta, who was following her master and lover, shirt front heaving, glasses gleaming. Alexander stamped down the stairs. Frightened orderlies and secretaries stood to attention. But from the courtyard outside there came crisp words of command and the stamp of marching feet; Pritwitz was sending the garrison to its appointed defensive positions, as allotted by himself. Created by himself, in fact, nests of machine-guns and mortars, concentrated firepower to resist any attempt to come at them from the Marshes.

Alexander continued on his way down to the cellar, and Olga Kaminskaya. Like Elaine before her, she hung from chains against one of the centre pillars. But her body was marked, a gigantic red and white weal. Everything that could be done to a woman had been inflicted on that body, save for actual mutilation. He had intended that for the last. But now he would have to change his plans. "Bring her out," he said.

Olga was dragged up the stairs. Alexander pointed to the next flight, and she was taken up there as well, forced on to the balcony, blinking in the sudden unaccustomed light. Two men had already prepared the rope, and the noose was dropped over Olga's head and tightened round her throat. "Well?" Alexander demanded. "Have you nothing to say?"

Olga spat at him.

"Aircraft approaching!" a loudspeaker boomed. Every head turned to look at the sky. There was no need to identify the aircraft: there were no German planes left in this sky. And besides, the bombers were approaching from the east. "Take shelter!" the loudspeaker instructed.

The men on the balcony looked at Alexander. "Finish her first," Alexander snapped. One of the men bound Olga's wrists behind her back, then lifted her from the floor and carried her to the balustrade, to which the rope had been secured. They could hear the crump of the bombs, and buildings were exploding into flame and black smoke. "Now," Alexander said.

Olga's body was thrown over the balustrade, to hang there, legs kicking. But soon they were still.

The partisans of Group One crouched beside the shattered railway line as the Ilyushins went in, flying low, hardly a thousand feet, pinpointing their targets, demolishing the town; that there were Russian civilians still in Brest-Litovsk was irrelevant compared with the business of killing Germans. Alex glanced from Tatiana to Elaine, one on each side of him, each grasping their sub-machine-gun, each staring into the debris in front of them. Behind them were Shatrav and Gregory, and all the other men and women with whom they had fought and died over the past year. Now their moment was come. "Go!" Tatiana said, and got up.

The town remained shrouded in the dust-mist caused by the bombs, and the planes were returning east, low enough to waggle their wings above the partisans. "Stay with me," Alex told Elaine, as they ran into the rubbled street. They passed a machine-gun emplacement that had suffered a direct hit; it was now a mass of shattered steel and men. A German soldier appeared in front of them; he had been sheltering from the bombs and was obviously dazed, although he still carried his weapon. Alex shot him through the chest and he fell without a word. Then there were others, but they too were obliterated by the automatic fire from the partisans.

Each group had its assigned target; Group One the headquarters, Group Two the barracks. Group Three, which had been responsible for the explosions west of the town, were to attack and destroy the railway station. Tatiana led Group One along the main street of the town, firing indiscriminately at anyone who showed themselves. Then they were in the square and facing the headquarters building. Here they were greeted by a hail of fire from the windows and doors, but they would have checked anyway, staring at the naked body of the woman dangling from the upstairs balcony.

"Oh, God!" Elaine muttered.

"Shatrav!" Tatiana snapped. He was their marksman. He stood up, leaned against the wall of the building where they were sheltering and fired several shots. At least two hit the rope, and Olga's body plunged to the ground. "Bring up the mortar," Tatiana commanded.

The squat weapon was pushed into position, the first projectile loaded into it. The partisans dropped to their knees, hands pressed over their ears, and the shell exploded on the front steps, near Olga's body. The body disappeared into fragments; so did the steps. The partisans screamed their "Ourrahs!" and ran forward, again to be checked by the fire. Several fell, and Tatiana waved the rest back to shelter.

Alex looked left and right, and found Elaine, unhurt, staring at the building. "Demolish it," Tatiana said.

The mortar fired, and again. Chunks of concrete flew

off the building, smoke began to rise from it. The radio chattered. "The garrison has surrendered, Comrade Commissar."

"Take no prisoners," Tatiana replied. "Shoot everyone in uniform." In front of them the headquarters building was silent, save for the sound of collapsing masonry. Tatiana waved them on again, and they ran forward. As they reached the foot of the crumbled steps, several people came out with their hands high in the air. Tatiana gestured them to come down to the street, and they obeyed, looking fearfully left and right. The partisans pushed the soldier to one side, while Tatiana inspected the officer. "Name?"

She spoke Russian, but guessed he understood her. "Major Frederick Clausen."

Tatiana glanced at Elaine, who was staring at the major, hands tight on her gun. "Was he one of them?" Tatiana asked.

"He was there," Elaine said in a low voice.

"Then he would have been there when Olga died," Tatiana said. Clausen looked from one to the other, licking his dustcaked lips. But Tatiana's attention had been caught by the emergence of the last two figures from the rubble. "Come down here," she commanded.

Jutta was shaking with fear, and she had lost her glasses; Alexander had to help her over the rubble as she blinked in the sudden daylight. Both their uniforms were smothered in dust. "That is Holzbach," Elaine said.

Tatiana stood before them. "Tatiana Gosykinya," Alexander said, wondering how he could ever have mistaken anyone else for this beauty. "We are related. By marriage."

"Where is your wife?" Tatiana asked.

"She is in Germany."

"And this one is your mistress?"

Alexander hesitated, and Jutta, seeking salvation, nodded. "Yes. I am his mistress."

"Then you will have to do. Shatrav," Tatiana said. "You and you and you. Rape this woman. Do it until you can do it no longer. Do it. Now. Here. Then cut off her breasts, and hang her."

Jutta screamed as the men threw her to the ground and began ripping off her clothes. "You cannot permit this," Alexander shouted. "You . . . Dr Mitchell, in the name of humanity . . ."

"That is what you did to my friends," Tatiana told him. "That is what you were going to do to Olga Kaminskaya. That is what you would have done to me, had you captured me." Alexander panted, as he realised his fate was next to be decided. "Strip them both," Tatiana said. She turned to Elaine. "Do you wish the pleasure, Doctor?"

Elaine stared at Alexander, and he stared back. For a week they had been almost intimate, in her defiance and his desire. Now she saw his lips trembling as the partisans pulled off his belts and then his tunic. "No," she said. "I would like them to be shot. Now."

Tatiana smiled. "You are still too soft for this war. Shooting is too good for such as these. Put them on the ground," she said.

Elaine turned and ran for the other side of the street. Alex went behind her, held her shoulders, both looking away from the sound of the men screaming, their sudden high pitch matching Jutta's. They listened to laughter and more screams, gasps and moans. They could not stop themselves turning back, to watch the three bodies being hung from the balcony by their ankles; all three dripped blood, and the two men's mouths were stuffed with their genitals. But they were still alive, swinging to and fro, "They are animals," Elaine muttered, "*We* are animals."

"Like I once said," Alex replied. "The caveman lurks just beneath the consciousness of all of us."

"I want to go home," Elaine said. "Can we go home, Alex?"

* * *

"Oh, my darling!" Priscilla held Alex close, then held him away again the better to look at him. This was her son?

He kissed her, then extended his hand for that of the tall, somewhat gaunt woman who stood beside him on the deck of the troopship that had brought them back from Europe. "You remember Elaine?"

Priscilla embraced Elaine as well. "We got your wire. Your parents are on their way. I've invited them to stay with us."

Elaine hugged her again.

Joseph shook hands with Alex and kissed Elaine on the cheek. "I guess yours was a pretty grim war," he said. "What do you want to do?"

"Go home," Alex said. "Have a hot bath, and a hamburger."

"Two hamburgers," Elaine suggested.

"And then, maybe, get married," Alex said. "As soon as Elaine's folks get here."

"Do you want to talk about it?" Priscilla asked. They sat in the drawing room of the Boston house, and Rollo served them champagne. It was a family occasion. A very small family, now.

"No," Alex said.

"I think we would like to forget about it," Elaine said. "If we can." Once she had said it would never end. But now it had to, for them at least. Whatever it had made them, they had to pick up the pieces of their lives

Priscilla had only the faintest idea of what the partisans had endured, what crimes they had had to commit just to survive, much less win. But she could remember the horrors of the civil war in her own youth, and she did not suppose what her son and his woman had gone through had been anything less cataclysmic than that. Compared with their ordeal, hers at the hands of Stalin had been, as he insisted, a holiday. "What of Tatiana?" she asked.

"Oh. Tattie and her people are still fighting. They won't stop fighting until they reach Berlin," Alex said. "But you and Joe. They told me you were wounded, Joe?"

"Some," Joseph said. "And I wasn't even a combatant."

Joseph and Priscilla looked at each other. They knew the question that was coming next. "How is Aunt Sonia?" Alex asked.

"I think she is dead," Priscilla said. Both Alex and Elaine stared at her with their mouths open. "She went with me to Russia. I shouldn't have let her. I was so sure she would be all right." She sighed. "I thought I would be all right. What a fool I was!"

"But . . . I don't understand," Alex said. "You say you travelled together . . .?"

"And we got to Moscow together. Then I was . . . invited to have lunch in the Kremlin. Sonia had lunch with Jennie. After lunch, she took a cab back to her hotel . . . and disappeared."

"Wait a moment," Alex said. "She took a cab? There weren't any cabs left around, when we were in Moscow."

"Yes," Priscilla said.

Alex turned to Joseph. "Can't the State Department help?"

"Not really. Official policy is that we are still bosom-buddies with Russia, and Sonia was travelling on a Mexican passport. The official line is that she was murdered by robbers. No one believes it, but . . ."

"Are we really going to go on being bosom-buddies with them?" Elaine asked.

"You fought beside them for two years," Priscilla said. "Don't you count them your friends?"

Elaine looked at Alex. "No," he said. "Comrades, yes. Friends, never."

Tatiana, Shatrav and Gregory stared at the gates of the concentration camp, the emaciated human beings who stared back at them. The Russians were no longer capable of being shocked, or of having feelings about these people. In the 18 months since they had stormed Brest-Litovsk, which they had had to evacuate again as the Red Army had not been able to get to them in time, before re-advancing to re-take the town in triumph, they had developed into killing machines who slaughtered the enemy, without discrimination as to sex or age, without the slightest hesitation or compunction. But this was something outside of their comprehension.

They stood with the other officers and watched the human wrecks shuffling past. These people were actually the lucky ones, who had been saved from the gas chamber by the arrival of the Red Army. But would they ever recover from their ordeal? And yet, Tatiana thought, some of them were quite sprightly, looked at their saviours, some even smiling. There was spirit there. She wondered if they would all have to be shot?

Then one of the women broke ranks. "Tatiana!"

Gregory and Shatrav instinctively closed in on their commander, protectively, while guards hurried forward. "There is nothing to be afraid of," Tatiana said.

"Tatiana!" The woman fell to her knees before her cousin.

"Why, Anna," Tatiana said. "I am glad you have survived."

If you could call it survival, she thought, as she looked at the emaciated figure, the hair which was just starting to sprout again from the shaven skull; it was no longer a glowing gold, but white. "Help me!" Anna begged. "For the sake of our name, help me."

"That is why we are here," Tatiana assured her. "To help you. But you must go with these people, now. They will take care of you. I will see you later." Anna allowed herself to be led way, looking over her shoulder and attempting to smile. "What will happen to her?" Tatiana asked the guard captain.

"She will go to a rehabilitation camp," the man said.

"They will all go to a rehabilitation camp. And then . . ." he shrugged.

Tatiana shivered.

The bells pealed, the people clapped. Red Square was packed, the crowd supervised by watchful guards, as one after another the heroes and heroines of the Soviet Union were led forward. Gregory's parents were there, to hug and kiss him after he had received his medal.

Shatrav no longer had parents, but one of the women kissed him anyway.

"Tatiana," Stalin said, as he pinned the Order of Lenin to the breast of her tunic, and then embraced her; like the others she wore a smart new khaki uniform and a matching sidecap, and her long dark hair was tied with a ribbon. "You are the true heroine. Now, there is so much for you to do."

"For you. For Russia," Tatiana said.

"Of course. There is so much for us all to do."

Tatiana stepped back, saluted, and then went to join her mother. "Tatiana!" Jennie hugged and kissed her. "Oh, there were times . . . But to have you back . . . you remember Galina Shermetska."

"Tell me how Sophie died," Galina said. She had only just learned that her daughter wasn't coming back.

"As a soldier, Comrade," Tatiana said. "Fighting the enemy." Galina's shoulders hunched, and then she straightened again, as the tall, moon-faced man with the pince-nez joined their group. "Comrade Beria!" Tatiana stood to attention.

"Welcome home, Major Gosykinya," Beria said. "I have an appointment for you." Tatiana raised her eyebrows. "You are to work for me, now," Beria said. "For the elimination of subversives. For the restoration of Russia. It is the wish of the Chairman."

*   *   *

The door of the cell opened and Sonia looked up. Then she stood up, a quick flush suffusing her face: behind Beria there were four people, two men and two women. If she had allowed herself to be lulled into a sense of security, of perpetuity, over the past couple of years she had always understood that today might come. The very moment she ceased to be of use to this horrible man. But she had always rejected the concept. She had almost enjoyed herself, with her books and the total absence of stress. These had been the most peaceful two years in her turbulent life. And now they were ended. "You are to leave this place, now," Beria said.

Sonia inclined her head. "I understand."

He smiled. It was as if an egg had cracked in two. "You are so brave, my Sonia. But you are not to be executed. I am removing you to a place of even greater safety than here." Sonia was incredulous. "Your time has not yet come," Beria said. "But it will. These people will look after you, until your resurrection."

"And then?"

"Then?" Beria's pince-nez glinted. "Then we will take the world apart, you and I."